L. E. Modesitt, Jr.

•••

GRAVITY DREAMS

WITHDRAWN

TOR®

A TOM DOHERTY ASSOCIATES BOOK
NEW YORK

GRAVITY DREAMS

Copyright © 1999 by L. E. Modesitt, Jr.

Edited by David G. Hartwell

A Tor Book
Published by Tom Doherty Associates, LLC
175 Fifth Avenue
New York, NY 10010

www.tor.com

Tor® is a registered trademark of Tom Doherty Associates, LLC.

ISBN: 0-812-56661-0
Library of Congress Catalog Card Number: 99-22966

First edition: July 1999
First mass market edition: July 2000

Printed in the United States of America

0 9 8 7 6 5 4 3 2 1

To Carol Ann,
who taught me that honesty is more than
accuracy in words

FIRST LOVE
FIRST KNOWLEDGE
FIRST SORROW

1

To that which is born, death is certain;
to that which is dead, birth is certain.

My eyes flashed to the rain-swollen stream, and then to the swirl of water that geysered out of the gray rocks of the defile. Heavy clouds melded with the granite to the north. Mist droplets clung to my hair, and water seeped down my neck and back. Sweat and fear enveloped me, a combined odor that the rain could not wash away, that would guide my pursuers through the ancient trees to me.

"The Demons' Caldron." The words mumbled from my chilled and chapped lips, and I looked eastward, seeing again the cart road.

A thousand meters or so to the right was the cart path that headed northward toward Rykasha and the Demons' Niche—*one thousand, seven hundred and ten point four meters* jumped into my thoughts, reminding me again of the demon I had become or was fast becoming. The paved path followed the once-larger road of the ancients, or so the maps showed, although it supposedly ended short of the boundary markers, and only a trail continued north into Rykasha.

I shook my head. Too close by far. I had thought I had been jogging farther westward, moving away from that serviceway, but my feet had betrayed me and carried me gradually downhill and back toward the gliders that tracked me. Back toward Foerga?

My eyes burned, and I shook my head. Poor Foerga, linked to a man who had become a demon, yet still loving him to the end, against the tenets of Dorcha, against the Townkeeper and the Shraddans. Against the Shraddans I had trusted and upheld in all my teachings of Dzin.

Underfoot the ground grew hard, with the ancient pavement that still endured around the Caldron. My stomach growled, a reminder that I had gone through all the food in the rucksack I had discarded kilos behind me, enough food for a normal man for weeks. It had scarcely lasted days for me.

An image of a vast glowing ball of light—an intense, yet peaceful, spinning pinwheel—rose before my eyes, and the grayness and the rain vanished for a moment. Just as suddenly, the image vanished, and I shook my head as I beheld the darkness of firs and rain-damped oak and maple trunks, and rain.

Rain . . . the mist was turning into rain, and I had no time to think about mysterious balls of light appearing. I forced my eyes back to the wet and gray granite and the twisted trees before me. From the Caldron, the green-and-white stream water swirled up in a foaming cascade, then subsided. I paused and took a deep breath.

Whrrrrr . . .

A glow of silver flashed through the trees to my right, the silver teardrop shape of a rough terrain glider—one with self-induction risers. I turned away from the stream and the Caldron and sprinted uphill.

The rain burst down in gusted waves interspersed with the near-continual rumbling of thunder, as I ran westward and then neared the crest of the first low rise, northward, trying to keep an even pace ahead of the gliders and the grim-faced Shraddans they contained.

So long as they could not get in front of me before I reached the border . . . I had to reach the border, if only for Foerga's sake.

The ground rose and smote me, doubtless because I had been thinking more of geography than where my feet should go.

I staggered up, ignoring the line of fire across my forearm, the blood that mixed with rain, and dull aches too numerous to count. Then I had to bend and untangle the boot laces from the root that had tripped me, retying them before straightening. The mustiness of damp leaves and mud filled my nostrils.

Two more gliders whirred out of the mist and over the stream south of the Caldron and began to climb the low hill.

I began to run once more, tired as I was, running like a hare compared to how I had once run, even in my younger years.

Benefits of becoming a demon . . .

The hill and granite outcroppings seemed to slow the Shraddans and their gliders, and the whining and whirring faded. Faded but did not disappear, lingering in my hearing, lingering in too many perceptions that had become too acute.

I slowed to a jog, insisting that one foot follow the other, then lead the other—any sort of mental imagery to keep moving, keep ahead of the Shraddans and what they wanted to do to me.

Lines of golden red fire filled the skies like arches holding back the depth of the void beyond the planet. That sky was not purple, nor blue, but nielle, blackness beyond black, with stars that jabbed like knives of light. I shook my head, concentrated on putting one foot in front of the other, and the vision vanished.

Some time later, when my legs ached into cramping, my lungs heaved, burning so that I could barely breathe, I lurched to a halt beside the dark-trunked fir. For a moment, all I could do was pant, although I tried to force deeper breathing.

Before I had taken much more than a dozen breaths, the silver teardrop shape of the first rough terrain glider loomed out of the rain to the east, whining and groaning as it forced its way through the undergrowth, not dodging bushes as I had done, but still weaving to avoid the man-thick pine and hardwood trunks.

With a gasp that was half sob, I dodged uphill around an outcrop of rain-stained rocks and back into the darkwood forest, forcing my legs, gasping for air, ignoring the agony that stabbed through my lungs with each breath.

Anything was better than starving in a stone cage. Than dying quickly by slow grams entombed in immovable stone. But I wasn't supposed to die. I couldn't let them kill me . . . not after everything that had occurred.

I pushed my body, using every Dzin technique I had ever learned. Once more, the whining and whirring faded to the edge of consciousness as I plunged northward, knowing another set of gliders followed the road to the east, ready to slide in front of me should I falter.

Did they wish to capture me? Or just drive me out of Dorcha?

Containment pattern, ninety-nine percent probability . . . Was that the demon, or was the demon liberating my own demons?

Having no answers, no time for answers, I avoided the berry patches, but even the other bushes ripped at my already-rent gown, and my boots skidded across clay and damp leaves and slick needles.

How had it all happened?

Less than a month earlier, I'd been a respected master of Dzin in Hybra. A low-level master tasked to educate the children of the town, but a master. Not quite a decade earlier, I'd been a candidate scholar in Henvor, learning the way of Dzin, learning the very skills that had stabilized the world and reclaimed it from the unbridled selfishness and chaos of the demons.

Now I was being hunted . . . as a demon . . . as an outcast and hated remnant of a despicable past forced on today's world by the unspeakable depravity of the ancients.

I slowed somewhat on a level stretch, a trail carpeted in rain-slicked needles, trying to catch my breath, to let jarred shins and fatigued muscles recuperate ever so slightly.

Me? A demon? Because I suddenly could think more clearly, run more quickly?

The long baying of a hound to the right spurred my flagging steps. Hounds were not used for herding and containment. Hounds were for the kill.

The blood on scratched arms forgotten, the cramps in overstrained legs ignored, I stepped up my pace, continuing to run up a gradual incline through the hills that never seemed to end.

Again, the sense and sounds of the gliders retreated. More important, that awful baying diminished. The mist cooled, became thin pellets of ice that bounced off my shoulders, off my soaked hair. In the stillness came the odor of sweat and fear, of panic.

The trees thinned, fir and spruce replacing the leafless oaks and maples. Fine snow sifted through the woods, settling on the needles and undergrowth not covered with the coniferous canopy.

In spite of my efforts, my pace slowed, and the whirring neared. Another pair of hounds bayed, their howling lower, more mournful.

The forest ended, and I stopped, caught by the openness running from left to right, an openness covered with snow. Flat, as though the snow covered pavement or grass, with no sign of undergrowth.

Fifty meters—*forty-eight point three meters*—to my left a tall silver pillar rose out of the ankle-deep snow, shimmering in the dim light.

A cleared swathe that cut off the tree growth as sharply as a knife or a laser ran east and west—marking the boundary between Rykasha and Dorcha, between civilization and chaos, and, incidentally, added that newly autonomous part of my thoughts, *the forty-fourth parallel.*

I shivered.

Behind me rose the whining of the pursuit gliders, a sound so faint I could not have heard it a month earlier, a sound so fearsome I would have pushed the idea out of my thoughts a decade earlier. The hounds bayed again.

I glanced back, sensing the approach of three, perhaps more, of the gliders, then looked at the pillar, then down-hill to where I knew there was another, and another be-yond that—a silver line marking the north boundary of Dorcha and the south boundary of Rykasha, the land of the demons.

Finally, as the whining rose, I shivered once more, then bolted past the boundary and into the land of my dam-nation.

The snow got deeper as I continued northward, seem-ingly centimeters higher with each few hundred steps, un-til I was plodding through knee-deep and clinging heavy white powder that soaked through the thin undertrousers and chilled my legs.

The trees grew farther apart, yet larger, and the mist became a white powder that filtered down from the dark-ness overhead.

I kept putting one foot in front of the other, glad at least that the whining and whirring of the gliders had been left behind at last. Bitter-glad, doing what duty—and love—required.

As I stepped out into a long empty space, with granite cliffs rising to the left and the right, another sound, more like a whooshing hum, intruded, grew louder by the mo-ment, seemingly coming from no direction and all at once.

I stood still, calf-deep in snow that chilled even my heated body, turning in every direction before looking up . . .

Light transfixed me—then darkness.

2

Dzin must be seized with bare hands and open eyes.

Outside the school, the late fall winds carried the fallen leaves past the half-open windows, creating a pleasant rustling. For a moment, rather than concentrate on the sixteen students sitting on their mats before me, I just listened, was just aware, holding to that single Dzin instant, accepting the moment.

Melenda held up her hand.

I nodded. There would be other moments.

"How did Dzin come into the world?" asked the long-haired young woman. "You tell us about it and teach us how to apply it, but . . ." Her words trailed off uncertainly.

"Dzin has always been in the world; we just need to discover it." I smiled. "That's both true and incomplete. Knowledge of Dzin extends farther than the great collapse. It could have existed long before that. We don't know." I paused, wondering how to connect what I had said to what we had been discussing. "What we do know is that Dzin is not like a mountain or a glider repair manual. It is neither an immovable object nor a step-by-step guide to life. It is the way to become *aware* of reality, not to explain reality or to describe it. That's why we don't spend much time on telling what it is or how it came to be. It is. We try to teach you to become aware of everything, not to explain everything."

"Is it like the clouds?" Wryan smiled broadly. "There, but you really can't touch it or feel it?"

"Like the clouds?" I chuckled. "Not exactly . . . although there is an old Dzin saying, 'The clouds are in the sky; the water is in the well.' But that's another reminder that Dzin teaches us to understand reality directly, without becoming lost in descriptions of descriptions."

There were several frowns at that, including one from Sergol, the blond fisherman's son in the middle of the second row.

"What's wrong with descriptions?" asked the thin-faced Sirena, squirming slightly on her mat.

"We need descriptions to deal with some aspects of our life. Yet we must recognize that while descriptions are necessary, they are only approximations of the world. That was one of the reasons for the downfall of the ancients. The ancients could describe anything. They had descriptions of subatomic particles so small that their most powerful instruments could not detect them, yet they described them. They described how the world was built from the smallest forces, forces so infinitesimal that they could be detected only by interactions created by machines that were as big as the entire city of Henvor."

The blank looks from the younger children in the second row told me I was well over their heads. I fingered my beard. How could I make what I'd said simpler, yet accurate? "Dimmel? Do you like chocolate?"

"Yes, Master Tyndel, yes, ser."

"Tell me about chocolate. What makes it good?"

"It's brown, and it's sweet, and it tastes soooo good."

I nodded, looking from student face to student face. "Lycya? Can you taste chocolate from Dimmel's description?"

"No, Master Tyndel."

I looked at an older face. "Can you, Erka?"

"No, ser."

"Can anyone tell me more about chocolate?"

"It has milk and sugars in it," added Wryan, "and it melts in your hand on a hot day."

"How does it taste? How do you feel when you eat it and after you eat it?" I pressed.

"Good . . . really good!" exclaimed young Dimmel.

"I'm sure you do." I paused, letting my eyes sweep over the group. "Do all these descriptions really tell you how chocolate tastes?"

A few heads shook, then a few more.

"You see how hard it is? And you know about chocolate. The ancients tried to explain things far bigger, far more complicated than chocolate. . . . Yet for all their explanations, for all their search for more explanations that they could use, they failed, and they perished. As the Abbo Sanhedran said, 'Explanation is not awareness.' " I paused. "What does that mean?" I looked toward the end of the first row at Dynae.

"Ah, ser . . . I am not sure. It wasn't in the lesson," replied the brunette, the Townkeeper's daughter.

I concealed the wry amusement I felt and looked back at the thin-faced older girl beside her. "What do you think, Sirena?"

"An explanation . . . it doesn't . . . it's not the same . . . as feeling something."

I nodded. "That's right. There's more. When you describe something you feel or see, immediately the truth of what you've seen becomes false."

"Oh . . . like the tale of the elephant and the blind men . . . except we can't possibly explain everything we see," interjected the redheaded Wryan. "So when we talk about it, we leave things out."

"That's part of it," I agreed.

"And there are things we feel but can't describe, and those get left out, too?" asked Wryan.

"You're right." I smiled and nodded. "That's enough for now. I want you all to think about it. We'll take a break before we start physical science."

I smiled. Not always did the Dzin sessions go so well, but I was pleased, though I took care to remind myself that all too much of what I imparted I had gained from others. Still, most of them seemed to understand, and some, like Wryan, had a feel for Dzin.

3

Truth is not somewhere else.

In the shadow of the cataclypt of Dyanar, two children kissed, and I let them, although in my new and deep aquacyan gown, I should have stepped forward, frowned, let the silence of my disapproval separate them, for such familiarity so young leads to the arrogance of unbridled knowledge.

Rather than act, I studied the carvings on the cataclypt, the images of the winged figures who represented the ancients and the tailed figures in the background, the representation of the demons who had been created by the technology of those ancient angels. Dzin had saved us, those of Dorcha, from degenerating into the soullessness of the north, just as, I supposed, Toze had saved those of West Amnord.

From the carvings, my eyes went back to the two children, kissing. That was the beginning, though I did not see it. Instead, I forbore intervening and smiled, for I well remembered a day years before when I had kissed Esolde behind the grape trellis in her parents' garden.

On this later day of my posting, in my aquacyn gown, with the slow swirl of the river below and the dampness of the morning mist in my nostrils, I let the two kiss unmolested and turned to walk along the foot-polished stones of the River Walk, the sun not quite warm on my right cheek as it struggled over the eastern hills and through the late-morning mist of spring.

Henvor is an old city, its origins on the banks of the Greening River lost in myths of time before the Great

Hunger and Devastation. The weather-auspexes claim that it was colder then, much colder, but now the winter rains were soft, and the morning mists and clouds of summer kept the sun's heat from drying the marshes that bordered the watercourse south of Henvor, the marshes and their grasses that purified the waters once again before they flowed between the Whitened Hills, winding ponderously toward the merchant cities on the Summer Sea, past Leboath and Wyns, and eventually to Mettersfel, where the sunships brought in the ocean nodules and carried the wines and cheeses of Dorcha eastward, eastward across the Rehavic Ocean south of the Pillars of Fire and around the Barren Isles to Thule . . . and occasionally to Dhura.

I hurried north toward the Hall, repressing a head shake. First my mother, then my father, then Umbard and finally Manwarr had cautioned me against the insidious and evil habit of open disapproval, even open disapproval of self, but still I had to fight that urge, calling on the precepts of Dzin, so much that I wondered what ancestor had gene-coded the trait.

Across the river was the equally old city of Teford, though it is closer to a large town than a city proper. There are the stone carvers, more properly called lithoidolators in their love of their craft, for it has been stone and Dzin that have held back the demons of the north.

The two river cities are the crown jewels of Dorcha, small but precious—unlike Halz and Mettersfel, which are large and filled with credits of all origins and denominations. Teford and Henvor are also far enough from the Sea of Summer to be comfortable, even if the merchants of Mettersfel call them provincial. Yet, how can a city such as Henvor, blessed with the hagiaphants of Dzin, ever be provincial, even to the merchant city-state of Mettersfel?

Behind me, there was the slap of softboots, and the children vanished into the Street of Iconraisers. I did frown at that. The iconraisers were tolerated throughout Dorcha, and indeed all of Amnord, but even I had to agree with Manwarr's view of them: "The universe we see is unreal; how then would one describe an image of unreality displayed upon a bed of light?"

The Street of Iconraisers contrasted thin and mean dwellings, scarcely more than caserns, with the gold and viridium shimmering pillars of wealth. How else could it be, when the electric current to power an iconscreen was dearer than pure bloodessence itself? Some claimed that the iconraisers were little more than coprophrologers who enslaved and transferred the souls of children to power their lightbed screens, but always are there superstitions among the less enlightened, even within Henvor. There are even those—Dzinarchists—who see Dzin not as a way but as a goal.

As the softboot steps died in sound and memory, I looked northward, toward the unseen granite ramparts that marked the south border of demon-ruled Rykasha, land of mystery and darkness, before hastening my steps toward the Hall of Unremitting Alertness.

At the old river gate to the city, now well within Henvor itself, I stepped through the narrow way of the Demons' Passage. After a decade under the hagiaphants, I no longer looked up at the twenty-meter-high-glass smooth walls, nor at the blocking stones designed to glide inexorably into place should a demon need to destroyed.

At the yearly ceremony of the old equinox, at each of the ancient gates, the blocks were tested. The first time, I remember, I stood behind Umbard, my head barely to his chest, my mouth open, as the niellen stones slid silently shut, creating a stone chamber that not even the strongest demon could escape. Then, my heart pounding, I had followed Umbard, as each new student had followed his or her first proctor, standing briefly alone in the square of judgment before being motioned to pass.

For all that two centuries had passed since the last demon had been caught and imprisoned in Henvor, my heart still beat a little faster each year, at least until the yin in the silver passlet on my wrist was renewed.

On the old city side of the demon gate, a constable in the dun red of the Shraddans smiled. "Happy awakening to you, candidate scholar."

"May the mists always be soft at dawn."

She nodded, and I passed, and before long, with the other twenty senior candidate scholars, I stood in the Hall of Unremitting Alertness.

Nearly so old as Henvor itself, the stone arches that bore the ancient oak cross beams and the niellen dark-slates soared into the dimness nearly thirty meters over-head, their size diminished only by their height. Aquacyn softboots remained motionless on the green ceramic floor tiles that showed no wear after nearly a millennium—yet another relic of the Days of Wonder and the time of demons.

Along the eastern wall stood the eight Masters of Dzin. Manwarr stood third from the left. Idly, I supposed that, had I been born in Klama, I might have been instructed by a Master of Toze. But speculating on the face I might have had if my parents had possessed others was futile . . . and meaningless.

"There is no ceremony to wisdom, and wisdom requires none," said Abbo Sanhedran. "The individual reveres wisdom because it increases self; the merchant because it increases coins; and the scholar because wisdom is the first step to ignorance. May the wisdom you possess truly be but a first step on that journey."

The words flowed over and around me, perhaps because I had heard them so many times before, just as the younger candidate scholars standing in the back of the Hall were hearing them.

I looked at the cream-colored sash worn by the Abbo, but once a year, wondering if someday I also might wear the cream.

After the ceremony, I walked to Manwarr's hypostyle, wanting to scurry, but, no longer a scholar candidate but a junior master of Dzin, I forced deliberation, even slow-

ing to savor the delicate perfume of the golden spring-
poppies in the garden without.

As I entered through the plain stone columns and
bowed, Manwarr returned the gesture, his faded blue
gown sweeping the polished stones of the columned west
meditation room, the one where he taught those of us who
had been senior scholar candidates. "You have been
called."

I waited.

"Townkeeper Trefor of Hybra has requested a junior
master now that Ainged has remanded his post and seeks
the Way of Ignorance."

My entire abdomen twisted in upon itself.

"You are fortunate indeed," Manwarr said, "for Hybra
looks upon Deep Lake. Years ago, in the time of the Fifth
Colloquium, the Master Vollod brought us, all the junior
scholars, to the precipice to behold the eels."

My stomach sank further. Eels were the last thing I
wanted to hear about. Hybra, where I would be schoolmaster to the offspring of foresters and trufflers. Hybra, a
town so small it barely needed a gliderway.

"I remember now what he said when the sun split the
crevasse and the light spilled like an arrow onto the waters."

I forced myself to nod.

"A true Dzin image renders insights beyond speech."
Manwarr was always like that, spouting forth platitudes
that were so obvious that they'd have been as threadbare
as the Abbo's ceremonial sash.

I reminded myself to consider that the obvious could
yet bear truth, even though I could not always see such.

"In Hybra, you will have the time to consider the life
you have not led. I would suggest, Tyndel, that you devote
yourself both to your duties and to your garden."

"I shall endeavor to follow your advice."

"Through disappointment, through the eye of the needle, lies shradda." Manwarr paused, and, in a way, his
words were fresh, recalling the definition of *shradda*—

"faith," perfect faith in the triumph of true ignorance. "Did you know that Abbo Sanhedran was once schoolmaster in Danber? It has not even a gliderway, not even to this day." A brief smile followed.

"I did not know that." I didn't, but perhaps times had not changed that much since Abbo Sanhedran had been young. I felt Manwarr was letting me know that a schoolmaster in Hybra could become one of the eight masters, perhaps even Abbo.

"I expect you'll be wishing to share your good fortune with your family. Come see me after you're settled in Hybra. It's not that long by glider—less than an hour."

With his dismissal, I walked slowly, reflectively, back to my room, back to the narrow pallet bed and the desk and scriber that I would leave to another.

There, Hywk came upon me as I packed the two black duffels that contained all I had, all I needed. He had another year, or more, at the Hall.

"The aquacyan wears well upon you, Tyndel."

"An aquacyan robe is an aquacyan robe." A safe enough platitude, and true.

"I wish you well on your posting. When you get where you're going, let me know."

"I know where I'm going, but not where I'm destined." I offered a laugh.

"The road not taken can be walked another day."

Hywk's words told me he had an idea that I wasn't sure whether to be pleased or not. But I didn't want to tell him that I'd been sent to Hybra, not after suggesting almost arrogantly earlier that I might have been considered for the undermaster opening at the Lyceum at Leboath.

"Perhaps even in the soft mists of morning." At least I had not been tasked to one of the floating cities.

"Or the fullness of evening, when the heat has fled." Hywk always grinned when he talked about evening, and most of Henvor knew why. That may have been one reason he had lingered so long under the tutelage of Master

Juab, the inscrutable. "I'll be late for my session. Do let me know."

A warm and crooked grin, and he was gone, and I needed but to add the last items to my bags. Then there wasn't much else to do but carry the duffels down to the gliderway above the river. I had up to three weeks before going to Hybra. That was the custom, and I hadn't been informed otherwise.

The orange ball of the morning sun was golden and near noon-high by the time I stood and waited for the next glider south. The glider was empty, and, after easing the duffels into a locker, I sat on the polished and curved wood of the first seat under the reflective overcanopy and watched the river as the glider carried me south toward Leboath, Wyns, and eventually Mettersfel. The faintest odor of ozone permeated the glider, a sign of impending maintenance.

The narrow grassy lawns that flanked the river near the center of Henvor, and Teford, since Teford was on the west side of the Greening and Henvor the east, quickly gave way to the marshes, the tall grasses, and the lilies. A huge blue heron stalked, darted his beak, and came up with a silver fish before the taller rushes to the south blocked my view.

A single-sailed tillerboard slid northward in the light breeze, a blond and white-skinned figure guiding the fragile craft more toward the pleasure docks at Teford and away from the eastern shore.

The late spring air flowed around the windscreen and caressed my face, and I watched the Greening, the occasional boaters, and the scattered dwellings between Henvor and Leboath. Older and smaller than Henvor, Leboath sits on a low plateau overlooking the river, and the glider slipped uphill toward the first boarding point on the north side.

As it slowed, I glanced at the smooth-faced green bricks that walled the antique waiting platform, bricks still unmarked, unvanquished by rain and weather, yet exuding age, and at the hard-finished and polished oak timbers that comprised each corner post and supported the roof. The design proclaimed the age of the timbers, as did their mellow aenous shade, but like most structures in Dorcha, the platform and its roof had been well built and better maintained.

A woman in a green tunic and trousers boarded at the north stop in Leboath, as did two couples, younger than I. The couples sat in the rear, but the woman sat across the aisle from me.

"On holiday, young master?" The white-haired woman's eyes sparkled as she settled herself and the glider eased at half speed toward the midtown stop. "You must be a teacher."

"Not yet. I'll be going to my first position after I see my family."

"Teaching is important, especially for the young." She snorted slightly. "Too many worry about being great masters in the Halls. You do, too. You've got the look. You'll be great someday, but not in the way you expect, I'd bet. In the interim, teach the young the best you can. That's anyone's true legacy."

"The dye is scarcely dry on my gown," I protested, half smiling.

She smiled. "You've the marks of greatness, but what kind is too early to say."

Marks of greatness? For a junior scholar master headed for a small Dorchan town?

"You smile, but I've seen my share of greatness over the years, and it's not a blessing. The only difficulty is that escaping greatness brings an even greater curse."

Was she one of the superstitious single-god believers? I nodded. "Your words are stamped with the imprint of truth." Safe enough to say.

"All words bear some truth."

The glider stopped once more, in mid-Leboath, and two men and three women boarded silently. All five, plus one of the couples in the rear, got off at the next stop—the south platform of Leboath, a roofless stand set in an extensive Barren Isles garden with maze hedges and topiaries shaped like fantastic birds with fanned tails. Outside of that one garden, I'd never seen such an image.

I did not speak as the glider accelerated southward, but watched the river once more.

"Good day and bright skies." The white-haired woman in green nodded as she rose to debark at Wyns.

"And to you."

"Thank you, young master, but at my age we take any day and whatever may be in the skies." The warm smile and soft tone further disarmed her words.

Two more stops in Wyns added more passengers, and the glider was nearly full as it whispered away from the south boarding point in Wyns. I withdrew more into my own thoughts. A teacher's post was certainly honorable, but what would I say to my father?

Yet even before the glider was close to Mettersfel, I was worrying about his disappointment. For the son of a merchant, the only mastership was one in a prestigious location. Dzin for the sake of Dzin was not enough.

Then, had it been so for me in the beginning? I forced a deep and contemplative breath.

4

[LYNCOL: 4513]

Explanation is not an escape from suffering.

Some nightmares don't end. I woke on a pallet not of snow, nor stone nor dirt nor leaves, but of some unyielding substance harder than steel or stone, and every muscle twitched. Yet I could control none of them.

Days earlier I had outrun gliders, and even heaved massive stones, but I could not move as I lay under a curtain of light that pulsed into my eyes, right through the lids even when I shut them. An odor of machines and power burned through my nostrils.

"Our boy here—he's got one of the really bad old versions—probably from the old Eibran massacre. We get one from there every few years, some form of ethical punishment or something." The man's voice, if demons were men, if demons had captured me, was deep, almost bass.

"Careful . . . he can still hear," cautioned a higher voice—a woman?

"It won't register. Never does. See . . . there's no violent feedback, and he's wearing aquacyan."

"A real hardcase for Jost or Cerrelle, if he makes it."

I understood the meaning of every word that penetrated the light curtain, and yet the sentences made no sense at all, except for the words about what I was wearing and about ethical punishment, which seemed like a redundant phrase to me.

How could any punishment in Dorcha not be ethical? How could those who truly followed Dzin not be ethical? How could following Dzin have led me to this? I would have cried out if I could.

My eyes blinked, and again I could see the arcs of golden red fire that seemed to web a black star-pointed sky. The curtain of light vanished, as did the words of the unseen speakers, and for a time I beheld bright stars in a sky blacker than any I had ever seen.

That image faded, and I was back under the light curtain.

"Another pulse from the En-field. Really dragged him down. There has to be an affinity there. He doesn't have that high a nanite concentration yet." The woman's voice was dispassionate, like that of a Dzin master, except that Harleya had been the only woman among the eight Dzin masters in recent generations.

"Old Engee must be having difficulties getting recruits these days. Or worshippers."

"We don't know that. It's a misnomer to call something like that a deity, anyway. You should know better."

"Whatever, Seana, whatever. If our boy makes it, he'll give Engee fits."

"If . . . if . . . if . . . Stop talking and help me with the reformulation insertion. He'll need the heavy-duty series . . . and that's more than iffy."

The light curtain flared, and I saw darkness . . . and nothing—again.

5

[HYBRA: 4510]

Better to see the face than hear the name.

Lessons had gone well. Even young Sergol had nodded his understanding of the parables of San-Merto, and I almost skipped, undignified as that would have been for a young Dzin master, as I headed home from the school. In the lane, well before the boxwood, the deep blue lilacs were about to bud. My nose twitched, anticipating their fragrance, a fragrance that I linked to Foerga, though her eyes were deeper than the lilacs.

"Strive not for beauty of raiment, nor for stately dwellings . . . behold the lilac." I laughed gently at my own attempts at a Dzin saying. The feeling was there, just not the conciseness and depth. With time, and more study, perhaps both would come. Manwarr had been right; Hybra had been good for me . . . good for both of us.

" . . . the sun is in the sky; the water in the river . . ." *And Foerga is here, creating beauty.* What more could any Dzin master ask?

When I opened the door to the house, I could tell Foerga was not there, but I could smell hot glass. Rather than call to her and possibly disturb whatever crystal she might be working, I slipped out toward her workshop, the small high-roofed and rectangular outbuilding we had added when Foerga had first joined me in Hybra. In the sunlit coolness of early spring, the door was open, and I stepped inside as noiselessly as I could.

Her back to me, Foerga drew the glass-bearing blow-pipe out of the furnace.

Holding my own breath, I watched as she blew, as the blue-tinged glass expanded evenly, and then as she deftly took the rod and twirled and shaped, in ways I could but watch and understand but not duplicate, until suddenly there was a long-stemmed, delicately fluted goblet, shimmering, standing where none had stood before. Truly, Foerga exemplified the Dzin ideal of perfection of the art, yet as an artist and a person, she also neared perfection.

When she eased back from the goblet, I did step forward. "It's beautiful. So are you, and I'm always amazed."

My words brought a shy smile, as though, even after seven years, acknowledgment of her beauty of soul and body yet astounded her. "They're for Elyancar. He has a customer in Leboath." She smiled more broadly. "He won't say who it is. So I told him he'd have to pay what she would, and he agreed."

"Who would not agree for your work?" And about that, I was right. Her crystal would be prized generations after my strivings with Dzin had vanished or, if I were fortunate, merged into the words taught to another generation.

"You praise me too much." She checked the furnace, then looked back at me. "I'd best do the last one."

"I don't praise you enough." For a moment, I saw the depth and the blue fire behind her eyes, those warm blue depths wherein I often looked and marveled. "After that, are you finished for this afternoon? Would you like some tea, then?"

She nodded, holding the glass pipe in one hand. "I very much would, especially the way you fix the Arleen."

"Good." I eased toward her, avoiding the pipe. She smelled of glass, and warmth, and fire, and I held her tightly. She returned the embrace, one-armed, and for precious long moments we remained an isle in a river. *The sun is in the sky, the water in the river . . .*

We kissed, then released each other slowly . . . eyes meeting for another timeless moment. After another brief kiss, I stepped back and went to prepare the Arleen.

6

[LYNCOL: 4513]

Where are you between two thoughts?

When I finally woke up, I lay on what seemed a normal bed with polished spindle posts on each corner. A wooden rocking chair sat in one corner with a table beside it, and a small glow lamp rested on the golden oak of the table. There were two other tables, one on each side of the bed, each also with a glow lamp, and a window that looked out over a rain-dampened and browning lawn and up at a slope thickly forested in evergreens.

I sat up slowly, swinging my feet to the side of the high bed and letting them dangle. I discovered I wore a green sleeping gown or the equivalent, silken against my skin. My face felt bare. As my eyes went to the mirror on the white wall, my fingers went to my chin—smooth as it had been back when I had been a scholar candidate. The brown hair on my head was also short.

A humming overhead, being paralyzed, lying under a canopy of light, and hearing voices . . . and now I was in a luxurious bedroom, with sheets and clothes as tightly woven as the finest silk.

The door opened, and a redheaded woman, as tall as I was, if not taller, stepped inside, closing it behind her. She wore a pale green shirt and trousers and brown boots. Her hair was short, for a woman, and her features sharp.

"I'm Cerrelle, and I'll be your guide." Her voice was girlish, but the piercing green eyes and the thin face were not, despite the welcoming smile.

I just looked at her. Guide? To what?

"To Lyncol, for one thing." She sat in the rocking chair and leaned back.

Lyncol?

"Lyncol—that's where we are. It's the coordinating center of Rykasha. Here." She took a deep breath. "I'm not likely to be as good as I probably should be. We don't get many converts anymore. That's if you can call unwilling nanite possession conversion."

Once again, I had the feeling of knowing most of the words and understanding little. All I really understood was loss. In the last few days, I'd lost everything— Foerga, my life in Dzin, my teaching, and nearly my life itself. Why? Because I'd changed a little?

"You really don't understand a word, do you?" She paused. "Some of this is going to be hard, especially for you."

For me? What did they know about me? "I would appreciate it . . . if you could tell me exactly what happened."

"You do speak. Good." A smile—sardonic, warm, wistful, all in one—crossed her thin lips.

I waited.

"You were infected with self-replicating nanites, and you happened to be one of the lucky ones with compatible genes. Relatively compatible. If we hadn't reengineered your system, you'd have burned out in another year or so. Painfully. About half who are infected die before they reach us—or get caught and killed by mites."

I just looked at her.

"Let me try again. In simple terms, nanites are subcellular organic machines that can undertake a wide array of tasks. Nanites immobilized you when they brought you in. They can block virtually any weapon short of high-powered lasers, particle beams, or nucleonic weapons. They come in various sizes, all of them submicroscopic. Let's see. How do I put this? A human cell averages twenty microns. Most nanites are one micron, although some of the specialized varieties are less than a tenth of a micron."

I struggled with the idea—something that capable that was a ten-thousand of a millimeter in size or smaller? My thoughts skittered away from the whole idea.

The woman frowned, not angrily, then smiled gently, almost as if I were a child. "I was afraid this was going to be hard for you. It will be harder than you think because, in a way, you've been subtly conditioned against higher technology."

Higher technology? What did technology have to do with where I was?

Cerrelle moistened her lips. "Somehow, one of those nanites infected you. They're old high technology. They changed you from being an unmodified human into a nanite-enhanced human. Weren't you able to run faster and farther and to lift heavier objects?"

"Yes." I nodded.

"That was because of the nanites," Cerrelle said.

My stomach tightened and sank. If what she said were correct . . . I was demon, and so was she. Me—a Dzin master—a demon?

"We call ourselves Rykasha." She smiled again, an expression warm and helpful, and just a hint patronizing. After a moment, she added, "People who aren't nanite-enhanced call us demons."

"But . . ." *Aren't those just words? Aren't you demons, the ones who brought down the ancients?* I didn't want to say anything out loud, but I might as well have done so.

Cerrelle shrugged apologetically. "Your legends are partly correct. The inability of the average mite . . . Dorchan . . . to cope with the advantages of nanotech was what destroyed the ancients."

My stomach growled.

"You need to eat. Your blood sugar's low, and you'll have enough trouble dealing with the changes in your life even when it's normal. Are you going to behave?" The green eyes glinted, humorously, directly, and that honest directness told me, again, how much I missed Foerga. I had the feeling I was going to miss her for a long time.

"It appears my choices are limited."

"For the moment. That will change once you get more settled." Cerrelle's lips quirked momentarily. "It might also be nice to know what to call you."

"I'm sorry. I'm Tyndel. All this seems like a nightmare. So much has happened." Hadn't I told her my name?

"It seems that way, I'm sure, but it's just the beginning. I'm sorry for being so direct in asking your name, but I had to ask because self-identification isn't the same as appellation. Early guides learned that." She stood and pointed to a sliding door in the wall. "That's a closet. There's a set of trousers and other clothes inside—and your boots. While you get dressed, I'll be waiting outside." She slipped out the door as silently as she had entered.

For a moment, I just sat on the high bed. Then I rose. The cool floor tile somehow reassured me as I walked to the closet. The pale green shirt and trousers felt almost silk-smooth, but I had the sense that they were close to indestructible. My own boots seemed crude in comparison, but I was glad something of my past remained.

I tried the other door—a shower chamber and toilet of odd design. I washed my face and hands before I stepped out of the room into a wood-paneled hallway where Cerrelle waited.

"You seem to be adjusting. It's hard, but try to take it moment by moment. Your Dzin might help with that."

I almost nodded to myself. *Concentrate on being aware of what is; seek no explanations; seek but awareness.* The mantra helped, and I squared my shoulders.

"If you're ready . . . ?"

I did nod then, and she turned and walked quickly down the white-tiled corridor, her boots padding on the hard surface. I had to stretch my legs to catch her, and by the time I did, she'd pushed through another door.

The low murmur of conversation caught me. Some of it died away as I stood in what seemed to be a dining common, then resumed.

". . . new convert . . . Cerrelle's charge . . ."

". . . keep her busy."

The redhead ignored the comments and walked along the end of the room to the far side. Cerrelle paused before a low console with several doors less than a half meter square and something like a miniature iconraiser's screen and keyboard. "There's a menu here, and it does have some Dorchan dishes."

I glanced around. There was no kitchen, yet the small dining area had a dozen diners, all with hot food. "Another demon miracle machine?"

"I guess it looks that way, but it's just a different way of processing molecules into food. Try to think of it like that." She lifted a card, one that was coated with a shimmering surface through which the printing appeared, and extended it to me. "There's the menu. If you see something you like, press the numbers on the board there. I'll show you."

Her own fingers tapped out the numbers, and a hum came from behind the far left door. Then a green light flashed over the door, and Cerrelle opened it, withdrawing a large slab of meat with an unfamiliar odor. Beside it was some form of steaming potato and what looked to be beans covered with buttered almonds.

"Steak. Beef protein. Rare. Quite good." She nodded

toward the tables. "Join me when you decide. Drinks are there." She pointed to a small table with several pitchers.

I read the list on the stiff and shining card. The printing was strange, angular, but recognizable, and that startled me momentarily. Somewhere half down the list was an entry I recognized—Orange Chicken Dorcha. I pressed the numbers, and the hum indicated the machine was at work.

I took the steaming dish to the table where Cerrelle sat, cutting her steak. She looked up and said gently, "Don't forget a drink. You'll need plenty of liquid."

So I got a large glass of water and seated myself, beginning to eat as my involuntary salivation told me just how hungry I was.

"How is it?" asked Cerrelle.

"It's good. Not the best, but very good."

"Another example of nanotech. The nanites rearrange the raw materials in the right order, and there you have anything you can program in."

"Is there anything they can't do?"

"They handle molecular rearrangement, not atomic patterns." She smiled. "They're like many machines, except smaller. They're like all technology. They don't do much for improving human intelligence or teaching people to think. And like a lot of technology, nanite systems can really create havoc when combined with human stupidity."

"Stupidity?" I wished the word hadn't escaped my lips, especially with the look Cerrelle offered.

"I wish I could explain everything, Tyndel, but I can't, not immediately. I can promise you that you'll get a history course, and a lot more, through nanopills and sprays. I know it would be easier if they could just stick all that in you right now, but body and mind, especially former mite minds, need periods of conscious and unconscious adjustment. Right now, I'll give you a few ideas to keep in mind. Ever heard of the free-birthers? The ancients had a lot of them—Saints, Roms, Buchs, Fals . . . so many ethnic and cultural groups I can't keep track of the names. There were close to eight billion people on the earth when nanotech became a functional reality, when the ability arrived to have every living human being a fully functional *and reproducing* organism for a thousand years. The free-birthers were producing five to ten offspring in a forty-year span and violently opposed any restrictions on reproduction. Now . . . anyone with any common sense could figure out the mathematics if even ten percent of the population practiced free-birth, and it was more like twenty percent."

"There wouldn't be enough food." I paused. "Except . . . what about machines like those?" I pointed to the console.

"That just made things worse. Every group wanted the health benefits, and self-reproducing nanites for an individual's system were relatively easy. Machinery, like those molecular food creators, takes capital, money, tools—and some power, and there wasn't enough. So . . . the ancients had lots of very physically healthy and strong people with even healthier appetites—those who had heavy weapons and food survived—about one hundred million, and the technology base was pretty much lost, except here and in Thule and one or two smaller enclaves."

"We have a decent technology base—"

"I should have said nanotech. Old-style technology is pretty limiting. It takes too much resource investment to maintain. That's even with a small population. It can't be done with a large population, and the ancients never did figure that out. That is one thing you . . . Dorchans figured out. You were successful in finding a self-reinforcing way to ration out goods and services that doesn't exceed the carrying capacity of the environment."

"So how do you do it?" I mumbled, angry with her veiled condescension and superiority.

"Some of the ancients had the right idea, and then they gave it up." Her words ignored my anger. "Each individual has a worth to society. All people are not equal, not in those terms. We reward people for their service to society and charge them for the resources that they consume, in general terms, just as the ancients did, and you mites do, with credits. We figure the basis for the credits differently. Those people who consume more than they earn have to repay the balance within a year or undertake compensatory service, like you will."

"Me?"

"Once you get medically stabilized and on your feet, you'll become a part of Rykashan society. Just like the rest of us, you'll need to make your way and pay for the goods and services you need. I'm here to get you started on making that adjustment."

That made a sort of sense, I had to admit. I looked at my plate. It was empty.

"You're still hungry, aren't you?"

"Yes."

"Go order another helping. You'll need it all. The nanites take extra energy. That's something you'll need to remember. As soon as you finish, Tyndel, we've got to get back to work. You've got a lifetime of knowledge and skills to catch up on. The sooner you understand where you are and how Rykasha works, the better off you'll be."

I didn't like the sound of that, or the idea of compensatory service, whatever that was, but the demons were treating me better than my own people had, except for Foerga.

I swallowed at that, and my eyes burned. I rose quickly and went back to the food console and studied the list, choosing something called Lemon Beef. Maybe the different taste would help, but I doubted it.

7

[METTERSFEL: 4503]

Wretched are all who work for results.

Mettersfel was large enough that it had smaller gliders that webbed the city, and large enough that private gliders or carts paid exorbitant passage-rights. Even so, at times one had to pause before crossing the wide and grass-centered boulevards.

After leaving the intercity glider, I took the harbor bluff glider. Because an older man already sat in the rear seat, I sat in front. When the glider reached the throughway at the top of the bluff and whispered across the polished stones, the Summer Sound spread out below the eastern bluffs. The sun danced on the gray-blue waters, and the foam of the small whitecaps glistened and subsided, glistened and subsided.

The stone piers shone almost white in the late-afternoon sun, although clouds were building offshore. Beyond the piers lay the low commercial buildings, most of gray or white stone framing the amber powerglass that supplemented the other solar and tidal power systems that supplied the city-state that was Mettersfel.

The older man watched, without speaking, as I left the glider at the Rim Park stop. The gold polished spruce of the exercise bars rose out of the lawn to my left. I'd never been that good at pure gymnastics, but I'd always liked the park, particularly the gardens on the downslope to the lower bluffs with their stone-walled terraces and the colors and scents of all the flowers.

The thought prompted me to pause and inhale, and to enjoy the faint smell of roses mixed with sunbursts. *What is . . . is.* I had to smile, recalling what I'd been taught in the middle of the park.

Beyond the park began the houses, all of one or two stories and situated to catch the sweep of the sound and the lower city. I was perspiring heavily by the time I had walked the half kilo from the park to the house and carried both duffels up to the low front steps of the two-story scaled-down replica of a Breaker house.

A low growl from the walled front side garden indicated that my parents, my mother, doubtless, had gotten another dog to replace Gershon.

My cousin Rhada opened the door. "They said you'd be here."

"I'm here. Where are they?" The duffels went on the spotless green marble, and I wiped my forehead with the back of my forearm. "It's hotter than I remember."

"Your mother's coming down from her studio, I imagine. Uncle Tynd—he's where he always is, trading and watching the markets." Rhada offered a crooked smile that bared perfect white teeth. "It has been hot this spring."

"Dear . . ." My mother was already halfway down the polished marble of the curving hall steps, steps that curved around the crystal chandelier that had been blown and cut nearly two centuries earlier by her grandmother. Artistic talent seemed to run in the women of the family.

"Mother." I bowed, then stepped forward and hugged her.

"You look wonderful in the blue."

"Aquacyan," I mumbled.

"Much better than in that brown."

Colors weren't everything, but mother was an artist. So perhaps they were.

"You must be famished. We should have tea. Up on the higher balcony." Mother turned to Rhada. "If you would give me a hand . . . I was having difficulty with the alcade's hair."

"You're doing the chief magistrate's portrait?"

"He finally conceded that only I was worthy to do it."
She laughed. "Why don't you put your bags away and
then go up to the balcony terrace?" Her words were really
a question, but a great deal of Mother's questions weren't.

My room was nearly exactly as I'd left it, except that
the bed frame had been refinished, as had the writing table. I set the duffels before the closet, then washed up,
enjoying the cool water on a flushed face. After that, I
went across the hall and out onto the balcony, where I
pulled up a chair. For some reason, I was tired.

From under the arches of the roofed second-level
balcony I could see the sound, and the harbor, and the
long and white-walled building that held Tynd Trading.
My father had purchased the older home that had once
stood on the site and totally rebuilt it—all so he could
watch the harbor when he wasn't down there.

I'd barely gotten settled when Rhada and my mother
arrived with two trays. Mother began to pour the tea, offered the tall and fluted cups to each of us, and eased into
the high-backed trader's chair beside me.

Rhada set down the smaller tray—nuts, sliced apples,
white cheese, and cakes and biscuits. "He looks older,
Aunt Kerisma."

I should have; it had been nearly six years since I'd
seen Rhada.

My mother's hand strayed to her thick and short silver-
gray hair. "Over six years, we've all aged, Rhada, Tyndel
the least of all, I imagine."

I didn't answer, but waited for my mother to touch her
cup, which she did, before taking a long and welcome sip
of the Arleen tea.

"I miss good tea."

"So why don't you come back to Mettersfel?" asked
Rhada.

"It doesn't work that way. The Dzin masters decide
where I teach."

"You don't have to do as they say."

"Of course not. I can leave at any time. But I can't

come back." I smiled. "I've learned a lot through Dzin."

"You'd be better off here. As a trader, or even as a private master in the trading school or in the Changers tutorial system. They pay Dzin-trained teachers well." Rhada smiled and took a swallow of the Arleen, so big a swallow that I wondered whether she'd even tasted it.

"Where will you be going, dear?" asked Mother quietly.

"Hybra. It's a small town on Deep Lake, northwest of Henvor."

"That's not far from the border with Rykasha." Rhada shivered.

"Rhada, don't exaggerate." My mother's tone was patiently exasperated. "The border's been stable for nearly a millennium, and no one's even seen a demon in Mettersfel for over twenty-five years. Or most places in Dorcha." She lifted her cup, sipped, and continued. "Besides, if Tyndel wants to teach there, it will be good experience. If he likes it, then that's good. If he doesn't, then the experience will be good for him and make him more desirable to the others here or elsewhere." She smiled, closing that subject.

Mother was nothing if not practical. I refilled my cup and had one of the butter biscuits.

"Have you heard about the Dhurs?" Rhada finally asked. The Dhurs were always a favorite topic of conversation. Everything they did was outrageous, impossible, and a form of insanity.

"What now?" I couldn't even guess.

"The Genchief of the Dhurs traveled to Mettersfel on a restored Second Confed warboat. He aimed the lasecannon at the MerChange and demanded that the Changers advance the credits for a Dhur floating city."

"And?"

"There's a new Dhur Genchief, and an interestingly shaped chunk of steel and composite that the Metalworkers are reclaiming. You can see the wreckage beyond the last pier. The salvage fees *might* pay off the damage claims against the Dhurs, including the power surcharges, but the Dhurs are claiming that it was all a misunderstanding."

"With the Dhurs, a great deal is." I took a surreptitious look toward the harbor. There was something that looked like a melted ship.

Rhada laughed.

Mother frowned.

"Have you run across anyone lately?" Rhada meant anyone she and Mother were likely to know.

"Outside of Khandet? He's still studying under Master Celvan. Not anyone else. Mettersfel doesn't generate a lot of interest in Dzin. I've lost touch with almost everyone." A thought struck me. "I should inquire after Esolde."

"Esolde? Is she the blonde you longed after before you marched off to the masters at Henvor? She is a scholar doctor with the healing masters in Halz, well above you now, Tyndel." Rhada was matter-of-fact, as she always had been, regardless of the impact.

So Esolde had gone to Halz? The great delta city of the River Dor? The only city to which the mighty merchants of Mettersfel paid heed, where healing raised more credits than trade?

"She was a lovely girl," Mother offered. "From a good family, too, and that always helps. Blood will tell." She smiled wryly. "In time, at least."

"I remember you spent a great deal of time around a certain grape trellis," suggested Rhada.

I couldn't help blushing.

"See! He's still mooning over her."

"Mooning over a memory, I suspect," said Mother. "But I do know another lovely young lady you should meet."

"Oh?"

"Her name is Foerga. She's a crystal worker—fine hand, very artistic, and really too sweet for most of the merchant types."

In spite of the suggested arrangement, I was intrigued.

And Mother had always had good taste. She had liked Esolde.

"Aunt Kerisma . . ." Rhada rose from the table. "I need to be going home, but it was good to get away from the twins for a little while."

I rose as well. "It was good to see you."

After escorting Rhada to the front door, I rejoined my mother on the balcony.

"I did mean it about Foerga."

"I know," I told her. "I've always respected your taste. I'd be happy to meet her."

"Good. She's coming for dinner tomorrow."

"Ah . . . all right." One thing about Mother—when she decided, she acted. Then, around my father, I supposed that was a necessity.

"I think I heard the glider enter the hangloft."

She could also hear the sound of butterfly wings, or delphinium stalks brushing against each other, from a kilo away, one reason why there had seldom been any secrets in the house.

With the steps echoing out to the balcony I stood, barely before my father burst onto the balcony.

"Son . . . it's good to see you." My father stepped forward and hugged me, moving as he always did, in quick bursts, with an energy that declared there was never enough time for anything. Then he released his bear hug and dropped into the chair where Rhada had been sitting. "So . . . you're a master of Dzin now. What does that mean?"

"Not a great deal," I had to admit. "I get to teach in out-of-the-way places or as a junior master under an experienced master."

"Someone has to, but you could do a lot more as a trader."

"No," I answered with a laugh. "If you were in my position, you could do a great deal more as a trader."

He laughed in return. "I suppose you're right, but I hate to see all that intelligence wasted in a schoolroom." He lifted the cup my mother had silently filled. "I know. I know. It's not a waste. Someone has to prepare children, and if the teacher isn't the best, we all suffer in the future." He shook his head briskly, as briskly as he did everything. "I still think you're cut out for something different. But I've tried, and you've tried, and we are where we are." He took a quick sip of tea. "How long will you be here?"

"Three weeks."

"Good. I understand your mother has some special treats planned for you. Besides your favorite meals, I mean." He grinned.

"She's alluded to one already." I grinned and leaned back in the chair, pleased that my father had decided to leave the past behind, and pleased with myself that I'd been able to rely on Dzin not to worry overly.

"There could be more," he said dryly.

We both laughed.

8

[HYBRA:4512]

All societies are evil, sorrowful, and inequitable, and always will be. Therefore, if you wish to help the world, you must first learn to live in it and then teach others the same.

The fields and gardens outside the school were sodden with the late fall rain, and all the students' boots rested on the spooled rack under the convective heater. The smooth, dark paving stones of Hybra, beyond the waist-high stone walls that surrounded the gardens and lawns and playing fields, shimmered with a reflective coat of rain.

I looked down from the dais at the fifteen students—

nine girls and six boys—seated on their pillows on the polished gold of the wooden floor, their lap desk stands set aside after their concrete mathematics lessons. The hint of dried apples and lavender perfumed the heavy air.

With a slow, deep breath, I looked at the book, although I knew the phrases by heart after eight years.

"Knowledge begets power.

"Power begets force.

"Force is applied from ignorance."

With a smile of habit, I looked at the blond youth on the end. "Sergol? Would you finish it?"

"Knowledge leads to ignorance." He frowned, and his thin lips turned down.

"You wonder how knowledge begets ignorance?" I nodded at the redhead beside him. "Wryan?"

"The twofold path," Wryan said confidently. "The total of knowledge is greater than the ability of any individual to assimilate. Because an individual does not comprehend what he or she does not know, the selection of knowledge by an individual is based on the knowledge possessed. The greater the knowledge possessed, the less likely the individual to discover ignorance. The less the knowledge possessed by the individual, the more likely ignorance is to be revealed. Thus, greater knowledge leads to greater influence by ignorance, and greater ignorance to greater influence by knowledge." Wryan bestowed a smile on Sergol.

Sirena—the girl to the left of Wryan—concealed a wince.

Sergol fidgeted on his pillow as the wind splashed fat raindrops on the clear permaglass of the high windows, and as the indirect breeze wafted through the room, bringing the faint scent of winter fern and pushing out the lavender.

"You doubt that all knowledge conceals greater ignorance?" I asked. Questions would not have been appropriate for older students, at the collegium in Mettersfel or in the Hall of Dzin in Henvor, but by questions must

masters draw out the misconceptions of the young before
they blossom into the knowledge-based power that is in
truth ignorance.

"Enlighten my ignorance, Master Tyndel." Sergol
bowed his head, keeping his eyes properly downcast.

"You do not believe that knowledge conceals ignorance," I said mildly. There was no use in anger; it would
only have bewildered him and weakened me. "To those
who seek knowledge, one piece of knowledge by itself is
not enough, Sergol. As the Abbo Sanhedran said, 'Of
making great knowledge there is no end, and much study,
and the knowledge therefrom is a weariness of the flesh
and a deadening of the spirit.' And we know what happened to the ancients, do we not?"

From the end of the second row, Fyonia bobbed her
head vigorously.

Keeping my distaste for such unseemly enthusiasm
from my lips, I inclined my head to the stocky daughter
of Hybra's most senior truffler, refraining from touching
my beard, finally beginning to show some gray, some visible indication of age and wisdom.

"The ancients wrested the secrets from the depths of
the earth and from the hearts of the stars, and with those
secrets they banished sickness, death, and all forms of
discomfort. And sickness, death, and discomfort gathered
together and created the demons, and the demons destroyed the ancients." Fyonia paused, then added conver-
sationally, "Most of them, but not all, or we wouldn't be
here."

The three bright faces in the back row were blank, as
those new to the school always were when the subject
first arose.

"The dangers of knowledge are threefold." I nodded to
Katya.

"There is the danger of not learning; the danger of
learning too much; and the danger of not understanding,"
she answered.

"But it is not like that, Master Tyndel." Sergol's words

tumbled out. "The big trout like the black worms. I put a black worm on the hook. I catch a trout. One piece of knowledge . . . one trout. I know that there is much I do not understand, but how can that one bit of knowledge lead to ignorance and evil?"

It was a fair question. That I had to admit to myself because I had asked it, years back. Yet I had been older than Sergol, years older, though my words had doubtless been more polished.

"Now, Sergol, you seek one trout. What happens when you are older? When you must provide your share of food for the town?" I shrugged. "You understand, but not all people do. And the ancients did not. So, they found ways to put many hooks on their lines, and ways to make their lines strong enough to hold many fish. In time, there were not enough fish. Then they grew the fish in ponds, but the ponds changed the land, and soon there were not enough birds to kill the insects, and many people sickened. Then the ancients killed the insects, and more of the birds died, and many small animals. To feed the people, and there were many people in the ancient times, their knowledge-seekers planted corn and maize and rice everywhere, and in many places the ground was too dry and blew away, and in others it was too wet, and the crops rotted. And people died. So many people died that there were not the numbers to count them." I paused.

Sergol was trying hard not to shake his head.

"That was when the ancients harnessed the powers of the demons, and the demons turned wastes and chaff and bark from fallen trees into food, good food, and for a time, all was well. For a time." I smiled and waited.

"But . . . that was better than people starving, was it not? People were not meant to starve, were they, Master Tyndel?" asked Sergol.

"Nor were fishes or birds. Too much of any good ceases to be good. All of you in the front row. Write me an essay for tomorrow on the excess of good." I offered a frown, not entirely for theatrical effect. "Now . . . out with your physical science assignments."

I wheeled the projection screen into place and waited, ignoring the slumped shoulders and the not-quite-hidden glares at Sergol, who still smiled brightly.

Physical science was straightforward enough, since we were dealing with the basics of material structure and chemistry, and not questions of Dzin. After science came language and rhetoric.

At the end of the day, after sweeping the floor, mopping it, polishing it with the cloth buffer, and setting up for the morning, I adjusted my hat and stepped out of the school into the rain that was more than a drizzle but less than the downpour that had pelted the roof tiles earlier in the afternoon.

The faint whine of a cart rose over the whisper of the rain and the light breeze. I watched as it lurched slightly— usually the sign of a fuel cell close to the end of its life— and several of the large pumpkins and squash in the carry bin rolled, but the driver did not turn, and I could not make out who it might have been through the rain.

I walked on, my waterproof and hat more than enough protection against the fast-falling drops, still wondering about the questions Sergol had asked. Scarcely questions from a truffler's and fisherman's family, and certainly the first so well posed in years. Yet Sergol had been blissfully unaware of the impact of his questions, even as the others in the first row had not. Fyonia and Wryan—they had understood, as had even some of those in the back, who had not heard my words before. So why had Sergol not understood?

"The unexpected only means that which you have not expected." That was what my old tutor Manwarr would have said, and he would have been right.

From the corner of my eye, the motion of the glider caught me, and I turned. Three people sat under the clear bubble canopy as the five-meter-long craft slid toward the kiosk that marked town center, apparently suspended in midair over the black, rain-polished stones of the glider-way.

I thought the figures might have been Eel-master Parsfal and Quella and their daughter, probably returning from shopping in Leboath, but a line of rain splashed over me, and I blinked, and the glider was out of sight.

Just before I reached our gate, so did the Townkeeper, and he waited for me.

"Master Tyndel." Trefor bowed the bow of the perfect third.

"Townkeeper Trefor." I responded, as necessary to the headman of the town, with one of a perfect fourth. "You look well."

"As do you, Master Tyndel."

"And of those you wish to speak?"

Trefor bowed again, then offered a smile. "Dynae has become a candidate scholar in the Hall of Dzin, under the Overmaster Juab. Much credit falls upon you."

"I can only take refuge in ignorance, Townkeeper. May she find it as much of a blessing as I have."

"I am most certain she will, Master Tyndel." He inclined his head, smiled, and continued toward the brown-walled house on the hill to the east of the square.

The drier and covered front portico of our home beckoned, and I sloshed the last few meters up the walk, turning and looking back once I was under the overhang. Was the yew hedge too large, its edge too close to the green ceramic border of the walk? The edges were clean, straight, and they should have been, but the hedge did appear oversized, slightly at least?

An ill-proportioned hedge would not be appropriate for Hybra's Dzin master, small as the school was, especially not after the Townkeeper's visit.

I repressed a shrug and opened the door. The scent of lemon-grass chicken filled the foyer, and my mouth watered as I took off my boots and donned the green house slippers.

I bowed to Foerga as I entered the kitchen. Foerga was

tall, half a head taller than I, and her eyes were the piercing blue of the west, for all that her parents and ancestors had lived in Dorcha all the days of their existences.

She nodded in return, and her eyes met mine, and we both smiled.

"My dear." I kept smiling.

"You looked troubled when you came in, Tyndel. Is it the rain?" She offered another of the warm smiles I treasured. "The tea is ready."

"I can't say it is the rain, but I am indeed ready for tea." We didn't go in for the long ceremony, just the short one, and I marveled, as always, at the precision and grace with which Foerga served and presented the tea. My own efforts fell far short of hers.

I sat at the burnished oak table set in the bay that overlooked the rear garden and the raven fountain that had been Foerga's first gift to me after she had joined me in Hybra. The warm scent of the Arleen wreathed my face, offering comfort.

"And your day?" I asked after the first sip, letting the warmth diffuse through me.

"Quiet. I finished the last of the goblets for Annynca. The turned ones, you recall?" She lifted her cup as gracefully as she had poured the tea.

I recalled. The area prefect's spouse had wanted unique goblets and hadn't even balked at the price—more than thirty credits each. "They're a bargain at thirty."

"Perhaps in Metterfels, but not in Hybra. Annynca and the Townkeeper's family are the only ones here who can afford my better work."

That was why Foerga often took the glider to Henvor or Teford, or down the Greening River to Leboath or even the Metterfels of her youth. There the great art dealers or even the household planners employed by the families of the wealthy clamored for her work.

"It's a pity, in some ways."

"In some," she conceded. "But it is far more peaceful here, and I'm happier and do better work where it's peaceful." She offered that open smile, so much more warming than even the Arleen tea.

"I'm glad of that."

"So am I." She refilled her cup, and then mine.

"I noticed the hedge. Does it seem slightly overlarge? Perhaps overpowering the balance between the garden rows and the walk?"

Foerga laughed gently, kindly. "You have always seen those balances more readily than I."

"You're too kind. I see your glasswork, and the balance and artistry."

"Glass and crystal are not living plants. There's a difference."

I let it go. She believed what she said, my all-too-modest Foerga. "Townkeeper Trefor was waiting by the gate for me," I mused. "It wasn't an accident."

"I would think not. There are not many accidents in any townkeeper's life." She slid the plate of wafer biscuits before me.

"Thank you." The butter-based wafer melted in my mouth, and I took another sip of tea, glancing out the window at the blue-feathered jay that alighted on the smooth brown bricks of the garden wall before shaking awkwardly, spreading wing, and vanishing into the mist and twilight. "Young Dynae had been accepted as a candidate scholar by Overmaster Juab."

"Overmaster Juab was at Henvor when you studied with Master Manwarr. You spoke of him."

"He always had insights, but seldom spoke." I sipped the last of the tea in the cup. "I did not recommend Dynae. Not even to Manwarr."

"His selection of Dynae troubles you."

"I cannot believe I was that mistaken. Yet . . ." I shook my head slowly. "To believe in one's own infallibility proves the opposite."

"You think that other considerations were involved?"

"I cannot believe that, either, although my mind says such is certainly possible." I laughed. "I don't wish to believe that Juab might be either fallible or venal, nor that my judgment was so erroneous."

"Sometimes, as someone I respect and love has said, all choices are unpleasant."

"You keep me more honest than I would otherwise be."

"More humble, I suspect. Not more honest. You're too honest as it is, Tyndel, my dear."

My dear . . . How I loved those words and the lady who uttered them. With a smile, I lifted the teacup. I could do nothing about Dynae, nor Juab, nor the Townkeeper. I could hold to the warmth of the past that we had built over the years in Hybra.

Had it been eight years? Closer to nine, actually. Nine years since I'd walked the River Greening and watched two children kiss by a cataclypt? Nine years since I'd found a blue-eyed artist who warmed my soul? Nine years bringing Dzin to the children of trufflers, fishers, eelmasters, and geoponickers.

Tomorrow, I thought. Tomorrow, I would prune the hedge, before anyone else noticed the imbalance. I smiled to myself at the thought. Who else would even notice? But once a Dzin master, however humble, always one, even unto pruning hedges.

9

[METTERSFEL: 4503]

Openness to the world, to what is, can never be aquired.

I paced back and forth across the foyer floor. Had allowing Mother to invite her young artisan friend been a mistake?

"Don't be so nervous," my mother called from the lower balcony.

That was easy enough for her to say.

"Your father won't be home for a while," she added, as if that were supposed to be a consolation.

I paced some more. At least I'd grown up with Esolde. What if I didn't like this woman? Mother would be telling me how good and how talented she was for the entire length of my stay.

"Stop pacing. You sound like a demon in heat. It doesn't become the aquacyan."

I stopped and shook my head. How could a demon be in heat? And what did that have to do with the color of my robes?

Then the bells chimed, and I took a deep breath before stepping forward and opening the door.

The woman who stood under the front portico was tall, at least half a head taller than I. The black hair framed a thin face, one dominated by deep blue eyes. The green-tinged blue tunic and trousers she wore neither added to nor subtracted from the clean lines of her face.

"Greetings," I offered.

"I'm Foerga. You must be Tyndel." Her lips curled into a warm smile, and her eyes sparkled.

I had to smile in return. "I'm Tyndel. Please come in."

When I closed the door, my mother's voice carried from the balcony. "Do bring Foerga out, Tyndel."

What else was I going to do? I wanted to roll my eyes.

Foerga's smile turned into a grin, and she murmured in a low and husky voice, "All mothers are the same."

I couldn't help grinning back at her, and I almost forgot how much taller she was as we walked out to the balcony.

"I'm so glad you could come." Mother was standing by the table. Steam curled from the spout of the teapot.

After seating the black-haired woman in the chair beside my mother, I poured three cups. "Would you like honey?"

"No, thank you." Her voice remained husky without being rough.

"Mother?"

"You know my habits well enough, Tyndel. One dollop."

I gave her one and took two myself before sitting down and glancing toward the harbor. It was still early enough that the overhang protected us from the descending sun, and early enough that my father was doubtless still wrestling with some aspect of exchanges or futures or shipping schedules.

"You have a lovely view from here," Foerga said.

"It is lovely, but Tyndel's father set it up more to view the harbor for commercial purposes. Not aesthetic ones." Mother laughed. "Tynd's never been one for aesthetics."

"Then everyone must be pleased." Foerga's summary was both matter-of-fact and delivered warmly.

I laughed. "You have a way with words that I envy."

"Foerga is one of the most talented artisans with crystal," Mother said. "Elexton told me that last week." If Mother said so, Foerga was talented, but I was more taken with the smile and the warmth in those blue eyes.

"I need to see to the dinner." With a knowing smile, Mother rose.

"As if she didn't have it planned to the last instant," I said with a laugh after my mother vanished from the balcony.

The dark-haired artisan laughed gently. "What else would you have her say? 'I'm going to leave you two alone in order to see if you can discover each other'?"

Her words were true enough, but there was no edge to them, no brittleness, no sense of revealed truth or self-importance. At that moment, I could sense that Foerga possessed an absolute understanding and acceptance of what was and would be. She understood Dzin better than I.

"Have you studied Dzin?" I asked.

"No. I read a little from my father's library, but"—a faint smile crossed her lips—"it seemed . . ." She shook her head.

"Obvious?" I suggested.

A slight frown greeted my question. "Not obvious. Anything that is obvious has more behind it." For the first time, she looked a little flustered, a little less composed.

I waited.

"The simplest crystal design is often the most difficult," she finally said. "You can feel how good it is, but executing it or explaining it sometimes feels impossible." She paused, those deep and piercing eyes fixed on me. "I think Dzin is like that."

I realized for the first time, but not for the last, that Foerga was like that—a simple goodness so direct that it was art and not artifice, a truth so obvious it could not be described.

For the longest time, I just looked into her eyes, far more blue than the Summer Sea, far deeper than any blue presented by a Dzin master.

10

[HYBRA: 4512]

You may know your thoughts, but you are not your thoughts.

The morning brume was thick, silver-white, and my breath added to it as the shears *snick-snicked* their way along the hedge in the postdawn glow. Each pruned piece went into the cart, none over a few centimeters, to be carried to the composter when I was done.

The scent of damp grass surrounded me, pervaded even the cold silver brume as my hands and fingers wielded the oiled shears. Ensuring the proper proportions of the hedge, that was easy, and rewarding, to apply myself to the task and become one with it. But why had I not seen how the boxwood had grown overlarge? Yes, the lines had been precise, but too near the green edges of the walk.

Why had I not seen the changes? Had I grown too complacent in Hybra? Too tolerant of the small deviations from the ideals of Dzin?

I walked back to the front gate and studied the walkside edge of the hedge. Another centimeter or two would be better. I lifted the polished wood and steel of the shears, shears older than I but still keen and functional.

When I finished, I did smile.

Then, after emptying the cart into the hopper and racking it on the garden shed wall, I turned the crank, regularly, slowly, and the finely meshed gears drove the grinder. A thin stream of shredded leaves and wood poured into the compost bin, from which I took the material that I used to build up the garden and mulch the trees, except that it came from the bottom, slanted so that it fed into the chute with a lifting door on the outside of the shed.

Dynae's selection by Overmaster Juab—that nagged at me, although I knew I was certainly not one who should question it. How could a lowly schoolmaster in Hybra question an Overmaster of Dzin? Yet the thought that criteria other than intelligence and receptiveness to Dzin troubled me, and I could not deny that unease.

Then, Sergol, a truffler's son, had questioned me, and not in the proper manner.

How had I failed? Had I not kept to the true ideals of Dzin in some subtle fashion?

I kept cranking the composter until the hopper was empty. Then I swung the grinder back into its rack and replaced the bin cover.

I would have to talk to Wolyd about his son, if only to discover who was planting such questions. Questioning to seek the truth was one matter. Questioning merely to cause unrest was another, and I had the feeling that Sergol's questions were not raised to seek the truth or the way of Dzin. I doubted Sergol himself had even raised them. But Dzin masters, even in small towns, were not supposed to let such questions and doubts arise.

I wiped down and oiled the shears, then racked them, closed the garden shed, and walked back through the fog and mist to the rear door of the house.

Foerga was up, heating the water and fixing breakfast. Her low song as she moved around the kitchen brought a smile to my lips, and I paused for several moments in the rear hall, silently listening, drawing in the warm of song and of the artisan who was my soul mate.

After laying out the exercise mat on the enclosed rear deck, I stripped to my shorts, then sat on the mat and tried to compose my thoughts. The key was to let the trivia of the world pass me by, concentrating on the now, on the sense of body and self and selflessness. The world did indeed recede, and physically I was refreshed, especially after my shower.

The questions pushed their way back into my thoughts by the time I sat at the table.

"You did not sleep well. I had hoped you would." Foerga smiled softly as she poured the tea.

"One cannot always sleep the sleep of the untroubled." I offered her a smile.

"You are worried."

"I am, but your words warm me." I took a slow sip of tea, then a bite of the apple biscuit, savoring the taste of each crumb. "They are but small matters—Dynae, Sergol and his questions." *And we have each other.* I smiled as I looked into her deep blue eyes.

"The tongue of the adder, visible only briefly, is a small matter." Foerga offered the slightest frown, and that expression worried me, for my artist soul mate saw more without words than I did with them.

Her expression told me more than her words that I was right to worry. Those small matters would have to be addressed . . . after I had considered the options through the perceptions of Dzin.

11

If the body is unmastered, the mind will remain unmastered.

I'd taken only one set of nanosprays and pills, but already my mind was filled with information and terms I'd never learned. . . . *adjudication may only be used after demonstrated irresponsibility and must be imposed by a class one adjudicator . . . Rykasha is comprised of eight geographic districts. . . . Amnord logistics for stellar transport is based in Runswi . . . facilities include . . . maintenance suits will be purple . . . the Authority will consist of no less than five, and no more than seven members . . .*

The seemingly unrelated facts tumbled and turned through my skull as if trying to find places, referents, someplace to which they could attach themselves, and all too often failing to find places of adhesion.

Then, too, somewhere deep within me was a coldness, a chill that would not lift, a chill tied to knowing I would not see Foerga again, or my parents, or even my cousin Rhada . . . but mostly I missed Foerga. She would have handled what I felt far better than I was.

I almost didn't hear the knock on the door to my quarters. Overwhelmed by the continuing flood of information, I tried not to stagger as I stood and made my way to greet the caller who had to be Cerrelle.

"You're having a hard time," she observed as I opened the door. "It will get better. I know."

I nodded, letting her close the door. Even after I sank back into the chair, my head continued to feel as though it were being split apart.

"You need to think through the information you're getting, try to talk about it. Talk to me, if it helps," she suggested.

I shook my head. "I wouldn't know where to start. There's so much."

"That's one problem," Cerrelle replied quietly. "Human beings are programmed genetically to be hunter-gatherers. We need to tie abstract information to real-world perceptions. That's why it helps to talk, even just to repeat what surfaces in your mind. Then, after you get a grasp on that, try to think where what you're sensing might be helpful in the future."

"In the future?" I laughed hoarsely. "I'm having trouble with right now." My eyes skittered away from her and toward the snowflakes slipping past the window.

"I understand."

I wondered how she could. She wasn't the one trying to assimilate the flood of random information.

"You're having trouble. That's natural. It's because you're still in the habit of experiencing and reacting. That's necessary for a mite—and deadly for a demon."

Mites, demons . . . what did it matter? So much of what she said, so much of what rattled through my mind, didn't seem to matter much.

"You have two problems right now," she said. "One is personal shock. You've been torn from everything you know and everyone you love. The second is cultural shock. You're in the middle of a culture you've been conditioned against from birth. You have to accept that those shocks are real, but you also have to go on."

"Why should I even care?" I asked.

"I could offer you warm words, but that wouldn't help you. You want someone to tell you how bad things are and how much you've been hurt. Well, you have been. We acknowledge that, but sitting and feeling bad won't help you get on with life. That's assuming you want to. And if you do . . ."

I couldn't just give up. I owed Foerga that much . . .

and more. "You really don't care how I feel, do you?"

"I care because you are an intelligent being, and right now you're confused, and you're upset, and your whole world has been turned inside out." Cerrelle stood and walked toward the window and the snowflakes that drifted by outside. "But there's a difference between caring between individuals and caring by society. That was one of the problems the ancients had. They always wanted everyone to feel good. They worried too much about how people felt and not enough about what needed to be done. How you feel and how I feel about you doesn't matter when it comes to society's basic principles. First, a society has to figure out what works. Then it must educate and condition people to accept it." She laughed softly. "I shouldn't be preaching, but it's hard to offer sympathy without being misleading. Adjusting to Rykasha is difficult, and dishonesty on my part will only make it harder."

". . . hard enough as it is . . ." I said, making an effort not to mumble. "Hard on anyone not born here."

Cerrelle turned her green eyes on me, eyes warm but honest, like a green version of Foerga's. I wished Cerrelle were somewhere else and anyone else. "Tyndel . . . every workable society conditions its members. Dorcha conditions its people. You should know that; you were one of the ones doing the conditioning. It's only hard when you have to learn someone else's conditioning." A tinge of bleakness colored her words, then vanished.

"Making it so cold . . . so impersonal . . . that's wrong. People aren't just numbers." I didn't know why I felt so strongly. Was it because I was an outsider, because I hadn't chosen voluntarily to become a demon?

"On the contrary . . . people have always been digits in any society. There have been numerous societies—and belief systems—that fostered an illusion of caring, but it was always an illusion, and we're not fond of illusions. We care about whether society works, but on the societal level, no one really cares about how you feel so long as you do what's necessary. We each have to find the individuals who care for us. That's always been true. Do you think that's changed in history? We deal with it more directly than most societies. We try to make honesty something more than lip service, and it isn't easy for us . . . for me. It won't be easy for you."

I just stared at her, not sure I'd heard the words she'd spoken.

"Tyndel . . ." For the first time, Cerrelle sighed, actually sighed, as she turned from the glass to face me once more. "You've spent your whole life learning and believing in Dzin. I don't fault you for that. Now that you have a chance to see more and learn more, you're fighting it. And you're reluctant to use what you learned from Dzin because it would prove that Rykasha is an improvement over mite society, and you can't face that. You want all your comfortable old illusions back." She shrugged. "You can have them back, or not, as you wish. But you're still responsible for yourself and, when you're able, for repaying us for saving you."

"I didn't ask to be saved."

"Then why did you flee Dorcha and come to Rykasha? Are you sure that you're not saying that you wanted to be saved on your terms and not ours?"

She was probably right, but I wasn't sure I really wanted to admit anything. Why couldn't things have stayed the way they had been?

"Because they haven't," she answered gently, "and nothing will change that."

I almost wished she hadn't been so gentle with her words. Then I could have lashed out. Instead, I swallowed. By Dzin . . . I missed Foerga . . . the certainty of the Dzin I had known . . . and even crusty old Manwarr.

12

*All is equally fair and good and foul and evil; only the
individual will claim something is but one.*

I went to talk to Sergol's father on sevenday afternoon.
Unlike many in Dorcha, fishermen do not rest, or
Wolyd did not, and I had to wait in the brisk chill wind
until he beached the dinghy.

The fisherman and truffler was small and wiry, his head
barely above my shoulder. His black beard was trimmed
short and square, like my own blond-brown beard, and he
paid me no attention until he had turned the boat on its
rack to drain and dry, and replaced all his gear in the small
barn above the rocky beach.

"What do you want with me, Dzin master?" In his
weathered gray clothes and grayed face, except for the
black beard and hair, he could almost have been a statue
or a full-sized carving.

"To talk to you about Sergol."

"Walk with me to the caves, then." He grunted and
turned, heading for an opening in the bushes. Not the one
that led to the cart road around the lake but one leading
toward the rocky slope to the south of the high cliffs that
seemed to plunge straight into the deep azure of the lake.

"Caves?" Even I knew truffles grew under oaks, not in
caves.

"Do mushrooms, too," Wolyd said over his shoulder.
"Where you think they come from? Come on. Don't have
time to waste."

I followed the wiry man down a well-trod path toward

another cliff, a mere fifteen meters high, unlike the hundred meter drop-off of the high cliffs.

"Sergol's a good boy." Wolyd eased back a sliding door that covered a long tunnel, reaching inside and touching a plate. A line of glow lamps illuminated the low-ceilinged and ancient tunnel, a tunnel long enough that I could not see the far end.

"He's a very good boy. He's also been asking some strange questions. Using fish as examples," I added blandly, then scrambled after the truffler as he walked toward the mushroom beds. My nose wrinkled at the dampness and acrid odor of manure.

"He should. Learn a lot from fish."

"Every creature has lessons to teach."

"What's the problem?" The truffler looked up from the long tray bed of mushrooms—portobello, I thought, but they were still small.

"I worry that he seeks knowledge for the sake of knowledge."

"You Dzin-folk do enough of that." A smirk crossed the man's face.

"If he wishes to follow the way of Dzin, then he will learn how to deal with knowledge." I studied Wolyd's blank gray eyes, eyes that said nothing and revealed nothing. The man bothered me, but I couldn't say why, even as I attempted to hold on to a state of unremitting alertness.

"He's a boy. Why worry about his questions?"

How could I phrase the answer? I wondered. "Sometimes . . . sometimes, children need to ask questions, and that is right, especially if the questions come from their hearts."

Wolyd cocked his head and studied me, a faint smile crossing his lips. "And you're worried that a poor truffler's putting ideas in his head?"

"I didn't say that you were," I pointed out reasonably.

"Who else would? His mother went back to Wyns years ago. Just Sergol and me." He paused. "You say you worry. Who worried about us when she left? Who worried when I had to pay a nurse? Now, boy asks a question or two, and you worry."

"I didn't know."

"Lots you Dzin masters don't know." He moved down the bed, studying the small fungi.

"I'm sure of that," I agreed, following.

"Anyone asks questions you don't like, and you start worrying about forbidden knowledge and demons . . . and the like."

Demons? I hadn't even thought about demons. What had brought that up? Was Wolyd a secret demon-worshipper? I tried not to swallow. "I wasn't talking about demons."

"What do you think about demons, Dzin master?" Wolyd's tone was too casual, and I wanted to step back.

"I don't know much about the demons. No one today does, except that anyone who crosses the border never comes back. Nor do any gliders. Sometimes, arrows of fire, or lasers, streak into the heavens." I shrugged. "They seem to want to be left alone, and so do we."

"Do not mock the demons. Those in Rykasha are but pale remnants of the ancient demons."

I stepped back, but the truffler narrowed the distance between us. What would a fisherman and truffler know about demons? And why was he angry at me?

"You do not believe me. Ah, well, I will tell you. In that, then, you will have the opportunity to brighten the mirror with cleansed perceptions."

I had to frown at the misapplication of the Dzin saying.

"In the time of the demons, each and every demon wore a magnificent suit of clothes. If folded, it was no larger than a man's fist, yet when worn the demon could lift weights of more than five hetstones and dash as fast as the glideways for nearly an hour." Wolyd bent down under one of the trays, as if he had dropped something.

A suit of clothes that would allow a man to lift the weight of, what, three glider cars? I smiled politely.

"So blind are you who do not see." With a laugh he stood and turned, and he held a polished gun, the kind designed to hold and stop even demons.

"I am no demon," I protested.

Whrrr . . .

My body convulsed, and I was held rigid by the current that froze my muscles, flowing through every dartlet that had pierced my flesh.

"Not yet."

What did he mean, this fisherman and truffler? I tried to speak, but I could sense nothing.

When I woke, I was bound to a wooden frame, and the loose sleeves of my gown and undershirt had been rolled back. Both arms ached, and I could see and feel that they had been slashed, or cut, and then dressed rudely.

Where was I? My eyes blurred as I turned my head, discovering I was in another ancient tunnel, a damp one, and one without glow lamps. The only illumination came from the portalight held by Wolyd.

"The rope will keep you bound. That's until you can get free. Then you won't do nothing." He laughed, nearly maniacally. "You Dzin types, you think you're so smart. You know phrases that others have repeated from the old days, and the sayings never change, and you never learn. The demons learned, and you drove them out because you were afraid of what they had discovered. Now you ignore them and drive out anyone who questions." Another laugh followed. "You Dzin masters, you are so high and mighty. And you, you, Master Tyndel, you are among the worst, for you believe what you say and would have my boy believe you. Well, Wolyd the truffler would have you see how you fare in a world where none think you are high or mighty."

Laughing again, he rolled a barrel next to me, lifted it onto the rock ledge by my head, and maneuvered a spigot covered with what seemed to be a rubber nipple close enough that it almost touched my mouth. An odor of rancid fish flowed over me, and I nearly gagged. "Not much better than pig slop." He nodded at the huge barrel. "You *think* you will not eat it, but you will. The little demons in your blood will see to that. You will need it all before you are strong enough to break free." A crooked smile crossed his face, revealing equally crooked and yellow teeth. "Then you will be a demon. And you will leave Dorcha or die."

"Demon?" I choked out stupidly.

"I know the secret of making demons. A demon died in these caves, long time ago, and in his dust . . . but you don't need to know that." He held up the demon gun. "If I must use this on you again, you will be carried to the demon cage in Hybra . . . and you will die."

A door *clunked* shut.

I was alone in the ancient tunnel, alone in the darkness, bound with ropes twice as thick as a truffler's thumbs. I, a master of Dzin, schoolmaster of Hybra, tied up like a pig for slaughter, tied up by a mad truffler in a place that no one would find. Tied up by a truffler convinced he had a mystical secret that would turn me into a demon.

I tried to wiggle free, but the ropes and the knots were firm, and all I got was rope burns and aching muscles. My stomach turned at the odor of rancid fish and at the fear of what Wolyd might have done. What poison had he introduced? Or had it all been a delusion, and had I been left to slowly starve in the darkness?

Was he angry at me? Or did he dislike all Dzin teachers?

I strained against the ropes, then tried to move my fingers, but my wrists were bound too tightly. Everything was bound too tightly, and the odor of fish too strong, far too strong.

I struggled until I was exhausted, with little result, and another darkness passed over me.

13

The objective universe is absolutely unreal.

For a moment, when I looked outside in the early afternoon, I thought fog had come to Lyncol, with the whiteness that obscured my view of the hillside trees.

Then a figure appeared passing the window, red hair blotched with white, and before I could reach the door, Cerrelle appeared.

"Greetings—"

She thrust a jacket at me, one I hadn't seen before. "Put that on."

"Why?"

"I thought it might be a good idea to take a walk. You're feeling sorry for yourself, and sometimes a walk helps."

"What if I don't feel like a walk?"

"Well . . . I'm supposed to help you adjust, and you aren't going to adjust sitting and looking at the wall. Life goes on."

"For some people."

"You think you're the first and only one who's ever lost everything he loved?"

Again, there was a hint of bleakness behind the overly cheerful facade, a hint of something I wasn't sure I wanted to know.

"Besides," Cerrelle continued, "it's snowing, and Lyncol is beautiful in the snow."

Snow? I shivered.

"You probably wouldn't notice it, even without the

jacket, but it will be more than enough with your nanite balance. Put it on."

Her tone didn't brook arguing. I didn't. She'd just keep being annoyingly cheerful. Instead I pulled on the jacket and followed her into the corridor and then out the side door and off the small stone porch.

The ground was white, and only one set of tracks marred the snow, the ones that led to the structure where I lodged and was fed nanopills and pestered and questioned.

I looked back. The roof was tiled. That I could see from the pattern, but not the color because the snow had already provided a white blanket. The windows were dark. I frowned. They didn't look dark from inside. Some form of one-way glass? Each wall stone shimmered a translucent green that almost seemed to glow.

"The stone shimmers—"

"Don't talk. Not now. You'll spoil it. Keep your questions for later. Just follow me."

I shut my mouth, wanting to protest her highhandedness, but what good would it have done? *Accept what is until you may understand it.* I held to that thought. You couldn't change anything until you accepted and understood it.

The snow squeaked, ever so faintly, under Cerrelle's boots, but I moved without a sound along the path that led into the trees to the north of the lodge. I *knew* it was north, but how?

Under the canopy of firs on either side of the path the snow cover was intermittent, and brown needles protruded. With no real wind to disturb, swirl, or blow it, the powdery white drifted down through and around the branches like a mist sifting groundward. The faint odor of pines or resin mixed with the not-quite-dampness of the snow.

We passed though a stretch of evergreens perhaps a hundred meters long. *Ninety-seven point three meters,* insisted the internal observer that had come with my transition to demonhood. Another expanse of meadow appeared, also snow covered, and a silver spire rose out of the snow-dusted evergreens to my right, rising perhaps thirty meters, although the silver seemed to meld with the snow and at times vanish.

In the open, the chill dampness of snow melting on my forehead and bare cheeks was strangely welcome, like cold tears. Foerga's tears? My mother's? I swallowed, paused, and then kept walking. The silver spire vanished behind us, just as the certainty I had placed in Dzin had vanished.

Out of the snow ahead rose an oblong black-pillared building, like one of the temples of the ancients, except those had been white. It stood on a small hill, around which ran water over a perfectly smooth bed, so smooth that the water looked like shining silk that caressed the gentle slope before collecting in a long pool lined with the same seamless black stone. Steam rose where the snow touched the water, and the scent of lavender puffed away from the pool as we walked past.

The snow kept drifting down, cool and welcome on my face.

The next structure was harder to describe—either built into a granite cliff or the facsimile of a cliff built around it—with balconies overlooking heated pools from which steam rose—or I thought it did. A diaphanous veil cloaked the entire dwelling, revealing only general shapes. A couple might have been bathing in one of the pools—or it might have been two statues given the illusion of movement by the shifting of the veil.

Then the woods got deeper and darker.

Cerrelle held up a hand for me to stop, and I did.

A dark, looming, four-footed creature, silent as the snow itself, slipped across the path in front of us. Dark and wide antlers, a good two meters across, topped a long fur-bearded face.

Never had I thought anything that large could have

moved so silently, but it had, vanishing into the darkness of the evergreens.

"What . . ." I whispered.

"Giant moose. Quiet." Cerrelle resumed walking, the only sound that of the squeaking of her boots in the dry snow.

A chittering sound echoed through the woods, twice, and not again.

For a time, we passed no other obvious structures, just walked through meadows and woods, and over a thin brook where the clear water splashed amid rocks that were half covered with snow. An unrailed bridge crossed the stream, a single seamless construction of reddish stone that leapt out of the ground at each side and arched over the water, stones, and snow-covered grasses—part of nature, and yet not at all a part.

Beyond the bridge and uphill was a small lake, and granite ramparts, natural cliffs, reared into the clouds at the north end of the lake, less than a kilo away across dark gray-blue water. Fist-sized stones, predominantly white, comprised the shoreline.

On the exposed shore, the wind gusted and small white-caps crested intermittently. A birdlike elongated shape, a black-and-white shadow on the water, glided away from us, then vanished beneath the chop, only to reappear a good hundred meters to the east.

Cerrelle stood and watched the lake and the diving bird. I watched the lake, the bird, the snow, the mountains, and Cerrelle.

Abruptly, she walked westward along the shore, then took another path downhill and back southward.

Beyond the first patch of evergreens was another dwelling, but no dwelling I had ever seen. The entire dome was comprised of hexagons, and each hexagon glittered a silver sheen, but each sheen was fractionally different from those that bordered it. The light snow slid away from the dome and piled around it. No walk, no steps, no footprints led to or away from the dome.

Cerrelle didn't even slow her even steps as we passed, and I had to hurry to catch up. A ghost of a past image—the lines of crimson fire across a nielle sky—flitted across my eyes and vanished, except I hadn't seen images like that before being entombed by Wolyd.

Cerrelle turned and frowned but said nothing, instead headed into the next patch of woods and the more gentle filtering of snow through the overhanging evergreen branches.

Once more, I had the feeling of cold tears on my cheeks, and I thought of Foerga, kind and loving Foerga, and my tears mixed with the snow, and I walked blindly for a time.

We passed more dwellings or structures, each different from the others, each standing separate, inviolate, and each, in a strange way, like the bridge we had crossed, springing out of the ground and forest or snow-covered meadows as though it belonged there.

The light was dimming, and our first footprints had been covered by the fine but continuous snow by the time we reached the lodge—or research or rehabilitation center. I wasn't really sure what anything really happened to be, and the dreamlike quality of that afternoon-long walk reinforced that feeling.

Cerrelle did not speak until we were in the corridor outside my door. "You walk through the snow like a ghost, as if you weren't here." A crooked smile crossed her lips. "But you are. Tomorrow, you start on the heavy-duty background education. I hope you can get some sleep, Tyndel."

She nodded and was gone, back into the twilight snow.

I went into my room and hung the jacket—already dry—in the closet.

Why the walk, except to show me . . . what? I shook my head and looked out at the falling snow for a long time, until it was too dark to see. Then I went and ate.

Dwellings, forests, lakes, images of fire in nielle . . .

what did they mean? Did they mean anything? And Cerrelle . . . patient on the surface but with a hint of something less patient, wilder, beneath.

I took a deep breath.

14

[DEEP LAKE: 4512]

He who would not be hammer will be anvil.

Wolyd the truffler had been right. In the end, I gulped and swallowed the rancid fish slop almost with an insane hunger. What had he done to me? And why? Why did he dislike Dzin masters so much—so much he raved about turning them into demons?

Eventually—was it days later?—I wrestled free of the ropes with a strength I did not know I had. The ropes did not give way. The wooden beam to which one of them was attached snapped with one of my desperate lurches. Then I squirmed and wiggled in the darkness . . . and worried myself free of the rest of my bonds.

Somehow, the tunnel had gotten lighter—or could I see better? Or was I seeing at all?

Once free of the rope, I pushed on the door, and with a creak and a shredding sound it opened. I looked down. The lock had ripped out of the wood, but the wood hadn't been rotten. It looked like good strong oak. The metal hinges were bent as well, and I couldn't close the door.

Rain and wind beat down on my face, but neither seemed that cold, though the season was early winter. In the gray light I studied myself. My gown was ripped and torn, my midsection thinner, far thinner. Scabs covered my upper arms, but scabs that looked mostly healed. Surely, I hadn't been in the cave that long?

Through the bushes, I could see the gray, white-capped waters of Deep Lake, choppy in the late afternoon. The light wind brought the mist raised by the waves lapping on the stones and the scent of decaying rushes and grasses from the marsh to the north.

Cold as it was, I washed my soiled gown and garments in the lake water, looking around every few moments. But it was winter, and no one came. And I marveled that I was not too cold as I stood on the rocky shore in the light wind.

Was I really a demon? Or was I hallucinating? How could I tell?

I hung the damp clothes on the bare branches of a blueberry bush for a moment, except for my damp drawers, which I slipped back on, hoping that my body heat would dry them sooner.

A good-sized boulder rested a meter beyond the bush. I laughed and bent to pick it up, knowing I could never budge it. It came out of the ground easily, and I almost dropped it on my foot. I staggered for a moment, then half threw, half pushed it toward the lake. A splash like the impact of ancient bombard rose from the gray chop.

I looked down at my hands and arms. They were no different, except thinner. My stomach growled with an emptiness that was almost like a hungry bear or mother cayute on the prowl.

My eyes burned, helplessly, as I pulled the damp gown and undershirt from the bush and pulled them on, ignoring their dampness. Whatever had happened, whatever I had become, I had to get home. I had to see Foerga.

Caution prompted me to take the path beside the cart road, but I only had to duck off the path twice as I hurried homeward, trying to avoid thinking too much about my ability to keep jogging longer and faster than ever before.

Instead, I just kept repeating one of Manwarr's mantras: "Explanation is not awareness."

As my feet and legs covered meter after meter, I forced the words through my mind and mouth. "Explanation is not awareness. . . . Explanation is not awareness. . . . Explanation is not awareness. . . ."

When I neared the house—the house of the master of Dzin in Hybra—not my house or our house, events reminded me, I left the path and entered the rear garden by the gate beside the shed. The boxwoods in back needed pruning, and I could smell the healthy mustiness of the compost pile.

The back door was not latched, and I stepped inside, calling, "Foerga?"

She stepped from the kitchen and stared at me, blue eyes deep. Then tears streamed down her cheeks.

"I'm here. What is the matter?"

"The Townkeeper . . . he said you had been carried off by a demon. He warned me."

"The only demon was Wolyd. He stunned me with a demon gun and tied me up in a cave. He doesn't like Dzin masters . . . or at least this one. It took me a long time to get free. I don't know how long."

"Ten days . . . eleven . . . oh . . . Tyndel . . ."

Without speaking we moved closer, then embraced, and I held on to her gently, trembling, afraid to squeeze, afraid of the strange strength that had burst ropes and a door and lifted a boulder I once could not have budged.

"You . . . are hot . . . so warm . . ." Her lips brushed my cheek, and she stepped back, eyes downcast for a moment.

"I . . . just . . . wanted to come home."

More tears streamed down her face—and mine.

In the silence, I was conscious of the smallness of the house, of the walls pressing in on me, each wall spotless and perfect, but close. And the scent of fresh-brewed Arleen tea drifted from the pot on the table.

Foerga hugged me again, shivering slightly as she did.

The ticking of the clock in the wall alcove echoed through the silence, loud as a drum.

My blue-eyed crystal artist stepped back once more. "You are so thin, yet your arms feel like iron." Her eyes went to my wrist and filled with tears again.

My eyes followed hers, and she nodded slowly. The yin in the passlet had nearly died. Only the palest flicker of silver remained.

"You are of the demons now. Look at your passlet." The tears kept streaming down her pale, thin face. "You must go. You must go. Trefor will gather his demon patrol, and they will stun you and cage you, and you will die."

I was already stunned. Me? How could this be happening to me?

"He or one of the others keeps checking to see if you have returned."

I lifted my head at the whispering whine of approaching gliders, the kind that didn't need glideways. "There's a glider coming."

Foerga tilted her head. "Your hearing is better."

Another small touch that clutched at my stomach—she had always been the one with the ears like a hare, able to sense the faintest of sounds.

"Demon or not, I love you." Foerga's arms went around me again, and they felt so comforting, so warm.

I closed my eyes, trying to ignore, just momentarily, the whining in the distance.

Foerga stepped back. "You have to go." She grabbed my old rucksack out of the pantry closet. "Put food in this. You look starved. I'll go out and delay them. Go out through the back."

"But . . ."

"Do it . . . please, Tyndel. For me. It's all I can offer now." She tried to blot her face even as more tears streamed from the corners of her eyes.

I took the rucksack, looking at it blankly as she wiped her face dry and scurried toward the front door, leaving me alone in the small kitchen holding a canvas rucksack. For another moment, I looked at the rucksack, until the front door shut with a dull chunk.

Then I began stuffing the sack—a loaf of bread, sunflower seeds, three apples, a wedge of hard cheese, a roll of crackers. What went in didn't matter . . . Foerga had told me to fill it, and I did.

I eased toward the back door and stepped into the rear garden.

"No! You will not!"

At Foerga's yell I ran along the side of the house, slipping up to the edge of the front hedge.

Only a single free-run glider rested by the gate, and Wolyd and Trefor, along with a single Shraddan, stood beside it. Another glider was at the end of the lane, but even with my sharpened vision, I could not discern who rode within, although I did see one dun-red uniform.

Foerga blocked the gate. "You just want an excuse to kill him." She held a staff, an exercise wand, and the Shraddan held his right wrist.

"He's a demon and she is, too!" Wolyd lifted his shimmering gun, turning it toward her.

Foerga flipped the staff into a thrust toward him.

Sssssss . . .

With the power of the guns, Foerga convulsed, the staff falling, clattering on the hard green ceramic tiles of the walk outside the gate. They kept pulsing the guns, and I realized they wouldn't stop, not until she died.

I dropped the rucksack and moved faster than I had thought possible, past the hedge and up behind the mad truffler, arms and legs striking, misusing the art of defense.

I felt Wolyd's neck crack. At least he would not poison any more Dzin masters.

Trefor seemed to move in slow motion, too slow, and I crushed his neck with my elbow.

The broken-wristed Shraddan ran back toward the other gliders, yelling, "The demon is loose! . . . demon loose!"

I bent down and cradled Foerga, black hair spreading across my arms, but it was too late. Her eyes were blank, and her body limp.

Behind me, the whistling *whirr* of the gliders rose.

I wanted to stay, but then Foerga's last effort would

have been worth nothing. The rucksack—I had to have food, any food. I groped for the canvas and came up with it.

The whining slowed, then grew louder.

Eyes nearly blind, rucksack dangling from one hand, I began to run. Away from the house of a master of Dzin and toward the uncertain future of a demon, death at my back.

15

[LYNCOL: 4513]

One can never conclusively prove an idea, only disprove it.

For days, interrupted periodically by gently frustrating conversations with Cerrelle, sleep, and dreams of Foerga and pursuing gliders and dun-red-coated Shraddans, my head swam or spun with the so-called background knowledge imparted through nanopills and sprays. Even when I lay down upon the silklike sheets of the bed, I felt as if my head and my entire body were bursting, like my very soul had been crammed with years of instructions by masters. But there wasn't any insight, no interpretation, just fact upon fact, image upon image, until my very self seemed ready to drown in information.

Some of the images were vivid—like self-assembling nucleonic weapons that destroyed much of the original coastline of ancient Dorcha. Others were prosaic—the basic idea of the food replicator. Others were mathematical—why would I ever need to calculate relative orbital mechanics? I thought that was what that series was about, but wasn't sure, because it had other math that applied to something called overspace, and how could there be something above real space? I thought there might be, but it wouldn't be practical if one couldn't get there, and the math didn't make sense. It seemed logical, but so had ancient speculations that the world was flat or that all other worlds held life.

Yet Cerrelle insisted everything was just background.

"You know all of this?" I asked her at another lunch in the same small dining area.

The green eyes glinted again in the expression I had come to see as a combination of warmth, wistfulness, frustration, and, I suspected, anger. "Much more."

"How can there be overspace?" I asked. "And if there is, how can one get to it? And of what use is it?"

"Overspace exists, and we use it for interstellar transport. There are special ships . . . you have that background. Why do you ask me what you know?"

"Because it doesn't make sense."

"It doesn't make sense to you because it's outside of your Dzin background." She set down her glass of lemon drink and looked at me. "Now that you know the basics, and when I talk to you and you don't answer, it's because of stubbornness, willful ignorance, or something other than lack of knowledge." She paused. "You're bright. The tests show that. Why are you so uncooperative? Was there a big wall you had to climb, Tyndel? Did anyone say you couldn't seek refuge here?"

"A barrier in the mind is as real as one in stone."

"I'll accept that." She nodded. "If you can tell me what barrier so that you can work on it."

I shook my head. How could I say I was angry she was alive and Foerga was dead? Or that I resented her probing and pushing and pressing? Or that I hated the arrogant superiority that seemed to infuse all of Rykasha?

A momentary expression of sadness crossed her face, and it was replaced with an equally vanishing look of anger before she sighed. "I'm sorry. It is hard for you. Sometimes, I forget. Let's try it another way. How did you end up getting infected?"

"Some daft truffler caught me off-guard, stunned me

with a demon gun, and somehow infected me with something that multiplied my strength and endurance and sharpened my vision—your original nanites, I gather. That qualified me as a demon." I glanced at my bare wrist. "At least it extinguished the yin in my passlet."

"The passlets measure certain body fields in reverse—fairly ingenious for mite technology. We can duplicate them and manipulate them, of course."

"Mite technology . . . mite stupidity . . . why do you call nondemons mites?"

The green-eyed redhead actually looked down at the table . . . with an expression somewhere between guilt and embarrassment.

I waited.

"It's a derogatory term. Short for termites."

"You think of us as low-level social insects?" My voice rose.

"You aren't one of them anymore, and you never will be. The tests would indicate you probably never were, not in mental outlook. And yes, old-style human beings aren't much more than technologically gifted social insects. As a group, they aren't any more able than termites to surmount their inability to overcome instinctual hardwiring. How many mite geniuses have been killed or stifled or exiled because they didn't fit the social norm?"

My mouth opened and closed.

"How many unwanted and unneeded children have been born and killed over the millennia? How many prophets have claimed to represent one deity or another with no proof, no evidence, except demonstration of powers available to every human being? And how many mites have swallowed the words of those prophets? Is that rationality or free intelligence?"

"Dzin holds society together." I forced myself to speak slowly.

"I didn't say it didn't." She took a swallow of her drink. "Instinct holds a termite colony together, instinct and accepted social practices. Dzin is a way of limiting human

social practices and abilities to ensure that human beings
don't destroy society and themselves. It's a declaration of
failure. It says that humans cannot reach their full intellectual and physical potential without becoming a danger
to themselves and to their society. So Dzin preaches and
enforces restraint."

"Of course it does. If someone eats too much, and there
isn't enough food, others will starve. If someone wants to
build weapons and use them on others, others suffer. Restraint is necessary in any human society." Was Cerrelle
blind? Were the demons that different?

"I'm sorry. I'm coming across as being angry at you,
and I'm not. I am angry at a society that turns people,
people like you, into fugitives and throws them out as
worthless or demons." She took a slow breath. "I am not
making myself as clear as I should. The nanites gave you
better vision, greater strength and greater endurance, and
over time, clearer thought processes. Yet Dzin resists
these changes. Why? Why does it limit you to less than
you could be?"

"Because those changes destroyed the ancients," I
pointed out as dryly as I could.

"That's my point. Human society is based on the lowest
common denominator. Or a fairly low denominator, anyway. Dzin, or Toze, or Dhur customs all limit the fullest
expression of human capabilities. Those capabilities are
not always or usually evil or antisocial."

I shook my head. "From what I've already learned, people infected with nanites require increased nutrition. There
wasn't enough energy or technology to feed those who
already existed, let alone meet the increased requirements."

"Exactly," answered Cerrelle. "And every intelligent
being who existed at that time, and for centuries before,
knew that. So did most political leaders. Yet few serious
efforts were made to curb population growth, and some
belief systems actually encouraged unlimited reproduction. Does that sound like an intelligent species?"

"When you put it that way . . ." I conceded, pulling at my chin. Humans didn't sound all that intelligent. But there was something about the redhead's argument that bothered me—the assumption of automatic superiority. "Where's your sense of responsibility?" I asked. "You can blame and denigrate the poor mites, but what have you done to improve the situation? You say all you demons know better, but what have you done?"

Cerrelle smiled—almost sadly. "Our borders are open. No one stopped you. No one tried to kill you. Your former colleagues have all the freedom they desire to do as they wish."

"What if they tried to take over the Rykasha lands?"

"They would be stopped. It has happened several times, but years pass, and people forget."

"You're so superior . . ."

"So are you, Tyndel. That's why they tried to kill you. And your beloved Foerga."

"Leave her out of this."

"Why? You believe she was a more perceptive and decent being than you are, and they killed her. Do you really think she was sacrificing herself to follow you to Hybra? Wasn't she also keeping herself away from jealous and scared mites? What better protection than to marry a Dzin master?"

Foerga? Worried about what others thought? "She wasn't a demon."

"I never said she was. I said she was a better being and that all mites turn against their betters when they can."

"Are you any better?" I snapped.

"We walked in the snow last week. What did you see?"

"Dwellings." I shrugged.

"Were they alike? Did they disrupt nature?"

"No." I paused. "They didn't seem to disrupt nature."

"Yet your masters of Dzin claim that demons are disruptive. Why? History shows that the greatest murders and disruptions were by so-called ordinary people, not by demons." Cerrelle snorted. "There are thousands of years of history, filled with villains, and everyone blames those villains, but most of the evil deeds attributed to them were actually carried out by ordinary people. Were those people weak—or did they secretly enjoy their work? I don't know that it matters. Either way, it's not a flattering image."

"And you're better?" I pressed.

"At heart? Probably not. Part of what we do is to force honesty. That and what else we do, both to those who grow up in Rykasha and those like you, isn't exactly ideal . . . but we don't have any real choice."

"Explanation is not awareness," I quoted absently.

"You've said that before. It's true, and it's also meaningless." She took another deep breath. "You should know this already, but you're fighting knowing what you know. Human beings are programmed badly for going beyond the hunter-gatherer stage." Cerrelle gave a wry smile. "We have to struggle with rationality because . . . rationality isn't necessarily good for survival on the species level."

I had to frown at that.

"Look . . . there are enough human beings out there so that your actions can't possibly destroy the species. That means all those altruistic responses that are gene-coded can be and are overridden by rational decisions for your own survival. Multiply that by billions, and that was the problem that the ancients faced. The other problem that humans face is lack of time. Our biological clocks are set by light and nutrition. The more exposure to light and the better the nutrition, the sooner the biological maturity. At the same time, with the civilization that creates artificial light and adequate food for most comes the need for greater knowledge, greater forbearance, and greater understanding, all of which require a greater social investment in the young over time.

"The ancients never did solve that problem. A burgeoning birth rate made the necessary investment in the young impossible for many societies—and there were many societies then, hundreds, if not thousands, from what we can tell from the records and traces, not the half dozen cultures that now exist. Add to that the biological urges to reproduce, which conflicted with the rational urge not to have so many children. . . . Anyway . . . a lot of things were tried, from abortion to war to contraception to infanticide—none of them worked very well."

"Dzin works," I pointed out.

"It does, and so does Toze, and even the Dhur customs work," Cerrelle agreed. "And they're all dead ends. They work because they've managed to create a consensual, custom-based restriction on the amount of knowledge and change allowed into their societies. That is, none to speak of. That was the appeal of ancient religions. A code was supposedly imposed by a god, something greater than the society and its people—a code that was usually an attempt at what was conceived as greater rationality. Usually, it wasn't. At least Dzin has a semirational basis."

Semirational? Even as I opened my mouth to protest, I wondered about the other phrase she'd said—the need for people to believe in something bigger than they were. Had that changed for the Rykasha? In what great dream did they believe? Did they even know what that dream was?

She held up a hand. "Look . . . I'm not saying that on the basic level we're not much better. We use nanites and technology to force knowledge and self-responsibility into people, almost from the day they can comprehend. Do you know what our suicide rate is?"

Suicide?

"We *force* true rationality on people. You'll see. Some people can't take it."

Not take rationality? A cold shiver settled in my spine, as though I already did know and feared accepting.

"Add to that the problem that our biological clocks *know* on the genetic level that we're time-limited," Cerrelle plowed on. "We can use nanites to extend our productive life enormously, to ten times that of the ancients, but those gene-coded responses still say that you have to reproduce in three decades or the species will perish. And we *have* to keep our numbers low because the earth's resource base is limited, especially after the Devastation.

"What we need, what all humans need, is a longer life span, call it the inverse of neoteny, where sexual matu-ration lags, rather than leads, cultural or societal maturity, something that's embedded on the cellular level. It might have been possible for the ancients, but we've lost a lot, and we have to be careful with tinkering on cell-gene level." She looked at the empty dishes and glasses. "We're wasting time."

"You never finish answering anything," I protested.

"I'm trying, Tyndel. I really am. But one person can't tell you everything. That's why you got all that nanite-implanted knowledge and why it's necessary for you to use it and sort through it."

"But you said it helps to talk," I pointed out.

Her lips twisted wryly. "I did, but talking doesn't help that much when most of your questions turn out to be variants on how far north is north." She stood.

North? What was to the north of Rykasha? Even before I finished formulating the question, I had the answer. There really wasn't anything north of Rykasha, because the demons had basically taken over the colder regions of Amnord.

There was no doubt that the demons were physically and technically superior to the older and numerically larger earth cultures . . . yet they had let Dorcha, the Dhur gens, the Toze peoples, even the floating cities—they had let them be. Why?

Cerrelle had been clear enough that the nanites that made demons out of humans did not change basic genetics or cellular-level programming. So the Rykasha weren't somehow more moral, and I wondered if even the masters of Dzin would have been as forbearing if they wielded the power of the demons.

Yet Cerrelle had denied the dream of Dzin, of faith. Was that why their suicide rate was high? Because even nanite-modified humans needed dreams, and forced rationality created too great an internal conflict? Or was there a hidden dream behind Rykasha?

For all the knowledge that filled me, I still knew so little—or had had so little time to sort it out.

"We can talk more later, if you'd like. Right now, you have another appointment." Cerrelle was always bringing me up short. Cerrelle—my keeper.

I held in a sigh as I stood, but not the bitterness in my eyes as I thought of another, gentler, keeper, and of a time I had not held dearly enough.

Was that to be the story of my life?

SCIAMACHY

16

Right in itself has no authority, but follows might as the smoke the wind.

When golden starbursts flared through my brain, recalling again the memory of those first days of nanite possession, I looked out the window at the hillside. The winter green of the conifers was pallid compared to the golden fires, weak compared to the more vivid greenery of a garden in Hybra.

I turned at the knock on the door. "Come in."

"Time for an educational experience," Cerrelle said.

"Like the walk in the snow?"

"This won't be as enchanting. We're going to some adjudication adjustment hearings."

Adjudication adjustment hearings? I scarcely liked the sound, and I racked my new stocks of knowledge. *Adjudication adjustment hearing: the procedure by which an individual's self-responsibility is assessed to determine whether specific actions merit permanent adjustment.*

"It's necessary so that you know how seriously we take personal responsibility. Like many things you get in the nanosprays, this is something that needs the reinforcement of personal experience. It may not be pleasant, but it's not yours. So don't worry."

How did the demons measure self-responsibility? And why was that a societal procedure? I stood up and followed Cerrelle. There wasn't any point in protesting, especially since it was clear she thought what I was going to see was in my best interest. I wasn't sure that what the demons felt was good for me was what I would have chosen, but until I knew more, I just accepted what arrived and did as she asked. In a fashion, I felt dead anyway, and it was easier.

We walked from the front foyer outside and up a low hill, then down another set of stairs from what appeared as a small building holding nothing but a staircase. There was, surprise of surprises, a tunnel platform and what looked to be a covered glider.

"Yes, we use gliders. Why wouldn't we? We believe in appropriate technology."

I sat on the padded bench seat beside Cerrelle, conscious for the first time of a faint floral aroma as she closed the permaglass canopy. Scent? From my prodding, demanding keeper?

The glider slipped into the darkness of the tunnel, except that I could see the outlines and sense the speed—far swifter than any glider in Dorcha.

Cerrelle turned on the seat to face me. "You've been here for weeks, and you still act as though you were in some sort of afterlife, like a nanite zombie. The diagnostics say you're metabolically and chemically extraordinarily well-balanced. I'm sure adjusting isn't easy, but you have to work on it. You keep acting as if nothing really affects you, and it does, whether you like it or not."

"It's difficult to believe any of this is real." I pointed out.

"It is real, Tyndel. Your Dzin should tell you that. Doesn't Dzin state that you have to begin by being aware of what is?" She gave me a sardonic smile.

Her use of Dzin bothered me. "It's still hard to adjust to a whole new culture."

"It is," she acknowledged. "It isn't easy, but there are others who've gone through a lot more than you have. If I were a little more sadistic, I'd give you a solid slap on the side of your face to let you feel some reality."

"You really don't like me, do you?" I asked.

"Actually, I do like you. That's what makes it difficult. You're intelligent, perceptive, and hurting. I think you have a lot to offer. That's why I keep pushing you. I think you're wallowing in self-pity. No matter how bad the transformation was for you, no matter how upsetting the past weeks have been, you have to live in the present. You have the ability to do well in Rykasha, and you keep shoving away the opportunity."

"I didn't ask for the opportunity."

There was a long deep breath from Cerrelle before she spoke again. "None of us ask for some things. We don't ask to be born where we were. We don't ask for those things which limit us. We have to do the best we can with what we have where we are. And we can try to change things, but you can't do any of that if you refuse to accept where you are." She paused so briefly that it almost wasn't a pause. "At least as a place to begin."

What if I didn't want to start again?

"Tyndel," she answered my unspoken question, "if you want to live, you don't have a choice."

"Can everyone read my thoughts the way you do?"

"First," she said patiently, "think about why you don't want to face reality. And second, the thought reading has been explained. You were injected with what might be called neural transmitter nanites. They form a network and broadcast, but only those people who have similar sets of nanites in their systems can receive your thoughts. They have to be close to you and attuned to you. Those nanites have a tendency to decay, and in a year most who are attuned to you now won't sense a thing."

"Most?"

"If you form an emotional bond with one of them it's possible the effect will last longer."

"That's hardly likely." I smiled crookedly in the dimness, and my smile had barely faded when the glider emerged into the light of another platform.

"The way you're pushing people away from you, I'd have to agree, but you never know." She stood as the glider came to a halt. "We're here."

Everything Cerrelle said made sense, but I was still having trouble with what she said.

We climbed four flights of steps from the glider tunnel platform. The stairwell was smoothed rock, polished to a luster and showing grains of stone I didn't recognize. Like every structure I'd visited in Rykasha, the adjudication chamber smelled clean, with the faintest hint of pine in the air. Despite the clouds outside, the indirect glow strips had the room bright.

At the far end of the stone-floored room was a dais. Two women and a man sat in a wooden-paneled enclosure on the left side of the dais. Each wore a lightweight headset. Below the dais were chairs, only about two dozen, a dozen on each side of a cleared space approximating an aisle.

A single woman wearing a deep black robe sat behind a white oak desk in the center of the dais.

"She's the adjudicator," whispered Cerrelle as she guided me into one of the empty chairs on the right side of the center aisle.

On the right side of the dais was a single wooden armchair. In it was slumped a blond man in a dark blue tunic and trousers.

"Are you Lartrel?" asked the black-haired woman in the adjudicator's robe.

The man in the low chair nodded slowly.

"Do you live in the dwelling you have called Remarque, below the Kangamon Slopes?"

"Yes."

"Do you have a daughter named Aberla?"

"Yes."

I glanced at Cerrelle, but she didn't look at me. So I watched the questioning.

"Please tell the panel what happened on the afternoon of five Decem."

"We were walking up the old log trail toward the quarry. We were below the upper ledge. I stopped to frame the scene. Beside being a tech, I also paint. Aberla kept walking. I told her to stop because there's a drop-off." Lartrel's voice slowed.

"Then what happened?" prompted the adjudicator.

"She didn't stop." He looked at the floor tiles. "She didn't listen to me."

"How old is Aberla?"

"She's four." Lartrel swallowed. "I told her to stop. I even yelled. She didn't listen."

"That isn't the question of this hearing. Did you willfully neglect your daughter's safety?"

"I didn't know she was that close to the edge."

"How close was she?"

"I had no idea that . . ." The man's face contorted, then smoothed. "She was about four meters—I think it was closer to three—from the drop-off when I called to her." Tears began to roll down his cheeks. "I ran. I ran as fast as I could. I didn't think. I . . . hoped that everything would be all right. I called the med-techs." He looked up at the adjudicator through reddened eyes. "They say she'll recover. They say that she'll be all right."

"Lartrel. Did you willfully neglect your daughter's safety?"

His eyes went to the panel, then to us. "I love my daughter. It's not as though I hurt her."

"Did you willfully neglect your daughter's safety?"

The panicked look intensified, and he looked down.

"Answer the question."

"Yes." The words were barely audible.

"Is this the first time you have let your own considerations jeopardize her?"

"I'm sorry?"

"Is this the first time you have neglected her safety?"

The panicked look reappeared, even more intensely, the look of a trapped animal with no way out.

Finally, the answer came. "No."

The adjudicator turned toward the panel. "Do members of the panel have any additional questions?"

The brown-haired man with a headset gestured, and the adjudicator nodded.

"Would you clarify why you are the primary care-giver?" asked the man.

"Her mother is a third officer on Web runs. My studio is at home." Lartrel did not look at either the questioner or the adjudicator.

"Another hearing is pending the mother's return," the adjudicator added. "Any other questions?"

"No."

"No."

Silence filled the room, and I waited along with the others. Perhaps five minutes passed before the adjudicator's eyes refocused and she turned to the blond man.

"Lartrel, you have been found lacking in supervisory care for your daughter. You will be adjusted, to ensure her safety, immediately following the conclusion of this hearing."

The blond man looked at the dais, then at the polished stone floor.

Two men in plain dark gray uniforms stepped through a door behind the adjudicator and walked toward the art-ist. The lower sleeves of the uniforms were black. The artist stood slowly. The two escorted him out.

"What . . . ?"

"Search your own data," whispered Cerrelle.

Adjudication adjustment? How was it carried out? I mentally scrolled through the volumes of data I'd re-ceived. That was the way it felt. Then I nodded. Each individual for whom adjustment was deemed necessary received a set of nanites programmed with an expanded code of behavior covering every eventuality. The same nanites administered a neural shock at any time the indi-vidual's actions violated the code.

I shivered.

Cerrelle said nothing.

I looked up as two more gray-uniformed figures—a

man and a woman—escorted a blond woman to the chair.
She glanced around the adjudication room.

"Please take the seat," ordered the adjudicator.

"No. It isn't right!" The blonde turned and started to
walk off the dais and toward the door through which we
had entered. Then she froze and slowly toppled to the
stone floor.

I winced.

The man and woman in the black-sleeved singlesuits
reappeared and picked up her form and carried her back
to the chair, where they held her upright.

After a moment, the woman staggered, but the two officials caught her arms and eased her into the chair.

"You don't have any right . . ."

"This is an adjudication hearing, and under the laws of
Rykasha we have every right to determine whether you
require adjustment." The adjudicator leaned forward. "Do
you wish to be released to the customs and laws of the
nearest non-Rykashan nation? That would be Dorcha."

"That's a death sentence."

"Do you wish to be released to the customs and laws
of the nearest non-Rykashan nation?"

"No." The blonde's voice was suddenly resigned.

"Are you Laranai?"

"Yes."

"You have been charged with corrupting an individual
into violence through a repeated series of actions."

"He struck me! I didn't do a thing."

"Veyt faces adjudication under another adjudicator.
Your actions are the issue of this hearing."

"I'm innocent! I didn't do anything." Laranai's eyes
went to the three individuals with the headsets and then
to Cerrelle. "You! This isn't right. I didn't do anything.
Tell them I didn't do anything."

Cerrelle said nothing.

"Please recount what happened on the afternoon of
eight Decem," ordered the adjudicator, ignoring the
blonde's outburst.

Laranai's face smoothed. "Veyt wanted to make love, and I said no. He insisted, and I told him I wasn't in the mood. He said I was never in the mood, and then he tore off my clothes and forced himself on me."

"Why do you think he did that?"

"I don't know."

"Please answer the question."

The blonde's face twisted. After a silence, she answered. "He thought I would be in the mood."

"Why would he think that?"

"I'd told him I would be."

"When was that?"

"Earlier in the day. I was trying to get the house cleaned up. I told him I'd be more in the mood when things were cleaner."

"And what was his reaction to your statement?"

"He helped clean things up."

"And then he took off your clothes and forced you? Right after the house was clean?"

"No. We had something to eat, and he had two glasses of wine. I had one. It was after that."

The adjudicator looked toward the three with the headsets. "Any questions?"

"Had this sort of behavior happened before?" asked the redheaded woman.

"It happened a week before. It was at night. We'd come back from the concert."

"What concert?"

"There was a string quartet—the Pollai Force."

"And he wanted to have sex?"

"Yes."

"Did he strike you?"

"Yes."

"Did he tell you why he was angry?"

The blonde, surprisingly, looked at the floor, and I got the strong impression that there was more, far more, to the questioning than was being vocalized.

"What did he say?"

After a long moment, Laranai finally answered. "He said I promised."

"Was that correct? Did you make some sort of promise?"

There was another silence. "Yes."

"What did you promise?"

Laranai looked toward the adjudicator, then toward Cerrelle. "He hit me. He kept hitting me. What does it matter what I said?"

"What did you promise?" asked the adjudicator again.

"I told him—I'd told him earlier—that I'd be more in the mood after the concert."

The man with the headset spoke. "Did you say or suggest that you would be more receptive to his advances if he took you to the concert?"

"I don't know. I might have."

"Did you make such a suggestion?" asked the adjudicator.

I had the feeling that the black-robed woman was having difficulty keeping her voice impartial.

"Maybe I did."

"Did you make such a suggestion?"

"Yes." The word was almost mumbled.

"What happened after you had sexual contact?" asked the adjudicator. "How did Veyt react?"

"He cried. He promised he wouldn't do it again. Then . . . he did it again the very next week. And he hit me again."

"How long has this been happening?" asked the adjudicator.

"Since the beginning of summer." The blonde sniffed.

Beside me, Cerrelle snorted quietly.

"How much has Veyt contributed toward your household, either in effort, or food, or capital goods?" asked the redhead with the headset.

"I'm sorry. I don't understand . . . he's been hitting me more and more."

"Please answer the question," said the adjudicator

tiredly. "What sort of things or help has Veyt given you?"

"Well . . . he's good with his hands. He built a console for Sylena, and he refinished the fresher walls . . ."

"He takes you places?" prompted the man.

"Sometimes."

"What do you do for him?" asked the redhead.

The blonde glanced at the floor.

"Please answer the question."

"I . . . try to be nice to him . . ."

"In what way?"

Laranai glanced down at the floor again.

"Do you offer him sexual favors?"

More silence.

"Do you?"

"Yes." The word was almost choked out.

"Do the monitors have any additional questions?" asked the adjudicator.

"No, Adjudicator."

"No."

"No."

There was distaste in all four voices.

"You will wait while we review the record and your responses," the adjudicator announced.

This time, the wait was considerably less. The adjudicator's eyes focused on the blonde woman.

"Laranai, you have been found lacking in personal responsibility, as well as engaging in antisocial and deceptive behavior. You will be adjusted immediately following the conclusion of this hearing."

"No! You're all against me. Veyt hurt me! Don't you see!" Laranai lurched to her feet, then froze.

The two men in the gray-and-black uniforms stepped through a door behind the adjudicator and walked toward the frozen figure, easily lifting her and carrying her out.

"Today's hearings are complete," announced the adjudicator. She adjusted her robe and stood, and the three monitors followed her through the door on the dais, leaving Cerrelle and me alone in the empty chamber.

"I don't understand," I whispered to Cerrelle, fearing that I did. "She never did anything."

"But she did. She promised sexual favors in return for certain actions. Then she didn't offer those favors after he carried out his end of the bargain. That's deception and a form of theft. His violence isn't excusable, but that's a separate question, and he'll be adjusted as well."

I frowned. In a way it made sense, but it also turned sex into . . . into what? Another item of commerce?

"Why not? All actions between humans are transactions. Why should fraud between individuals—especially fraud that leads to violence—be less a concern than a public fraud?"

It made sense, but it bothered me.

"We don't make an artificial distinction between those who create violence and those who carry it out. That woman was evil," snapped Cerrelle. "She was pretending to trade on sex, and being totally dishonest about it."

I swallowed. "Would it have bothered you if she had . . . paid off?" I stumbled through the sentence.

"No. We all provide services for others. What services are an individual choice. I wouldn't offer sex. I try to help ex-mites like you."

At that point, I felt very much like a mite. "What will happen to her? And to the man?"

"They'll be rehabilitated." Cerrelle shrugged. "You know that. Each will receive a set of nanites programmed with an expanded code of behavior covering every eventuality we can think of. It's not perfect. There's some loss of higher reasoning and discrimination, but they'll be able to go on with their functions, and most people won't even notice."

"So . . . why . . . don't you do that with me? Wouldn't it be easier than your having to spend all this time with me?" I could hear the bitterness in my voice.

"You don't have a very high opinion of yourself, do you?"

"What does that have to do with . . . all this?"

"You have a well-trained mind. You're in good physical condition. You could offer a great deal to Rykasha and benefit personally as well. We're trying to keep those choices open for you. That's one reason why I brought you here." Cerrelle offered a slight smile, not exactly open, as she stood.

I wanted to shiver. Just what did the demons have in mind? Something even worse than what I had just seen?

"No. We can't coerce you into a positive action, and we wouldn't want to." Cerrelle stood and motioned toward the door through which we had earlier entered.

We can't coerce you ... But what were they doing if not coercing by showing me the adjudication? Or was it that it just didn't matter to me?

"You thought a Dzin master would change his mind?" I asked after a time of silence as we stood in the empty chamber.

"I thought you had some potential for intelligence. True intelligence changes as it learns." The words were mild, but the piercing eyes were not.

"Why is it that you demons think that intelligence equates automatically to your point of view? Or that I would change to accept that?"

"You're a demon, too," she pointed out.

"It wasn't my choice."

"You chose to live. You didn't stay in Dorcha to be starved to death in one of your mite deathtraps. You ran to Rykasha."

Because of Foerga ... I couldn't waste that sacrifice. I just looked at the redhead for a time, not avoiding the piercing green eyes. For the first time, I realized that Cerrelle looked at me, and at the world, in the same way Foerga had. I hated it. She had no right to be alive while Foerga, who had hurt no one, was dead.

"I didn't kill Foerga. Your friends the mites did," Cerrelle said quietly. "Maybe you should have weighted yourself with stones and drowned yourself in that damned Deep Lake of yours."

Maybe I should have.

"You don't need that lake. You're still carrying around enough self-pity to drown everyone in Lyncol."

"If I have so much self-pity . . . if I'm so worthless . . . why do you bother?"

"You could contribute a great deal. You could be worth more than you know, but you're still as stubborn as ever. You'd rather bathe in self-pity than face the hard and the unfamiliar."

There was more than anger in her words. Pity, perhaps, and I didn't need that. "I didn't ask for you to look after me. I didn't ask that of anyone."

"I know that. You wouldn't. You're a Dzin master, self-contained. You have all the answers." Although the words were harsh, her voice was almost soft.

"I don't have all the answers. You don't, either."

"None of us have ever said we did. You keep insisting that we do. That's because you don't like our answers, and you can't come up with any that comfort you. You're looking for old-fashioned truths of the sort that Dzin masters pounded into you, and they don't exist in the real universe. Not once you've left those ancient stone walls that hold a history that has taught you nothing."

"Truth always exists. We may not see it, but it is here."

"Then perhaps you had better look harder, Tyndel." Her voice was almost a whisper. "Much harder."

"You seem to forget that I didn't ask to be rescued."

She looked at me as though my words were the babbling of a child protesting going to school. I'd found that expression on my own face in Hybra when Foerga had called it to my attention, ever so gently, as only she could.

"You ran into the middle of Rykasha . . . just to die?"

I had to look away.

"Don't you understand?" asked Cerrelle, her voice that of a teacher to a very young student. "No child asks to be born. No member of any society is given that choice. The only choice you have—the only real choice any of us has—is whether you will be a productive member of society. Society doesn't owe you anything. Neither do you owe society other than your share of the cost of maintaining that society." She shrugged. "You either pay your debts or you can go back to Dorcha or Dhurra, or the Toze Confederacy. Or you can become a Follower."

I chose not to ask what a Follower was. The distaste in her voice made it clear I wouldn't get an objective answer. I didn't want to be indebted to her for anything more, either. "Some choices."

"They're the same in any society that survives. Do you have a better answer? One that works?" she asked.

How could I answer that? I didn't even know how their world worked, and I was supposed to come up with a better system?

"You haven't exactly worked at learning our system," she pointed out. "It's all inside your skull, and I'll be happy to answer any questions."

I couldn't think of any . . . or didn't want to.

"Come on, we might as well head back." Her voice reverted to a tone of professional cheerfulness.

I followed her, my thoughts churning.

17

[LYNCOL/RUNSWI: 4514]

As soon as a thing is named, its essence is limited, if not lost, for nothing is limited to its name.

The next morning, Cerrelle took me on another subterranean glider trip, to Runswi, a place supposedly holding the transport complex. This trip lasted much longer.

"If Lyncol is the local administrative center, why is the transport center so far away?" I finally asked as the dim-lit glider slid swiftly through the darkened tunnel.

"The arrangement's not ideal, but Lyncol is too mountainous. Also Runswi is far enough from Dorcha that most mites ignore the lights and dismiss it all as the work of the inscrutable demons—if they say anything at all."

Certainly, I'd been one of those mites, half aware that Rykasha existed but not really focusing on the boundary with the unknown. Why didn't people think that much about Rykasha?

"Because through the last millennium, the curious ones either migrated to Rykasha or were eliminated by other mites. All the mite cultures have great and hidden restraints, restraints so powerful that no one even talks about them."

I got tired of Cerrelle answering my unspoken questions, even as her answers demonstrated yet another facet of the nanite superiority, and I hoped it wouldn't be too long before the nanites degenerated enough so that she couldn't sense every strong thought I had.

"How long will you keep reading my thoughts?" The faintly spicy scent she wore tickled my nose, and I rubbed it.

"It's getting harder. Unless you get another injection of the heavy-duty types we use for adjudication . . . not much longer than another few months. By then, though, unfortunately, I probably won't need them."

"My thoughts aren't that bad."

She laughed . . . once. "Did you notice that you didn't even want to question my statement about your hidden restraints?"

"What statement?" I couldn't resist teasing her.

"That's another humorous way of avoiding the issue."

"Humor helps."

"So long as you don't use it to avoid facing things. That's merely humorous dishonesty."

"Why are we going there?"

"To get you evaluated. To see what your potential might be."

"You haven't been exactly supportive of my potential," I pointed out.

"I've been supportive of your potential, but not of your efforts to avoid acknowledging it."

"Can I say something?" I kept my voice even.

She nodded. "You're suggesting I've missed something. Maybe I have. Maybe I've judged you too harshly."

I wanted to swallow. She hadn't fought me, and the words felt honest. For a moment, that unhostile directness reminded me of Foerga.

"I'm not Foerga. I think she was probably a better person than I am."

I did swallow, but managed to get out the question. "Why are you so against Dzin and yet keep telling me that it's trained my mind well?"

The redhead frowned, but I could tell the frown wasn't directed at me. Finally, she spoke. "That's a good question. I'm not sure I can answer it all the way, but let me try. Dzin is a tool, a way of perceiving reality. We don't dismiss the effectiveness of the tool, but we have problems with the way Dorcha uses the tool. The way Dzin is used in Dorcha isn't just to develop awareness of the world but to emphasize an acceptance of what is."

"Dzin isn't like that at all," I protested.

"Dzin isn't," she agreed, "but the way in which Dzin is used to teach students is a means of conditioning. Look at you, Tyndel. You *know* that. As soon as you realized what you had become, you ran. You understood that there was no place in Dorcha for you."

That wasn't quite true. I'd sought Foerga first.

Cerrelle smiled sadly, and I hadn't the faintest idea why. "You understood, subconsciously, that without you, she might not fit in Dorcha, that she was too much of an artist."

"Too much of an artist?"

"Artists are dreamers. They seek beauty, perfection, an artistic expression beyond their culture. And Dzin is used to promote acceptance and understanding of what is, not how to transcend what is."

I really wanted to find the words to cut down her argument, without even knowing why I needed to, but I couldn't. And that bothered me. So did the fact that Cerrelle understood Foerga, in a way, better than I had. What did that mean? That Cerrelle understood me better than I wanted her to?

When the covered glider came to a stop and the canopy slid back, we stepped out onto an embarking/disembarking platform and walked along the tunnel to a single set of steps. At the top of the stairs was a small glass-walled structure perhaps four meters square. A single carved and high-backed pine bench stood in the otherwise vacant and spotless space. I wondered how they managed to keep everything so clean. I'd never seen anyone scrubbing or wiping.

"Cleaning technology is easy, comparatively," Cerrelle said as she opened the door.

I had to stretch my legs to catch her. She marched along the stone-paved lane toward a rambling structure perhaps two hundred meters north of the largely subterranean glider station.

Runswi consisted of a series of scattered low structures spread on a low plateau that overlooked a marsh that extended to the eastern horizon. The lane paralleled the western shore. In the midday light, tall stalks of browned grass bent in the light breeze that carried the odor of the sea.

"Ocean?" I gestured vaguely in the direction of the marsh.

"Ten kilos east. That's far enough that our shuttles are above normal radar scan patterns of the ocean shipping lanes."

Shuttles?

Cerrelle gave me a disgusted glance, and I began to ransack my stored and not-too-well-assimilated knowledge. Shuttles, magshuttles, orbital transporters . . . vehicles that carried people and equipment off earth.

"You see?" she said. "Although you have all this knowledge, you subconsciously shy away from recognizing it or using it. That's because it's outside the framework of your Dzin. You could use Dzin to understand and accept it, you know? We've pointed this out to you. It's not new."

Why? Despite her explanations, I had to wonder why my thoughts skittered away from demon technology and the ancients. Was it the Dzin conditioning? Or some other sort of conditioning? Genetic selection? My own lack of interest?

Cerrelle said nothing, and the only sounds were those of our steps on the stones and the whispering of the marsh grasses in the light wind. I took a deeper breath, gathering in not only the smell of distant salt but of fish, and mudflats, and the faint hint of decaying vegetation.

The leather soles of our boots scuffed the polished surface of the lane. Cerrelle's heels hit harder than mine.

We drew nearer to the long rambling building, its low mortared rock walls surmounted by glass windows and then by a gray slate roof that shimmered almost silver in the winter morning light.

"That's the medical center."

It didn't look like one, not like the tall structures in either Mettersfel or Halz. Esolde—what sort of evaluation would she have given me? Probably a fatal one, I concluded morosely.

"Tyndel . . . you have to stop feeling sorry for yourself. I know it's not easy, but it isn't doing you any good, and I don't think you want to end up before an adjustment adjudicator."

I had to agree with that as I followed the redhead into the building and down the glass-windowed corridor almost to the end, where Cerrelle knocked on a wooden door, then entered without waiting for a response.

The small room was spare, with two chairs, a wooden cabinet that was taller than I was, and something similar to a console with an iconraiser's screen, except the screen displayed an image of mountains and a river falling through a cleft.

The sandy-haired man stood from behind the console and nodded as we stepped forward.

"This is Bekunin. He's a medical specialist," Cerrelle said to me before turning to the thin-faced doctor. "Tyndel is the one we discussed."

Bekunin nodded to her. "I'll run the tests."

Then she was gone, and I was standing there with Bekunin.

"Apparently, you were a Dzin master. You might have what it takes to be a needle jockey." Bekunin nodded toward a straight-backed chair. "Sit down."

I sat. "Needle jockey?"

"Interstellar pilot. It was in your briefing sprays. It's a challenging and rewarding profession."

"Thank you." I paused. "And if I don't want to be a needle jockey?"

"Then you'll become a cargo handler on the most distant and unpleasant stellar outpost we have." Bekunin smiled, a cold expression, so unlike Cerrelle's smile. "And don't make some comment about it not being fair. The way mites treat anyone different, including you, is even less fair."

He was right about that, but I wasn't certain I didn't expect a higher standard from Rykasha, and my face certainly showed that.

"We do expect a higher standard. We expect everyone to be a contributor to society over a lifetime, and this is where we start. Without us, you'd either have starved to death in a stone cell or be dying of cellular burnout. It takes resources to deprogram those old nanotech reformulators, and we need to see what you're fitted to do. Anyway, you need a systemic audit. Please lean back in the chair. This is going to be rough. Not physically, but it's going to be disconcerting mentally."

"Wait a moment."

Bekunin paused. "It's physically painless, and you'll have to go through it sooner or later."

"What am I going through?"

"It's a complete physical diagnosis." He went over to the wooden cabinet and pulled out a gray metal canister with a spray nozzle. "Sit still, right there."

"What . . ."

"Just a trillion or so diagnostic nanites. They'll scan every cell in your body and report back. If that's positive, then we'll go for the higher function assessment."

Matters were once again flying past and around me, but I tried to concentrate. Why was I having such trouble? Every time we got to nanites and what they could do, my thoughts skittered sideways. Cerrelle had warned me that mites . . . Dorchans, whatever I was or had been . . . had a tendency to react rather than to anticipate, but I was having trouble even understanding my own reactions. I wondered if I'd ever be able to anticipate.

Bekunin touched the stud on the side of the canister, and a mist swirled toward me and then vanished—inside me, although I couldn't feel anything. I just sat as he held a sheet of metallicized plastic in front of me and waited, looking at a screen. After a time, the scene on the screen vanished and a grid structure appeared.

Bekunin set aside the sheet and sat at the console, studying the information. I waited. Then he stood and went to the cabinet. "First stage is good. Excellent. Cerrelle has good senses about these things." He took out a smaller canister, one that was a pale green, and turned back toward me. "This could be disorienting, but it should be temporary. You'll understand more later when you get your in-depth briefings."

He pressed the stud on the green canister.

Another mist fogged around me, then vanished. Sparkles flared across my field of vision, growing into dazzling stars that left me as blind as I'd been in the truffler's cave. The darkness faded into green, veils of green that marched down an unseen hill and past me. Then came a squall line of purple hail that smashed through my thoughts.

More darkness. I squinted, but the darkness remained.

A line of fire arched before me, followed by a second, and then a third . . . a fourth . . . until a fountain of golden red rose and fell in the blackness.

Later . . . later . . .

Both the words and the fire fountain faded, and a series of gauzelike red veils swirled before and around me. In time, they vanished.

I blinked, trying to focus my eyes on the doctor, or evaluator, or whatever he was.

His image slowly swam into focus.

"Excellent." He frowned. "Almost too good. Very high sensitivity, and there were some residuals from the earlier engee probes, but you suppressed them nicely, almost instinctively. Necessary for a needle jockey . . . very necessary. It goes with the Dzin background."

I blinked again. "Engee probes? Someone mentioned engee someplace. I don't remember where. What's that, and why is this sensitivity necessary for a needle jockey—"

I broke off at the disgusted look on his face and began to rummage through my own recently acquired knowledge. I was getting to hate that look, the one that said "Dumb mite, use your brains!"

He waited quietly while I scrambled to put it together. Interstellar transporters . . . overspace . . . the Web . . . the pilots called needle jockeys . . . who threaded the narrow and constantly shifting wormholes on the upper plane . . . guiding their ships around the energy vortices. Nanotechnology didn't solve all problems, as Cerrelle had pointed that out. Subatomic transmutation was beyond the capability of nanotech. And it still took massive energy concentrations to lift anything out of a gravity well and send it across stellar distances . . . even using overspace and the Web. My knowledge was limited enough that I couldn't follow the math exactly, but my assessment was probably close enough.

I licked my lips before I finally spoke again. "Why does having been a Dzin master improve the success of a would-be needle jockey?"

Apparently that was a fair question, because I didn't get "the look" again.

"It has to do—we think—with your conscious and sub-conscious reality acceptance and assessment. Needle jockey talent runs to about ten percent of the Rykashan population and about five percent of mite baselines. The historical sample is too small to be significant—statistically speaking—but over the past half millennia between fifty and sixty percent of mites who'd had Dzin or Toze training have possessed the raw outlook talent." Bekunin shrugged. "That's one reason why the center in Lyncol was willing to spend the extra effort to deprogram and deactivate those old nanites in your system."

"And what about engee?"

"Right now . . . we don't know too much about the . . . phenomenon. You can think of engee as an energy field that permeates known space and broadcasts . . . signals . . . that can affect sensitive individuals such as you. That kind of sensitivity is also necessary for a needle jockey."

"Mental signals?"

Bekunin shook his head. "We don't know exactly their basis. They affect certain people in a relaxed state, and sometimes in a highly emotionally disturbed state. We can duplicate the signals and read your reactions, but the signals mean nothing in any way we can discern. They're definitely discrete energy patterns, and they stimulate visual signals. . . ." He shrugged.

I had the feeling that everything he said was true . . . and very incomplete, but I couldn't find enough information quickly enough to ask an intelligent question.

The door opened, and Cerrelle stepped inside.

"He's as good as you suspected." The doctor nodded to the redhead.

"Good for what?" I wish I hadn't spoken. Bekunin had just told me.

Cerrelle shook her head, but she didn't say anything.

"I—" I decided more words wouldn't help. It was just that questions about some things didn't come easily. In a way, I felt it was grossly unfair. The Rykashans expected me to pick up information and concepts instantly when they'd grown up with them.

"You're right," said Cerrelle. "But we're working to give you the information and the skills to make the effort, and you keep resisting. Don't you understand? The universe doesn't really care about fairness. It responds to actions. Your survival depends on you, your understanding, and your actions. Rykashan society isn't structured to baby-sit adults. We're trying to make the transition as easy as we can, but you have to help. Otherwise, you'll end up adjusted or dead or in the nastiest and dirtiest scut job we can find you."

I couldn't help nodding. Her words weren't even a threat—just an absolute cold statement of fact. I tried not to shiver.

Bekunin nodded gravely. "I think you finally impressed him, Cerrelle."

"It's hard for him. I know how hard. It was—" She shook her head abruptly and cut off her own words, looking directly at me. "Let's go. There's nothing more Bekunin can do, and we need to get you new quarters. Then we could use something to eat. I could, anyway."

I was ready to leave, leave Rykasha, but where could I have gone? And what could I have done? I took a deep breath. And I'd thought Master Manwarr had been difficult.

18

Truth is one, although the sages call it by many names.

As usual, Cerrelle wasted no time, marching me to another lodge or dwelling area—except this time I got two rooms and a refresher, and an introduction to Thaya—a blocky young woman in charge of transient quarters and a lot more, I gathered, in Runswi.

"Tyndel, here," concluded Cerrelle, "is still having trouble with using nanite-implanted information. He's at the stage where his first impulse is to look to others for the answers." She smiled. "Please don't you do it. He's got to learn to be his own Rykashan."

"I'll try not to," said Thaya with a warm smile under her blond thatch. She turned to me. "The basics are simple. The Authority pays for your training, and that includes lodging, clothing, and food here at Runswi, plus a basic stipend . . ."

She kept talking, but my mind scattered around the word "Authority." *Central decision-making body of Rykasha, composed of five senior controllers . . .* The demons just accepted that kind of power in the hands of five people?

". . . use your personal code for such things as links, food elsewhere, special clothing, transport—you'll get it figured out. It's on the screen in your quarters, under 'Candidate Basics' . . ."

Just like that—given once, and I was supposed to recall it all.

"Any questions?" Thaya finally asked.

"I'm not going to remember all that. Is there some-where I can look that up?"

The two exchanged glances, and, again, I felt stupid. Why? Why was I still asking stupid questions, reacting . . . not thinking?

"Everything I just told you is on the screen in your room. Look for the icon for 'Candidate Basics.' You use your personal code. I'll write it out for you." Thaya found a yellow card and wrote out something and handed it to me.

I looked at what she had written: "Tyndel-IP-red-95."

"That's your personal code," Thaya repeated.

"You're reacting because that's the way you were con-ditioned," Cerrelle said gently. "This training will help you change that . . . if you work at it. Also, your blood sugar's low, and your system's not used to the extra en-ergy demands of the nanites. Low energy levels don't ex-actly help with thinking."

"Get him something to eat before he falls over," Thaya suggested.

"That's where we're headed, off for some old-fashioned nourishment." Cerrelle whisked me right out of the tran-sient lodge and back onto one of the ubiquitous polished stone lanes under the clear blue winter sky.

"You take advantage of her good nature, Tyndel, and I'll make you wish you'd never been born or that you were back in a stone cell in Dorcha."

Even though Cerrelle had offered the words humor-ously, I felt she would have.

She then dragged me through a gymnasium with ex-ercise rooms and then along the side of a black-tiled pool where one man swam back and forth endlessly, watched by another tall bronze man who could have been an an-cient gladiator. That kind of swimming was a form of physical conditioning that seemed both masochistic and futile.

We kept walking, past a series of two-storied long structures with smoothly finished stone half walls topped with metal-and-glass window panels and glistening gray slate roofs. Several had odd-shaped metal devices mounted above the roofs—devices that my internal information bank identified as antennae.

"This is orbital operations . . . and there's logistics." Cerrelle's voice was clipped and rapid, as though she were trying to ensure she pointed out everything to me. To try to help me integrate the knowledge thrown into my brain by nanites? "That's where you show up tomorrow morning at zero nine hundred—they use old-style military time here."

Logistics? Why?

"Someone has to plan cargo distribution over the Web. It just doesn't happen. And that's where your training starts."

"I understand that." I did understand trading and transport. It was just hard to imagine that the Rykashans so matter-of-factly shipped goods between the stars.

"We don't ship that much—usually the few items that can't be replicated or the machines and technology necessary to set up replication facilities."

I wasn't sure I wanted training to start, but did I have that much of a choice?

"There's where we're headed now." She pointed at another stone and gray metal-and-glass and slate-roofed building half sunk into a low hill—or perhaps the hill had been formed around the side of the building. Who knew with the demons? "It's one of the lounges. There are almost a dozen in Runswi. Sooner or later, you'll find those that are most comfortable to you. They all have food formulators, and the menus are similar."

Once through the wooden doors and the empty foyer, we entered a room where one side was entirely windows.

"Let's sit down for a moment."

I looked out at a brown-grassed meadow when we sat, waiting in the small lounge that held five tables widely spaced. The tables were a dark oak, polished, bound at the edges in shimmering brass. The dark oak chairs also were brass bound, with a dark gold-and-blue brocade over the upholstered seats.

"I'll be leaving later today. You scarcely need me around for your basic training." Cerrelle's eyes went to the doorway, then back to me.

I paused, searching through the information already fed to me. "I don't seem to have anything on basic training for interstellar pilots."

"You looked. That's good. To begin with, you'll probably be given exercises to help integrate all that data. Then more information and more complex exercises. Then the first round of physical training . . ." The redhead shrugged. "You'll get the pattern." Her eyes went to. the doorway again.

I wondered if I wanted to understand the pattern.

"Good. They're here."

With Cerrelle's words, my eyes turned to the couple even as they entered. She was dark-haired, slender, well endowed, and moved with almost an erotic grace. He was red-haired, tall, broad-shouldered, and athletic. Both were obviously young.

"An attractive pair, aren't they?" asked Cerrelle.

"Yes," I answered warily.

The two walked easily toward us. I decided to stand. Cerrelle did also.

"I appreciate your coming," said my keeper. "This is Tyndel."

"Alicia deSchmidt." The name came with a smile.

I repressed a frown. I hadn't ever heard anyone call someone by a double name in either Dorcha or in Ryka-sha. Only the ancients had possessed the population density and the mobility that had made such conventions necessary.

"And this is Tomas Gomes," added Cerrelle, sitting again herself.

"I am pleased to meet you." The red-haired man had an accent—faint, but a definite accent. Tomas—or was he

Gomes?—slipped into the chair to the left of Cerrelle, while Alicia deSchmidt sat to my left.

"Tomas and Alicia," Cerrelle whispered, although the whisper had to have been a courtesy, since any demon could have heard.

"You're the latest refugee from Dorcha, aren't you?" Alicia's girlish voice carried an accent of sorts, one I couldn't exactly place. Perhaps she was from one of the Rykashan interstellar colonies?

"I'm definitely a refugee," I said. "I don't know about being the latest."

"He's the first Dzin master we've had in a while," added Cerrelle.

"In time, we are all refugees. Strangers finding our way in a world that grows ever less familiar." Alicia grinned girlishly.

I blinked at the conflict between the girlish voice and the philosophical tone, between the almost childlike sensuality and the weariness of the words.

"Don't play with the boy, Alicia," said Tomas almost languidly. His tanned skin seemed to glitter, even in the indirect light of even intensity that cast no shadows.

Boy?

"Dzin master or not, he still places too much emphasis on appearances," added Alicia.

I still couldn't place the accent. It didn't seem like any Dhurr or Toze, or like any of the demons I'd met.

"Time for tricks?" A hint of weariness infused the young man's voice as he glanced at Cerrelle.

"It's easier," answered Alicia.

"As you see fit," agreed Cerrelle.

I didn't know what to think, and suspected that was exactly what the three had in mind.

The dark-haired girl slipped out of the chair and stood beside the heavy wooden table, then abruptly jumped straight up—turning the impossibly high jump into a dive that ended with her balanced in a handstand on the middle of the table. I looked again. Alicia's entire figure was balanced on one finger. Unwavering, she balanced on the center of the table, then improbably flipped herself back to the floor—off a single finger.

I wanted to shake my head. Were they playing with my vision, my perceptions?

"Is the table expendable?" asked Tomas.

"Don't waste it," suggested Cerrelle.

Tomas nodded, then picked up one of the knives laid out in place settings. His arm blurred. The knife was buried to the hilt in the heavy oak.

"Try to remove it," he suggested politely.

I couldn't. Instead, I ended up snapping it in half, leaving several centimeters of metal protruding above the table.

Alicia stepped up to the table. This time it was her arm that flashed, her flattened palm driving the ragged metal flush with the table. She smiled and turned her unmarked hand to me. "Would you like to try it?"

"No, thank you." I paused and added, "I know my limits."

"They won't be what you think they are," said Tomas mildly, the softness of his voice emphasizing the accent. He picked up a fork and a spoon. His hands blurred, as though he were rolling them together, and steam—or smoke—rose from them. He extended his hand—then flipped the cylinder onto the table, where the finish blistered under the hot metal that had been separate utensils moments before. "I am sorry," he said to Cerrelle. "It is harder to minimize the collateral damage."

Collateral damage? His words, soft as they were, chilled me.

"Tomas always has been tenderhearted," said Alicia in the same girlish voice. "Will that do?"

"I hope so," said Cerrelle.

My eyes flicked from her to Alicia to Tomas. Tomas shrugged apologetically.

Alicia stood. "We're outbound again. Halcyon Four. There's been a rash of democratic heresies."

"Democracy," snorted Cerrelle. "Mob rule."

"It's slightly better than a despot." Tomas stood.

"Only slightly," said Cerrelle. "Thank you and good luck."

I watched as Alicia smiled bemusedly, and the two turned and made their graceful way from the lounge. What could I have said? Instead, I walked slowly to the built-in counter in the corner where the reformulators waited and got myself a mug of tea, very hot tea. Arleen tea. After a moment, I added a plate of Dorchan spiced pork.

Then I sat and ate and sipped the tea. The food and sipping helped the emptiness in my stomach and the light-headedness, but not the questions that kept piling up in my mind.

Tomas and Alicia—who could bend and shape metal barehanded, balance on tabletops with one finger, and drive steel through hardwood. Tomas and Alicia, younger than I, seemingly, with an accent I had never heard. Tomas Gomes and Alicia deSchmidt, with two names in a world—human and demon—where people had but a single name.

Then there was the almost casual application of force with the hint of incredible restraint, a hint that was equally casual, matter-of-fact, so matter-of-fact that what it implied should have been obvious.

It should have been, but it wasn't, as so often had happened since I'd left Dorcha. Cerrelle had assured me that, shortly, I'd notice the lack of focus on such things as demon technology and new information less and less. But I was acutely aware of my sluggish thoughts at that moment. After finishing all the pork, I sipped the tea to the dregs and still could not focus my brain.

"We send Alicia and Tomas to where there are problems," Cerrelle said. "Usually that's Halcyon Four. It's the only outsystem colony with multiple governments—and that's meant trouble for a long time."

"They apply brute force?" I asked, recalling Tomas's

comment about it being hard to minimize collateral damage. "Colonies?"

"Once—well before my time—we sent them to Mettersfel to raze the old guildhall there."

Before her time? I pursed my lips.

"It's in the records. You'd find it. That was almost seven hundred years ago." She sipped whatever she was drinking.

"They can't be . . ."

"Why? Because they look so young?" Cerrelle snorted. "Have you seen anyone in Rykasha who looks old? Or who is physically old? What do you think nanites do for humans?"

"But . . . can you drive a steel knife through a table?"

"No. You *might* be able to someday. I don't know how they balanced your system. I wouldn't try it now. You'd drive the steel through your palm."

"Would you explain?" I finally asked.

"They're from the days of the ancients," the redhead said. "We've lost a lot of that technology, although we're slowly regaining some of it. They're just about invulnerable to almost all mite technology, except a bank of high-powered lasers, and they can move fast enough that no one could keep the focus on them."

"To be so young for so long . . . so powerful . . ."

"What do you think you'll look like in a century or two?"

I hadn't thought about it.

"You'll look like they do. Have you seen any old-looking Rykashans?"

"No," I answered after a moment. "I don't know about this . . . immortality, isn't it?"

"Not for most of us. Tomas and Alicia are the exceptions. They're close to five thousand years old. Things fell apart before the ancients could modify nanites on a personal basis for more than a handful of individuals. Theirs are intertwined with their gene structure."

"I thought you said—"

"No. Yours, mine—they have to be compatible, but there's a difference between actual link-ties and compatibility. We don't have to worry about growing old or disease, but we're not immortal."

"Accidents?"

"Usually. Or starvation or asphyxiation."

Starvation? I couldn't see any of these people getting trapped in a mite stone cell.

"From accidents. Say there's a malfunction on a needle ship. Your nanites will protect you so long as there's any oxygen anywhere and so long as you have any food or fat cells left to cannibalize. But space is big. We've had the same thing happen to people exploring. Once in a while, some needle jockey ends up mistranslating and the ship goes into a stellar mass. Nanites won't protect you from that. The probabilities are low . . . but they mount up over several millennia."

I was supposed to become a needle jockey, a Web-ship pilot. My thoughts scrambled back through my information bank.

"Don't bother," said Cerrelle. "We all die of accidents—or suicide. The only question is when."

I pursed my lips, wanting to shake my head but not wanting to enough to endure any more comments from Cerrelle.

"It's time for me to go," she said. "You need to get settled so that you can get on with your training."

We stood, and I wondered if I would regret her departure.

19

To the work alone are you entitled, never to its fruit.

Beginning the next morning, things got harder.

I followed Cerrelle's instructions and appeared in the logistics building at 0855 the next morning. One thing I had learned was that Rykashans didn't repeat themselves—not often, anyway, from what I'd seen.

"You're Tyndel," observed the round-cheeked and hollow-eyed woman who met me in the corridor. "I'm Andra. Along with long-range logistics planning, I also handle preliminary indoc and training."

I wondered how many needle jockeys there were.

"Not just potential needle jockeys, but everything from the basics of maintenance to muscle-powered cargo lugs. Especially with nanites, the human body is the most adaptable equipment there is, and we try not to waste it." She offered a flat smile, a smile that should have told me more than it did. "In here."

I followed her into a small room flooded with light from windowed walls on two sides. There were half a dozen wooden chairs with upholstered cushions. Each cushion had a different design. I sat on a bluebell.

Andra sat backward on the chair across from me, her trousered legs curled around the chair back, her arms crossed and resting on the squared off wooden frame. The mid-toned green tunic and trousers set off her strawberry hair and pale freckled complexion.

"If you were one of our youngsters, I wouldn't bother with the verbal part, just start you on the education and let it run, but . . . you're not. Your payback for being reclaimed is ten years of being a needle jockey. That's ten years personally experienced elapsed time, not earth standard objective time."

I still wanted to wince at the thought of being an interstellar cargo pilot. The ancients had gone to the stars, and the result had been total disaster.

"Forget that business about the ancients and the stars. We know what you're thinking, Tyndel. You've got enough telemetered nanites in your gray cells to let me—and Cerrelle—know what your inclinations are before you know. The ancients barely got to the gas giants. They had to invest too much in capital structures for those who didn't pay their way. You'll get more information on that as you go along. What you need to know is that we have colonies in the dozen or so systems with habitable or potentially habitable planets that we can reach through the overspace Web. They're all out from Galactic Center— we're pushing to reach the rim and cross the void, but that may be a while, and it's hard to do it all in weightlessness. All of this requires transporting infrastructure goods—essentially power systems and basic nanite equipment and structures, as well as specialized biologic templates. That's where you and the other needle jockeys come in."

"Aren't the ships infrastructure, too?" I asked, trying to elicit more information or statements that would tie to what had been poured into me.

"You're right. They're the most expensive and hardest to replace. That's why good and motivated needle jockeys are important. That's why your payback is only ten years if you make it to be a needle jockey."

Only ten years?

"Cargo handlers or ship support types—that would be fifteen years, at times more."

"What about regular demons?" I asked.

"Everyone has an initial obligation. It's twenty to forty years for someone born here in Runswi. Forty years if you stay planetside. Then there's an additional obligation every century of personal elapsed time. You don't think we just dumped this on you because you're an outsider, did you?"

That was exactly what I had thought. I looked down at the polished and shimmering golden oak planks.

"You former mites don't like to think through anything that's unpleasant or at variance with your belief systems." Andra looked at me without compassion, without anger. "You're going to have to get over that."

Easier said than done, I thought.

"A needle ship," continued the strawberry blonde, "what is it? It's basically a long chunk of composite filled with stored energy that jockeys thread through the Web of overspace. Overspace isn't, but it can be thought to be, the magnification of normspace to the degree necessary to magnify natural and artificial wormholes and quantum chinks to the size where a needle can be threaded through such passages." She smiled dryly. "Or, I suppose, the analogy could be that overspace shrinks needle ships enough to let them penetrate such quantum passages. Either way, the effect is the same."

Some of it I understood. Composite was used as much as possible because metal tended to make the control fields that drove the ships unstable or less controllable or both. The same was true for operating fusactor power plants.

Some of it I didn't, even after scrambling through the still-disorganized information piled in the corners of my brain.

"Any questions?"

I had lots, and scarcely knew where to begin. Finally, I sputtered out some words, as much to keep things going as anything.

"You seem to imply that a lot of cargo needs to be carried. Why so much, when nanotechnology can create materials—"

"Nanites are very good at rearranging existing materials, but not every place in the universe holds the diversity of elements that earth and our solar system do—or in places that can be easily reached." She shrugged. "As for transmutation, that doesn't work. Quantum mechanics still applies. To locate and move a lepton precisely enough to rearrange a subatomic structure does horrendous things to its velocity, not to mention a few other properties . . . and you don't want to do that, especially if a top quark's involved."

Even with all the information funneled into me, her words made little sense beyond the fact that there was a mechanical and/or practical reason why nanite technology couldn't be applied.

"As a matter of fact, using quantum mechanics that way has been suggested as the basis for another doomsday weapon. We haven't done it because we have more than enough in the arsenal. The ancients were good enough at that to create destructive systems for a dozen races."

"But exactly how does . . . a needle jockey do this?"

"You'll be coupled into the ship, into the fields, and you'll feel and experience what all the ship's sensors register. By reacting and willing, you move the ship as if it were your own body. In a way it is—while you're in overspace. Being a needle jockey is like dodging three-dimensional blocks fired at you by a cannon, except that the blocks you try to weave the ship through are blocks of colored sound, sounds that run from . . . say, the most beautiful and harmonic music you ever heard—do you know Beethoven?"

Another name I'd never heard.

Andra's mouth smoothed into a neutral smile before she spoke. "For a supposedly educated people . . . Never mind. Cargo pilots go under the Web and into overspace—that's explained, too—and it feels like you're dodging blocks of harmonic or jagged sound. Those blocks have edges sharper than a laser scalpel. Add to that the complexity of high-speed, three-dimensional chess and you have an idea of the job. It sounds impossible, but it's not, not with reflex boost and the training. You've certainly got the raw ability, and we can provide the training, if you'll just stick with it. What can make it hard is that you can never relax, not when you're under the Web."

I had the feeling that none of the demons ever relaxed anyway, but I mused, almost absently, about the emphasis on pilots when they obviously had both nanotechnology and computers that made the iconraisers' screens antique toys by comparison.

"Computers? Nanite implants? They can't feel their way above the now. They make it all possible by translating the inputs, but being a needle jockey is reflexes, perception, and feel. No machine can feel and sense the way a trained jockey can."

In a way, her words told me little more than that the demons needed trained pilots because pilots couldn't be replaced by technology, but I couldn't verbalize any more comments, not at that moment.

"All right. Let's get started. You've got a great deal to assimilate." She stood and walked through another door into a small room. On one wall was a rack of canisters, the kind the doctor had used to spray me with nanites to evaluate my physical condition. On the opposite wall, less than two meters away, was a large metalicized plastic screen—presumably for collecting the nanites. Andra closed the door, and we stood in the small room.

"This is basic technology." The canister Andra lifted had a scoop—almost shaped to fit a human face. "Not really even technology, but the theory behind the technology you'll need to be using."

She eased the scoop almost against my skin and pressed the stud. A mist rose around me, then vanished. I thought I felt thousands of tiny needles penetrating my skin, but that had to have been my imagination.

What came next wasn't imaginary, but a rush of phrases, images, terms, and interrelated equations, information . . .

. . . *xenon discharge . . . elevates atoms . . . wave forms above the quark level . . . releasing additional energy in photonic form, tuned to a specific frequency, which replicates the effect . . . creating two phased photons and a cascade effect down a crystalline channel . . . parallel wave forms pass through openings the same size as their wavelengths . . . diffraction occurs . . . intensity drops inversely as the square of the distance . . . color does not exist except as a perception of different wavelengths . . . failure of initial fusactor technology lay in unstated assumption that no wavefield interference would occur from plasma and magfields, despite superconductivity . . . deuterium and tritium resonance on the quantal level . . . maximum span potential directly proportional to the strength to mass/weight ratio of materials . . . disregarded superconductivity and gravfield variations . . . galactic oscillations reverberate through overspace at frequencies inversely proportional to the age of the specific galactic center . . . supercooling phenomena can create harmonic vibrations on the supraquark level with the superposition of two coherent-state wave packets, thus creating a dual presence of a specific single atom . . . from within overspace incorporates a complete embedded minimal surface of finite topology . . . requiring subjective superposition navigation . . .*

I wanted to scream as the weight of all that information flooded through me. If I'd thought the information that Cerrelle had fed me was concentrated, I hadn't understood what intensive really was.

Although I swayed on my feet, I managed to stay erect.

Another image blasted through me, like a starburst that came and went—the golden fire fountains, but that faded almost as it streaked through my thoughts, somehow above and beyond all the images and words that sloshed through my information-soaked synapses.

Andra watched a small screen beside the plastic collector, then nodded. "Good."

Good? I wondered about that.

She opened the second door and gestured for me to

follow her into another small room. This one had windows and was warm and bright. Andra's arm extended to a small console with a keyboard. "Sit down there. The instructions are written on the panel. It's simple enough. A question will scroll onto the screen. You search through the information you received and press the key that represents the most nearly correct answer. This will help you integrate what you've just received."

She looked at me, nodded, and left.

Except it wasn't that simple—not at all.

Take the first question: "Light can most nearly be described as which of the following?"

I just thought about light, and the flood of information slammed through me. Drowning in phrases and ideas, I was trying to sort out old ideas and newly acquired information.

What was light?

Visible radiant energy ranging from 3,900 to 7,700 angstroms? Electromagnetic radiation with a wavelength of between 400 to 800 nm? Quanta of photons following geodesics in four-dimensional space-time? Radiation in semicoherent wave form approximating chaos in five or more space-time dimensions?

I closed my eyes and massaged my forehead. That was just the first question, and sections of supporting texts and background information flooded over me.

Never . . . never had I felt I knew so little. I tried to think about what Foerga would have done, but trying to call up her memory just left me asking why I bothered.

With a slow exhalation, I opened my eyes and looked at the screen. I had to get on with the exercise. Hoping that every question didn't generate the same reaction, I finally punched out the key that indicated all of the answers were correct. They seemed to be, and that gave me a headache as well.

A second question appeared: "What are the properties of a star?"

My head began to ache and split simultaneously, and I

wondered how many questions the console held before I closed my eyes and massaged my forehead. However many it happened to be, that number was far too many.

That much I did know.

20

Every individual's face is no more and no less than a mask.

The silver brume swirled around the hedge, thickening ... rising out of the very ground, out of the grass, out of the stones of the walk ... a silver as cold as Deep Lake in the depths of winter, as impersonal as a Dzin master, as unforgiving as a demon.

I bent down, trying to reach Foerga's still face, and the mist deepened so much that I could see neither her face nor even my own hands. The misty chill seeped through my face and hands and into my bones.

I kept groping, and my hands dipped into the grass, and through it, and through the stones, but I could touch nothing, and her dark hair writhed and turned silver, and she was the brume. And then she was gone.

"The demon is loose!"

SSSSSssss. The susurration of the demon gun shivered the leaves and branches of the boxwood hedge above my kneeling figure. The leaves shriveled into fragments and then powder as I rose, then dove at the dun-red of the Shraddan.

My fingers twisted around his neck, then found each other, as the constable faded into silver mist, as had Foerga. I straightened, and all around me was the brume, silver, cold, and endless. I wriggled my fingers, and they glistened silver, then seemed to meld into the encircling brume.

I tried to open my mouth, but no sound issued into that endless silver that swirled ever closer.

Was everything fading into the mist, everything from my life?

"No . . ."

I bolted awake in the middle of the night and sat straight up in bed, sweating and shivering simultaneously.

Had it been Andra's descriptions, or Cerrelle, or the adjudication hearings? Something had bothered me more than I'd thought.

I realized I was breathing fast, panting, and the sweat was rolling off my forehead. After a moment, I eased back the sheet and blanket and swung my feet onto the cool wood of the floor.

Then I stood and padded to the window.

A few points of light glittered across Runswi, few indeed under the endless stars, and the flat of the sea marsh stretched toward the dawn that would come—must come.

I just watched the stars for a time, letting my breathing return to normal, trying to organize my thoughts.

Item: Not only could the demons ingest vast quantities of information, they expected me to do the same.

Item: Through nanites and headsets, Cerrelle and Andra could determine absolutely whether I was telling the truth.

Item: The demons attempted to ensure personal responsibility, whether or not the individual wished to assume such responsibility.

Item: They had virtually no sympathy for the human failing of self-deception, and they attacked that disease with particular virulence.

Then, they attacked every weakness with virulence. But why?

I wiped my forehead again as I discovered that even that brief analysis had speeded my breathing and started my sweating again.

Why? Why anything?

Because the nanite technology had granted humans powers beyond the average human's design capability for responsible action? Because humans were essentially irrational creatures gifted with the power of rationality?

I didn't have answers. Or if I did, I couldn't seem to find them. Did I want to? That was another question I couldn't answer.

In time, I went back to bed, lying on top of covers too heavy and too warm for my body to bear, and, eventually, I drifted back into an uneasy sleep, a sleep that seemed filled with blackness.

Then . . . there was neither blackness nor fog, but the arching fountains of fire filled my dreams. Fountains of fire rising out of a point of light set in endless darkness. Was that point of light a star? An unimaginably powerful star?

I sat up shivering again, shivering and sweating.

Why would I dream of points of light or stars? The Rykasha had gotten rid of the mismatched nanites . . . hadn't they?

I sat up and put my head in my hands, and the afterimage of fire fountains faded.

Who or what could I believe?

After a time in the darkness that had begun to turn to the gray that preceded dawn, something else struck me.

I didn't care. I didn't care if I repaid the Rykashans for saving my life. After all, it had been their technology that had taken away my old life. I didn't care if I disappointed Cerrelle. I didn't care if I lived up to my "responsibilities" as a newly enlisted demon.

I just didn't care. Why should I care? Foerga was gone. The certainty of Dzin was gone. I wasn't ready for suicide. That would have made things too easy for Cerrelle, and it would have been a betrayal of Foerga. But there was no reason to strive endlessly and mindlessly for a goal I hadn't set, but had been demanded of me without anyone even asking me.

No reason to strive that way at all.

Whether I got to be some sort of interstellar cargo pilot or not seemed immaterial, like the silver brume that had filled my dreams. Like the images of fire fountains in a niellen darkness. Like approval from Cerrelle or Andra. Like anything else that might benefit Rykasha.

21

[RUNSWI: 4514]

Symbolic forms have always been the supports of civilizations, their laws, and their morality. Since symbolic forms are illusions, and illusions sustain civilization, those who rule must maintain illusion.

The next morning, back in the logistics building, I didn't even let Andra get out another set of canisters or set up console exercises. "I don't care if I would make a good needle jockey. I don't care if I owe a debt to Rykasha. Don't you see? I don't care!" My words were so forceful that I had to pause and take a deep breath.

"It doesn't matter whether you care or not," said Andra, putting aside the green-shaded canister that she had held and setting it back on the shelf. "You owe a debt. You will repay it one way or another." She didn't smile, and she didn't frown, and every one of her words was cool, as if she were discussing the weather or the technology of food formulators. She just stood there in front of the shelf rack.

"You really don't care how I feel, do you?"

She turned and studied me. "Cerrelle should have gone over this with you, but maybe she didn't, or maybe you were too upset to take it in. We try to avoid illusions. That everyone should care about someone who is upset is an illusion. Yes, we care to the extent that we try to solve problems, but not to the extent that individual concerns overwhelm the functioning needs of society. That was a critical problem for the ancients. They always wanted everyone to feel good, and in the end, perceptions of personal welfare influenced decisions more than hard facts. It wasn't the cause of the Devastation, but it was one of the things that made any early recovery impossible." Andra carried her trim figure toward the window, then stopped and turned. Behind her, beyond the glass, a wide-winged gull flapped over the edge of the marsh. "In a working high-technology society, adherence to basic principles comes first. We try to design and operate those principles so that they represent the greatest good for the greatest number, but any set of principles will impact someone more adversely than another. You're upset, on a deep level, perhaps subconsciously, that we won't all recognize your pain and grant you some special consideration. But we do, and we have. First, you have a far lighter obligation than someone born here. Second, you're being offered specialized training that will make you a highly respected and responsible member of Rykashan society."

"I understand that, but you haven't given me any choice."

"You can refuse the training," she pointed out. "We offered you the most rewarding and quickest way to repay your obligation, but you don't have to take it. You do have to repay the obligation, though."

"That's it. The obligation means more than I do. People mean nothing to you. I'm not the only one who feels this way. I saw that in the adjudication hearings."

"I'm sure you did. That's why those people were in adjudication." Andra smiled faintly, then glanced back through the glass, her eyes on another seabird.

"It's all an illusion, all this caring . . . you just need another needle jockey."

"Of course we do. Did we lie to you about that? We told you that it was a hard job to fill, and that was how you could fulfill your obligation with the least time commitment. The training and the job would have benefited both society and you. Is that wrong?"

"You make it so cold . . . that's wrong. People aren't just numbers."

"Every human being who ever lived who wasn't a hermit has been a nanite in his or her society. Some have been important nanites; some have been almost superfluous. The greatest danger to a developing society, one that hopes to progress and improve itself and its members, is pandering to self-idolatry. Fostering an illusion of caring is a form of self-idolatry, and it's been tried, and it fails, unless you're talking about a static society where the idolatry is used to reinforce the status quo."

Cerrelle had said something similar, but I'd passed it off.

"She was probably too gentle with you," Andra said. "She was trying to be honest without dropping you into the cold vacuum of reality."

"Reality? Caring is real. People do care. Why do you insist that's wrong?"

"Tyndel . . . you're twisting my words. People should care about others. But when you talk about the survival of a society or the human race, you don't change principles that work because of one individual. Each individual believes his or her circumstances are unique, and they are. If we threw out our principles every time they impacted one individual harder than another, then we'd have no society. In a way, that was what happened in Amnord. I won't retell that, but if you're interested you can find it in the histories available through your screen. Even Dzin follows our principles. Don't tell me that you don't create the impression that acceptance of the way of Dzin isn't necessary. Isn't that just another form of saying that society's principles, even in Dorcha, come ahead of an individual's needs and pain?"

I looked down at the polished gray stone floor tiles.

"You can go back to Dorcha at any time," Andra reminded me.

I recalled hearing the same words at the adjudication hearings. "I won't be a needle jockey," I said firmly.

"That's your choice. If you don't want to go through training, then you'll be a low-level technician and cargo handler on one of the more dangerous orbit stations."

"What if I won't do that?"

"We'll find another way for you to repay your debt. That would mean adjudication. Do you really want that?"

"No." I didn't have to think about that. The last thing I wanted was another batch of nanites in my head, monitoring and regulating everything I did or didn't do.

"There might be some hope for you . . . someday." Her eyes strayed once more to the window, to the free-flying seabird unchained by digits and cold reason.

Hope? Not if it meant being like Cerrelle and Andra, there wasn't.

That I knew already.

22

To oppose is to maintain what one opposes.

Andra wasted no time.

That afternoon I was escorted toward a long paved strip—*permacrete*, insisted my recently acquired database before I pushed the term away—that ran for more than two kilos eastward from behind the logistics area and partly out into the marsh. The winter-browned grasses that flanked the strip swayed in the cold breeze that carried the odor of salt and mud. From my left hand swung a single small duffel bag, pale green, not even half full.

"There's your orbit shuttle," the strawberry blonde announced, gesturing toward a sleek gray craft with stub wings that stood on the tarmac. *Magshuttle*—the identification came unbidden.

The craft was scarcely mine, not even by desire. I followed Andra to the ramp that extended from behind the stub wings, and then up it, noticing the pitted and browned gray of the fuselage.

"Take one of the seats in the last two rows. Those are for low-techs, and you're definitely low-tech now. Put your duffel in one of the lockers in the back." Andra's tone continued to hold that mixture of sadness, frustration, and regret, as if she'd failed to make me understand something basic.

My lack of understanding wasn't the problem. I understood. I just couldn't accept being pushed around for my own good. I couldn't accept that Foerga was gone and no one even cared but me. I couldn't accept that the Rykashans just expected me to go on as if nothing had happened.

I nodded at Andra and left her there. After I slipped my minimal belongings into a locker, I sat and strapped the harness around me.

Andra reappeared beside my seat. "There will be other passengers. Someone will meet you at orbit station to get you on the right needle. You're headed for Omega Eridani on the *Tailor*."

"Thank you," I managed. There wasn't much more to say, and I didn't.

"Some real thinking wouldn't hurt, Tyndel. It would be a shame for you—not for Rykasha, but for you—to waste all that ability on self-pity." With an abrupt nod, Andra turned and walked forward and out the shuttle door.

Self-pity? I was considered self-pitying because I was angry over losing Foerga? Because I wasn't slavering gratitude and saying *Of course I'll take your needle jockey job? Just to be alive, I'll do anything you want?* No matter how impossible and dangerous? I snorted to myself. I'd repay them, but more on my terms than theirs.

The section where I sat was windowless, even at the

front where the apparently more desirable couch-seats were. The sides of the craft rose and joined in a seamless gray curve overhead, perhaps a meter and a half above my head. I could smell a faint odor of oil and metal mixed with the salt air that drifted through the open door.

After a time, a slender man wearing a shimmering one-piece black coverall entered and sat in the front couch-seat. Then a woman in red trousers and tunic sat across from him. Neither spoke to the other.

A man and a woman in dark gray—both well muscled—literally lifted a small, dark-haired woman into the shuttle and carried her toward me. Her hands and feet were bound with clear shimmering straps. Silently, the two strapped the woman into the seat across the aisle from me.

The female guard looked at me. "Please don't unstrap her. You both could get hurt. They'll release her at her destination."

"Bastards . . ." hissed the bound woman to the backs of the two guards as they left. "Think they can order folk to slave for them."

From what I'd seen, the Rykashans could do just that. I could be a low-level slave, a high-level slave, or dead. I didn't want to die. That would still have negated everything Foerga had done. But I didn't want to reward the Rykashans by becoming a needle jockey. That left being a low-level slave, not that I was pleased with that option, either.

"They seem effective at that," was my response.

"Bastards, all of them."

Five people in gray-and-green uniforms trooped into the shuttle and deposited themselves in the seats behind the more colorfully dressed two in the front. One woman glanced in my direction, then at the bound woman, before shaking her head.

"Them, too," added the bound woman.

Almost silently, the door slid shut, leaving the shuttle

cabin illuminated by a pearly light diffusing from the gray walls.

"Please make sure your harnesses are fastened. We will be lifting shortly."

The warning was not repeated, and almost immediately the craft shivered slightly and then began to slide forward, perhaps to rise as well. The silence of the craft's hover, and the smoothness of its acceleration, prompted me to search my mental dustbin of information until I confirmed the earlier unbidden identification—magfield drive.

Based on the sketchy yet voluminous information poured into me earlier, I tried to sort out an understanding. From what I could deduce, a magfield drive was a further adaptation of the glider principles, the tapping of the planetary magnetic field and its use as a basis for some form of induction propulsion—I thought.

In the silence, and to take my mind off the disturbing feeling that my stomach was going to turn itself inside out, I looked over to my left. "I'm Tyndel. Who are you?"

"I can't believe you're sitting there."

"Why not?"

"Do you think you'll ever come home?"

"No." Even if I returned to earth, it wouldn't be home. Home had vanished with Foerga and the mad truffler.

"That doesn't bother you?"

"I can't do much about what can't be changed," I pointed out.

"You sound like the rest of them." The bound woman snorted and turned her head away from me and toward the blank shuttle wall. "Real courage in men vanished with the ancients."

The whining outside the shuttle continued into higher and higher frequencies, until it felt like my teeth would shatter. I tried closing my eyes, but that was worse, with images of Shraddans and demon guns flickering through my mind, followed by endless canisters of nanosprays and nanites weaving invisible and unseen webs around me, webs that pushed me in one direction, then another.

I opened my eyes and waited.

How long before there was a *clunk* that signaled docking at Orbit One, I didn't know, not until my internal demons observed *forty-three standard minutes since lift-off*.

I could feel myself drifting upward against the restraining harness, my stomach seemingly climbing faster than the rest of me. I swallowed down acid and fear, but it took several gulps. I wanted to burp, but dared not. My eyes flicked to the bound woman.

She glared at me, and I asked, "What did you do to end up here?"

"Questioned the wisdom of Rykasha. They know not the greatness of the True God. Nor do you, although you could, if you would but look."

If she happened to be so insane, why was she being shipped off earth like a package for delivery? Why hadn't she been adjusted?

"They can't adjust Believers. We are the Angels and the Followers of the True Lord." She laughed. "The old demons won't tell you that, but adjustment doesn't work on us. So they have to send us home."

"Home?" I blurted.

"The home of God, among the nearer stars."

I did not answer. What could I have said? My internal data store offered no suggestions or answers. All I had absorbed contained nothing on angels or followers or gods. I frowned. Cerrelle had mentioned the Followers, with great distaste, but even with that insight I could find nothing. Then, I didn't know for what exactly I was searching. That was half the problem with nano-implanted knowledge. Without the right referents or key words, a lot of it was useless.

Instead, I waited for the various uniformed figures to pull themselves out of the shuttle, partly out of stubbornness and partly because my stomach wanted to turn itself inside out, and I was fighting it on that, mostly from pride, calling on old Dzin muscular control techniques.

Suddenly, the bound woman retched a spray of stuff that drifted up and toward me. Hastily, I unfastened the harness and bumbled my way back toward the lockers, banging my shoulder into the corner of the lockers. My fingers felt like thumbs as I fiddled with the locker latch, glancing toward the nauseating mess in midair.

"Tyndel?"

I tried to turn and found the motion bounced me off the opposite bank of lockers. I grabbed the back of the last shuttle seat and swallowed to try to quell a rebellious stomach before turning toward the voice.

A slender dark-haired woman in a dark blue singlesuit gestured. "Stop flailing around. Use the overhead guidelines. That's what they're for."

The purpose of the lines against the shuttle ceiling was obvious—after she had pointed them out and explained—like everything else put together by the Rykashans, except half the time they didn't bother with the explanations. Duffel in one hand, I pulled myself toward the open lock door, past the white-face bound woman, avoiding the mess she had made.

"Bastards. . . . God will smite them. . . ."

So these true believers couldn't be adjusted? Interesting . . . if true.

The guideline ended short of the shuttle door, and I looked around, then grasped a railing and pulled myself down until I was approximately level with the woman who had called me.

She extended a hand. One of her boots was somehow attached to a metallic-looking strip in the tubular tunnel that melded with the shuttle portal.

I took her hand. It was cool, long-fingered, and muscular—like Foerga's.

"There. Use the bulkhead handholds until we get to the transition lock. I'm Martenya. Cerrelle told me you've had trouble adjusting to some of the requirements of Rykashan society. So she asked me to see that you got to the *Tailor*."

"Cerrelle?" Why had she made the arrangement and not Andra?

"She can be hard on people from whom she expects a lot." Martenya shrugged. "Some people won't use their potential, and she's never accepted that, even though she understands that it happens." She turned and pulled herself along the tubular tunnel, leaving me behind in the grayness that from appearance could as easily have been drilled through the cliffs overlooking Deep Lake or set anywhere underground in Lyncol—just rough gray walls with handhold bars at waist height.

Martenya waited at the transition lock—scarcely more than an oversized barrel big enough for three people. When she touched a stud, the portal through which we had entered closed. Then, after a moment, the lock shivered and seemed to move. Abruptly, I could feel myself reorienting, and my feet swinging down. We left the lock at right angles to the way we had entered, stepping into a narrow corridor lit indirectly. These walls glistened a muted metallic blue.

My knees tended to go up too far, and I felt like I had to take steps that were nearly babylike to keep from bouncing into the ceiling or whatever it was called.

"The overhead." supplied Martenya. "Walls are bulkheads. Enjoy the gravity while you can. We don't bother engineering for spin forces on the smaller outstations, and you're headed for one of the smallest."

I almost asked why, but forced myself to go through the mental sorting process to see if I could discover the reason buried in the mass of data I'd been force-fed. "The highest payback for unskilled interstellar labor?"

"Exactly."

A man passed us going in the opposite direction, using a long gliding stride, with his feet barely leaving the dark gray carpet underfoot. I tried to imitate his gait. The motion seemed to help keep my knees from rising so high.

"That's better," observed Martenya. "We still have another quarter of the wheel to go to reach the locks to the

upper transition ring. You don't have that much time before the *Tailor* leaves. You can use the canteen on board
while the ship's on ion boost."

She offered nothing more, and I asked nothing.

The second transition lock was like the first, except that
the gravity—or centrifugal force—was markedly less by
the time we reached it.

The passenger section of the *Tailor* was less than half
that of the orbit shuttle, if more luxurious, with eight rows
of upholstered couches, two in a row, each with wide
straps, and each seemingly formed out of a solid block of
some sort of plastic. *Synthcomposite*, my internal demons
supplied. Above each couch was a shell-like block that
apparently descended over the couch to form a monolith
around the passenger.

"Gee-foam and restraints—they're all nanite-based.
While the needle's accelerating or between insertion and
exit, you'll be unable to move at all. A good thing, too,
since you'd be jelly on the bulkhead if you could."

"Ah . . . what . . . how?" I didn't like that idea at all,
and what knowledge I'd been nano-fed didn't explain
why. Or perhaps I didn't know how to access what would
explain it.

"Try thinking about Hawking wormholes for starters,"
suggested the dark-haired woman. "And take one of the
front couches. You could sense the differentials."

What kind of differentials? As I pulled myself along
the handholds I found my mind scrolling through all the
half-mentally-filed information that still felt unfamiliar
and awkward.

"You'll figure it out. You Dzin types do—eventually.
Have a good trip to Omega Eridani." With a brisk wave,
she was gone.

I half slid, half pulled myself down into the front couch
and studied the wide straps, then tugged them into place,
shifting my body until I was as comfortable as I could be.
I looked up at the shell-like block poised to mate with the
couch assembly—with little room for my body. Looking

up at that massive restraint block, my body trying to expand in all directions, I was even more certain that I
wanted nothing to do with being a needle jockey.

My stomach growled, but I wasn't sure whether it was
from hunger or protest at the null gravity.

A man in a uniform that was somehow both silver and
green half-glided through a hatch at the front of the compartment, and the entry lock irised shut. "You're the only
passenger on this run. Not many go this far out." A wry
smile crossed his face. "What did you do?"

"Refused to be a needle jockey." I kept my voice level.

"You'll change your mind. If you're lucky and smart
enough to live to do that." He shook his head. "Now . . .
we'll be going on ion boost for about a standard quarter
hour to get clear. Stay in your couch until the bells sound.
The small gee-force, like gravity, will go on for ten to
fifteen minutes, and you can walk around—if you want.
It's a better time to eat, and it's best to eat early."

I could definitely understand that, the way I was still
half fighting my stomach's desire to invert itself.

"There's a head aft, and a small canteen. When the bells
sound the second time, you have five minutes to get
strapped in. If you don't make it, you're dead. The captain
can't change the insertion envelope at that point, not without destroying the ship. So . . . you're out of luck. Understand?"

I understood. It was like everything else the demons
did. How could it have been otherwise?

23

Enlightenment shatters the illusory realities of the world.

There is but the slightest hiss before all the force lines shift.

A tug . . . there. A twitch there . . . and I and the ship—we shiver through a shower of gilded mist, clawing up a cliff of violet. A carillon of trumpet chimes cascades from the violet. A long straight channel of red beckons to my right, regular and even . . . sharp and hard beats on twin tympanies.

I ignore it, for regularity means solid matter, not the swirling of vacuum and gases between the stars, and the channels are traps.

Along the footlighted strands I dance, each strand the strobe of a quasar that flashes across the overspace, singing lyric notes that Dzin never recognized. Silently, for the ship and I are unheard against and amidst the waves of sound, I edge farther upward across the linked lines of stars visible only in powder blue puffs that vanish as I stretch-and-fly across each, and violins vibrate in long strings against my back.

Flame burns at my fingertips as I push away from a black wall that echoes the heavy tempo of kettledrums rumbling ever lower. I search for a gap, any gap on the far side of the star-stage, grasping the strands that reach above me and stretch before that black wall.

Two channels open—red and green—on each side of the wall. I hesitate, then leap, grasping, digging fingers into the diaphanous fabric of the Web, letting the fire sear through me, for I am being dragged down by the leaden spines in my guts, as a chorus of tympanies marches up my backbone.

Another leap, another grasp, showered with cerise explosions and discordant polyphony from at least two unseen harpsichords, and we totter edgewise up the strands and across the high wire of yet another stage, a circus ring, our feet poised on hot coals. The scarlet fumes circle inward, twining to the tinny silver of a tambourine snapping out a flamenco beat.

I sense the deep white of the beacon, the faintest of clear lights in a swirling universe, centered in a smaller whitened web.

Three black spears loom from beneath, exploding upward toward my guts, lead-copper rock, punctuated with the reverberating twanging of massed steel-strung and hard-twanged guitars.

I point-toed leap, and drop, whirl, and dodge, lunging around the spears and toward the clear amber light, toward the soft and golden harp strings. One spear slashes across my laggard back, but I totter onward, stifling the scream.

Lilacs and the perfume of spring explode around us, silver strings soothing the chaotic polyphony below, and, while I breath deeply, we dance upside east, the pattern carrying us around a cliff of violet, past a red channel, and over a green ditch. A single, longing high C rides over the harp. Somehow, my feet stay upon the strands of the Web which suspend me above the now, dark and solid below, even as my back burns.

And I stretch and grasp the handle of the old-fashioned kerosene lantern, ringed in a circlet of lilac, centered in that smaller web. We are almost there, almost to . . .

24

*No society that places the individual above itself will survive;
but neither will any society that places the individual below
itself.*

The unnamed crewman and Martenya had both been
right. Had I not been in the solid, gee-foamed, and
nanite-restricted monolithic cocoon, my body would have
been less than a thin film of jelly spread across the
walls—bulkheads, rather. Beyond what I felt, I could
sense the forces, almost like blocks of music somehow
solid and massive or knifelike and deadly.

Then, after another twisting, screaming wrench, the music and the forces vanished. Shortly, following an initial
acceleration, we decelerated. The cocoon opened, and I
found that I had sweated so much that my greenish singlesuit was soaked through.

Using the faint "gravity" provided by the deceleration,
I made my way to the head, and then to the canteen, but
I only drank some mixed fruit juice and ate an orange-
mond pastry. I knew that total null gravity would return
soon enough.

"Return to your couch. Approaching destination station." The words were clipped, as if an afterthought.

I strapped in and waited.

Even after the *clunk* that announced the needle ship's
docking *somewhere*, the passenger compartment remained
sealed, and, while I loosened the restraints, I did not remove them. I preferred not to fight the null gee when I
had nowhere to go. So I sat under the loosened padded

restraints until the ship's hatch or lock irised open and a figure appeared.

"I'm Gerbriik, and I'm the maintenance officer of the station." The thin man who floated in the needle ship's open portal had a long square face, clean-shaven and large in proportion to a body even smaller and slighter than mine. He wore a shimmering silver one-piece suit. "You're Tyndel, and you once were a mite Dzin master. None of that matters. What matters is that you're here for a ten-year tour. That will repay two thirds of what you owe."

I'd known I owed; I'd recalled something about ten or fifteen years, but I'd never pursued it. It didn't matter. So I waited.

"Unstrap. No sense in wasting time." He glanced around the compartment, then sniffed. "Good thing you didn't make a mess." A laugh followed. "You'll appreciate that more and more."

His eyes raked over me as I pulled myself along the guideline toward the portal. "Green, eh? Here, you wear dull gray. Nothing else."

Aquacyan, blue, green, gray—what did it matter? I nodded.

"See how accepting you are in a year." Gerbriik snorted. "You call me ser, just like any other station officer. That's anyone in solid blue or black. In fact, anyone in a solid-colored uniform."

"Yes, ser."

"Let's go. Sanselle will be coming through here." Gerbriik turned in a single effortless motion.

I pulled myself after him, conscious of my awkwardness, with one hand on my small duffel, the other grasping along the lines. There were no transition locks, just the ship lock, a tube, and a second lock leading into the station proper. The corridors of OE Station were small, barely wide enough for two people abreast, and smelled of humanity and new materials simultaneously. The walls were brownish gray and reeked of age, though I doubted they were near so old as they felt or looked.

We had traveled no more than fifty meters when he stopped by a green-rimmed hexagonal-shaped hatch. "All the levels are connected by transverse shafts. There's more on that in your briefing spray. The double hatches are nanite-sprung to stay closed." Gerbriik nodded and slipped inside the door, pulling one thin door toward him and pushing through another that swung in the opposite direction.

I followed, finding myself in another tubular corridor perpendicular to the one we had just left. Gerbriik was already ten meters above me, past one hexagonal hatch and floating opposite a lower one. Then he pulled the inner door and pushed through the outer one.

It took me longer, because my duffel caught on the inner door and jerked me backward, practically back across the corridor.

Gerbriik's face was blank when I finally emerged. Once I was clear, he pushed off down the corridor, stopping less than thirty meters from the shaft hatch door. I didn't stop and swung past him. I finally managed to grab a guideline on the wall—bulkhead—and slow myself. Weightless I might have been, but my body retained all its inertia, as my hand and fingers testified with the strain of slowing and stopping me.

The maintenance officer pointed to another hatch—a smaller hexagon. "This is mid-deck three, space four. Remember it. This is your cube. You're not important enough to rate space. You get it because it's more convenient for everyone else. There's one space that's yours to keep spotless, and you will keep it spotless, Dzin master, all by yourself, with your multiple talents. It has an inside latch for privacy, but that's it." He pushed the hatchlike door inward and open. "Go ahead. Look."

I wondered at the inward-opening design until my demons supplied the answer—*protection against depressurization.* If the station were holed the internal pressure of the cube would keep the door almost welded shut against the seals.

"Go ahead. Look inside."

"Yes, ser," I managed. The space beyond the door was small, no more than three meters by two, with built-in drawers and a narrow closet on one side. There was no-where to sleep—just six rough gray surfaces.

"You don't need a mattress in null gee, but you get a sleeping net with a pallet pad on one side. It's rolled up inside the closet. Use it. Otherwise you'll be working with bruises and cuts, and those sting in your gear. Oh, there should be two gray work coveralls in there, too. They're nanite reinforced. You should be able to move a good two hundred kilograms, even in full gee. You can move more here, but stopping that mass would be something else. I have a few more things to show you. Leave your duffel."

Lifting two hundred kilograms or more on a routine basis?

Before I could extricate myself from the small cube, the maintenance officer was a good twenty meters down the tubular corridor. I shut the hatch door and scrambled out of the cube to follow, catching up while he waited by another hatch, this one rimmed in blue.

"Here's the low-tech canteen. It's big enough for all three of you. That's Sanselle, Fersonne, and you." Gerbriik laughed. "Same food replicator as in the officers' mess. Same menu. Even has traditional Dorchan dishes. You can eat as much as you want, whatever you want, and whenever you want so long as you're not working." The long-faced maintenance officer handed me two nanite-spray cans. "These hold all the station info you'll need. Go back to your cube and take them two standard hours apart—unless you want a splitting headache. Report to the maintenance office at zero eight hundred station time tomorrow. Eat first." He laughed again. "Enjoy your time off."

With that, he glided away, leaving me floating by the canteen.

My stomach had barely settled, and I didn't want to risk upsetting it again by eating immediately. So I began to ease myself back the few meters to what amounted to my own private, and very gray, casern.

The gray walls were as depressing as the mad truffler's cave had been, even more depressing than the cellars and caserns scattered through old Henvor. The gray bulkheads offered even less hope of early escape. *Abandon hope* . . . Those words came from somewhere, but I didn't recall them. There was much I knew now that I did not recall. I looked down at the nanite-spray cans. There would be more of those as well.

25

[OMEGA ERIDANI: 4515]

Those who err without understanding shall die without comprehending.

Even two hours apart, the two nano-sprays had split my skull, as more figures, charts, diagrams, and specifications flooded through my brain and synapses. Some of the knowledge would be helpful, such as the plans of the station's decks and the various lock locations, but what did I care about the various moduli of elasticity of shear for the bearing truss joists? Or the decompression pressure stress bright lines? Or the acceptable atmospheric pressure variances? It wasn't as though I would be in any position to do anything about them. Not as a maintenance laborer or low-level tech.

The jolts to my brain hadn't helped my stomach or my adjustment to null gravity, either. Or my attempts to sleep. The sleeping net—even tethered at four points—swayed all night long with every motion I made. At times, I felt like I was choking in my sleep. I didn't sleep, but dozed, or so it felt. Learning to sleep in null gravity was going to take some learning. Then, what else did I have to worry about besides learning to sleep and be a high-level laborer at the end of the universe?

I didn't think about clocks, or timepieces, but I didn't need to worry.

My briefing spray included something along those lines. Internal demons jolted me out of my dozing state. *Zero seven hundred. Zero seven hundred.*

The null grav shower was also a joy, but at least the food formulator delivered, and I ensured that I was in the maintenance office before eight hundred. The space was perhaps five meters by ten, and one wall was nothing more than covered bins of various sizes and shapes. Built into the wall to the right of the entry hatch was a desk space, above which were mounted various screens like those of the iconraisers of Henvor. I could not help but wonder about the amount of electroessence they required and how they were powered. *Null gravity fusactor, design beta-one.* Nuclear fusion—a form rejected by the ancients?

Gerbriik pushed himself away from the various consoles, turning in midair as he did so. "Good morning, Tyndel."

"Good morning . . . ser." I barely managed to tack on the honorific.

"We'll start you out on something simple but necessary. You all work twelve standard hours. That's really fourteen, because you work four, then get an hour break." Gerbriik pointed toward the equipment floating on a bulkhead tether—a cylinder three meters long with an attached hose. "That's yours, Tyndel."

I paused, trying to rack my memories and ill-sorted knowledge. Nothing. There was nothing about shiny cylinders with flexible brown hoses.

"That's a SARM—separator and recovery module. It's just a nanite sorter with an intake suction feed powered by a blower."

That didn't leave me any wiser.

Gerbriik smiled condescendingly. "In short, former Dzin master, it scoops up elemental dust and gas molecules and sorts them into bins in the cylinders. Understand?"

Even with my aborted recent reeducation, I knew enough to know that was possible, since essentially it was a modification of the food formulator principle. But what was I supposed to do, and why was it necessary?

"No."

"No, ser!" snapped Gerbriik. "If you don't show respect, I can recommend your exile, your physical exile to one of the borderline colonies, like Nabata. There's no place for disrespect on an orbit cargo station."

"Yes, ser," I answered, recognizing, belatedly, the authority in his voice, that and the desire for power that the maintenance officer barely kept in check. I doubted he had that kind of authority, but my doubts had been wrong before about the demons, and now wasn't the time to test my judgment.

"That's better." He offered another condescending smile. "We have nanite housekeepers here. Two kinds— the microscopic disassemblers and the collector-scrubbers installed in the ventilation system. The disassemblers are programmed to break down certain molecular chains into constituent atomic structures, and most of those chains are waste materials. The disassemblers are ten-micron-sized, and they go anywhere in the station. The scrubbers collect and store everything that the air returns pick up. Now, do you understand?"

"I think so. Ser," I added hastily. "Materials too heavy to get carried, or those trapped in corners and too big for the disassemblers—"

"Exactly. Your job is to put on a breather mask and poke that hose into every square millimeter between deck one and deck two. Tomorrow, you'll do the same thing on the next interdeck."

I waited, then asked. "Is there a manual or instructions? I have some questions."

"Ser."

"Yes, ser. Does it signal if it's full or not working?"

"When any of the bins are full, it buzzes, and you bring it to maintenance. Sanselle will empty and clean it. No brains or instructions necessary, Tyndel. Eventually, you might learn enough to do that." He handed me a purplish mesh with a clear faceplate and a heavy squarish lump on the bottom. "That's your breather hood. We could use a more sophisticated nanite system, but they have to be tailored individually, and they're costly. This works almost as well, and it's just fine for you. All you do is pull it on and make sure it fits flush against your maintenance suit."

"Yes, ser."

"Here are your work gauntlets." He extended a thin gray pair of gloves.

I looked dubious.

"They're nanite-reinforced. You'll need a maintenance belt and tool kit. This one's checked out to you." He extended a dark gray belt with several flat pouches fastened to it.

I slipped it around my waist and then took the gloves, heavier than they appeared at first, and pulled them on. They went halfway up my forearms.

Gerbriik pointed to a flat screen on the wall. "I've called up the interdeck schematic. That shows where you'll be. Study it, and then haul yourself to entry port two and start cleaning from there."

I stepped forward and looked at the interdeck schematic, trying to memorize it or something, but the effort called up a similar map in my mind, and I tried to integrate the two, looking for entry port two.

"You got it?"

"Yes, ser."

"Then take the SARM and your hood and get to work." Gerbriik twisted back to the consoles as if to indicate he'd said all that was necessary.

I wondered, but I clipped the hood to the belt that had come with the dark gray coverall and towed the SARM along the corridor outside the maintenance space to the access shaft that would bring me closest to entry port two.

Entry port two was another type of hatch. I recognized it belatedly from the information that had been dumped on me through the latest nanosprays. Not only was it double-sealed, but it contained a third sliding metal panel between the outer and inner hatches. The middle panel required a maintenance wrench. I thought, and then fumbled out the wrench from the small tool packet fastened to my belt. It was the wrong one. After three tries with various wrenches, one worked; I had the middle door open.

Then I tried to ease the SARM module through. The SARM power stud banged on the side of the hatch, and a whining started up immediately. When I scrambled to turn it off, I ricocheted off the side of the hatch with my ribs, then put up a gloved hand to stop myself.

The nanites in the glove protected my fingers by stiffening, but that threw me sideways in the other direction and slammed my thigh against the door. I had to duck to keep my head from getting mashed on a girder that flanked the other side of the portal.

For a long moment, after finally stabilizing myself by clutching the plasteel beam, I hung in the gloom, sucking in deep breaths, realizing that I was seeing mostly by nanite-enhanced vision. Moving gingerly, I closed the portal. The built-up odors told me why Gerbriik had sent the breather hood.

After locking one leg around a support beam, I pulled the hood over my head and sealed it. While I could breathe without gagging, I began to sweat almost immediately.

Slowly, I levered myself down to where I could recover the SARM. Then I began to thread my way toward the far corner between the two air return ducts that dwarfed me. The cleaning pattern suggested by the briefing nanites started there, and I felt less than terribly creative with sweat coating my face and hair while pushing a three-meter cylinder that massed half what I did.

With the restricted view through the faceplate, I didn't see the conduit for some type of cable that protruded from the lower deck, and the toe of one boot caught. I spun, and trying to avoid crashing the SARM into the diagonal girder to my right, found my hooded head banging into another brace. The hood reduced the impact to a jar, but I bounced sideways. The SARM hose twisted around one leg, and my other hip scraped something.

I finally managed to stop colliding with sections of the station, but I'd barely started, and I had bruises along both legs, a twisted calf muscle, sore ribs, and other bruised muscles in places I'd probably rediscover over the next few hours and days. I'd never thought about how difficult not having gravity would be, and wondered if I'd dream longingly of full gravity in the days and years to come.

In time, I managed to figure out how to move the equipment and myself with a minimum of effort, and thus a minimum of reaction. But I kept sweating.

After about a standard hour I found myself squinting through the faceplate as I pointed the nozzle of the SARM in the direction of an enclosed metal rectangle with nodules on it. A jolt ran through my system. *Restricted equipment! Restricted equipment!* I shivered and wanted to shake my head, beginning to understand, once more, just how effective nanotech conditioning could be. No wonder I hadn't gotten that much of a briefing. The briefing sprays had just applied the warnings to my nervous system somehow.

While I was recovering from that jolt, the SARM canister rebounded against my left calf, giving me what would be another bruise.

I had swept out most of the crevices and hidden areas on the inboard section of the interdeck when my internal demons announced *twelve hundred hours.*

Almost simultaneously, another figure in a breather mask tapped on my shoulder, then reached down and flicked the power stud on the SARM. The other person also wore dark gray and gestured back toward entry port two.

Outside the port, I followed the other's example and pulled off the breather hood. Sweat still streamed down my face and down the back of the coverall singlesuit, leaving it an even darker gray than when I had started that morning.

"Time to eat. We get a standard hour to eat and rest each four hours. I'm Fersonne." She was angular, and as tall as I, with brown hair not much longer than mine.

I followed Fersonne, pulling myself after her through the tube down to mid-deck three and the canteen, a gray windowless space that would have fit into a prehistoric castle, except for the formulator. The spiced orange pasta and chicken dish was good. But I was certain that was only because good food cost no more than bad with a nanite food reformulator. Fersonne had something else, something that was mostly rice, and she ate without talking.

The sticktites on the chair seat held me in place. I wondered why they even bothered with seats in null grav, but supposed it was part of the effort to re-create the familiar ... or something. There was nothing on the reasons for anything in the briefing sprays, just facts, fingers, and schematics.

"Tyndel?" asked Fersonne, her mouth half full.

"Yes?"

"Why are you here?"

I shrugged. "Because I wouldn't be a needle jockey."

There was a definite silence before she spoke again.

"They offered you that kind of chance? And you turned them down? Do you know what kind of life needle jockeys have?"

"No. No one explained very much of anything."

Fersonne looked at me with those wide brown eyes, and, for some reason, I wanted to duck under the table.

"I'm on an extra two years' objective here, Tyndel. You know why?"

"No. I don't know much, I've discovered." I followed the words with a shrug.

"I'm adjusted. That means I can't do much on earth. More on an outplanet, maybe. A year's station stipend here is almost ten years what I could earn anywhere else, and they'll let me choose any open outplanet after station duty." Fersonne shook her head. "A needle jockey gets ten times that, or more, I hear."

"After the first years, I suspect."

"They live well even then." She dropped her eyes.

There was little enough I could say without making matters worse. I took another mouthful of the pasta, wondering how long before the gray bulkheads would start to close in on me, if I ever would regard OE Station as anything more than the demon equivalent of a Dorchan stone demon trap with food.

Fersonne's guileless brown eyes studied me. Meeting them was hard, and I didn't know why. Or was it that I didn't want to think about why? I sipped Arleen tea that was already lukewarm from a squeeze bottle, as much to avoid speaking as from thirst.

26

Freedom and ignorance are incapable of long coexistence.

I half glided, half scrambled toward the maintenance office as my internal timepieces warned me—*zero seven fifty-five . . . zero seven fifty-five.*

Every muscle ached from the maintenance details of the preceding five days. I never would have thought how muscles could ache in null gravity, especially with the extra strength provided by both personal nanites and the nanite-reinforced coveralls. Gerbriik found ways to use every bit of that strength.

Beyond that strength, as a Dorchan I still sometimes had trouble believing that the demons had returned to space and the stars, apparently so easily. That was inconceivable, yet, as a Dzin master, I could see that it *had* happened. The conflict between what my Dzin training and perceptions told me had happened and what my upbringing had told me couldn't have happened sometimes gave me a headache if I thought about it for long. Why? Because all my early upbringing had emphasized that the return to space was inconceivable? Because my Dzin training had also conditioned me to accept what obviously was? Because the ancients' dream of the stars was considered impossible? But if the demons had the stars . . . what was the next dream? Was there one beyond just stars and more stars? Somehow, conquering the Void didn't seem like a real dream.

I wasn't ready to think more about that, and I didn't. Instead, I slid into the maintenance office and closed the hatch behind me. Gerbriik waited by the large wall screen, drifting in midair in the null gravity. Fersonne floated beside the maintenance officer, her wide brown eyes expressionless.

"Tyndel," began Gerbriik, pointing to the image on the screen, "this is a cargo sled. Fersonne and Sanselle will help you practice with it. That practice is not because I'm babying you. That's because of all the jump-credits it takes to get one out here. I don't want one of our sleds damaged. Neither do you, because I can charge the damage to your contract time."

"Yes, ser." I looked at the image of the sled—nothing more than an open-topped box with dark gray reinforcing beams on the bottom and both ends, and with netlike webbing on the front, back, and top.

"How do you think it works?"

Rather than ask, I searched the briefing data, a mental chore that continued to feel like rummaging through piles of unread papers in my skull. "Magnetic induction, ser?"

"What does that mean, O former Dzin master?"

"The sled centers itself on the guides on the left side of the cargo spaces and transit corridors."

The maintenance officer nodded abruptly toward Fersonne, in a motion that was swift and effortless, the kind of movement that created no reaction in null gravity. "Have him run it up and down Beta Corridor—quick stops, turns, shifts to the opposite rails."

"Yes, ser," answered my brown-haired colleague.

"Tyndel, you do exactly what Fersonne says. Do you understand?"

"Yes, ser."

"Good. Over the next few months we're scheduled to get three ships' worth of cargo for the terraforming project. You'd better be as good as Fersonne by then."

"Yes, ser."

Gerbriik turned in his usual manner to signify he was through with us.

I followed Fersonne to the transit shafts and then all the way to the bottom—where I'd never been before.

"Lower level's all cargo stuff," she announced as she opened the three-door hatch from the shaft. Her fingers were deft with the wrench key for the middle door.

"Does the station get much?"

"No. Just supplies and stuff for the projects."

"Gerbriik mentioned terraforming . . ."

Fersonne gave me another of those wide-eyed looks that made me feel embarrassed that I hadn't searched my internal knowledge before opening my mouth, and I began to rack my brains once more.

After I moment, I nodded. The whole point of the out-stations was terraforming—for those stations in systems without habitable planets, and that was more than half of the dozen-plus systems linked by the needle ships. Nanotech made general trade uneconomical, and none of the outcolonies had the education and resources yet to develop technology or knowledge superior to that of the Rykashan demons of earth.

The idea was simple enough—spread people far enough that no single catastrophe could wipe out the human race. I frowned. Which human race? The one from which I had sprung or the demons? Or were they one and the same?

"Cargo handling's better in some ways," Fersonne said after my continuing silence. "Sometimes you get to talk to the crews or the super or even a passenger."

"Other people."

"You notice no one on station talks to us except to give an order? Or information necessary to carry out an order?"

I hadn't, but I took her word for it. She led the way down the dimly lit cargo corridor with the gliding movement everyone but me seemed to have mastered. The corridor was a good three times as wide and high as the tubular corridors on the other station levels and gave me the impression of a vaulted basement of an ancient building, for all that the walls were seamless gray, shaded slightly with brown.

Fersonne eased to a graceful stop. Behind her were

three bays or hangars with closed doors. She touched a stud, and all three doors rose. The cargo sleds were just as pictured on the screen, except smaller than I expected, only about four meters long and two high. Each was inside its own enclosure, tethered to heavy bolt anchors from six points. The tether lines didn't seem that strong-looking, but who knew what kind of nanite reinforcing they had?

Fersonne pulled a square box from a strap pouch at one end of the leftmost sled. The box was attached by an electroessence cable to the sled. "Here is the control box. Same as on the small sled. You seen that?"

"I didn't even know there was a small sled."

"Use that for moving stuff around the station, but it's self-powered. Could really rip things up if it got out of hand."

For a moment I had to think, and run through what I knew but really hadn't assimilated once more before it became clear. The big cargo sleds only ran on the cargo corridor and were held by the energy fields that bounded the corridor. The little sled was self-contained, with far less mass but with no external restraint. I blinked and looked down at the box in Fersonne's hand.

The sled controls looked simple enough—four arrow-shaped studs surrounding a circular stud. Outside the arrow studs were two square studs—one glowing green, one red.

"The power switch is under the toggle cover."

I hadn't even noticed the shielded cover in the corner. I nodded.

"Center button is the stop button." Fersonne smiled. "Only works if the sled's within range of the guiderails. Use the others to move the sled. Green is up; red is down. Others mean direction."

"If I push up and the side arrow . . . ?"

"Don't. Only want to move in one direction at a time."

I nodded.

"We'll untether it first. Don't want to pull out the anchors."

Another example of the demon outlook. The sled had enough power to rip out the anchors, but they wouldn't use the materials or effort to reinforce the hangar. They expected the users to be careful. When the maintenance officer could recommend someone's exile, they could expect care.

I followed Fersonne's lead and undid the tethers on the left side, then returned to stand beside her while she eased the sled out of its bay and into the corridor. Once it was well away from the others, she handed me the control box. "Remember, it keeps going in whatever direction you move it. The controls are supposed to feed back so it doesn't, but don't trust them all the way."

Trust? What could one trust? How much? I took the control box, wondering if I'd ever be able to trust Ryka-shan society's rules as much as I once had trusted the way of Dzin to make my way in Hybra.

27

[OMEGA ERIDANI: 4515]

Those who reward vain attempts encourage such and discourage true accomplishment.

Sanselle glanced across the narrow canteen table at me. Her green eyes seemed overlarge in the pinched face, and her short, sandy hair was strawlike. "Fersonne says you could have been a needle jockey. That true?"

I finished the last mouthful of Dorchan mushroom pasta before answering. "I had a chance. I do not know if I would have been successful."

"You'd 'a been." She took a swig of a dark brown beer

from the squeeze bottle. "When you're not around, Gerbriik says you're worth two of most lugs. So how'd you get here?"

How had I? It had seemed so simple. Was it? I could feel myself somewhere else, somewhere with red arcs of flame, golden-red flames in a niellen night . . .

"Tyndel? You all right? Your eyes . . ."

I shook myself. "I'm sorry. I didn't mean . . ."

"We all got pasts. You want to talk, I'll listen. You don't, that's fine."

"Things . . . I'm still not sure."

"Whatever." Sanselle laughed easily. "You being here makes things easier for us. Nathum—fellow before you— he broke two SARMs and jammed a sled. Tried hard, he did, but trying's not doing."

Simple as they were, those last words echoed in my thoughts. *Trying's not doing . . . Trying's not doing . . .*

"How did he jam a sled?"

Sanselle shrugged. "Somehow got it crossways going into its bay, then tilted it. Mite-damned job to unwedge it. Ended up taking out some panels and one of the guiderails."

That explained why Fersonne had suggested I not attempt multidirectional commands with the big cargo sled controls.

"Ready for the orgnopaks?" asked Sanselle.

"Ready as I'll ever be." Carting replacement materials paks for all the food replicators from the storeroom to each mess wasn't nearly so onerous as cleaning the between-decks spaces, but it was nearly as tedious and time-consuming.

Theoretically, the replicators could have been built able to shift molecules of any structure, but the side effect was that such full-range replicators took a great deal more electroessence and generated far more heat, and heat dispersion was more of a problem on orbit stations than heat retention. So the maintenance crews replaced the materials paks with new ones containing trace elements, hydrogen, nitrogen, and carbon, as well as other elemental forms necessary for food synthesis. The paks weren't labeled with the actual contents—just with the class of replicator they fitted.

I loosened the sticktites and let myself drift toward the disposal slot below the replicator. It wasn't a disposal slot, since the waste material was shifted by nanites into a separate waste-orgnopak and reused as it could be. After shoving in my plate and cup, I turned in midair to follow Sanselle.

"Fersonne says the small sled is acting up." She lifted her eyebrows.

That didn't surprise me, either. Little in my ambit had, not even OE Station, not since the comfortable world of Dzin had vanished when the Shraddans I'd trusted and justified in my teachings had killed Foerga and sent me running.

Was I still running? I tried not to shiver at that thought as I followed Sanselle.

28

[OMEGA ERIDANI: 4515]

The shape of a container is not the nature of that which is contained.

I pushed the SARM canister around the gently curving corner that followed the arc of the station's hull. Ahead was a mist, fulgurant and full. I tried to slow the heavy SARM, but I couldn't halt it before it plunged through the mist, its inertia dragging me through the curtain of pinlights. Each tiny light seared, cutting like a white-hot needle.

There before me, beyond the sparkling curtain, I stood

amid a black nothingness. The orbit station corridor had vanished. Arcs of golden-red fire webbed a sky blacker than any I had ever seen, a heaven whose stars shimmered so brightly that I had to slit my eyes.

The fire arcs sprayed out from a pinwheel that sputtered before me, except it was a star twirling ever so slowly in the darkness. A face slowly swam from the center of the spinning and sputtering fire into the center of that light. Short black hair framed a thin face, and out of that face shone deep blue eyes.

Then the light brightened even more. I had to close my eyes against the glare, and I found myself unable to breathe, unable to move, with fire coursing through my closed eyes, hot winds desiccating the skin of my face.

I lurched up in the sleeping net, still squinting. I found myself coated in sweat and shivering. My face was burning, my body chill.

I could not swallow, so dry was my throat. After opening one side of the sleeping net and slipping out, I floated to where I could reach the squeeze bottle. The coolish water helped—some.

So did a towel, to dry my sweaty face. Then I eased back into the net and reclosed it. I needed more sleep. Perhaps I would dream of gravity, where I would not be lost in the aimlessness of null gee.

My eyes wouldn't stay closed, nor my thoughts quiet.

Foerga's face in the middle of a spinning star? The arcs of golden-red fire. I had seen them before. Where?

Why would they return to a dream now?

Stars? Now that I thought about it, I hadn't seen a single star since I'd left earth, and yet I was on a station orbiting a planet circling one of the most distant stars to which the demons had sent their needle ships.

A laugh started within me but died away, cold and distant, as I recalled the insight in Foerga's face. Foerga's face, and penetrating deep azure eyes and niellen hair.

I shivered again, cold all over now. Hybra seemed far away, much farther than mere stellar spacing, an infinitely distant land of auspexes, lithoidolators, and dzinarchists.

29

The passion for analysis does not reflect upon the accuracy of the analyzer.

Eventually, even on a demon orbit station as far from Rykasha as possible, as low as a maintenance tech was, I settled into a routine. Gerbriik's voice became bored when he issued me orders, as it was with Fersonne and Sanselle. I began to recognize the names and references to the needle ships that called, and their officers, even though none of them ever looked at maintenance crews as more than high-level AIs with organic limbs designed to off-load cargo and carry out simple tasks.

I developed a consistent exercise routine in the gym and the full-gee spin chamber, even if I never exercised when the station officers or Sanselle did.

Finally, for lack of anything else to do, I began to study again—this time what there was on the background of nanite development and engineering. And I did it the way that seemed to work for me—by reading the information from the station's databanks on a portable screen.

The Rykashan history that had been pumped into me had never made much sense, nor did the additional bits and pieces I overheard. Initially, the history of nanite technology implementation made just as little sense. Whole sections of the text referred to events that were not in my basic indoctrination history. Nor did they correspond in more than vaguely general terms with the history I had learned in Henvor.

Sorting all that out required more research to fit historical developments together with nanite technology evolution. Even so, seemingly rational passages made little sense, especially when I was tired after three straight shifts. But I persisted, after a fashion.

In the dimness of my cube, I blinked at the words on the screen clipped to one side of my sleeping net, then blinked again.

. . . the implementation of the first nanite-based psychohistory projects (circa 530 A.S.) in the Amnord nation precursors to Dorcha and Toze established the applied feasibility of accurate projection of political behavior on the first true microaggulatinated-socioeconomic basis . . . despite the so-called Free Action massacres that followed . . .

. . . although uncontrolled nanite-based organic rehabilitation developed by Dretias and Kestmayer (see *Prehistory of Nanosystems*) was cited as the cause of the Demon Gluttony Famines (515 A.S. and 510 A.S.) . . . analysis indicates that climate readjustments caused by industrial greenhouse offgasing played an equally pivotal role . . . such changes . . . led first to global geoponic restructuring, to silval reengineering, and to the forced development of advanced low-cost formulator technologies . . .

. . . Dorchester compact rejected use of formulator-derived nutrition . . .

. . . of nanite-fisheye invisibility was deployed by the Risen Shin (?) Empire against the Chungkuo Republic in approximately 490 A.S. (2060 AD or old era measurement) . . . led to the sterilization of the archipelago . . . reclamation was not begun until 200 PSE . . .

I clicked off the screen. The information was too detailed and created too much conflict for me to digest more than a few thousand words at a time—and there were many thousands of words written about the technology that had created my world and then thrust me from it.

As my eyes closed, the blackness was filled with red-golden arcs of fire, arcs that cascaded across a starlike pinwheel circling in blackness. I opened my eyes quickly, and the fire arcs and pinwheel vanished into the dull blackness of my cube, fuzzy and indistinct compared to that niellen-backed tableau of stars and flame.

Sleep came less easily—far less easily—as my facility with maintenance duties improved.

30

[OMEGA ERIDANI: 4516]

When the complexity of social patterning is reduced, so is individual freedom.

One of continuing menial duties of the maintenance crews was to cart up linens and supplies for the transient guest quarters on the upper station levels. The job wasn't onerous, merely menial, and often a welcome relief from tasks such as using a SARM between decks, or unloading needle ships, or patching scars in corridor bulkheads too large for the maintenance nanites.

I was halfway though unloading the clean linens for the guest suites on the uppermost level of the station when Gerbriik appeared at my elbow. It wasn't Gerbriik, but a nanite-generated image from my own commpak, but he might as well have been there, square-faced, sharp-nosed, black-haired. Would that Manwarr had seen such icon-raising. I held in an amused smile, thinking how he would have called Gerbriik far worse than a cophrologer.

"Tyndel."

"Yes, ser?"

"You should have finished by now." The maintenance officer scowled.

"Yes, ser."

Gerbriik's eyes seemed to go to the small sled—two-thirds empty—tethered loosely on one side of the corridor. "You'll have to finish later, and you will finish it before you go off-shift."

"Yes, sir."

"Glide your corpus down to lock three. *Hay Needle*'s on final approach. You and Sanselle need to unload it quickly."

Quickly? What difference did it make with all the time dilation involved whether we took a few minutes or hours longer? It would still be weeks or months before the *Hay Needle* returned to one of the earth orbit stations. So much hurrying was because people thought that haste saved time for something more valuable. The *Hay Needle* was likely to lose more time from a poor insertion than from a few more minutes spent unloading.

"There's a big singularity in the overspace Web, and it's angling toward us. The pilot wants his cargo off. Otherwise, he'll be here for a long time." Gerbriik smiled coldly. "You wouldn't want a needle jockey mad at you. Or me."

"No, ser." I tightened the tethers on the small sled and refastened the straps over the linens I hadn't unloaded. The transient guests needed linens because their beds were more like pallets into which they were netted. Towels we all needed to mop up the water around us after null grav showers, as well as what clung to us that wasn't recovered by the nanite collectors.

"You'd better get moving, hadn't you, Dzin master Tyndel?"

"Yes, ser."

As I glided toward the transit shaft, I tried to access what I knew about singularities. *Singularity—a region of space-time where one or more components of the non-standard curvature tensor become infinite. Singularity—a* *discrete but dimensionless discontinuity in the supra-wave-vector space. Singularity—the result of an object collapsing with a mass of $S^{(s-1)}$ and with a gravitational radius greater than its physical radius.* Were they all the same? Or were there three kinds of singularities? The second one sounded like what Gerbriik was talking about, but I wasn't in any position to ask.

Sanselle had the sled waiting by the big cargo lock by the time I got there. While the station's lock was open, the ship's cargo lock had not opened. Snowlike crystals fell away from the outside of the hatch as the station's air roiled over the dull surface like a miniature storm. The crystals melted as they struck the warmer sides of the cargo corridor beyond the one open lock.

"Is there someone in charge of the cargo—for the ship?" I asked as we waited for the chill to abate.

"The junior officer—most ships only have a crew of three," Sanselle said. "Needle jockey and two others. They handle everything else. Don't want anything worrying the pilot."

With a hiss, the ship's lock opened. After a moment, the green-clad third officer looked down at the pair of us and the cargo sled. "Captain Adgar wants all this clear as soon as you can. Stack it in the corridors if you have to, but get it off."

"Tell the officer that the mass is too great." Gerbriik's voice was in my ear.

"Ser," I said respectfully, "the cargo mass is too great for the station to do that. We'll move it as fast as we can, but we can't put it all here."

"Is that from you, crewman?"

"No, ser. The maintenance officer."

"Do what you can." The red-haired third officer nodded reluctantly. "We've already started inspecting for departure. I'll check back in a bit. Start with the red cases."

Sanselle had eased herself into the hatch opposite the officer. "Those? The spines?"

"Right."

I followed Sanselle's gesture and made my way to the heavily tethered containers set within a braced semienclosure comprised of composite beams.

"See," murmured Sanselle. "Gerbriik used you."

"That's because he's following me. You know what you're doing."

"You do, too. You've been here near-on a year."

A year personal objective? Had it been that long? Or longer? *Eleven standard months, two weeks and one day,* announced my personal demons, as if to confirm something, perhaps no more than I was no longer a true follower of Dzin.

The containers in the enclosure were small—small and massive—no more than a meter long and ten centimeters by ten in cross section. For the first time since I'd come to OE Station, I could feel the effort to move one of them—one single container—and Gerbriik had assured me that the combination of personal nanites and the coveralls could handle well over two hundred kilos with no strain at all.

"What are these?" I eased the first one onto the cargo sled—most carefully.

Sanselle, moving more easily than I, slid hers beside mine, bracing herself against the corridor wall to kill the container's inertia. "Fusactor spines, I'd guess."

I winced. Fusion power? The different kind of demon that had led to the wars of destruction? Images flashed across my mind—the old illustrations from Manwarr's library showing glowing shells of stone that had failed to hold the nucleonic devils, the images of undersea warships whose metallic hulls glowed enough to illumine the lightless depths of the Summer Sea millennia later. Those old images from Henvor conflicted with others more recently nanite-implanted, fought with the Rykashan assertions that fusactors had supplied the environmentally beneficial power necessary for the great cleanups. For a moment, I froze.

"You all right, Tyndel?" asked Sanselle softly, the

green eyes gentler and suddenly more concerned.

"I'll be fine." I forced a smile. "Image conflicts." I'd had them all along, but I really hadn't quite understood them. I supposed that was part of what Cerrelle had tried to warn me about with the bits about honesty. Honestly— or accurately—addressing the images seemed to help, once I'd understood the problem. Not all accuracy reflected the Rykashan viewpoint, either, I'd decided.

"We'd better get moving, or Gerbriik and that third will both be yelling at us."

I slipped back into the hold of the *Hay Needle*. While the needle ship's hull was thick, a third of a meter or more, it was nonmetallic—a sophisticated form of high-level composite. I studied the hold for a moment, noting that almost everything seemed to be nonmetallic, confirming what I'd learned.

We kept at the unloading, but I let Sanselle move the sled once all the fusactor spines were unloaded. With that much mass on it, the more experience the better, even if I had been using the sled for almost half a year.

I did maneuver the second sled into place and began to remove the other containers—everything from a handful of orgnopaks to odd-sized and individual shipping packs that could have contained anything from station system replacement components to supplemental terraforming supplies and equipment. I wouldn't have known.

I had the second sled half loaded by the time Sanselle returned the first one empty.

"Had to store those," she said. "Gerbriik said we can pull everything else off, stack it along the corridor if we need to."

I looked at the half-loaded sled.

"After this one is loaded and moved," she added.

The redheaded officer reappeared. He did not speak to us, but looked through the hold and then vanished again, frowning.

"Worried," murmured Sanselle.

We had the second sled loaded to mass limits far more

quickly than the first. Again, I let her move it. After she left, for a moment, I studied the lock and the empty first sled. Then I eased the back of the sled practically into the lock, the way Sanselle had. Using the sled would still be faster, even if we only guided it thirty meters down the cargo corridor.

Sanselle returned far more quickly this time. "Just tethered it at the other side of the station. Gerbriik said the mass would balance. Have to unload it later."

We both worked on the sled, and when it was full, we both were soaked in sweat. I rode on the back while she guided it fifty meters beyond the sled bays, where we stacked everything on one side of the corridor. We repeated the process three more times before we had emptied the needle ship's cargo bay.

The third officer watched as we stacked the last, and very irregular, containers on the sled and started to ease it away from the cargo lock.

I wiped my forehead with the back of my sleeve.

"You got that clear faster than the captain hoped," the third officer said. "He's recommending a bonus. So am I." His grin was one of relief. "Stand back. We're sealing. He wants clear of here now."

As the *Hay Needle*'s lock hissed shut, so did the station's lock door.

"Must be in a real hurry," said Sanselle. "They usually stay and rest ten, twenty hours, anyway."

Within moments of the closure, there was a scraping thump of sorts followed by a slight vibration that ran through the station. Gerbriik's image appeared between us. The maintenance officer was smiling. "Captain Adgar was pleased. You'll get the bonus he recommended, but you still have to store all that cargo. The station's partly out of balance."

"Yes, ser," we said together, keeping our faces expressionless.

At that moment, I could sense Sanselle's thoughts, or

closely enough, and mine were the same. *Nothing ever satisfies Gerbriik.*

Was that why he was maintenance officer? Were the demons using his continual dissatisfaction to assure better maintenance on a distant orbit station that had to be more costly to maintain? Was every person judged and fitted for such a slot in demon society? But had it been any different in Dorcha? Had the Shraddans come after me because I had become a demon or because demons were different and did not fit the pattern?

That question echoed something that Cerrelle had asked, and not for the first or the last time. Had I feared her honesty and perception because I needed it and didn't want to accept that? I shivered within myself, then glided along the composite gray walls toward the masses of cargo that remained to be stored for station use or trans-shipment.

31

[OMEGA ERIDANI: 4516]

Be not afraid of the universe.

One day on OE Station was much like another, and time passed, sometimes quickly, sometimes not so quickly. On one of those slow days, Gerbriik's silver-clad image appeared in the canteen, where I was finishing my break meal. "Tyndel. Meet Fersonne by passenger lock three—gauntlets and breather hoods. Now!"

"Yes, ser."

The image vanished like brume under a summer sun. I gulped down the last of the nanite-produced, fresh-tasting orange juice. Gerbriik's tone had been more than enough. I hurried along the corridor and down the number three

transverse, but both Fersonne and Gerbriik were waiting
by the time I glided to a halt outside the number three
upper lock.

Fersonne had brought the small sled, and it was loaded
with gear. Some of it was initially unfamiliar, and I had
to search my nanite information bases. The green-striped
drum with the flexible nozzle was a sealant system. It
created a nanite barrier against atmospheric loss. The
yellow-striped canister was a composite-bonding unit.

I frowned. Shouldn't we have had the equipment by the
cargo lock?

"We have a problem," Gerbriik's long face was
drawn—the first time I'd seen any sign of concern. "You
two wait here. The *Costigan* ran too close to a singularity.
Pilot managed to bring it in most of the way . . . before
they lost power. We're using the bugs to drag it close
enough to lock. The ship's overstressed—the bugs have
been pumping air into it, and the outside crew is hooking
up a direct feed. It's still leaking. So as soon as the crew's
out, you two need to start patching. Tyndel, you'll be
spraying anything that looks like a stress fracture in the
hull." Gerbriik gave me a grim smile. "Better call up
everything you got briefed on. You won't have much
time." He said nothing to Fersonne. He must have talked
to her before I had reached the passenger lock deck, just
above the cargo locks.

A dull *clunk* shivered through the corridor, and Gerbriik
twisted away from us, his eyes glazing over as he linked
into the commnet on levels not open to either Fersonne
or me.

A medtech I didn't know appeared beside Gerbriik.
"Maalorn will be here in a minute or so, ser."

Gerbriik offered the smallest of nods, eyes still half
glazed. He barely nodded when the second medtech arrived. His eyes did snap open when a blond man in blue
appeared. "Commander Maestros."

I'd heard the name but had never seen the station commander in person.

Maestros was tall and lanky, almost wispy, but his eyes were as hard as any demon's. "Officer Gerbriik. Your crews did a good job of wrestling her in." The station commander's round and unlined face looked more drawn than did Gerbriik's.

"Thank you, ser."

"I'll go aboard with the medtechs. Your crew ready to seal her?" Maestros's eyes examined me and then Fersonne before glazing over into the haze of someone on a commnet.

"Yes, ser."

The only sounds were those of breathing and the hissing of the corridor ventilators. Both Gerbriik and Commander Maestros continued to wear the glazed look of men whose thoughts—and concentration—were elsewhere.

Holding our breather hoods, Fersonne and I waited outside the front lock of the needle ship. Gerbriik floated before us, the two medtechs beside him. My thoughts were on the sealer system: *nanite-to-nanite shuttle bond . . . effective for eight standard hours . . . maximum coverage per unit . . . five thousand square meters . . .* At that thought, my eyes went to the sled. There were four of the green-striped units on the left side.

"There aren't enough for the whole ship," Fersonne said. "That's why you spray where you think there are leaks. I'll try to bond the big gaps. Need to work fast. Cold in there."

Commander Maestros loosely, absently, grasped the holdbar beside the lock as the inner door slowly opened. A blast of chill air burst from the opening, followed by a cascade of ice flakes that billowed out across us as the station's atmosphere boiled across the exposed sections of the *Costigan*'s outer, mostly retracted lock. That breath of winter reminded me of Lyncol, even of Cerrelle, but only for a moment.

The man in blue and the medtech were first through the lock. When they vanished into the darkness of the ship's lock, Gerbriik turned in midair to face us. "There's more damage than we thought to the ship. You'll have to work fast if we're to save the cargo."

"What's the cargo?" asked Fersonne.

"Gene templates, nanite modules for planoforming—the usual." Gerbriik shrugged. "Could be some datablocs for the station." His attention went back to the lock, where mist still churned around the edges. The warmer station air blew past us into the ship, and the ice clouds swirled around the inside of the ship's lock.

I shivered and pulled on the gray gauntlets. Fersonne already had hers on, and she was doing something with the composite bonder. I eased myself over to the first green-striped sealing unit.

The medtech or Commander Maestros or both were returning. The voices were loud, but the words were indistinct—and then very clear.

"Music! The music—"

"It's quiet here. Take it easy. . . ."

Fersonne and I looked at each other, then back to the lock, where the medtech and the commander floated out a figure—a man—strapped to a stretcher of some sort.

"The music! So loud—think! Think!" The man's head jerked from side to side in the restraints despite the calming and quiet words from the medtech. What had been the whites of his eyes showed a yellow-green cast, a color clear enough from the three or four meters between us and the stretcher.

"That has to be the second officer, or the third," murmured Gerbriik. "Captain Adara is a woman."

Behind the commander came the second medtech with another stretcher, one bearing a dark-haired and pale-faced woman.

"That's Adara," Gerbriik supplied. "Good jockey."

Good jockey or not, she was unconscious, and two nanopaks—each barely fist-sized—rested against her neck.

"Music! Too loud . . . too loud!" the second officer

yelled from behind us as he was floated toward the transverse shaft.

Gerbriik waited, and so did we.

Singularities? Closeness to a singularity had left the second raving and the captain unconscious? My own nanite demons responded. *The disruptions caused by a singularity's discontinuity follow the path of least resistance along pre-established transits of the supra-wave-vector space.* Pre-established? *Event horizons already existing constitute pre-establishment. The overspace trajectory of a supra-wave-vector craft exists simultaneously with entry and also constitutes pre-establishment.*

Not even all the words made sense. Their meaning was beyond me, except I had this feeling that it meant somehow singularities were drawn to needle ships, or worse, the other way around.

The first medtech returned with an empty stretcher and eased himself back inside the *Costigan*. Station air kept whistling past us and into the leaking ship. The temperature in the passenger lock area continued to drop.

"Go!" snapped Gerbriik. "Survivors are clear."

Before I had my breather hood down and the first sealer to the edge of the ship lock, the medtech shoved out the covered stretcher. Someone hadn't survived.

"Start forward with the cockpit, Tyndel," Gerbriik ordered. "Get a fast coat on everything. Then the passenger cabin. Take the rear hatch down and get the cargo holds. I'm putting the other sealer units inside the *Costigan*, just inside the ship lock. We're sealing the lock again. You'll need to hurry."

Sealing the lock? I suppose they had to in order to keep from losing too much air, but that didn't reassure me much.

Gerbriik made it sound matter-of-fact. Sealing the *Costigan* wasn't quite that easy.

Clouds of swirling ice crystals rained around me from everywhere. Frost coated every surface, and my boots slipped off *everything*—bulkheads, decks, overheads. The

sealer unit was more massive than a SARM, and the reaction from the nanites streaming from the nozzle kept
pushing me back from where I needed to go.

It was *cold*. Before I managed the ten meters from lock
to cockpit, I was shivering, despite the heating elements
in the heavy gray coveralls. Frost began to fringe the
breather hood's faceplate, and gusts of departing atmosphere tugged at me. The coveralls began to bulge, and
that meant the air pressure in the *Costigan* was continuing
to drop.

Then the pressure from the nozzle wasn't pushing me
back. I looked down and could see a red light flashing.
Empty—unit is empty. Back to the lock for a second
sealer. I couldn't feel much in the way of air currents in
the passenger section. So I gave the place a quick treatment and headed down to the cargo area.

Cold! The cargo hold made the upper level feel like
Deep Lake in full summer, and the coveralls stiffened so
much it was hard to move, even in null gee. My gauntlets
were freezing and stiff, too, as though they had turned to
the cold-hammered bronze of a statue to be set on a pedestal along the riverway in Henvor.

Fersonne was already in the cargo hold, had been all
along. She was using the bonding unit to weld and fill a
stress fracture that had to have been more than twenty
meters long when she started. She was working on the
last few meters. Back from the five centimeter-wide fracture itself, a line of frost had built up. The area closest to
the fracture was clean, sucked clean by escaping atmosphere.

I started spraying where it felt coldest and kept spraying
until that unit was done. I went for another, and finished
it. I was working on the fourth unit when Gerbriik's voice
broke through my shivers. My fingers and hands trembled
inside the gauntlets.

"You've got the *Costigan* sealed. Get back to the ship's
forward passenger lock, but stand back. We're going to
open it and get you out."

"Yes, ser." We bolted up from the hold and waited by the *Costigan*'s inner lock door. I stamped my feet to keep them from freezing.

More cold mist and ice crystals erupted once the cargo lock opened, but the gusting winds that had been there before were absent.

"Get back into the corridor," ordered the maintenance officer.

We did, taking off the damp and frigid breather hoods—coated with frost and ice. Then Fersonne and I hung in midair outside the cargo lock, somehow sweating and shivering at the same time.

Gerbriik's image appeared between us. "Good job. Commander Maestros wasn't sure you could seal that much damage, but you did. You two take off the rest of the shift. Get some rest. Sanselle and I will unload the cargo before the seals go."

"Yes, ser."

"Yes, ser." Fersonne's voice was as ragged as mine.

I wanted to grin—for a moment. If Gerbriik and Sanselle were unloading cargo, then we had to have done a good job.

"This cargo had some unique biologicals," the maintenance officer added. "Could have taken years to get them replaced. Commander Ferstil on Alaric will be very pleased. Your telltales say you need to get warm and eat. Do it." Gerbriik's image vanished.

Neither Fersonne nor I said much as we pulled ourselves back through the shaft to mid-deck three. We found ourselves outside our quarters and canteen, still shivering.

The heaters in the gauntlets had begun to warm my hands, if slowly, too slowly.

"Tyndel?" Fersonne's voice was gentle, as gentle as I had ever heard it.

"Yes?"

"Know there must be someone else . . . out there. Seen your face at times." She swallowed, then moistened her lips. "I won't ask."

I waited.

"You see something like that. The *Costigan*, I mean. You do something like that . . . gets you cold all over."

"I know." I thought I understood. I was cold all over inside, as well. I eased toward the brown-eyed woman and put my arms around her, just held her, and let her hold me, taking comfort in being close to another soul, and being alive.

That closeness, so welcome, led to a greater joining in her sleeping net, more of a full-body bare-skinned embrace than mere relief or carnality—lust limited partly by physics and weightlessness and by the need to comfort and be comforted . . . and by old and hidden memories of a darker-haired woman who had also loved me and given to me.

In time . . . we eased apart.

Fersonne looked at me, the brown eyes deep, not asking for more, not rejecting—just there. "Thank you."

I embraced her again, clinging to her, to her acceptance of the now, to the moment she represented, for both that moment and the understanding that, while the past could not be changed, or eliminated . . . I had to take another step forward into the present.

In a sense, she was almost Dzin-like, while I had been required to learn Dzin.

After another long interval, she brushed back my hair. A gentle but warm smile preceded her words. "We'd better eat."

We did. More than I would have thought possible.

32

To see what is, make your mind like a mirror, to reflect what is as it is, not as your heart or mind would see it.

On another slow day, after we'd serviced an inbound needle ship the day before, I had just refilled the linen storage closet on the uppermost level when the man and the woman in shimmering blue singlesuits glided and floated awkwardly toward the guest quarters. Blue usually meant senior controllers—those who made the decisions that guided Rykashan society. I had never met anyone in blue, only those in green—like Cerrelle—or silver, like Gerbriik. Or the medical types, in red.

I slipped to one side of the corridor as they neared, paying no attention to me.

"I hate null gee, Ermien." The woman was short-haired and dark-skinned, and her voice was firm but not loud. "You'd think someday we could master artificial gravity."

"Not in our time, I think. Not while the physicists still come up with inconsistent and anomalous measurements for gravitons."

"That's only in the engee fields."

"Where else would you better measure them?"

"Engee doesn't follow the rules for anything else. Why would graviton measurements conform there? Or bosunic condensate density?"

My internal demons informed me about gravitons— *particles defined as the quantum of a gravitational field with a postulated, if unmeasured, rest mass and charge of zero and a spin of two.* I understood every individual word of the definition, and the definition not at all. I had no idea what bosunic condensate density might be, and even my nanite-provided knowledge base was silent or empty on that definition or set of definitions. Again, I wondered about engee . . . the mysterious . . . something . . . that wasn't in the databases, or not the ones I could access.

"Like it or not, we're here," the man replied. "Someone has to oversee and evaluate the project's results."

"Should we really have expended all the resources necessary to reach the stars? Do we need all these planets? Have you ever thought that some other intelligent organic life might evolve there? Ever?"

"That's why you're here," he pointed out, scraping a knee on the side of the corridor and rebounding awkwardly, stopping himself with a hand—a dangerous move in null gee. "To raise and answer questions like that. We're only talking about a dozen worlds, or less, and all are Vee-type—highly unlikely to develop any kind of life for billions of years, if ever." The man laughed. "We won't be around then, one way or another."

Their voices faded, even from my enhanced hearing. Neither had so much as looked in my direction, but their words in passing had raised more than a few questions. Where exactly was engee . . . where the rules of physics didn't exactly apply? How could they casually raise the types of questions I had raised and not be sent off to some outplanet station?

I half laughed, realizing as the question crossed my mind that we were all on the same outplanet station in the middle of nowhere—except they could leave and I couldn't, not for another eight years or so. The only gravity I'd feel would be in the exercise centrifuge, and in my dreams.

I looked down at the half-unloaded small sled, then shrugged. Where would I go? Back to the stone demon traps of Dorcha? Or the faithfully fanatic Shraddans of Hybra? I smiled wryly at my own rhetorical questions.

33

Life is merely a succession of appearances.

Gerbriik gave me a curt nod as I finished reassembling the SARM. "You do that well, Dzin master. You could have been a maintenance officer . . . or a needle jockey. If you'd shown more common sense. You still could be. You wouldn't have to sweat and grub between decks. You wouldn't have to fight inertia unloading needle ship cargos."

"Yes, ser. That's probably true, ser." Infrequent as it was, unloading needle ships was more interesting than such duties as pushing SARMs between decks or carting supplies from one point in the station to another or accomplishing low-level repairs here and there. Most years, according to the station records, OE Station saw about one interstellar ship every third or fourth objective station month, if that.

"At the very least, you could be a junior engineer out there putting the *Costigan* back together."

I'd seen the engineering types using lock number one, but I didn't feel like responding directly. I nodded.

"Or reloading stuff to the local vacuum boats." Gerbriik offered a wide, yet sneering, smile.

"Yes, ser." I replaced the last of the SARM cover clips, then eased the unit toward its stowage bin. Far more frequent were the local ships from planets two and three—Alaric and Conan, respectively, named after some ancient figures no one had ever heard of—there wasn't even anything in the station's library base on the origin of the names.

"If every mite you knew is going to die before you finish your duty here, you might as well be doing something that challenges you, Dzin master. Or do you intend to delude yourself for the rest of a long and boring life?"

I ignored Gerbriik's overstating of the time dilation. "Ser, I have not found life boring." Hard, unfair, difficult, but not boring. At times, it was hard to believe that close to four years had elapsed on earth, or would have if I had started back at that moment. Overspace detoured the limits of real-space, near-light travel, but there was still a time dilation effect. There was also the space-time curve effect. While I hadn't bothered to explore all of that mass of data, one of the last that Andra had pumped into me in Runswi, I understood the general effect without much effort. Time was relative to mass and the curvature and the closeness of overspace to real space. That meant objective time flows differed slightly in different parts of the Galaxy or universe. Not a lot in most locales, but measurably. Black holes, singularities—there time differed much more.

Like much of what the Rykashans thought important, I wasn't sure it was. To get from one part of the Galaxy to another required travel. The dilation from needle ship travel was so much greater than other factors that locale time flow differences were insignificant by comparison.

"For a Rykashan, you're young. The boredom will come." He laughed mockingly. "Perhaps your outmoded Dzin will keep it at bay."

Dzin outmoded? What did nanotechnology have to do with outmoding Dzin? Or Toze? Or any belief system? Except Dzin wasn't a belief system. I frowned, realizing that was what I'd been trying to put into words. There was a difference between using Dzin and accepting the Dorchan history of Dzin.

"Tyndel . . . don't you understand yet?" Gerbriik's voice had turned softer. "Dzin was designed to restrict human aspirations and human accomplishments. That's why it's outmoded. It's a mite crutch, and you're not a mite anymore."

"No." Even Gerbriik didn't understand. Dzin wasn't the problem. It was a tool, and could be misused, like any tool. The problem was that I wasn't a demon in heart and spirit, either, and I didn't know what I was except that being a demon in body had taken everything I had been. I could recall two children kissing in the shadow of the cataclypt of Dyanar, walking the ancient stones of Henvor, holding Foerga in her workshop beside the heat of her furnace, even trimming the hedge by the walk in the brume of late fall. All that had been taken, and I had no dreams. Then, did any demon? If so, what?

"Why don't you study the schematics for the sleds?" suggested the maintenance officer. "When Fersonne leaves, you'll have to help Sanselle with them." He turned fluidly in midair and glided back to his console.

When Fersonne leaves ... Logic told me she would. Dzin told me I'd accept it. And I felt that, even if it were years, she'd be gone before I ever really knew her.

34

[OMEGA ERIDANI: 4516]

The ancients sought their gods in temples, in worldly goods, in the technology they created, and lastly in the stars. They found neither gods nor enlightenment in the materials of the universe, nor will any wise soul find aught in such but the reflection of sorrow.

Fersonne pointed to the oversized coverall, helmet, and boots floating beside her in the maintenance bay. Behind them were a green cylinder and some other items I couldn't see behind the silvered and bulky coverall. "This is the outside suit. It's like a breather and coveralls, but heavier," Fersonne said. "We don't even try to have someone use it until they've been on station more than a year."

"Because of the null grav adaptation?"

"Mostly." Fersonne's smile was warm. "Gerbriik also likes to see how maintenance types do. Never did put Nathum in one."

"Would have lost him and the suit," added Gerbriik from the other side of the maintenance bay. "Too much explaining, then, and too much work for the rest of us."

I had to wonder why the suits were necessary. Theoretically, from what I had studied, a nanite-based unit could have held atmospheric pressure around anyone without the suit at all.

"You're wondering why you need the suit?" asked Gerbriik.

"Yes, ser."

"Heat. Mostly. Also, the suit form confines the nanites to a barrier area. That reduces the power needs. Besides, how could you do anything out there?"

The answer to that question took me a moment—before I realized what the long-faced maintenance officer meant, and I flushed, realizing once again I'd already known the answer from my experience with the *Costigan*. Nanites could hold an atmospheric field around someone, but they wouldn't do much for heat loss—especially if you had to use tools or touch something. I'd breathe for about as long as it took to take the few breaths before I froze solid.

"You need to try this on, to see if it fits." Fersonne eased the suit forward. It shimmered more than coveralls, was heavier, bulkier, and, once I had it on, considerably hotter, even without pulling on the gauntlets attached to the sleeves, the headpiece, or the boots—overlarge and puffy.

"Except for now, you don't put this on until you're ready to go out," Fersonne said. "Try on the headpiece, then take it off for now."

"Heat retention?"

She nodded. "You'll get cold anyway, chill enough after a time to freeze a mite."

I returned her nod and reached for the headpiece—more like a soft helmet, not like the more free-form and clinging breather hood, and the faceplate was almost wraparound. I could feel the heat building up and the sweat starting to flow. I removed the helmet and suit quickly.

"See? It's not terribly heavy." She brought forward two other items. "Here's the rebreather tank and a reaction pistol."

The rebreather tank was small, a cylinder not more than fifty centimeters long nor fifteen in diameter. The reaction pistol—*hand-held, free space, gas-powered propulsion device*—had a bulky grip and a barrel that tapered to a fine nozzled point. Like so many Rykashan devices, its dull gray finish appeared antique and weathered.

"You'll have a broomstick outside, but the reaction pistol is for emergencies—if everything goes wrong."

"If it does," commented Gerbriik, "the pistol probably won't do much good. But there's a chance."

I understood. Anyone who made enough mistakes to need the pistol probably would be so flustered that he couldn't use it soon enough or correctly enough.

"Unless your problem is caused by a mechanical failure," added Fersonne. "They don't happen often."

"Have you ever had one?" I waited for her reaction.

"No. Sanselle did once."

My eyes studied the equipment and the suit. Bulky as it was, it scarcely seemed enough to protect one against the chill of space, not after I'd seen the thick composite hulls of the needle ships.

"Take him out," Gerbriik said. "Give him the long tour." His eyes went to me. "Pay attention. You owe that to Fersonne, even if you don't care that much about yourself."

I had no doubts he knew we took comfort from each other, but beyond that, as well, he was right. "Yes, ser."

Fersonne dragged out her own suit from somewhere, circled it with a net, and waited while I found a net to hold all my newly acquired equipment. Then she inventoried mine again before we took one of the transverse shafts all the way down to the cargo level. The equipment-filled net kept bumping me all the way down. Nonrigid things always had a tendency to oscillate in null grav. Even though I'd adapted, I missed gravity. Why hadn't the demons ever mastered gravity control?

Because it would effectively require the creation of a gravitional geon, and translation of other energies into those which affect, create, or modify gravitons ... while theoretically possible, practical translations have never been successful ... I wasn't sure what all that meant, and pushed it aside as I followed Fersonne.

She led me to the personnel lock between cargo locks two and three, tabbing the entrance plate.

"There are locks on the upper levels," I noted as the composite door retracted into the side wall of the cargo corridor. "We could take the passenger locks."

"All ESAs are from the lower locks, except in emergencies."

My autonomous database called up the fact that there were no quarters on the lowest level—and automatic seals on the shafts, and that the lower levels were more heavily braced, even the passenger level right above the cargo corridors.

The lock was like a cargo lock, but smaller. Grayish brown composite bulkheads melded into composite decks and overheads, the simple right angles where they met still fusing together in a way that left the eye wondering. Was it the identical coloring? The even and indirect lighting from the glow strips?

Broomsticks—five of them—were clipped in brackets on the left wall, each holder about a meter from the one beside it. They appeared as little more than a hard composite seat and a flat panel before the seat, both mounted upon a long tube. According to my briefings, they were effectively nanite-enhanced, gas-propelled, low-power rockets.

"Look at the panel." Fersonne gestured. "See the big

rheostat thing. That's the power control. When the red stud is out, you get power from the back. Push it in, and you get power from the front."

I waited.

"There's a spring in the tubing. It you're moving too fast, let the tube hit the hull." She offered a crooked smile. "It's designed to absorb that kind of inertia. Your hands aren't." After a pause, she added, "We'll go over that again when we're outside."

After I had everything on but the soft helmet, Fersonne checked over all the seals—between boots and suit, and suit and gauntlets. "The nanites can maintain suit pressure without perfect seals, but there's no point in making them work harder."

Work harder? Fersonne talked as though the nanites had intelligence. Could micron-level constructs manifest intelligence? Then, we were like nanites compared to the suns that were stars. *Poor comparison . . .* But was it?

For a moment, that half-forgotten, half-familiar cascade of golden-red flames arced across my vision, flame arcs against a spangled darkness edging the fires, then blurring the brown-gray bulkheads before the momentary vision vanished.

Fersonne clipped a small reel to my equipment belt. "Safety tether. A quarter kilo of monomer. First thing you do outside the lock is clip on, before you let go of anything."

Like all demons, she didn't repeat the warning, but donned her helmet. She checked mine after I put it on, then eased two of the broomsticks from their racks. They also had tethers, and I found myself tethered to a broomstick, holding on to a safety bar as the inner lock door closed. Ice crystals swirled around us, then vanished. The indirect light from the glow strips lost its diffusion, and, while I could see the lit panels, the only illumination they cast was on the deck itself, giving it a barred appearance, except where broken by my shadow or Fersonne's.

Then the outer door opened, and I followed Fersonne's

example, hand-over-handing my way through the open outer lock door. In the darkness outside, I clipped the end of the tether to the half-circular ring protruding from the station hull beside the door.

"Good," murmured Fersonne. "Get on the broomstick." Her words relayed through the helmet were soft, yet close enough that her lips might have been touching my ears. My skin tingled as though it recalled when her lips had touched my ears.

I managed to slide onto the broomstick by concentrating on moving as little as possible and holding on to the tether ring with one hand. Finally, sitting on the seat of the broomstick, I looked out away from the station to the endless spangled points of light that were the first stars I had seen since leaving Runswi. I found myself taking a long breath and holding it, my eyes on those points of brightness and at the depth of the blackness between each.

"Above" us and a kilo away was the hull of the *Costigan*, where lights flitted intermittently, presumably from the engineers finishing up the de facto refit of the over-stressed needle ship.

After a time, Fersonne spoke. "You all right, Tyndel?"

"I was looking at the *Costigan* . . . and the stars."

"Takes your breath away." After a moment, she added, "Your broomstick is slaved to mine, until you get the knack of riding it. I'll show you what I mean. I'll unslave it for a bit."

An amber light on the panel before me winked out.

"All right. Give the broom the tiniest bit of thrust . . . just move the dial a bit, then move it back."

I did and could feel the broomstick move ever so slightly under me—or try to move away from me, and I began to drift away from Fersonne.

"Now . . . remember the red button?"

"Yes."

"That's reverse thrust. You push that in until it stops, and the dial controls the thrust from the front of the broomstick instead of the back."

Very simple—and very easy to get in trouble. I could feel that even more hanging in the darkness beneath the wall that was the station.

"Try to stop yourself."

I punched the red button, then repeated the movement with the dial. I could tell I'd overdone it because I found myself headed backward past Fersonne toward the station. Another correction found me moving back away from the station, if at a slower rate. That required a smaller brake. That led to yet another micro puff of gas . . .

Despite the chill that seeped in from outside the suit, I was sweating by the time I hung motionless beside the other maintenance tech.

"Not so easy as it looks." She laughed gently. "Like a few other things in null gravity."

I blushed in the privacy of my helmet.

Fersonne did something to the panel in front of her. "You're slaved back to me now."

My broomstick's being slaved to hers made me feel helpless rather than relieved. The station loomed over us like a dull dark gray wall, its edges fuzzed where composite met the darkness of space and the pinlights of stars. Logic said that without atmosphere the station should stand out clearly. Logic was wrong.

My fingers began to feel cold, and I flexed them.

"Better show you what you need to see." Fersonne guided us along the lower level past the three large cargo locks. "Three cargo locks are all we have, but we could use the personnel locks if we needed them. Or the emergency locks on the upper levels."

"The locks all look the same, and both locals and needles use the same locks. But the local ships are built differently." Their holds were larger, for one thing. I could have ransacked my internal database that still didn't seem fully integrated, though more and more often I was finding I *knew* things without really knowing where I had obtained the knowledge.

"Gerbriik says it's easier on the station. Local ships are

built bigger and not nearly so tough as a needle ship. They need the dampers to protect them. The needle ships are tougher than the station—to survive the Web. So we need the dampers to protect us."

Every reference to needle ships confirmed my feeling about the dangers involved. I nodded within my helmet.

Fersonne eased the broomsticks "up" toward the higher levels of the station. I felt like a hummingbird in the dusk and beside the great precipice of Deep Lake, the one that dropped into the depths that held the eels.

Deep Lake . . . Foerga . . . such a short time ago, even as lives go, and yet so far away. My eyes burned, and I could do nothing, not in an outside suit and a helmet. That distant yet unforgotten loss coupled with guilt to silence me once more, for Fersonne guided her broomstick less than three meters from me, Fersonne, who had also given without demanding. Fersonne, who had suffered more than I knew, who would never have the chance to be a needle jockey or to return to earth except as a submenial. Yet she had given, asking nothing, hoping for human comfort and little else.

I felt as though I had given nothing, demanded without words, accepted without gratitude, and understood giving not at all.

In the silence, in the star-splotched darkness, I swallowed wordlessly, ignoring the cold dampness on my cheeks, the dampness with the bite of forming ice crystals, almost welcoming that bitter chill.

35

There is no "truth," for the very term requires both
conformity with physically verifiable reality and adherence to
the underlying belief system of the "truth-seeker." Belief
systems, by definition, place faith in the unknowable above
factual verification,
while facts stand independent of faith.

I should have been getting some sleep, but I was restless, and turned in my sleeping net, still reading a Rykashan history of the postcollapse period and the building of Rykasha. I didn't know how much to take figuratively and how much as literal truth.

Clunnnk! Someone pounded on my hatch.

I clicked off the small screen, far less satisfying than the honest paper and cloth of a real book—not that I had seen such since I had left Hybra—and turned in the darkness toward the hatch to my cube. Who sought me? If Gerbriik had needed me to help Sanselle and Fersonne unload the needle ship that had been scheduled to dock during my off-swing, he would have used my beltcomm to alert me. His image would have been glowering over my shoulder in the dimness of my cube.

"Yes?"

There was no answer, and I slipped out of the net, half clad, and flicked myself toward the hatch.

Thrap!

"I'm coming."

A half-familiar face appeared as I eased open the hatch. Her hair was red and short, the face and body thin, and

the eyes green and as piercing as ever. I blinked, just
hanging in space in the open hatch.

"Hello." Cerrelle's voice was soft.

I just floated there, speechless.

"Aren't you going to welcome me?" she asked.

"Ah . . . I wasn't exactly expecting you."

"You're wondering why you should."

"I didn't say that. . . ." What could I say?

"I've stepped out of my life for a year to check on you.
You were always saying that no one cared. I'm here, Tyndel." A faint smile, warm but uncertain—or something—
appeared and vanished. She had ship boots on, and her
foot braced to hold her in place in the corridor, showing
a certain competence in null gravity.

"You came all this way because you . . . why? I didn't
think you cared, except to make sure I became a productive member of Rykashan society." As I finished the
words, I wished I hadn't ever uttered them.

"I do care," Cerrelle said. "I cared enough to treat you
as an adult. I cared enough to tell you what is instead of
offering you comfort through falsehoods and inaccuracy.
You respected your poor Foerga for her honesty, and you
need honesty, and yet you rejected it when I offered it. I
cared enough to travel light-years and then some to see
how you are faring." Her lips tightened momentarily.

I could feel the numbness encase me, and I didn't even
know why. "Is it part of your duties as guide?"

Cerrelle's face blanked for a moment, even as she met
my eyes, not flinching, not attacking. Somehow, she reminded me of Fersonne, though they looked not at all
similar. That bothered me, too. Was I creating partial rep-
licas of Foerga out of all women?

"Would it matter? You wanted Rykasha to care about
you. Not me."

There was something there, something I knew was
there but couldn't find.

"I told you that I cared, that it wasn't Rykasha's job to
care." She paused. "And I'm here. How are you doing?"

"I'm fine." Why had she come all the way to OE Station? It made no sense . . . unless she did care, but no individual could afford that. So . . . someone had sent her. I could feel myself tightening inside.

"You've been here a year and a half—personal objective time. Are you willing to try training again? Or are you ready for eight more years on OE Station?"

I knew she wanted me to go back, to accept training as a needle jockey. But I couldn't. Not with a whole society pushing the idea. I just couldn't. I looked at her, trying to be honest. "I can't."

Hanging there in the middle of the corridor outside the hatch to my cube, she smiled sadly, a sadness that faded into melancholy, then pity. "I'll see you in eight years. . . ." After a moment, she added, "You have a lot of thinking to do, Tyndel. I hope you do it. Do you really think that just because you see things as they are that means you have to accept them as unchanging? Or unchangeable?"

She turned and glided down the corridor, never looking back.

I said nothing, half waiting for her to turn. When she didn't but disappeared into the transverse shaft, I finally shut the door, sliding back into my cube, where I floated beside my sleeping net, looking blankly beyond it at the dull composite bulkheads and the even duller deck that seldom felt the force of boots. Why had she come?

I had wanted to follow her down the corridor, but I couldn't. Not so long as I could not accept being a needle jockey. Yet my eyes burned.

How could I believe she didn't care? But why had she asked that last Dzin-like question? Because I was accepting a current reality as an eternal one?

Somewhere, deep inside, I could almost feel a mirror shattering, and I didn't know even what image had been held on the unseen glass. Even though I turned off the dim light and climbed back into the net, I did not sleep. Too many faces floated through the darkness, and the only one I did not recognize was mine.

36

*The world is a mirror lit by consciousness: in the darkness it
is empty.*

Both Fersonne and Sanselle took me on outside orien-
tations twice before I started joining them on outside
repair tasks. First, I did simple things—like inspect the
station's hull. I understood that nanite-enhanced human
vision could see more than all but the best scanners and
interpret what was seen better than any AI available. It
seemed anachronistic in one way, and in total accord with
Dzin in another. That provided me with a rare chuckle,
as I considered what Manwarr would have thought to have
one of his pupils standing on a dull gray hull in the middle
of a field of stars studying the composite with demon-
aided eyes.

After the two other techs determined that I wasn't hope-
less, I was pressed into service replacing the dampers and
cradles on the center cargo lock, the number two lock.
That took the three of us—and Gerbriik—nearly a standard week.

I didn't know what Gerbriik had in mind when he next
summoned me down to the station's number one cargo
lock. Sanselle was waiting, but the maintenance officer
wasn't there. Nor was Fersonne. I stepped through the
open inner door.

The sandy blonde waited until I was well inside the
lock before she spoke. "Every other station objective year,
we resurface the hull. This time, you get to help." Sanselle
grinned, not quite maliciously. She gestured toward the
big cylinder webbed to the deck of the number one cargo

lock. "This is one of the outside bonders. We're behind schedule some because the engineers needed both bonders to finish the repairs to the *Costigan*."

I looked at the dull composite of the cylinder's exterior—more like a small barrel with a snout at one end and an attached seat at the other end. Mounted on the blunt end of the barrel facing the seat was a control panel.

"The skin gets scratched by every stray micrometeor. Some impacts aren't so small. Rebonding makes sure that the only way the station gets destroyed is by something large and swift." Sanselle's thin lips curled away from the even teeth.

All demons had perfect teeth. Mine were as well, though they had not been when I had been the Dzin master of Hybra.

"The outside repair bonders are like SARMs," she continued. "The controls are more complex; they're more massive, and you have to anchor them. . . ."

As she continued the explanation, I wondered why someone couldn't just put the bonders on tracks or channels and let them circle the station endlessly. Instead of asking, I searched all the knowledge, useless and otherwise, that had been poured into me since I had left Dorcha. The answer was simple enough. The bonders—undirected—would fill every crack they perceived, including lock edges and joints for exterior mounted equipment. The sensors and AI capabilities necessary to direct the bonders were too costly and too sensitive to transport by needle ships except with special handling and packing. In short, we were far cheaper.

I had to shake my head at that. I could repay my debts to demon society by working fifteen years in high-level menial labor—a repayment rate nearly three times or more the norm from what I could calculate. And I was cheaper than the transport of mid-level AI equipment and sensors, or the kind that could operate in vacuum.

". . . because of the reaction force of the bonding, what we do is weld a track in place on the surface and run the bonder along the track. First, we'll weld three lines of track onto the station's hull. Then you run the bonder down the first. While you're running the bonder, I'll lay out the fourth and fifth tracks. Then I'll shift the bonder to the second track, and you weld down the fourth and fifth tracks."

I'd read about tracks and the ancient steam-powered locomotives, but those weren't what Sanselle had in mind.

"Here's the track we'll start with." The sandy-haired blonde pointed to the pallet webbed down on the far side of the bonder. Each section of track was a length of gray composite three meters long with the cross section of an inverted trapezoid.

I wondered how the track was welded.

The nanite-based composite spot-welder she thrust at me must have massed twenty kilograms. "I lay out the track. You weld it."

Instead of asking how, I called up the knowledge from the briefing spray. Theoretically, it was simple: Put the not-quite-right-angled welding head adjacent to hull and track and press the welding stud.

In practice it proved more difficult.

Sanselle tacked each rail in place with a nanite-based space glue, and each was set parallel to the first, exactly point seven-five meters between rail edges, as measured by the marking laser she employed. She moved easily along the tether line stretched between two rings, using the line as a brace.

I still didn't move that easily. The outside gauntlets were bulkier than the inside ones, and my fingers didn't feel quite where I thought they were. Then I had to line up the welding head mostly by feel, and I was a visual person. The stickpads on the outside boots didn't grip unless I set them down squarely, and I'd never walked quite squarely.

I tried to ease the welding head down in place, ever so gently, but my boot slipped, and so did the spot-welder. Cold and salty sweat ran into my eyes. Some felt like it had pooled in my boots, and I sweated and shivered simultaneously.

"Are you still on that first section, Tyndel?"

I was still on the first spot-weld of the first section. The track wanted to bend up from the hull because the glue didn't hold much once I banged the track with the welder. When I pressed the stud, the energy from the welding head wanted to push me away from the track and the hull, despite the pads of the boots and the tether line.

Just short of halfway through the shift, I had managed to weld down the first line of composite track—all of eighteen meters—six segments. I got a second line down in a third that time.

"Let's get the bonder. You can run it while I weld." Sanselle's orders were half amused, half disgusted.

"It's getting faster."

"I'm freezing."

"How do we get this up when we're done?" I pulled myself along the tether line after her and toward the number one cargo lock, one hand on the spot-welder.

"We don't. The machine fuses it into the hull. It's part of the composite feedstock."

Sanselle guided the bonder out of the lock, and I pulled myself back along the tether, wondering why I'd bothered, feeling dwarfed by the bulk of the bonder and minimized by Sanselle's crisp expertise. After she settled the bonder in place on the ridge of composite, she took the spot-welder from me.

"Watch. You just strap in and follow the monitors. This one on the top right is for composite supplies in the bins. The track only supplies about a third of what's used. This is available power. . . ."

I sat in the control seat and watched as the bonder vibrated along its predestined way. The hard work was welding the track. The bonding operator really just sat there and watched to see that nothing went wrong. Riding the bonder was easier, but it was colder, far colder, and I went back to welding another section of track after the bonder finished smoothing and flattening track and composite into the hull along the first less-than-meter-wide strip of hull, a strip but fractionally smoother than the untouched hull on either side.

We alternated once again, and after four standard hours my coveralls were filled with cold clammy sweat, despite the best efforts of the scavenger nanites, and the sweat that had pooled in my boots and extremities had begun to turn to ice.

"It's time for a break," Sanselle announced. "Move the bonder down to the end of this run. We'll ease it over and tie it down on the next section of track."

She watched as I sat and monitored the bonder. It lumbered and vibrated the last half meter of track, then hung on tethers above the hull after bonding the last centimeters of composite track. We switched places, and she guided it onto the next section of track, where we added tie-downs. Then we pulled ourselves along the tethers and back to the open number one cargo lock, standing there and shivering as the air filled the space and ice crystals swirled around us.

The cargo locks took longer to warm up than passenger locks, and more ice crystals formed. I was shuddering, rather than shivering, by the time we had our soft helmets off and floated out of the lock and into the lower corridor.

"Everything comes off, Tyndel. Send it all through the cleaning unit and put on fresh stuff before you eat or shower. You'll need it dry and clean after the next shift."

I wondered if I'd survive the next shift.

The null grav shower was a cylindrical tube with water jets all around. The nanites scavenged the water after it bounced off skin or walls. Usually I didn't care much for the steamy mist, but after a shift in an outside suit, this mist was more than welcome.

My sandy-haired coworker and supervisor was already eating when I reached the canteen.

I glanced at the dish before her, the food trapped under the shield that was transparent to the null grav fork. Then

I sniffed. Coriander, saffron . . . curry? "That's a Dhurr dish."

"My mother was Dhurr. Always liked food with taste."

I nodded, my mind trying to grasp the idea that there were Dhurr demons. "Did she come from Dhurra?"

"No. Great-grandmother did. She just walked across the border and announced she was tired of being a Dhurr and wanted to be a demon." Sanselle laughed. "She tells the story to anyone who will listen—when she bothers to stop working."

I had to force a swallow after the casual references to someone three generations older who was still active. My mind accepted the idea; my emotions and conditioning didn't. "What . . . who does she look like?"

"My cousin Eldroth says we could be sisters. Great-grandmother and I look more alike than Ellsinne and I do." Sanselle laughed. "Once she wore a festival dress—back from the old traditions—and when Isjant came to pick me up, he thought she was me and began to flirt with her. She still jests about that. She'll make some comment about young Isjant within minutes after I come home."

Sanselle had a home of sorts.

"How did you get here?"

"I chose it. I'm lazy. I could spend fifty years paying my debts to Rykasha for the next three centuries—or I could spend ten. My debts are high." Sanselle smiled. "That's the first personal thing you've asked."

Had I been that cool? "Adjusting to demon . . . Rykashan . . . life has been hard."

"Fersonne said you were a Dzin master."

"I was a Dzin-trained teacher. I hoped I'd get to be a master." After another bite of the hot Dorchan riced shrimp, I added, "Matters didn't work out that way."

"They never do." She frowned. "I didn't think I'd be back here."

"Back here?"

"This is my second time. I do free rock climbing. Most climbers don't make three centuries."

I managed not to swallow as I considered to what lengths the Rykashans had gone in enshrining athanasia. "You don't sound like you want to last three centuries."

"I don't want to live hoarding my life. Do you?"

Hoarding my life? Was that what I'd been doing? Or denying it?

"Oh . . . they always talk about how the forebearers sacrificed to create what we enjoy, but they didn't hide in dwellings or avoid the stars." After a pause, she added, "I like working the outside better than inside the station. It's another way to live, but it is living."

I sipped the last tea from the squeeze hot bottle and asked, "Is it always like this? The hull rebonding?"

"We started with the easy sections. Wait till you have to weld track around the cargo locks. Or the upper emergency locks."

I nodded solemnly, but my thoughts remained on the sacrifices of the forebearers—and another sacrifice, one far more personal and closer.

"Do this for a tour on a station," Sanselle muttered, "and it's near as dangerous as being a Web jockey. But you don't get the pay or the perks. Or the company." She slipped the sticktites and pushed away from the canteen table. "I've got another shift. You've got two."

I followed her down to the number one lock and the rebonding that awaited us both, idly considering how much easier the job would have been with any sort of gravity.

Amazing how what you didn't have kept coming to mind.

37

When you seek a cause, you have already created a result.

I was back on the top level of the station, hurriedly replacing the ballast for one of the glow strips outside the guest quarters. Glow strips lasted for years, but the one I was replacing had chosen to gutter out just as a needle ship with unexpected passengers had popped out of overspace and sent a comm announcing its arrival.

Gerbriik's image appeared beside me. "As soon as you finish, head down to cargo lock three. The *Reichmann* has more cargo to transship."

I eased the edge louver back in place, eased the old ballast into the flap pocket of the tool pack, and glided down the corridor to the lowest level. Sanselle had the sled out when I got there, but the lock door was closed. The *Reichmann* hadn't yet docked.

"Took you a bit," she commented from beside the cargo sled.

"Fixing a glow strip on the upper level. For our passengers."

Gerbriik's image appeared. "The captain's about to blow the lock. You're to unload all the cargo that has a violet lumntag on it. Nothing else to begin with. Then take that sled down to lock one and secure it there. Use one of the other sleds for the rest of the cargo—it goes in the transshipment bay."

"Yes, ser."

Sanselle nodded, and we waited as the lock door opened and the scaturient ice crystals billowed out and around us in their transitory glory. Two figures in green with silver bands across their sleeves were in the cargo hold, watching as we surveyed the stowage before beginning the muscular work of moving it all up the shaft from the hold and through two locks onto the sled.

After an initial silence, the two began to talk, inaudibly at first, their voices slowly rising, perhaps to be heard over our efforts.

". . . still think there's something wrong on Thesalle?" The angular woman glanced toward me. "Be careful with the green-striped case."

I nodded without looking directly at her and eased the case toward the sled, netting it high on the side frame. I wouldn't secure it firmly until all the other lumntagged cargo was off-loaded.

"There's not a thing in all the data. This is the fourth full survey, and not a one has shown anything," replied the round-faced man in green. "T-type planets are so rare that everyone rushed the surveys, and Thesalle is pretty, not like Actean or Halcyon Four."

"Pretty, yes," agreed the angular woman. "The holos don't show everything . . . couldn't believe what—was like. Vegetation . . . that green . . . everywhere, and I felt like I was moving in a dream."

"Nembret says that the air has an unidentified hallucinogen." Those words came from another man in green. "Here! I'm taking this with me." He looked at Sanselle, who was reentering the ship's hold, and gestured toward the oblong container.

"If you would let me scan the tag number . . ." Sanselle's voice was polite.

"Of course." He eased the meter-long container past the half-webbed cargo cube I'd been working to sort through.

Sanselle scanned the tag, and he floated awkwardly back into the main section of the *Reichmann*, leaving the other two.

". . . could be some inroads by engee . . . on the same side of the Arm."

That was yet another reference to engee . . . but I still

had no idea to what the term referred. There was nothing anywhere in all the nanite-loaded information I had absorbed, nor in the station's data banks.

"Who cares? We've got to recheck Alaric . . . something about polar ammonia dispersion reinforcing the greenhouse effect. Qualcon's worried about an imbalance . . ."

I muscled the last lumntagged crate onto Sanselle's cargo sled, then began to web everything in place, strapping the green-striped case on the top.

"You get the other sled," she suggested.

So I did, and I had it locked in place before she returned.

"Not bad, Tyndel."

"I learn."

Only the *Reichmann*'s third stayed around to watch us unload and stow the remainder of the cargo. She was angular in a way that reminded me of Cerrelle. Her eyes were muddy brown, not the deep blue of Foerga's or the piercing green of Cerrelle's or the honest full brown of Fersonne's.

Neither Sanselle nor I spoke much. In ways I did not try to analyze, the presence of the officials in green had damped our normal interest in unloading. We wanted to get the job done and return to other duties.

"That's it," the third finally said. "We'll close up."

We nodded.

Then we had to unload the sled in the transshipment bay. It was easier without anyone looking over our shoulders, although we both knew that Gerbriik monitored us periodically. He didn't trust anyone. That was why he was maintenance officer—and why he'd never be more.

Afterward, when we got to the canteen, I stuck myself to the seat and glanced across at Sanselle. I preferred to ask her questions where I might look stupid, rather than Fersonne or Gerbriik. Sanselle took everything evenly, and I hoped she could help.

"Sanselle . . . ?"

"Another question?" Her eyebrows arched.

"I was fixing the glow strip. The *Reichmann* came in with those passengers Gerbriik didn't expect."

"Right."

"They were talking when they kept looking over our shoulders."

"I didn't care much for that. They couldn't do any better."

"No, they couldn't." I paused. "They used a term I've never heard, and I can't find it anywhere."

Sanselle's blond eyebrows rose. "*You* couldn't find it anywhere?"

I flushed. "I searched the station database, and the library's, and all the information that's been pumped into me."

She half grinned. "You think I'll know?"

"You know more than you ever say." That was true enough.

"What's this mysterious term?"

"Engee . . . or something like that."

Her visage clouded momentarily, before another grin appeared, shakier. "That's what some folk called the Anomaly. The Believers think their God created it and lives there. Engee is short for nanite-god or something like that."

Anomaly? *The angle between the radius vector to an orbiting body from its primary (the focus of the orbital ellipse) and the line of apsides of the orbit . . .* That wasn't it. I tried searching my personal data stocks again. *Deviation from rule, irregularity . . .*

"Why isn't there any reference to it?"

"There isn't any evidence," she pointed out. "They teach that in all the early histories. That's what brought down the early system nets—all sorts of information that wasn't even true in some cases. Anyone can get anything, just about, off a net, but you have to know the protocols to add stuff. Adding stuff without clearance is cause for adjustment."

Just adding information to a data system could get a demon adjusted?

"A main system. You can put anything you want in a local system, but it can't be lifted by outside access. There are ways around it." She grinned, but the grin faded. "Most wouldn't try it. Not worth the risk."

Another hidden and cold aspect to Rykashan controls. I pushed on with my first line of inquiry. If I didn't, it would get lost in all the other questions for which I had yet to find answers. "I've heard people talk about the Believers. I met one on my way here. She was absolute about going somewhere . . . where this engee . . . was the true God. Something like that, anyway."

"They have a deep-space colony somewhere. They have to go by slow boat. Photon drive all the way. That takes years objective, but only weeks subjective."

"Near this Anomaly that no one recognizes?"

"That's what they say." Sanselle's words were wry and flat simultaneously.

I laughed, but I wondered.

"They also think free rock climbers are suicidally antisocial. We have to carry a positive societal balance at all times."

My laugh stopped.

"Or we face adjudication adjustment."

"Because . . . ?" Because what? I wasn't sure even how to frame the question.

"It's costly to rescue a climber who's stranded or injured. 'A waste of scarce resources' I believe is how the adjuster put it." She shrugged. "I'm inhibited from climbing unless my resources are sufficient to cover rescues and medical disasters."

"You build up a credit base . . . ?"

"Exactly. Then no one can say anything. Or do anything. Not even the little monitors they stuffed inside me."

I did shiver at that.

"It's better not to be adjusted, Tyndel."

I'd known that already, if not so strongly.

38

Desire always seeks to deceive pure thought.

Fersonne slipped onto the seat at the canteen table across from me, a canteen as dim as the caserns of the soldiers of five millennia earlier. She readjusted the sticktites, then smoothed her dull gray coveralls and took a sip of the hot tea from the bottle. A spheroidal droplet floated sideways, an extravasion propelled toward the gray composite walls, where it would be ensnared by the housekeeping nanites and added to the other wastes for molecular reconstitution.

Fersonne's brown eyes studied me before she spoke. "Gerbriik offered me a bonus of another full year's credit if I'd stay for a half year more."

"Are you thinking about it?"

"I could leave on the next outbound, or the one after that if I don't stay." She took another sip of tea from the squeeze bottle.

"What will that mean for you?"

"It's not that anyone's waiting. When he didn't renew the contract, I decided I'd do something. I wanted to earn enough to have my own place on Thesalle or Actean—a bigger place, I mean."

Fersonne had never mentioned, even when we were close, who "he" had been, and I'd never asked. She had never asked about anyone in my past. I was grateful for that.

"Where you owed no one askance?"

She nodded briskly. "Had enough of that at home."

"You're from Runswi or . . ."

"Vanirel, north of the mite Thule."

"Are the Rykashan lands always in cold places?" I shook my head, realizing that I could have phrased it another way. "Or maybe it's because the Rykashan lands are in cold places that the older folk are in the warmer lands?"

"You're not a mite, Tyndel." Fersonne looked at me. "Not sure you ever were. You look at things different-like. Bet some of them knew it, too."

"I'm not a Rykashan."

"You are. You don't want to admit it."

Why did I have such trouble admitting what was so clearly a fact? I didn't even want to call it "truth." Was that because if I acknowledged such a truth I had to give up my past? But my past was mine, no matter what I became. I had to accept that. "Do you want to stay here any longer, or is it the idea of a better place?"

"A better place. I want to see the stars without looking through a faceplate. I want to run again, and not in a station treadmill that smells oily and sweaty." After another sip of the tea, she studied me again. "Why do you stay here?"

"Do I have a choice?"

"You could leave on the next needle ship if you agreed to train as a Web jockey."

"You think so?"

"Gerbriik's as much as said that. Rykashans are stubborn, too, Tyndel. No one's going to beg you to be a Web jockey."

"I didn't ask to be a Rykashan. Or a Web jockey."

"Why don't you do it because *you* want to—not because you're opposing them?"

"I don't know. Maybe because I don't want to."

"What good does it do to keep refusing? If you want to change things, Tyndel, you have to do *something*."

"Why? Anything I do benefits them."

"Anything any of us do that's good is good for someone. Do you hate everyone so bad that you won't do something good?"

That was the sort of question Foerga would have asked. Or Cerrelle. I didn't answer.

"Do you still think of me as one of 'them'?"

"No. You know that."

"A lot of folks are just like me, Tyndel." A soft smile went with the words. "Most of us aren't Gerbriiks or Web jockeys or planoformers."

"I understand."

"You don't act like you do."

"You're hard to lie to, you know." A muttered laugh went with my words.

"You have trouble lying to yourself. I didn't have anything to do with that."

But she did. I swallowed silently at what I had refused to see. Foerga, Cerrelle, and now Fersonne. Fersonne wasn't brilliant, but she was honest, and I'd always needed honesty—and never wanted to acknowledge that need. By pressing me to be honest, Cerrelle had angered me, and it hadn't been her fault. Neither Foerga nor Fersonne had pressed me . . . and that said what? I wasn't sure.

"Are you going to stay?" I finally asked. "For the extra half year?"

"I'd never have to come back." Fersonne looked down at the table. "I could go to Actean, even." She didn't look at me. "I'll probably tell Gerbriik I'll take his bonus. It's at least doing something." The brown eyes met mine, and she smiled . . . faintly.

"You don't have to . . ."

"I know. It's for me, Tyndel."

Her smile bothered me, despite the denial, long after she'd gone back onto her shift and I to my cube, where I climbed into my sleeping net alone . . . wondering. *Anything good benefits someone . . . do you hate everyone so bad . . . ?*

39

Illumination cannot be communicated.

After my work shifts, before I slept, I continued to try to read something. I'd located an antiquarian text in the station library base, one that hadn't been accessed in decades from what the records showed. The title had intrigued me—*The Nanite Perspective*—as had the opening sentences framed in the reading screen clipped to my sleeping net.

> . . . once worlds have changed, those who live in the new world fail to understand the perspective of those lost in the old . . .

I certainly empathized with that, for I still felt lost in the old even while being forced to live in the new, and half hoped that the words of the forgotten author might help—somehow.

> . . . all the changes in the world were as nothing compared to the Nanotech Revolution. . . . While some few saw the seeds of destruction, early obstructions to implementing the technology were seen as final barriers beyond which few peered. . . . Greatest of the bars to widespread implementation of nanite technologies was the early difficulty in developing a usable scanner technology. After the Heylstron scanner was developed . . . escalating economic dislocation corraded the very fabric of society . . . economic disintegration was rapidly followed by military appli-

cations of nanite technologies in an effort to halt the
restructuring of cultures and societies . . .

That made sense. Even in Dorcha, the sealords had first
claim on the taxes of the state and resources necessary to
maintain the fleets. The Dzin masters came last, for all
that they taught the coming generations and the next set
of sealords.

Despite the banality of the opening, I kept reading, my
eyes fixed on the screen in the darkness of my cube.

. . . first recorded deployment of nanite disassemblers
occurred in 505 A.S. with the attempted reconstitution of the Mogul Hegemony . . . casualties on both
sides reached eighty percent . . .

I winced at that, long ago as it had been. No wonder
the masters of Dzin and Toze and the Dhurr genchiefs
opposed the demonic weapons. After swallowing and pag-
ing ahead, I settled into a section on the arts, except that
it didn't quite stay on the arts.

. . . the impact of nanite replicators effectively destroyed the economic use of fine art as a means of
storing wealth, since a nanite-scanned and repro-
duced replica is indistinguishable from the original
by any nondestructive test . . .

Art as a way of storing wealth? Not to be used and
enjoyed, the way Foerga's crystal was? Or my mother's
paintings? The ancients had actually done that?

. . . values of previously precious metals and gems
also declined precipitously, especially those of dia-
monds, rubies, and sapphires . . .

I closed my eyes for a moment, images crossing my
mind, figures in stained silks and satins, or ancient fabrics

once rare, wearing gold chains, their faces gaunt, their eyes sunken, their limbs shriveled from hunger.

Dorcha and the rest of the mite world still relied on the economics of the so-called natural world—prices of goods determined not just by their composition but by their scarcity, a scarcity repealed in Rykashan society. A nanotech culture changed all that in more than the most obvious ways. Almost any substance could be duplicated through electroessence and nanites, except the most rare of elements, and such were not a good basis of a currency or an economic system.

I rubbed my forehead, wishing I could chase away the images.

So what was the basis of the Rykashan economy? *Skill and applied dedication.*

The power requirements for a food replicator were far less than those for organically grown materials, and if the replicators were programmed correctly there was no difference in terms of nourishment. The replicated food also had less chance of contamination. So what happened to the trufflers and eelers, the gardeners? Anyone could duplicate credit notes perfectly, undetectably. What happened to currency? Nanotechnology had been demonstrated to produce horrific casualties in battles. What happened to war? *Those without nanotechnology are destroyed or contained. Those with it develop a system without war or perish.*

What kind of system?

I wanted to shake my head, but that wouldn't have helped. In hindsight, so much seemed so clear, but that sight had been a long time in coming, because I had known, had fought the understanding, that nothing indeed would be the same.

I flicked off the reading screen. I had already absorbed too much history and background.

When I finally drifted toward sleep, the arcs of fire were pure gold—not golden-red. They were like golden chains, spinning out through black space to ensnare me, to shackle me to ... I didn't know what.

"NO!"

I sat up in the net, shaking it against its anchors, and bounced from the bottom to the top and back again, feeling like a beaker of alcardia shaken so long that it foamed tastelessly.

I was beginning to understand, beginning to comprehend why I had not wanted to understand—and now I felt as though something were trying to ensnare me. The new world in which I was caught?

After a time, I slept—fitfully at best—in a dim darkness so unlike the niellen depths through which arcs of fire had reached toward me.

40

[OMEGA ERIDANI: 4517]

All life is sorrow.

After a quick shower and a change into clean coveralls, I sat in the canteen alone, eating curried Dorchan strip beef and noodles, and sipping orange tea.

Sanselle's image appeared beside me in the canteen. She seldom called up an image from my commpak. Her face was, pale, her eyes slightly swollen. "Tyndel ... cargo lock three ..."

The image vanished.

I pulled free of the sticktites and quickly disposed of the remains of my meal, then flung myself into the corridor toward the transverse shaft—number four—that would drop me closest to lock three. I was supposed to be off-shift, but the strain in Sanselle's voice negated that.

What could have upset her? Why had she called, instead of Gerbriik? Had something happened to the maintenance officer?

Whatever it had been, it wasn't Gerbriik, because he and Sanselle stood anchored in the corridor by the lock. A cold tension flowed between them.

The lights on the lock control panel, and the dull and muffled *thud*, confirmed that an inbound ship was docking.

Both faces blanked as they saw me. Gerbriik's visage remained impassive, unlike Sanselle's. The darkness remained behind her eyes, and her cheeks were blotchy.

"I'm sorry," she said softly.

Sorry? For what? "What happened?"

"There's been . . . an accident," Gerbriik answered, his voice edged. "Fersonne—she was hit by the *Hook*'s braking blast."

Sanselle nodded slowly, her eyes preternaturally bright.

"How . . . ?" I didn't understand how it could have happened. ESAs weren't allowed with incoming ships. Fersonne? She was so careful, more so than either Sanselle or me.

"The usual for something like this." Gerbriik didn't look at me. "The *Hook* arrived early, with less than five minutes' notice. She came in too hot. I called Fersonne to get inside. I told her to leave everything and get in. She torqued up the thrust on her broomstick to hurry. She was on her tether and tried to use it to swing her in toward the open lock. The *Hook* was hot and had to brake later and longer. Fersonne tried to kill her thrust, but she'd been out more than half a shift, and the gas reservoir of the broomstick was low and gave out. She tried to reel herself back in, to shorten the arc. She wasn't fast enough, and the shorter arc sped up the swing—right into the *Hook*'s blast." He shrugged. "A few degrees either way and nothing would have happened."

A few degrees . . . a few moments . . . if I had been a few moments faster in Hybra, Foerga might have lived.

If Fersonne hadn't extended for the bonus. Or for me? If . . . but ifs don't change death.

I glanced around, half expecting to see the brown eyes looking at me, accepting me. I just saw the gray of the cargo corridors and lock doors. My eyes went back to Gerbriik.

"Even an outside suit won't protect you from the ion exhaust of a needle ship's thrusters." Gerbriik's voice was flat. "There's nothing . . ."

Sanselle shook her head.

So did I. It didn't make sense—but it did. The unexpected, combined with a lot of little errors . . . and Fersonne was dead. The least likely to be killed that way. Perhaps the best person I knew on the station, or since I'd left Dorcha. Dead.

I could feel the chill beyond the thick composite of the hull, and the chill rising within me, like the brume off Deep Lake just before it froze.

"I'm getting the sled," Sanselle offered as she glided away down the corridor.

"The sled?"

"You still need to off-load the *Hook*," Gerbriik said slowly.

Fersonne was dead—she'd just been killed—and we needed to off-load the incoming needle ship. Life—even demon life—went on.

"Yes, ser." My voice was flat.

"I couldn't have known," Gerbriik said quietly. "I wish I could have."

"I know, ser." I was angry, but I wasn't angry with the maintenance officer. How could I have been? Gerbriik was a perfectionist. That might have been what killed Fersonne. Because he worried, he'd asked her to hurry. Because she'd hurried . . . That was the awful irony. Because he had been concerned, he'd set up the coincidences that had killed her, and he'd worry the situation to death, perhaps his own death, over the years ahead. "I know," I repeated, not knowing where to direct that formless rage that seethed within me. "I know . . ."

The faint hum of the cargo sled rode over the silence. Sanselle guided it along the side of the cargo corridor and brought it to a halt less than three meters from me.

"Still waiting for them to unlock?" she asked.

I could almost read her thoughts from her face. *They've messed up everything else . . . what else should we expect?*

The lock hissed open, and we were showered with ice crystals and hull-chilled air. The nanite fields that completed the seals didn't stop heat loss. Not much.

The *Hook*'s third stood amid the swirling ice mists that cleared from the open cargo lock, waiting expectantly, as if he expected us to move to him. After a moment, Gerbriik did. Sanselle and I followed.

"Treat this off-load carefully. It's special equipment they need at the Alaric orbit station. They pulled us in to bring it out." He winced. "There's a great deal of metal there. It's expensive metal."

Gerbriik nodded as if the fact that the cargo contained expensive metal explained everything, justified Fersonne's death. I knew he didn't feel quite that way, but I wouldn't have been surprised if the third officer did. We all felt the deaths of those close to us, but merely regretted and justified the deaths of those we did not know. Only in small communities was it different. . . .

At that thought, I wondered. Hybra had been a small community, and I doubted there had been much slowing of the town from my disappearance and Foerga's death.

The third returned the nod, then eased back from the lock door. I wanted to grab him and stuff him outside without a suit. *Life goes on, and the careless ones don't even know the loss they create.*

"It's all yours." Gerbriik looked at the two of us, then turned in midair and glided away without another word.

"He isn't going to say anything about Fersonne?" My eyes flicked sideways to Sanselle.

"Commander Maestros already let the Web jockey know over the comm."

"And no one said anything?"

"What could they say? It wasn't their fault, not exactly, anyway," pointed out Sanselle. "They never would have picked her up on their sensors . . . not quickly enough."

I swallowed. Personal responsibility again. Fersonne had been responsible for her own safety, and she had failed. I wanted to hammer the bulkhead with my bare fist.

Instead, I followed Sanselle through the lock and into the hold.

The third waited. "This bay first."

My eyes were colder than the space beyond the ship's hulls, and the junior ship officer looked away from me quickly.

Sanselle began unwebbing the bay, then eased a cubical container about a half meter square toward me. "Careful—more mass than it looks like."

My hands and arms recoiled at the seemingly inexorable inertia. I glanced at the description stenciled on the side of the small and heavy cubical container: "Section two (b), formulator analysis microflakes." The words slid off my mind, and I forced myself to concentrate on them. Why were such microflakes so important? Or was any cargo more important than the life of a maintenance technician?

Sanselle followed with a matching cube. All in all, the first bay contained two dozen of the identically labeled cubes.

When we had finished, the third gestured toward the next bay, avoiding my eyes.

The second bay held oblong containers with the appellation: "High pressure microvessels[Spec. A-4c]."

More cargo bays and more not totally comprehensible labels followed, until we reached the fifth or sixth bay.

"Aerostat frame assemblies"—I murmured the words

as I eased the three-meter-long container toward the cargo sled.

Sanselle helped ease it under a flexible web, and we went back for more.

Filling the rest of the hold were thin sheets of material roughly a meter square, webbed into sets of ten, so light I could move three bundles easily. Those were labeled: "Insulation, High-Temp[Spec. 5-XXX]."

Aerostat frames, high-temperature insulation, high-pressure microvessels, special formulator microflakes— and none of it could be built or created around Omega Eridani? So special that it required diverting a particular needle ship?

"What's the matter?" Sanselle studied me. "Besides the obvious."

"The obvious," I said. "Nothing changes that."

"There's more . . ."

"All this cargo." From what I knew, the cargo didn't make sense, but in the mood I was in, I didn't want to ask anyone. I had questions, questions I should have thought about months or years earlier, except I hadn't cared.

"Not much different from what we've been unloading all along. Heavier, and more of it, that's all." Sanselle shrugged. "Don't want to take all shift, either."

I agreed with that, but I hadn't wanted to touch anything on the *Hook*, not once I'd reached the cargo lock.

After a deep breath, I forced myself back toward the *Hook*'s lock—and the few containers remaining, trying to ignore the questions seething through me.

Why did the Rykasha have three orbit stations off Omega Eridani? That answer came from within me easily. *One outer system main station and two planetary stations minimize interstellar transit power requirements and maximize needle ship cargo efficiency.* In short, send one needle ship to the system, and let the locals unload it on their time.

What did nanite formulators have to do with planoforming? And why did they need special equipment shipped interstellar distances rather than build from plans in-system?

And why did it have to be Fersonne?

There wasn't any real answer, just as there hadn't been for Foerga's death. Or I couldn't find an answer. Not for me.

I eased the sled's webbing around the last container.

An image of Gerbriik, monitoring our actions, appeared between us. "Don't unload the sled. Just tie it down in lock one. The cargo boat from Alaric will be here in thirty hours, and there's nothing else inbound."

"Yes, ser."

I followed the sled to lock one, then helped Sanselle anchor it in place.

"We're done," Sanselle finally announced. "You'd better get some sleep. We're going to be working short-handed for a good while."

I hadn't even thought about that.

As I made my way back toward my cube for a very short rest—I wasn't likely to sleep—I thought about needle ship cargos and death. What was in the cargo that was so special? Or were certain types of planoforming equipment so complex that they could only be created and built on earth? So complex that Fersonne's death meant almost nothing? Meant nothing personal to anyone but me, and perhaps Sanselle . . . and maybe Gerbriik.

The ancient economists would have theorized that death would have meant more in Rykashan society—because there were fewer people and because those people lived longer. And they would have been wrong. Except for the occasional great person or hero, or tragedy, death has always been personal, affecting one individual and the handful of people who cared about that dead individual. The rest of society went on, and that had been true as far back as the ancient pyramids and great walls, and remained true, and would doubtless remain so into the far future.

Death had two meanings—the loss of resources to society and the personal grief of the few who cared. Fersonne's value was less than that of one cargo, and this time, I was one of the few who cared, and I wanted there to be some meaning behind Fersonne's death . . . and there wasn't *Unless you create that meaning . . . unless you do . . .*

As I tossed in the sleeping net, another thought drifted through my fevered reveries. *We all need meaning . . . and it's different for each of us, but what gives meaning to society?*

Dzin gave meaning to Dorcha . . . Toze to Klama . . . what provided a dream or a meaning to the Rykashans? Did they have one?

I lay in the darkness in my sleeping net for what seemed like a long time, too many questions yet unanswered, too many feelings churning.

41

[OMEGA ERIDANI: 4517]

Pride is a dim lamp on a dark road.

Over the next standard week, I kept asking questions about death, and about what mattered, but the answers never changed. Death was personal, and society went on.

I did figure out an answer to one question: What would give Fersonne's death some meaning? It was a very small answer, but it was the best I could do. So I finally swallowed and went to Gerbriik at the end of my last shift for that day. He looked up from the main maintenance console with eyes as dark-rimmed as mine or Sanselle's.

"Ser?"

"Yes, Tyndel? I can't change the shifts. I know you're being worked too hard, but with Fersonne's death . . ."

"It's not about that, ser."

"I'm sorry about Fersonne. I am. I know you two were close." His face was impassive, the eyes blank, waiting.

"There's something else, ser . . ."

Gerbriik raised his eyebrows. "You're beginning to understand?"

I hated the faint tone of pity, but my feelings weren't important this time. As a former Dzin master, I should have found it easy to keep my feelings out of things. I never had, and that might have been why I'd been sent to Hybra. *Might have been?* "Yes, ser. If it is possible, I'd like to request training as a Web pilot."

"If it's not?"

"Then I keep working here. Doing as well as I can. Until my obligation is complete." What other choice did I have?

"Whether they accept you—that's up to the authorities in Runswi." He nodded. "I thought you might. I'll send the request with the next ship."

"Thank you, ser."

"I am sorry about Fersonne." He nodded and looked back down at the console. "I am, more than you know . . ." The last words weren't really for me. That I knew.

I glided back to the transverse shaft and down to my cube. I didn't even try to sleep . . . or read. I lay there, in darkness that wasn't black enough to shut out everything that swirled around me, hoping that I'd found one solution, hoping I wasn't deceiving myself.

42

*When facts are combined into an assemblage of verifiables,
their illusion becomes reality.*

Sanselle and I had just finished unloading the *Hay Needle*'s cargo and getting it stored in the transshipment
bay. She was guiding the cargo sled back to its storage
bay.

I glided beside her, wiping my forehead with the back
of my forearm, then stifling a yawn.

"Tired?" she asked.

"Aren't you?"

"I've adjusted." She laughed. "No reading. No exercise
except maintenance. Just work and sleep. Time passes."

"That's really not true." I raised my eyebrows, then
smiled.

"No . . . but it feels that way sometimes."

Even as I understood the feelings, I wasn't sure I'd
adjusted even that well. Both on-shift and off-shift were
lonely, and after two years plus on the station, with nearly
eight to go, they would probably get more lonely. At that
moment, Gerbriik favored us with his image.

"The maintenance bay, as soon as you're free," he said
before his visage faded.

"Yes, ser."

We looked at each other.

"Replacement for Fersonne," suggested Sanselle.

"If it is, they didn't waste much time." It had been ten
standard months, and with overspace dilation—far better
than photondrive slowboat but far from instantaneous—

that meant that if Gerbriik had a replacement they'd sent someone by return ship.

Sanselle handed me the control box. "You can stow it."

I took the controls and edged the sled into the bay. After two years, I could do it as well as she did.

"Do that well, Tyndel."

"Thank you."

Then we went up the shaft and along the upper mid-level corridor to the maintenance bay. Gerbriik had a muscular black-haired woman beside him, bigger than any of the three of us. "This is Seriley. She's the new maintenance tech. She spent a year already on earth orbit station, waiting for an outspace billet." He gestured toward Sanselle, then me. "The sandy-haired one is Sanselle. She's the head tech. The brown-haired fellow is Tyndel. They're both glad to see you. So am I."

Seriley smiled more than politely, but not effusively. "It's good to meet you."

"We are glad to see you," Sanselle replied.

I smiled and nodded. Seriley didn't seem all that pleased to be on OE Station, for all that Gerbriik had said.

"After I finish showing her around, Seriley will work with one or the other of you until she knows all the duties," Gerbriik concluded with a vague smile.

"I'm looking forward to it," added the muscular new tech. "I really am."

Looking forward to what? I gave a last smile.

"You hungry?" asked Sanselle as we left the maintenance bay.

"Yes."

In the canteen, Sanselle had the formulator prepare another of the spicy Dhurr dishes—a type of fish packed with chilies and then deep-fried and covered with a plum sauce. I had a truffle cream beef with steamed almond beans.

"You like the bland stuff, don't you?" she asked.

"I don't find it that bland, but you burned out your taste buds and olefactors with those chilies years ago."

That got a grin from her. "Used to think you were so stiff, Tyndel." She brushed back the short-cut straw-colored hair.

"I am."

"Not so much. Quiet." She paused for a mouthful of the chilied fish. "Wondered what I'd have to talk about if no one knew the things I grew up with."

"Work. After a time, you share that." That was what had happened. The longer we had worked together, the more common experiences we had, and the more to talk over. I missed talking things over with Fersonne. That loss made me even more aware of how much I missed the quiet evenings with Foerga. In a way, I even missed Cerrelle, even if I couldn't quite say why . . . except she'd traveled out to OE Station, and it hadn't been just to recruit a pilot. I'd not seen a lot of things, but I'd been so numb . . . how much had I missed?

"Some things, about you, no one will understand. We didn't live as mites. Some things about us, they'll take you years to understand, Tyndel."

"I can see that." I could—at last.

"You'll understand them. Won't feel them. That's why they'll make you a Web jockey."

I was afraid I understood what Sanselle said all too well, even if I could not have articulated the logical basis for her words. I'd heard nothing about my request, and doubtless wouldn't, not for a while. Considering my request, even for Rykashans, apparently took longer. It might take eight years, although I doubted that from what I had seen on OE Station.

Sanselle was right, and I knew it. I didn't know enough about Rykashan culture, and parts of it I'd never feel. *Like what hopes drive Rykashans or what dreams hold Rykasha together? Or those dreams that even Rykashans do not realize they dream?*

Later, I stretched out in the sleeping net, yawning. Some things were beginning to make sense. Seriley had been waiting to get an outspace billet. If they were so rare, why had they thrown me into one so quickly? Why were the stations so meagerly staffed? With fusactor power and food and oxygen replicators they could easily support more people. How could they repair a complex needle ship at OE Station but have to ship certain fabricated equipment across long interstellar distances? Why could they act as though I were valuable, and yet replace Fersonne without even a tear or a sigh, except from Sanselle and me?

I was all too afraid I did understand, and I still wasn't sure I wanted to.

I finally closed my eyes.

43

[OMEGA ERIDANI: 4518]

A shadow in darkness reveals more than it conceals.

"You can give Seriley her outside orientation," Gerbriik told me, barely gliding back from the maintenance console, his eyes half glazed as he remained partly intermeshed with some part of the station. "She's been outside off earth orbit station. So it's more of a familiarization with the differences."

Between us, Seriley nodded, her short and shining hair bobbing.

The maintenance officer's eyes glazed over fully.

Taking that as a dismissal, I looked at the muscular new tech. "We might as well start."

"That's fine with me."

I eased out of the maintenance bay and started along the corridor. She caught up without being flustered or even looking hurried.

At the top of transverse shaft number four, the black-haired Seriley looked at me. "You're not like the others."

"No." I shrugged, starting down the shaft.

"Are you an outie?" She kept up with me.

"No. I've never set foot on one of the colony planets."

"You will. Gerbriik says you're going to be a Web jockey."

"I don't know," I admitted. "They asked. I refused. They sent me here. I reconsidered. Now they're considering." I braked at the bottom of the shaft, reaching for the handhold beside the hatch.

The black eyes softened. "You must be a convert—one of the mites who got infected with an old nanovirus."

"It happened. Not quite like that. What about you?"

"I used to be a Follower. Or I thought I was. I know better now. Delusional break, that's all it was, but I didn't want to spend the rest of the next sixty years repaying the treatment." Her words were even, but the pain behind the words said I shouldn't ask more.

I didn't. Were all of us who were furcated across the Web misintegrals of one sort or another? From religious delusionals to obsessed perfectionists? But what was it about engee that inspired such delusional faith? Was engee real? Some sort of ancient relic venerated by the unbalanced? An alien intelligence?

Shaking myself mentally, I had to smile. In a way, it mattered little. Engee was whatever it was. Then I caught myself. *That . . . that is the difference!* Dzin taught one to discover and be aware of what was. The Rykashans sought to advance and improve, but not necessarily to become fully aware. Dzin-instinctively, to me, outside of my personal curiosity, it didn't matter what engee was, but I had a responsibility to become aware of what he/she/it might be had I ever the chance.

I opened the triple hatch and gestured for Seriley to follow me toward the bays that held the cargo sleds. There I stopped. "Based on the specifications, these are larger than any used in the earth orbit stations, but they stay down here. There's the smaller sled that can fit in the transverse shafts and doesn't require the heavy guides that these three do." I kept walking. "We do all ESAs from the lowest level. The passenger locks are on the level above, but we only use them for receiving, and there are emergency locks higher on every upper level."

"That's standard in all stations. The lowest level is the most heavily braced."

I almost asked if she'd studied them all before I realized that I already knew it myself. I just hadn't looked. Or remembered? That was the trouble with nanite-carried information. After a time, you didn't—or I didn't—know what you knew or didn't know.

Since no ships were docked or off-loading, I took her to the middle personnel lock. We pulled on outside suits and soft helmets, checked the supporting fields, checked each other. Remembering Fersonne, I checked the pressures on both broomsticks a second time before I pressed the evacuation stud.

Momentary swirls of minute ice crystals flew, then the chill followed. We slipped through the bars of light thrown by the glow strips and out past the lock dampers. Seriley didn't have to be reminded to clip her tether.

When first I swam out from the light of the lock, again, the rampart that was the station reared upward and outward like a wall of the ancients. The featureless expanse stretched endlessly toward the starry pinlights that cut the niellen blackness like tiny knives. Somewhere, if my visions and dreams were accurate, behind all those stars lay arcs of golden-red fire that burst from a spiral of stars . . . somehow linked to the mysterious engee.

If they weren't . . . then I was the delusional one. I eased the faintest puff of gas to the broomstick. Then I turned on the stick's seat and gestured. "We replaced the dampers on the cargo locks about fifteen standard months ago. Gerbriik thinks they'll be good for another five years."

"They only last two years or so on the earth orbit stations."

"Higher traffic," I pointed out.

"Much higher," she added.

I gestured toward the brightest star in the sky, a pin-disc. "There's Omega. You can't even see discs of Conan or Alaric from here. Dust density's higher than normal. They put the station farther out, well beyond the VeeTee range."

"The hull's pitted already. Earth orbit stations are smoother." She laughed. "But we're hit with more junk."

"Remnants from history?"

"Some of that. Also the comet belts are more erratic and denser. Something to do with the placement of gas giants in the earth system."

We slid past the end cargo lock, past the personnel lock, and around toward the back side of the station, the dark side where the coolant fins from the fusactors melded into the darkness of space, not even lit by the photons from distant Omega.

Every station has a dark side. So does every life, even that of a demon, and I was a demon, no matter how long I had resisted accepting that.

44

[A. FELINI: 4530]

Your concern alone is the action of duty, not the judgment of that duty.

From the depths to my left, to the massed pipe organ sounds of a march orchestrated by an ancient Baroque composer, gallop cavalry troops of rectangles—bright blue—arrayed in rows not quite symmetrical. Underneath the music is the weight of something—something massive, and yet being flung swiftly—and behind the rectangles and their accompaniment come the words.

Even the mighty are limited . . .

"That's a tautological paradox," my mind replies, concentrating as I am on avoiding the deadly rectangles that threaten me/us. "True mightiness would have no limits."

Any being within a universe is limited by that universe. Any ordered action in any universe results in a total increase in disorder.

I have no answer, swooping to my right, maintaining the gradient I need, knowing that to flee downward will allow the rectangles to pierce and bury us/me.

Even gathering and creating information is an ordered action, and as such, there is no way even a god can create more information than is destroyed through the creation process. Golden-red starfire punctuates the words.

"Then how can any being increase knowledge?"

By linking two universes, by using the energy from a collapsing high-entropy antimatter universe to power the creation of order within this universe.

"That would take more than a god." I dismissed the thought and concentrated on the white/black warmth of the beacon ahead, mustering my last energy to control the descent that would bring us back to Sol from the greenness of Thesalle, that greenness I pondered, as had who knew how many scientists . . . and all without an answer.

45

[OMEGA ERIDANI: 4519]

All beings have gods to worship: not all gods respect those who offer worship.

The end of my third year on OE Station was rapidly approaching. Seriley was pleasant enough, but I missed Fersonne. I even missed Cerrelle.

One shift break, Sanselle, Seriley, and I sat restrained

by sticktites in the canteen, finishing meals of great diversity. The way the schedules rotated, the three of us seldom ate at once. The odor of Dhurr spiceroll drowned out the mild basilic flavor of my chicken creamed truffles and whatever Seriley had been eating.

"How long will you be here, do you think?" Sanselle asked me.

"I don't know. Another three months, another eight years. I haven't heard."

"What about you?" The sandy blonde turned to Seriley.

"I'm here for five. Six if I want, if I can take it." The muscular woman shrugged.

"You'll wear out the exercise area by then."

I could understand that, lax as I had been. The nanites helped, especially on the cellular level, but we'd all been briefed on the fact that after two years we'd need nearly six months of intensive physical reconditioning to regain full gravity well ability, more as the years off-planet built up.

"I don't want to lose too much muscle tone." Seriley sipped something from a bottle, then asked Sanselle. "How long for you?"

"I've been here four years—this time—and I need another two."

The slightest frown crossed Seriley's face.

Sanselle massaged the back of her neck with her right hand. "I'm one of those suicidal risk-taking free rock climbers. I've got a place in the White Peaks, do some work for the ecology restoration folks. Working here is for rescue and medical rehab."

"Have you ever needed it?" asked Seriley.

"That's why I'm back. Got careless on a trip to the Old Rockies. Took a flitter to get me out—and two years of spinal rebuilding."

I held in the wince, taking a last mouthful of the truffles.

"You're going back there again," said Seriley.

"Of course." Sanselle laughed. "Next time, I won't be so careless."

"Why do you do it?"

"To be alive. Life has to be more than just existing."

"Life doesn't insist on that." I finally spoke. "We do. Most creatures do little more than exist and perish."

"That isn't exactly Dzin, is it?" A wry smile crossed Sanselle's lips.

"Hardly. Dzin says that the concern is the perfection of the work, not the perfection of the worker."

"Like termites." Sanselle laughed. "The nest is all."

"There's not much difference in Rykashan society," I pointed out. "The nest is bigger and more complex, but look at you . . . us." I realized that I was no longer insisting that I wasn't a Rykashan. "To find the meaning you want from life, you have to work twice as hard to ensure your freedom doesn't endanger the nest or waste its resources."

"What if there isn't . . . meaning, that is?" asked Seriley.

I shrugged.

"I mean it."

"I know." I shifted my weight against the restraint of the sticktites. "I'd say the universe doesn't have a meaning or a purpose. Throughout history, people kept inventing gods because they couldn't conceive of or imagine that creation and existence were an accident or occurred as a result of purely natural processes."

"Dzin . . . does it . . . ?" Sanselle shook her head.

"Dzin avoids the issue," I admitted. "It provides a set of rules for a meaningful life within a society and assumes that the meaning is provided by the continuation of an orderly society. Society is, in effect, God."

"I'll bet that would get you readjusted, or whatever mites do," suggested Seriley.

"Executed or exiled," I said.

"I'm glad I'm not a mite." Seriley tossed her head.

"Rykasha isn't that much different." I grinned at Sanselle, then smothered it and waited. "Society still makes the rules. We don't call it God, but, so far as controlling us, we might as well. What with nanotechnology and micronics, we either live by the rules or get readjusted one way or another to live by the rules." I smiled. "The difference is that we can talk about it."

"What if there is a god?" asked Seriley.

"He hasn't shown much interest in us," answered Sanselle. "Human beings have been building cities for something like ten thousand years, and it's been a long time since anyone's documented a god's presence."

"Why would a god care? Would anything that mighty worry about our opinion?" I asked.

"Probably not." Sanselle finished her bottle of whatever Dhurr beverage she'd been drinking.

"The Believers say engee is a god," offered Seriley. "There's *something* out there. Even the astrophysicists say so. They just won't say what."

"Except that it sends forth signals that affect some people," I added.

"That something doesn't change things here or anywhere else," countered Sanselle. "We still have to play by the rules that people set up."

Gerbriik's image appeared in the space between Sanselle and me, his lower extremities cut off by the canteen table. "I beg your pardons for interrupting your theological discussion, but the *Tailor* is coming in. Sanselle and Seriley need to get ready to off-load."

"Yes, ser."

"Yes, ser."

"There's God," said Sanselle after Gerbriik's image vanished. "For now, anyway."

Seriley frowned but did not speak.

I let them go, then slipped back to my cube and the reading screen. What really was the point of discussing God—or gods? Discussion wouldn't determine the existence or nonexistence of a supreme being. Nor had any such supreme being ever directly affected the conditions under which we lived, not in any scientifically demonstrable way.

Yet, even in the rational culture of Rykasha, people believed—some, anyway—in a god called engee. Yet in what seemed an unlimited universe, far more was possible than Rykashans or mites had envisioned.

But if the improbable occurred, the proof of a god, an alien intelligence, a cosmic catastrophe, a great many people would overreact, as if the merely unknown or improbable had been heretofore impossible.

What did that say about people? *That most don't understand the universe? Or Dzin? Or themselves?*

I knew all that already, including the fact that I didn't know as much about myself as I once had thought, and I laughed to myself as I climbed into my sleeping net, flicked on the reading screen, and called up more history—hard history.

46

[OMEGA ERIDANI: 4519]

The universe has no destination.

I had just climbed out of sleep, four hours after the *Tailor*'s arrival, awakened by my internal timekeeping demons, and was stowing the sleeping net, when Gerbriik's image appeared. "Once you're cleaned up and ready for duty, see me first." The image vanished as quickly as it had come.

I showered, put on clean coveralls, grabbed an egg-cheese pie from the canteen formulator, washed it down with lukewarm tea, and scrambled up to the maintenance bay.

The area was empty, except for the maintenance officer

himself. Gerbriik's eyes snapped from their glaze—totally—when he turned from the console. "The *Tailor* brought back the response to your request."

"Yes, ser?" Was I to remain on OE Station for another seven years? Or two? Three? I waited for the cold words.

"You're returning to Runswi for training as a Web pilot. On the *Tailor*. Immediately. Apparently, we need Web pilots more than maintenance techs." Gerbriik smiled, one of the few times he'd done so. "And we'll see you in a few years."

"I hope so, ser." I paused. "I'm sorry . . . if you're shorthanded. I don't want the others to work too hard."

A second smile crossed Gerbriik's face. "They did send a replacement. So Sanselle and Seriley won't be muttering imprecations at your hasty departure."

"Sanselle wouldn't."

"No . . . but I might have."

I didn't have a ready answer, but Gerbriik went on. "Don't waste any more of your life, Tyndel. You have more to offer than you realize."

"The time here wasn't wasted, ser." It had been necessary, all too necessary, because it had taken the time on OE Station for me truly to learn how to apply Dzin.

"I hope not. You were a good tech, even if you took some educating."

"Thank you."

"We'll look forward to seeing you bring a ship in. Good luck. You need to hurry. The *Tailor* will be sealing locks in less than two hours. I let you sleep because you'll need it." His eyes were on me, fully on me, until I left the maintenance bay.

In the end, I didn't bring back as much as I had brought, and I wore dull gray coveralls, not the greens I had worn out to OE Station. I'd earned the grays.

HYSTERESIS

47

You may know your body, but you are not your body.

Once away from Earth Orbit One on my way down to Runswi, I sat halfway back in the shuttle's window-less passenger cabin, beside a redheaded woman in a blue-trimmed, silver suit—the colors indicating some type of support to a senior administrator or controller. She kept her narrow face averted from me.

Most of the dozen on the shuttle wore blue or red, although a slender man near the front was dressed in green, a darker green, with a gold collar pin in the shape of a triangular web. *Web pilot*, supplied some source within me. No one sat in the couch adjacent to him.

The shuttle slid down the invisible magfield slope and along what I knew to be the permacrete strip at Runswi even if I could not see it.

After the shuttle came to a near-silent halt, the hatch swung open, and tendrils of the moist hot air of summer merged with the ozone-oiled air of the shuttle itself. I waited until the narrow-faced woman was clear of her couch and the others in red and green and blue were filing out into the diffuse sunlight beyond the cabin before I stood. Then I rose slowly and went back to the lockers to retrieve my single small duffel.

Despite four weeks of high-gee reindoctrination on the orbit station, I felt logy and tired, too massive for legs that wobbled like straws supporting a hog ready for slaughter. I stepped down the ramp with great delibera-tion, pausing at the base, and glanced around.

After a time, I turned toward the operations building

and began to walk, stopping frequently to both catch my breath and to rest already aching muscles. Sweat coated me, and my heart pounded by the time I reached the operations desk. I didn't know where else to go. I stood there, breathing heavily.

"Candidate Tyndel?" asked the dark-haired man behind the console after a time. The sleeves of his silver gray singlesuit were striped with green.

"I'm Tyndel."

"Good. Coordinator Andra asked me to convey her apologies for not being here." He extended a folder. "That has all the information you need—your room assignment, your gymnasium and exercise schedule, and your first week's re-indoc activities. Oh, there's a map there, too. Try to get plenty of sleep and exercise." He offered a smile. "The first month back on earth is hard. Good luck."

I took the folder and opened it, noting that he'd summarized the contents exactly. "Thank you."

"There's an electrocart through the back way, ser. You'd better take it." His tone was wryly amused.

"Thank you."

In slow steps I made my way to the rear of the building and stepped back into the heat under a shadowed overhang.

A stocky brown-haired woman dressed in dull gray coveralls, much like those I still wore, stood as I neared the six-seater cart. "You're candidate Tyndel?"

"That's what everyone's calling me." I let the duffel rest on the permacrete as I blotted my forehead. I'd forgotten how hot true summers could be. I'd never known how heavy full gravity felt after three years in null gravity.

"Hop in, ser. I'll run you over to the transient quarters. They're expecting you."

I set the duffel on the cart floor behind the first two seats and eased my too-heavy body into the seat beside the driver. The deep breath as I sat was in spite of my efforts not to sound like a stuffed boar.

"Even with nanite support, the first month's hard. How long have you been off-planet?"

"Three years personal objective, more than four elapsed time."

"They must have sent you a long ways." As she spoke, she eased the cart out of the shade and along the stone lane.

"Omega Eridani." The sun smote me like a wall of fire, and my eyes slitted involuntarily. Even so, I could make out the half-remembered two-storied long structures with smoothly finished stone half walls topped with metal-and-glass window panels and glistening gray slate roofs. The antennas on several, especially those of the operations building we had left, glittered in the full sun.

"There's logistics," offered the driver. "Trans quarters are just ahead, on the left there."

The transient quarters had no shaded overhang, and I continued to sweat as I carried my duffel into the front foyer. Finally, sighting an open door, I trudged toward it, having to make an effort to lift my feet.

The blocky blond woman who stood as I peered through the door was familiar, and I searched for her name. "Ah . . . Thaya. I'm Tyndel, and I've been sent here."

"Again," she confirmed with a warm smile that was also slightly sardonic. "Cerrelle said you'd do it all the hard way."

"She was right." I lowered the duffel.

"I see you've got your schedule. Come on. Let's get you to your quarters before you fall over." She stepped around and started down the corridor.

I followed, less expeditiously. Climbing the one flight of stairs wasn't agony, but scarcely pleasant, either. She held the door open as I staggered into the sitting room and study and set down the duffel that no longer felt particularly light.

"Same as before. There are candidate greens in the closet, to your measure, as well as exercise clothes and a few other necessities. Your quarters and food here at Runswi are paid by the Authority. Your stipend goes to your free balance. You pay for anything else out of that. You need anything else, see me or Yrila—she's my assistant."

"Yrila . . ." I mumbled. My mouth was dry. "Thank you." Free balance—I'd almost forgotten about that. I hadn't even cared when I'd been in Runswi before. Did I have a balance? I could worry about that later.

"You've got two hours to rest. Then you'll go to the pool." She paused. "Do you recall where that is?"

"No. I didn't use it before." I forced a grin. "I didn't get that far."

"It's on the map, about two hundred meters south of here. Start early so that you can take your time. You'll spend a lot of time there for the first month. Believe me, it feels better than walking around. Then they'll really start the physical conditioning program."

I sank into the straight-backed chair before the built-in data console.

Thaya shook her head. "Two hours."

"I know." The words came out like a groan.

"It's too bad you had to do it the hard way, Tyndel."

There hadn't been any other choice for me. So I just nodded as Thaya closed the door and left me.

As before, the two rooms and a refresher that I got were comfortable and large, especially compared to the cube I'd had on OE Station. And I could barely wait for Thaya to leave so that I could stretch out on the bed.

One thing bothered me as I stood and walked slowly into the bedroom, where I sat on the edge of the bed. Cerrelle or Andra could have had the cart meet me at the shuttle, short as the walk had been. Why hadn't they? Because they wanted me to understand what terrible condition I was in? Had I been that difficult before?

I pulled off my boots and laid back.

Yes, came the answer before my eyes closed.

48

All life is structure.

The late summer rain fell like cool steam across Runswi, except where the fine droplets struck the permacrete of the magshuttle landing strip. There, hot fog from the strip rose to meet the sultry mist that seeped downward from the thick gray clouds, following the rain.

I walked slowly toward the logistics building and my first nanite indoc or briefing since I'd returned. Ten days of mainly physical therapy—interspersed with tests designed to measure something about my mind and personality—had left my legs much stronger. I'd actually come to enjoy the work in the pool.

For the first time since I'd returned to Runswi, I finally met Andra—in the logistics building. Her pale gray eyes were flat as she studied me.

"Greetings," I offered.

"Greetings, Tyndel. Are you willing to work . . . this time? You're not going to oppose what we're trying to do?"

Oppose? I remembered Fersonne's words—"Why don't you do something because you want to, not because you're opposing something else?" Then I nodded. "No . . . I mean, I'll be working."

"Good. The first briefing spray will be the same as the last one you had. We'll need to check the retention level." A brief smile crossed her narrow lips. "That will also make it easier for you to get back into the feel of training." She stood and walked through another door, into a small room, as she had years before, and lifted one of the canisters.

My eyes went to the large metalicized plastic screen on the wall. I'd forgotten about the collection systems.

"We'll give you the basic technology again." Andra lifted the canister. I'd forgotten the scoop shaped to fit a human face. "You shouldn't have trouble with this. It's just the simplified theories behind the technology you'll need to be using."

The scoop felt cool against my skin, cooler when the mist permeated my face. I still sensed thousands of tiny needles penetrating my skull. Then came the rush of phrases, terms, and definitions mixed with interrelated equations . . .

. . . xenon discharge . . . elevates atoms . . . wave forms above the quark level . . . creating two phased photons and a cascade effect down a crystalline channel . . . parallel wave forms pass through openings the same size as their wavelengths . . . diffraction occurs . . . intensity drops inversely as the square of the distance . . . color does not exist except as a perception of different wavelengths . . . failure of initial fusactor technology lay in unstated assumption that no wavefield interference would occur from plasma and magfields, despite superconductivity . . . deuterium and tritium resonance on the quantal level . . . maximum span potential directly proportional to the strength to mass/weight ratio of materials . . .

Her eyes on the screen beside the plastic collector, Andra nodded. "Not bad." She motioned for me to follow, then walked into the adjoining room, the one with windows. "You remember this. Sit down at the console. A question will scroll onto the screen. You search through the information you received and press the key that represents the most nearly correct answer. This will help you integrate what you've just received."

I nodded back and wondered if the first question would be the one about light.

She looked at me, then left.

The first question was: "Light can most nearly be described as which of the following?"

As before, when I thought about light, information flooded through me, but less overwhelmingly than four years earlier. Half-familiar as the questions were, I was still staggering mentally when I completed the exercises on the console.

Andra appeared almost immediately after I selected the last answer, beckoning me back into the nanite spray room. With rubbery knees, I followed.

"From here on in, based on the test analyses, what you get will be different from the last time." She lifted another canister and pressed the scoop to my face.

The second blast of information was more soul-shivering . . . far more.

. . . *invariance translations . . . result in no changes in charge conjugation, rotation, or transformation . . . modification of the real space inversion in dimension "n" of the multiverse . . . equivalent to the curvature of overspace . . . requiring spinless state . . . conservation of parity . . . not apply with weak interactions or under overspace inversion insertion . . . apparent suspension of parity selection "rules" and potential frame cascade . . .*

The definitions and equations and explanations went on and on—and kept going.

Andra took my arm to steady me but said nothing, guiding me back to the windowed room and the waiting console.

She left once more, and I held my head in my hands, trying to keep it from falling off, for a time before I glanced at the message on the console screen.

"Describe in simple terms the theory which allows needle ships to employ overspace translations to cross interstellar distances in apparent contradiction of light-speed constraints. When ready, press the *speech* stud and talk distinctly."

I looked at the question again. I hadn't been required to formulate answers before. Did that mean I was farther ahead? Or that they expected more as a result of my time on OE Station? Did the information I had received allow me to answer the question?

After searching and sweating, and moistening my lips, I finally began to talk, wishing I could have written it out first.

"Ah . . . the overspace translation system allows the needle ship to transverse overspace as a soliton . . ."

The screen blinked. "Please explain the theoretical basis of the system."

"Under normal space conditions all inertial space-time coordinate frames are in uniform motion with relation to all others. In overspace, while the total motion of the coordinates must . . . balance . . ." I paused, knowing my paraphrasing of highly technical theories was probably so simple as to be totally wrong, then plunged on. "Direction and time may vary inversely, allowing a greater distance to be covered in less elapsed time than in normspace."

The screen remained blank for a moment, then scripted, "At how many points must a partially curved frame over-space-time surface intersect real time?"

I punched the letter beside the answer indicating none.

"What is the optimal interrelation between real-space velocity and overspace insertion velocity?"

I wiped my forehead. This was the beginning? The next question wasn't any better. Nor the one after that.

After the last question of more inquiries than I wanted to count, I put my head down in my hands and closed my eyes.

"Tyndel?"

I looked up.

"That's all for today. Nine hundred tomorrow. Ileck is expecting you at the pool." The pale gray eyes offered neither sympathy nor disgust . . . just a trace of amusement.

I stood. "Can you tell me what I have to look forward to? And how long?"

"In general terms"—Andra frowned—"no Web pilot or

needle jockey is trained exactly like any other, not until you get to Web bugs and shiphandling. Then it gets pretty standard, I'm told. Our job here is to get you ready for that." She paused. "You're weak on the concepts, but your sense of logic and organization is strong. That's the Dzin. If you stay on path, we'll finish with your basic structuring and indoctrination in another month." She nodded. "Then you can start learning what you'll really need to know."

"This is all material that any Rykashan should know? Right now?"

She shook her head. "Any well-educated Rykashan."

At least I'd end up a well-educated Rykashan, even if I didn't turn out as a needle ship pilot.

"You can be a pilot. You have the skills. Whether you have the mental toughness is another question."

"Is this all just for education? For what I don't know?"

"No." A faint smile appeared, and I had hope that someday she might regard me as more than a spoiled Dzin master. "Do you still have the feeling that you know something and yet you don't—all at the same time?"

I had to nod to that. "Not so much anymore."

She laughed. "That will get worse as you learn and apply more knowledge. Some of what we do won't seem to have much to do with training. It's designed to integrate knowledge and experience from all data inputs."

"It's going to be a long fall."

"And a long winter," Andra promised. "Now . . . you're going to be late for physical training."

So I stood and headed for the pool.

49

The effective use of symbolism is a key with knife edges.

In chest-deep water I leaned against the side of the swimming pool, my forehead against the cool black tile, panting, trying to recover from swimming several hundred meters at full speed.

"Better." At close to two meters tall, with golden bronze skin, jet-black hair and eyes, Ileck was the image of a prestabilization god. He was also the taskmaster set to recondition me. "In another month, you'll be able to go twice as far—say, eight hundred meters—at a sprint."

I nodded, not looking up, waiting for the queasiness to subside.

"When you're ready, come on down to the deep end."

I finally heaved myself out of the water and padded along the side of the pool, the dampness of my footprints lost on the gritty surface of the black composite that composed the deck of the enclosed pool. The water looked black as well.

Ileck handed me a singlesuit that had seen better days and pointed to a pair of boots on the pool deck. "If you would put them both on . . ."

I began to pull on the suit, glancing at the apparatus that now spanned the deep end of the pool. A polished wooden beam ran between two pedestals—one on each side of the pool, a distance of more than ten meters. Each pedestal was three steps high. The beam—less than ten centimeters wide—was a good two meters above the water—and the water depth was at least five meters. After the suit came the boots.

Ileck looked at me. "You're going to walk across that."

Fair enough. I started toward the pedestal before me.

"No . . . not like that." He held up a blindfold. "You get up on the second step, and then I'll fasten this in place."

Walk the beam blindfolded?

"This is just the beginning," Ileck added.

Keeping my thoughts about that buried, I stepped up and waited as he fastened it across my eyes. "What might be the reason . . . ?"

"Symbolic analogue. You're better off if you don't know much beyond that yet: I'd appreciate it if you didn't ask."

From his tone I could tell I'd be seeing more symbolic analogues, even if I had no idea what their purpose might be. The old Dzin philosophy insisted that true ignorance was far superior to shallow knowledge. I smiled wryly. I was truly ignorant at the moment.

"Try to sense the beam, to visualize where it is. Take your time."

Take my time? I certainly would.

I felt for the beam with my left boot, and it slid. The beam surface was as slick as wet glass or oiled tile. Slowly, I eased my left foot onto what I felt was a centered position before shifting my weight onto it. I could feel the sweat forming on my forehead, then slowly oozing down my back. I repeated the maneuver with my right booted foot. Foot by foot I struggled across the beam, a beam that neither flexed nor bent.

By the time I managed to get all the way across, if wobbling several times, I was soaked with sweat. On the other side I stopped and reached for the blindfold.

"Turn around and start back."

"Now?"

"Now."

Slowly, I turned.

Not three steps had I taken when a blast of trumpets shivered the air around me, almost palpably pushing me sideways. I shifted my weight, but I was too off-balance and—rather than plunge awkwardly—I stepped sideways and pointed my booted feet, dropping past the beam.

The blindfold ripped off as I plunged into the cool water, and I bobbed to the surface and swam toward the side where Ileck waited. The drag of the wet singlesuit and the waterlogged boots turned a decent overarm crawl into an elbow-dragging, pseudopaddle.

"Climb out. You need to try it again." Ileck gestured.

My exit from the dark water was graceless and left puddles of water along the black composite. Ileck had another blindfold waiting. I wiped water from my face and stood on the step pedestal and let him fasten it again.

"You have to concentrate on where *you* are, Tyndel. This is not a meaningless exercise."

None of what the demons did was meaningless. Frustrating, exhausting, difficult, but never without meaning. I stepped onto the beam once more.

In the middle of my very first step, instruments of all types—horns, strings, harps, and drums—as well as tones I'd never heard, assailed me. I staggered but managed to put my foot down on the glass-smooth surface of the beam despite the power of the music. It was music, not cacophony, though I had never heard its like before.

With my second step, the music swirled into a dance of some sort, and my third brought a ballad, faintly familiar. Although the beam remained firm, my legs trembled with each step and the variation in music volume.

Salty sweat built up under the blindfold, and my eyes burned with the last few steps before I felt the pedestal underfoot.

"Good," declared Ileck. "You can take off the blindfold."

I almost shook myself as I stood there, blotting the sweat from my eyes.

Ileck stood below me, his eyes level with mine, holding a stained grayish canvas pack filled with something. He lifted it easily and extended it to me. "Here. Put it on."

So heavy was the pack—a good fifty kilograms—I

nearly dropped it, and holding on to the straps left me teetering on the edge of the pedestal and struggling not to topple into the water below. After straightening, I struggled into the straps, pulling them in place over the wet green singlesuit. My feet were not unwelcomely cool inside the soaked leather boots.

"Turn around." Ileck had another blindfold in his hand.

I blotted my eyes dry, then turned. He fastened the blindfold in place.

"Start across."

I managed two steps before a wall of sound—an ancient organ as loud as a shuttle first breaching the atmosphere?—slammed me off balance, and the weight of the pack toppled me into the dark water below. Swimming to the edge was a true struggle with the weight on my back, but I knew that was part of whatever Ileck had in mind.

"You need to try again." That was all he said.

I clambered out of the pool and trudged to the pedestal steps once more, where I handed him the soaking blindfold. Silently, he replaced it. For symbolic analogues, he was certainly putting a great deal of verisimilitude into my training.

It took two more attempts before I could get across with the heavy pack on my back against the walls and arrows of music and sound.

"Be careful this time," Ileck said after the successful effort.

I turned and took a step.

Not only did an off-tempo march with volume enough to shiver my very skull strike me with the first step, but my second was greeted with a beam of heat that seemed to sear me, followed as quickly by a gust of ice-chilled air that felt as though it froze my soaked singlesuit to my skin. My fourth step took me into the water, colder by far, or so it felt, than earlier.

I had to hang on to the edge of the pool for a time before I could pull myself out.

"Once more," insisted Ileck, his voice impassive.

I made one more slow trip across the slick beam carrying the heavy pack, assaulted by music and other sounds, and the heat and chill. My knees trembled, and moving each leg had gotten to be agony.

At the other side, Ileck waited, as usual. "That is enough for today."

I took a deep breath. "Thank you."

He smiled, almost ironically. "This is the beginning."

The way I felt, I didn't ask exactly what I was beginning.

Below, in the locker room, I took an old-fashioned hot shower, luxuriating in the steam, before I dried and dressed in my pale green singlesuit. Then I walked slowly to the nearest lounge, since the dining area in the transient quarters was somehow depressing.

The lounge held five tables widely spaced, all of dark oak, polished, bound at the edges in shimmering brass. The dark oak chairs also were brass bound, with a dark gold and blue brocade over the upholstered seats.

After scanning the menu on the reformulator, I picked both the Serian chicken and the Dorchan hot noodles and a mixed fruit salad, with Arleen tea. I'd eaten about half of the enormous meal when a woman in green and silver walked into the lounge, followed by a wide-eyed younger woman with braided hair coiled at the back of her head. The wide-eyed one was scarcely more than a youngster.

The Rykashan glanced at me, taking in my pale green singlesuit, and murmured to the girl. "He's a Web pilot trainee. You can tell by the light green of the suit and by the eyes. You'll learn more about Web jockeys later. Very respected . . . Now, this is a lounge. Anyone can eat here . . ."

I sipped the last of the Arleen tea in the mug, then rose to get another.

The woman—dressed in the same deeper green that Cerrelle had worn—did not look up, but kept talking to her charge. "Runswi is very different from Dezret . . . women are equal . . . women administrators, pilots, and specialists . . . have you meet Alicia deSchmidt sometime. You'll see."

I took the tea and returned to my table. Alicia de-Schmidt—for a moment I tried to recall the name, then nodded to myself—the dark-haired and erotically graceful special operative who had driven a metal knife through the table—perhaps the one at which I now sat. Glancing toward the door, I almost expected her to appear. Or Cerrelle.

After more than two months, I still hadn't seen Cerrelle. Part of that time, I'd been too tired even to think about much more than getting through the day. Belatedly, I recalled Fersonne's words. "Rykashans are stubborn, too . . ."

Cerrelle had come across a chunk of the Galaxy to check on me . . . and I'd dismissed her. Now I expected she would seek me out? I found myself shaking my head. "You hoped? Think a bit more, Tyndel—and sooner."

I swallowed the last of the Arleen. In the end, I was going to have to eat sour eel. I hoped I could manage it.

On the way back to my quarters, I turned toward the logistics building, pausing for a moment to watch the near-silent approach of a magshuttle shining silver in the afternoon light. Clouds were gathering to the west, just above the trees that marked the horizon.

Once the shuttle dropped behind the building, I entered and stepped up to the information console, behind which sat a slender young woman in silver with blue-striped sleeves.

"Yes, ser?"

"Ah . . . this is going to sound unintelligent, but I'd like to know how I might get in contact with someone in Lyncol."

"Not at all." She laughed generously, and despite her girlish appearance, the laugh was that of a woman, yet not at all malicious. "They teach you candidates everything but the important matters. You're far from the first to ask something like that." A smile followed. "All you need is the person's name and personal code. If you don't have their personal code, you can link to information and describe what they do if you know, or where they live, and see if you can obtain their professional locator code. That's not a personal code, but you can leave a message with their outlink, and they can get back to you. You have to leave your name and code, of course."

My code? I didn't even know I had one. I frowned, then nodded. I knew, somewhere in the depths of information that had flooded through me over the past years, but I'd never needed to call it up.

"Any console will give you access to the link. When you get farther along, you'll be able to access the system directly." She gave another smile. "Does that help?"

"Thank you." I returned the smile and walked down the side corridor, hoping to find Andra. Her door was open, and her eyes widened as I peered in.

"Andra?"

"You don't have another session until tomorrow."

"I know. I had another kind of question." I found myself looking down at the polished natural wood floor of her work space.

"Which is?"

"I was hoping you might have one of the codes I could use to contact Cerrelle, or at least leave a message."

"After two months?" Andra raised her eyebrows.

I forced a laugh, tasting the bitterness of sour eel as I did. "I never said I was perceptive. Nor did Cerrelle, I think. I need to apologize. It's late, but I need to."

"You're right about that." Almost without pausing, she added, "Her personal code is LY-green-forty-four."

"Thank you." LY-green-forty-four—I concentrated on holding that.

"Tyndel?" The words were softer than the flinty expression in Andra's eyes.

"Yes?"

"Cerrelle's my friend, and you have not been that helpful. Nor kind. Nor even close to understanding. She tried very hard for you, perhaps harder than you know."

"I know."

"Please try to remember that."

"I will." Forgetting it would have been hard. I nodded again. "Thank you."

"I'll see you tomorrow." The door closed.

I walked through the afternoon heat, past an electrocart carrying a group of pale-faced and sweating individuals who had obviously just come off the shuttle that had landed earlier.

Not understanding, not kind, not helpful—and Andra was right. I hoped I could stand the taste of all the eel I was planning to swallow.

For a long time, I sat at the console in my quarters, ignoring the supplementary reading Andra had recommended, just looking blankly at the screen itself, on which images appeared and vanished, images of mountain peaks, then of lakes. I'd selected the images, but I suddenly wondered why I'd chosen lakes and mountains.

As the late-afternoon clouds rolled across the sun, and rain began to patter down outside my room, I turned to the screen and tapped in the codes.

An image flashed onto the screen—that of a thin-faced redhead with piercing eyes.

I opened my mouth, but the image was faster.

"This is Cerrelle. Please let me know you linked."

After a moment, I finally spoke. "Cerrelle . . . this is Tyndel . . . I'd like the chance to apologize. If you don't wish to speak to me, I understand." I paused. "You were right . . . and thank you." I swallowed and broke the link.

Sour eel didn't taste that good, either literally or figuratively, especially since I'd had to taste it twice so far, with Andra and then Cerrelle's link answerer, without even talking to Cerrelle.

I rose and got a mug full of Arleen from the formulator downstairs.

Then I accessed the first of the supplemental readings. Andra had insisted that the more I read, the faster the nanite-supplied information would meld into an integrated mental database—or whatever organic equivalent that meant for the brain of a man who had been born a mite and re-created as a Rykashan demon.

I looked at the words as they appeared. Sometimes, material in the manuals or from the nanospray briefings sounded perfectly logical but left me no wiser. This was another case in point.

> The limits of nanite-based AI capabilities are determined largely by the specifications of the applicable conglomeration/agglutination blocks . . . function as synaptic limits . . . work of Foulst and Henrica to remove second-level blocs . . . eventually led to development of functional overspace translation insertion systems . . .
>
> . . . first-level blocs encoded within actual leptonic spins . . .

That made no sense at all, and I took another sip of Arleen. Andra had told me that some of the material would probably be beyond my current understanding but not to stop at everything I didn't comprehend, since the breadth of what I read was as important as the depth.

About that, I wasn't sure, but the console reference section didn't have anything on first-level agglutination blocs.

I took another sip of tea and went back to the supplemental readings, trying not to wonder if Cerrelle would return the call.

50

When the symbolic images developed by the society no longer work, and the images which do work are not those of the society, the individual has nowhere to turn.

After a particularly long afternoon with Ileck, I made my way to one of the lounges, the one overlooking the section of the marsh that resembled a lake, where the open water glinted blue-gray and seabirds wheeled in off the ocean. Some long-legged plovers or rails or something strutted along the small sandbar I could see through the wide window that flanked my table. A turtle lounged on a wide root in the warm sunlight of fall. Behind the turtle was a spit of land that held mostly bushes, except for a stand of a dozen trees, pseudomangroves whose roots arched down into the water.

One helping of the chilled crayfish wasn't enough. So I took my tray back to the formulator and punched in another order and took another cup of steaming Arleen tea. Then I turned, and she was there, so close to me that I couldn't move, not without bumping into her.

"You come here a lot, don't you?" asked the young woman. "You always sit alone." Her eyes were open wide, a deep guileless brown, under an unlined brow. Her sandy hair was short, and she had small ears with almost no lobes. Her narrow face angled from high fine cheek-bones to a gently pointed chin. Her lips were almost too full for the elfin face.

"I'm too tired to go far," I said, accepting the flattery of her approach and glad for company for at least a time. "Would you like to join me?"

"Are you sure? I wouldn't want . . . I mean . . . you must have a lot to do."

"Not at the moment." I paused. "What would you like?"

"Oh . . . I can get it myself."

I stepped back, careful not to brush against her, especially since her red-cuffed silver singlesuit was somewhat more than formfitting.

After a minute or so, the reformulator blinked. She slipped what looked to be a beer and a plate of noodles and sauce onto a tray. I smiled and gestured toward the table, then followed her, standing until she sat. I eased the tray back onto the table and glanced outside.

The light across the water had become more golden, not quite sunset but getting close.

"It's pretty here. Sometimes, I just sit and watch as the sun goes down." She turned in her chair and faced me. "I'm Aleyaisha. I work in the medical section for doctor Bekunin."

Bekunin—the name was familiar, but I couldn't recall why. "I'm Tyndel. I'm a trainee of sorts."

"You're going to be a needle pilot, aren't you?" The eyes widened more as she looked directly at me. "I mean . . . you wear the light green, and no one else besides . . ." As her words trailed off, she moistened her lips.

"I'm trying." I gave a soft laugh. "That's up to other powers." She wasn't that guileless, and yet she was somehow embarrassed. I wondered why.

Aleyaisha nodded, then twirled the pasta deftly around a fork and cut it with the side of a large spoon. She ate neatly, and not a dab of the cream sauce strayed from the pasta or her mouth.

Two women walked past on their way to the formulator. One was thin-faced and black-haired, with pinched lips, the other brunette and more ample. Both wore silver with full red sleeves. The brunette swayed as she walked. The thin-faced one glanced at Aleyaisha and gave the faintest of headshakes.

"Do you think you'll like being in space?" Aleyaisha

asked as though she hadn't seen the disgusted look offered by the thin-faced woman, and she might not have.

"I've been there. I was a low-technician on an outspace orbit station for a while." I took a mouthful of chilied crayfish.

"You were? What was that like?"

Again, I had the feeling that she knew more than she was saying, but a gust of warm air swept over us as two men entered the lounge, glancing around.

The taller man's eyes spotted the women who had come in earlier. "They're over there, Haifez."

". . . could have waited for us . . ." Haifez snorted.

The taller man, fresh-faced and in maroon, a color I hadn't seen before in a singlesuit, passed us on his way toward the pair at the table.

". . . know her," murmured Haifez. "Works in medical . . . wouldn't even look at me."

"That's the way it goes . . . candidate, not even a needle jock yet, and they're hanging on him."

I tried not to flush at the taller man's comment.

"He wasn't very interesting." Aleyaisha smiled at me. "Do you have a lot of other women who hang on you?"

"I don't think anyone hangs on me," I admitted. "No one that I know."

"Look!" Aleyaisha's whisper was intense, and I followed her finger.

A great blue heron had swooped down to stand, first on two feet, then one, in the shallows beyond the mangrove spit. So still he might have been a statue, the heron waited. The light flooding across the marsh lake from the west grew more orange-golden, and the heron remained motionless. The shadow cast by the lounge inched across the water toward the mangroves.

Flick! The heron's bill stabbed and came up. Impaled on it was a shimmering sliver of silver that twitched once before the heron gulped it down.

"You see why I like it at this time of day?" Aleyaisha smiled impishly.

Since I was chewing crayfish, I nodded.

"There's always something. Last winter, when there was ice on the edge of the water, I saw a pair of black swans. They had red bills."

Last winter I had been . . . where? OE Station? Or had I lost the end of winter to the time dilation of overspace travel? "Do you think they'll return?"

"They might. I'd like to see them again." She took a small sip of the dark beer, then a second.

The two couples at the table farthest from us laughed, loudly, and I hoped the sound didn't carry beyond the permaglass and send the heron flying.

". . . birds . . . get him with birds."

"Why not? He's another kind of bird . . . flies the overspace . . . think they're little engees . . . most do." .

I winced.

"Don't listen to them," Aleyaisha suggested. "They're jealous."

"All of them?"

"The women wish they had the nerve to talk to you. The men are angry because you can do things they can't."

"Everyone can do something unique." I sipped the last of the second mug of Arleen.

"There aren't many needle pilots."

"How many are there?" I wondered if she knew or would tell me.

"According to the medical records, right now there are ninety-three active needle pilots. There are four they could recall."

"Ninety-three?" I couldn't believe that. The Rykashans had almost two dozen outspace colonies or stations serving planets being planoformed into something habitable. Then I wondered how she knew.

"You'll be the ninety-fifth if no one goes off active status. There's one in flight training at Orbit Station."

I frowned. I suppose I could have tracked the information—or maybe I couldn't have—but the thought that there were so few had never occurred to me. "Is that because we don't need any more?"

Aleyaisha shook her head. "The skills are rare."

Rare? How rare? Rare enough to justify structuring a death to coerce me? I felt small at the thought, *knowing* that was something none of the Rykashans I had met would do. For a time, I sat there. The four in the corner rose and left, and shadows covered the water outside, all the way to the mangroves.

She finally broke the stillness. "They say you were a Dzin master. Is that true?"

"I studied Dzin and might have been a master, in time." I thought about the words and added. "I thought so then. Now, I don't know."

"You would have been."

"I don't know."

I knew I could have invited her back to my quarters. Although holding and touching her would have warmed an empty evening, whenever she had left, both the evening—or morning—and I would have been far emptier. Emptier than the darkness around OE Station or than my soul on the day when I had fled Hybra.

She wanted something, not an image, but perhaps to console me, and I wanted to be consoled—but not out of pity. It had to be out of honesty, and the only ones who could have done that were Foerga and Fersonne . . . and Cerrelle, except she wouldn't have wanted to, and I couldn't blame her.

Honesty demanded that I be more than an image, more than an image to myself. So I smiled. "I'm glad you wanted to talk. Maybe . . . another time."

She smiled back, not quite sadly. "Another time."

We walked in different directions, and I stayed up later than I should have, poring over Andra's supplemental readings, readings that never quite answered as many questions as they raised, occasionally half wondering about why Aleyaisha had really sought me out, but not sure I wanted to look that deeply.

Vanity? My lips twisted into a smile of sardonic self-awareness. *You're afraid it's all professional, and you want to hang on to the illusion that you're personally attractive to someone?*

I knew the answer to that question.

51

[RUNSWI: 4519]

Do not seek truth through brighter light or inspection of appearances.

With the scoop's cool surface barely against my face, Andra touched the canister stud, and the nanoneedles slipped under my skin, ferrying yet more raw information to various neurons and structures within my skull.

Engineering, this time, I thought, my eyes looking over the gray edge of the scoop at the scene beyond the window, the west side of the operations building lit by the crisp sunlight of late autumn and the high clouds beyond that promised a thundershower by evening.

. . . potential interaction of sublimation pressure with molecularly compressed inert pseudometals (composite) . . . avoided by formation under high-temperature multiple-gee-force containment . . . use of discharge nozzle to maintain ionic supercriticality to maximum duration . . . plastic deformation of composite occurs . . . difference between maximum and minimum principal stresses equals twice the yield stress in shear . . .

As the images and words, and equations and phrases, swept over and through me, I couldn't help but feel that engineering was different. Unlike the physics and the theories, where the words had been initially as unfamiliar as the meanings they conveyed, in engineering I thought I knew all the words—but the way in which they were used made them a different tongue entirely.

Andra stepped away, but the faint fragrance of flowers I did not recognize lingered for a few moments. Half bemused by the floral scent and thoughts of engineering terms, I stood and followed Andra into the adjoining room and the all-too-familiar console.

"You know what to do," she said.

I nodded as I seated myself.

The console scripted: "Which of the following most closely approximates the process for producing interstellar-grade composite?"

Each of the answers was more than a paragraph long, and I had to reread each twice and then pore through the newest mass of information spinning within my skull. I touched the console, and the next question appeared.

When I finally sat back from the screen, morning had vanished with the fall sun starting its descent into afternoon. My eyes were blurred, and my head ached.

Andra reappeared.

"Not bad. The engineering section is hard for most pilots."

"It's the use of familiar words in an unrelated context."

"You're eloquent, Tyndel."

"I wish I were." My fingers massaged my forehead, and I closed my eyes for a few moments. "This all seems endless."

"You'll be finished here—with the information and indoctrination—before Ileck finishes your physical conditioning and readiness. You're a natural, Tyndel." Andra shook her head, and the reddish blond hair rippled. "I've had astroengineers who didn't pick up understandings the way you do. Why did you fight it?"

"It wasn't the knowledge." I felt like shrugging but didn't. "I've always enjoyed learning about things."

"You don't mind hard work, either. The reports from OE Station confirm that." She stepped back. "I won't pry." A half grin followed. "Not more than I have already."

"They sent reports to you?"

"Not until you'd returned."

"Has anyone else—any other Dzin type—refused training and changed his mind?"

"It's happened. Not recently."

"That's because you don't get many refugees anymore, not Dzin types," I countered. *Nor that many possible pilots.*

"You could be dangerous, Tyndel, if you used your brain more." Andra gave me a faint smile. A grin and a smile in the same session—far more than she usually expressed.

"I am working on it."

"Good. Until tomorrow." With that, she was gone.

I didn't have time to walk to the lounge and then back to the pool. That meant I had to hurry to get something to eat at the transient quarters. Besides, while I wasn't avoiding Aleyaisha, I didn't want to give the impression of courting her, either. So I settled on my usual standby when I really didn't know what I wanted—Dorchan orange strip beef with flat noodles and Arleen. I only ate enough to dull the edge of hunger, knowing my stomach wouldn't take more with what Ileck had in mind. The second mug of tea was rushed.

When I reached the pool in my swimming briefs, Ileck—impassive as always—was waiting, black-booted feet standing on the black composite deck. The exercise singlesuit and boots, and the heavy and weighted canvas pack, were waiting for when I finished swimming laps.

"First, your warm-up exercises. Then . . . the weights. After that, sixteen hundred meters, four hundred fast, four hundred slow, four hundred fast, two hundred slow, and the last two hundred a sprint."

I took a deep breath, recalling how pointless I'd thought the lap swimming on my first indoctrination to Runswi. Now I was one of those undertaking such exercise. I had to admit that it was better than wrestling SARMs in null gravity on OE Station. I hadn't forgotten the sweat and the grittiness seeping into every pore on my face—and all the bruises I'd garnered from bumping into interdeck beams.

The warm-up exercises and the weight training ended too soon, and I was swimming lap after endless lap through the clear but black-tinted water. Much later, after the long, too long, sixteen hundred meters, I slumped against the black tiles of the side of the pool.

"Come on, Tyndel. The real work starts now."

I could hardly wait, but I dragged myself out of the water and pulled on the suit and boots, then shouldered the pack. "No blindfold?"

"You'll wish you had one," Ileck promised with a grin that faded. "Up on the pedestal."

I was the one who raised his eyebrows, but I doubt Ileck saw the gesture because he touched the portable console he held. The entire pool area turned black, so dark I couldn't have seen my hand if I'd touched my nose with it.

"Go on." Ileck's voice vibrated the darkness, creating an even deeper blackness than the sightless black that enfolded me. Blacker than black isn't possible, but that was the niellen depth that I experienced.

I glanced down. The beam displayed the faintest line of luminescence, but a shimmering length that illuminated nothing else. I felt suspended in nothingness. If I'd been in null gravity, I could have been in starless space, except I wore no outside suit and the air was far too warm.

I edged my left foot forward, a black blot on the shining line that cast no radiance. My whole body wobbled. I paused, concentrating on what I felt, knowing that I was more sightless than if I'd worn a blindfold.

"Don't close your eyes," Ileck ordered.

I could feel myself flushing in the darkness, since I'd been contemplating just that.

The sound of ragged trumpets thrust at me, and, this

time, actual notes half shaped like spears flashed toward me from the left. I winced, then tottered, trying to catch my balance. Abruptly, the deep bass of the ancient organ-like sound rumbled from the other side, and a rectangle, luminous and knife-edged, swept toward me from the right.

A hot wall of air—or something—shoved at my back, and I did lose my balance. All I'd taken had been three steps before I plunged into the dark water.

I convulsed at the electriclike shock of hitting the water. *That* hadn't happened before, but neither had I been assaulted by shapes and actual musical notes before, either.

Abruptly, the darkness vanished, as did the electric knives within the water.

Ileck stood at the edge of the pool. "Get out. Try from the other side."

Soaking wet, I heaved myself out of the water and trudged around to the other pedestal, the pack spewing water down the back of the singlesuit's legs, my feet squushing in the wet boots.

Ileck waited until I reached the top of the pedestal, where the smooth and narrow surface of the beam stretched before me and across the black waters below. Water oozed down my back as blackness closed around me, and the beam glimmered before me.

The first step was easy enough, for there was silence before the roaring of thunder, and the rush of surf segued into some sort of massive chorus supported by hundreds of instruments with explosions in the background. I took a second step, then a third, against the pressure of the music, ignoring the cubes that flashed at my face.

The scent of lilacs, impossibly powerful, smothered me, nearly gagged me, and I found myself tottering on the beam once more. I did straighten, just in time to hold against another gentle but unseen cold pressure accompanying a spearlike blade that knifed upward from below, seeming out of the black depths beneath me. The wince that my body gave was enough to unbalance me into the water.

As I struggled to the black-tiled edge of the pool and slowly extricated myself, Ileck laughed. "Never met a male needle jockey yet who didn't flinch at a thrust to the groin. The first time, anyway."

Not for the first time, I wondered about my reconsideration of being a needle ship pilot. They called what I was undergoing basic orientation and indoctrination. I decided not to think about what came next. Back to the first pedestal I walked, the boots heavier than ever.

Ileck waited until I stood before the beam once more.

When the blackness again swept across the pool and me, trumpets blasted so loudly they shivered my eardrums and spine. With the trumpets came the odor of sweet roses, and jagged-edged peaks seemed to march down from above, as if to crush me.

Heat and cold pressed from one side, then the other, but I edged along the beam until I reached the other side. Despite the damp singlesuit and waterlogged boots, sweat was flowing down my face, salty in my eyes, by the time I stood on the pedestal.

Light flooded across the pool area, so bright that my eyes watered. I stood very still on the pedestal. My knees were quivering.

"You made it." Ileck sounded as though my crossing were to be expected.

"For analogues, some of those felt and smelled rather more substantive than symbolic."

"They're supposed to, Tyndel. Being a needle pilot isn't sweet pastries, flowers, and music."

"I've gotten that idea." I tried not to grin, since Ileck's training seemed based on flowers, music, and geometric shapes with a definite kick.

"You need to start moving faster and more smoothly. You can't crawl with a ship on your back. Not in overspace."

"How much more do you plan to put me through?"

"You're coming along well. Not spectacularly, but well." Ileck lifted his well-muscled shoulders. "Don't ask me to predict. You still have trouble screening out certain emotional keys in the music, and that could be a problem."

"Why?"

"Because a Web pilot is the ship. Without emotion, you can't employ full-body intelligence, but you have to harness emotion, not be harnessed by it." His lips closed firmly. "Tomorrow."

As I left the black deck and the dark water behind, I wondered how many tomorrows I had yet to face with the physical trainer, how much more he wanted from me.

With the rest of the late afternoon mine, after I cleaned up and changed back into my clothing, I walked eastward to the edge of the marsh that stretched beyond the permacrete transporter strip toward the ocean, farther to the east. The marsh wasn't Deep Lake or the Greening River or the Summer Sound at Mettersfel. The grasses were showing faint traces of brown, and the warm sun on my back was balanced by the cooler breeze on my face.

Why was I here? *Because too many people gave too much for you to give up?* I nodded to myself. Even with the knowledge that the Rykashans needed me, I still had trouble accepting the idea that I owed society. I had far less trouble believing I owed Foerga, or Fersonne, Sanselle, even Gerbriik and Cerrelle.

Except I had yet to hear from the red-haired Cerrelle, and that nagged at me. If she didn't return the link in another week, I'd try once more. *Why?*

Did I want to pursue that?

Because she tried to be honest with you without being nasty, and you need honesty more than you want to admit? Because you feel guilty because she reminded you of Foerga?

I turned and strolled slowly into the setting sun, back toward my temporary quarters. Then, I'd learned all quarters were temporary.

Ileck's comments about intelligence and emotion piqued my interest, and I wasn't sure I wanted to think too much about Cerrelle—not yet. So after I ate, I settled in front of the screen and began to access what I could.

. . . emotion . . . strong feelings based upon/arising from sensio-cerebral reaction or stimulus . . .

There was more, but the majority dealt with the cellular and glandular mechanics that created the transformation from the stimulus to physical reality.

Only one small paragraph grappled with what Ileck had suggested.

. . . measurements on the hormonal, electro-cellular, muscular, and brain wave functions have confirmed a clear, but nonlinear link between strength of emotional reactions to spacio-symbolic-abstract intelligence . . . development of either emotional reactivity or intelligence remains an intertwined function involving both genetic predilections and environment (see "nurture versus nature") . . .

The "nurture versus nature" section confirmed what had been known from the time of the ancients, that separation of the influence of environment and genetically based development was impossible in a practical and meaningful sense, and varied greatly from individual to individual and from environment to environment.

What about emotional reactions and reflexes? I tried the search functions again but came up with nothing.

In the end, I went back to reading the supplemental materials on Andra's list, wondering if Cerrelle would ever return my link effort. Then, I supposed she had no real reason to do so, not with the way I had behaved.

I concentrated on the words and phrases on the screen, just those words and phrases.

52

[RUNSWI: 4519]

The most absolute lie is the presentation of an irrefutable fact based on unassailable numbers.

Outside my window, left ajar for the cool air of the fall evening to seep in with the scents of leaves about to turn and the dampness of the not-too-distant marsh, insects chirped. Small creatures rustled through the brush to the rear of the quarters, all sounds I could not have heard five years earlier. Senses that were far better than those I had been born with were far easier to accept than the social structure that accompanied them, but I continued to struggle with both.

I sat at the console, eyes closed, yawning. I rubbed my forehead. The days continued to rush by, and my sessions with Andra had been spread out to every other day, while Ileck's training was increasing until it filled most of the daylight hours. That effort left me exhausted. The more I could do, the more he demanded. I was swimming over three thousand meters a day, half of it at sprint speeds, and lifting multiples of weights that would have had me confined in a demon cage in Dorcha. I continued to get soaked in the black pool by the assaults of ever more sophisticated sensory illusions and pressures, partly because Ileck insisted on my working up to running and stopping and other gymnasticlike maneuvers with the heavy pack on my back. The boosted shocks of hitting the black water were also stronger—much stronger.

With another yawn, I opened my eyes to see the screenborne images of mountain peaks and lakes that appeared and vanished, one replaced by another, all of them collected from the image library of the Rykashan data system, none of them familiar.

Aleyaisha's words of how many weeks before continued to trouble me, more than they had at first. Only ninety-three needle ship pilots, and one more ahead of me in training?

No one had said anything from the first day I'd returned to Runswi? Or had Aleyaisha been sent to let me know that and a few other things? To comfort me—or to see if I needed comforting? How would I find out? Did it really matter? Except that I was an extremely valuable commodity to the Rykashans. The problem was that they were treating me as more valuable than what I knew would make me, much more valuable.

I swallowed another yawn and tried several searches on the screen, tallying up the number of needle ships and the number of outspace stations and colonies. Sixty-one needle ships and five colonies, with another nine orbit stations serving worlds undergoing planoforming. One needle ship per objective quarter per station—perhaps only three a year for some stations.

I frowned. The numbers could be lower for stations other than OE Station—or higher.

The system had no information on ship departures or schedules, at least I couldn't find anything, but that clearly could have been my lack of knowing what keywords or fields to search. So I tried getting information on the ships I knew about—the *Hook*, the *Costigan*, the *Hay Needle*, the *Tailor*—setting the search based on their names. All that came up was a description of each—no schedules, not even when they had been built. I tried synonyms for "needle" and related terms, but only managed two more ships' names, the *Darning* and the *Tatter*. The descriptions were similar to those of the ships I'd known.

I shook my head. The Rykashan data system was totally open—and still restricted, since one had to know where to look.

Closing my eyes, I tried to concentrate on why the

numbers of ships and pilots bothered me. If the Rykashans trained two pilots a year, as they were, it would take nearly fifty years to have gotten ninety-three. Yet . . . Cerrelle had said that my obligation would only be ten years personal objective. Even with the time dilation factors, that made no sense. The Rykashans couldn't possibly keep the pilots they needed. Unless they were lying. Or unless they expected I would *want* to be a needle pilot well beyond the obligated service.

Cerrelle had never lied to me. Not that I knew. Nor had any demon type. That fact, combined with the numbers, sent a shiver through me. *But they haven't always told you everything . . .*

I finally touched the studs on the console and attempted to place another link to Cerrelle. Cerrelle and LY-green-forty-four—I'd held that separate from the flood of information that continued to inundate me. Why? Because I'd realized that she'd been the most honest from the first. Brutal, at times, but honest, too honest to let me deceive myself. And I was coming to recognize that for all the pretension, I was a self-deceiver. Maybe all intelligent creatures were. That I didn't know.

The familiar image dominated by piercing green eyes flashed onto the screen, breaking through my musing reverie. "This is Cerrelle. Please let me know you linked."

"Cerrelle . . . this is Tyndel. I didn't know if you got my last message, or if you're traveling somewhere. I still would like to apologize—in person." There wasn't much else appropriate to say on a link message, and after a moment of silence I broke the connection.

The succession of mountains and lakes reappeared on the screen. Although they looked familiar, when I studied them, they were not. That was life, looking familiar, but totally unknown when examined.

I turned off all the lights in my quarters, as well as the screen, then walked to the window and looked into the darkness outside—a grayish darkness, for the clouds had thickened, and not one star nor the moon was visible. Grayish darkness—was that what I was trying to pull my life from—and I hadn't even known it?

Ninety-three pilots, and I'd be the ninety-fifth?

53

[RUNSWI: 4519]

All that is material decays, unlike virtue and sincerity.

The tips of the marsh grasses beyond the lounge window were browning and ruffled in the wind that was raw in the misty and cloudy late afternoon. Two of the other tables were taken, one by a couple—both wearing the solid blue of senior administrators—and the other by two men in brown. The man and woman who were administrators kept their voices low. The other two did not.

". . . can't hold a flare to the Noctet . . ."

"Flare? How about a pinlight? Hierxal's got more assists with his left toe than the entire high line of Jynx . . ."

"High line . . . hardly . . ."

The conversation went on, but all I could tell from the context was that they were talking about some form of sporting contest—I thought. I'd chosen a lemongrass chicken from the formulator with brown rice and was halfway through it when Aleyaisha slid into the chair across the lounge table from me. She still wore silver and red, but the singlesuit was not nearly so tightly tailored. She still looked good, and her brown eyes were beautiful.

I waited for a moment before smiling. "You're the gentler, kinder approach?"

She flushed. "Tyndel, it's not exactly new. Cerrelle tried that, and you weren't exactly . . . receptive to information that conflicted with your biases."

"You're right, but most of you don't have to deal with having your entire life torn apart."

She looked down, the short sandy hair brushing the tops of her small ears.

"Would you like something to drink or eat?" I asked.

"I don't know."

"I still like you," I said. "I need friends."

"I like you, and I'm glad you didn't ask for more."

She would have given more, and that bothered me. "Get something to eat. I'm still hungry and have to get more anyway."

That got a faint smile. "I am hungry."

"Good."

The low sound of the wind whistling through the tall grasses sifted into the lounge as we stood and walked to the wall counters with the reformulators.

"What were you eating?" Aleyaisha glanced at my tray.

"Lemongrass chicken with brown rice and chili peppers."

"I think I'll stick to lobster and sweet butter with greens."

When we walked back to the table, I pulled out her chair and waited for her to seat herself.

"If you keep such courtesies, Tyndel, every unattached woman in Runswi will arrange to bump into you."

"Flattery . . ." I mumbled, aware that the two men at the table beyond the empty adjoining one were studying us.

". . . needle trainee . . . and look at her . . ."

". . . don't see why . . . gone half the time . . ."

"Maybe they're twice as good when they're home . . ."

Both men laughed.

I could feel my face redden. "You do bring me a certain . . . attention. This doesn't happen when you're not around."

"They were talking about you, Tyndel. Not me." She sipped the dark beer from the tall and fluted beaker. "I'm just another wanton woman throwing myself at a Web jockey." She grinned.

"Did you set up those couples who were here, too?"

"I didn't have to." She laughed warmly. "There really is a mystique about Web pilots. You'll see. There will be other women. They'll be far less restrained." She leaned across the table and looked soulfully into my eyes. "You really are a needle pilot . . . I've never known anyone like you . . ."

I had to laugh.

Aleyaisha straightened. "Andra was worried that you didn't have anyone to talk to. So was Cerrelle. That's what Andra told me."

"I didn't. I still don't . . . unless you're still interested. Just in talking," I added hurriedly.

"I know." She nodded. "You find women easier to talk to, don't you?"

"They listen," I pointed out. "Most of them, anyway."

"You've been fortunate. We do have some ruthless women here, just as in any culture. Worse, probably." Aleyaisha dipped a chunk of the white meat in butter. "They'd . . ." She shook her head. "Trust me . . . you want to be careful."

"How? I don't even know who they are."

"If you're not sure, ask me. Or Andra."

"I just might." I paused. "What about Cerrelle?"

"She's a lot like Andra. Direct but not a dominatrix. You like her, don't you?"

"Yes, but I don't know why." I forced a shrug. "There's something there, but I was hurting too much when I met her, and she reminded me . . . well . . . things got worse. Probably will stay worse."

Aleyaisha nodded that she had heard what I said, and I ate some of the second portion of chicken, and then got up and refilled my mug with more Arleen. I also refilled Aleyaisha's beaker.

After the two administrators rose and slipped into the

twilight, I looked directly into those brown eyes. "Is my data screen censored . . . restricted?"

"No. You can search for anything that any director of the Authority could, and it would come up. We don't censor what people take off the net."

"In a way you do," I countered. "You have to have a certain . . . knowledge . . . to know what to ask."

"That's true in any system. If you have the time, or persistence, you can find it here."

Was it that I just wasn't persistent enough? Or that I wanted the solutions immediately? I didn't like either possibility. "Everything I do is monitored, isn't it?"

"Mostly. Everyone is."

"Everyone?" I took a mouthful of chicken and chewed, thinking. Given the minuscule size of nanites and their capabilities, such monitoring had to be easy enough. "Who plays Supreme Being?"

"No one. Anyone with the ability could tap into anyone else's monitors, but they're designed so they also record who undertakes such taps. Repeated unauthorized tapping can lead to attitude adjustment. It's a consensus sort of thing."

"I can't believe some people don't abuse that sort of power."

"They do. They just don't do it again." Her lips quirked. "The systems know everything about everyone, and everyone knows that. Think about it."

I did, and shivered.

"The only antisocial acts that aren't known immediately are those committed in isolated areas, and even traces of those will show up in the perpetrator's nanite support system. It's very hard to escape justice."

"Living in a glass house with telescopes trained on it," I murmured.

"Every house has telescopes trained on it. Adjusted people don't look; maladjusted people don't look for long."

"Do what's right, or we'll make sure you do," I suggested.

"We allow people to choose what is right, if they will. If they don't, they lose that choice. Do you have a better idea? Isn't that what Dzin is all about when you strip away the beautiful language?"

"The idea of what's *right* bothers me."

"Here . . . it's simple enough. We don't like people who hurt other people or manipulate them. Don't hurt or manipulate others and you can do whatever you have the resources to do."

"Humor me," I asked, finding my voice turning skeptical. "What is manipulation?"

"The use of psychological force, the implication of physical or administrative force to persuade another to commit actions against the well-being of another, including himself or herself."

I nodded. "Who defines well-being?"

"Who needs a definition, except someone who's intent on abusing the system?" she countered.

That did stop me. If you needed to define someone's well-being . . .

"See what I mean?"

I saw, or saw well enough. "Glass houses . . . so no one throws stones."

"There are always a few. Fewer here than in most places."

I savored the Arleen, the Arleen and a friendly face. We talked for a long time.

54

When the windows of perception are cleansed, the individual sees the universe appear as it is.

The lower edge of the late-afternoon sun touched the split-stone ridge cap of the transients' quarters roof, and silvered light spilled across the slates for an instant. I blinked, and the silver flow had vanished, and the cool and not quite raw air of late fall gusted around the stones of the building and ruffled my damp hair.

Internal nanites or not, months of conditioning to the contrary, my body ached after Ileck's swimming, exercise, and weight conditioning—followed by the strain of the black sessions in the pool. Symbolic analogue sessions, no less, where the blackness represented space or over-space, except that the impassive Ileck refused to speculate or explain beyond what he had already said, and I was left in the dark, literally and figuratively.

I took a deep breath and stepped inside the front foyer, turning to the left and heading down the corridor to my quarters. My door was ajar. Had I left it that way, rushing out that morning? I pushed it open.

A redheaded figure stood by the couch.

The smile crossed my lips unbidden, without thought.

"I hope you don't mind my waiting here," said Cerrelle. "After all, I did travel across half known space to check on you once."

"I don't mind at all. I am surprised. I wasn't sure I'd ever hear from you again."

"You almost didn't." There wasn't any humor in the statement.

My smile faded. "Have you eaten?"

"Not enough to spoil my appetite."

"Would one of the lounges be all right? I can't eat much before Ileck's sessions, and I'm starving."

"From what I've seen, you probably are. You've put on more muscle. You don't look like a scrawny Dzin teacher any longer."

Scrawny? I'd thought of myself as slender, but I'd done my exercises and conditioning work even in Hybra.

"You were scrawny," Cerrelle reaffirmed as she started past me and toward the foyer.

I followed, closing the door behind us. Cerrelle walked quickly enough that my muscles twinged as I hurried to draw abreast of her. I appraised her solid figure, seeing a feminine muscularity I hadn't noted before. "Did you do a stint as a trainer—like Ileck?"

"Not like Ileck. I was a patrol trainer."

I did a quick mental search. *Patrol . . . entrusted with monitoring the Rykashan borders with lands populated by unmodified humans.* "In Lyncol or somewhere else?"

"Elena."

I had to search for that, too, managing to discover it was in the northwest of Amnord and as far north as Lyncol, but even rockier. It was the largest Rykashan enclave geographically and bordered Dezret.

"Did you patrol or train or both?"

"You don't train until you've spent five years on the border." Her voice was cool . . . very cool, and I fell silent as we neared the lounge—the larger one opposite the operations building, not the one overlooking the marsh.

Only three others were there—two men and a woman—and they sat at a circular table almost next to the entry arch. None of them looked at us past a casual glance. Because we both wore green—if of different shades?

Cerrelle called up some game meat whose odor I didn't recognize, and, of course, her lemon drink. I settled on spring rolls, a crispy lemon duck, and jasmine rice, with Arleen tea. We took the corner table, the most secluded of the dozen in the lounge, nearly twice the size of the marsh lounge.

Cerrelle settled into the green velvet of the chair, then fixed her eyes on me. "Before we go back to meaningless small talk . . . what changed your mind?" Her voice carried an edge, but one softer than when I had been in Lyncol and Runswi before. "I didn't."

"It took three of you. Someone asked me some honest questions." I paused. "Then she died."

"And you want me to be her? No, thank you."

I swallowed what might have been a bitter comeback, since I probably deserved her skepticism. *Besides, you want her honesty, Tyndel.* "That was almost two years ago. I don't want you to be her. I don't want you to be Foerga. I thought. I waited to link you. I don't know why . . . not exactly . . ."

"Tyndel. You may be on the way to being a great Web jockey, but you don't know what you want from women. You never did."

She was mostly right about that. "You're right. Mostly. Can you still understand what I think?"

"I might be able to if I really tried, but most of those nanites would have degenerated. They're not self-replicating, for very obvious reasons."

I nodded.

"I'm too old to play games, Tyndel. What do you want?"

I swallowed. I'd known it would get down to something that simple. *What do you want?* "I still don't know. You're part of it. You have an honesty—a directness. That sort of directness has scared me, always. But I've used things—Dzin, family—to avoid looking at life directly. I pretended I did, but I didn't."

"I'm not a mindtech, either." Her voice was neutral.

"I don't want a mindtech. I don't want a nurse. I want someone who looks at life as it is, and who will talk about it that way."

"And . . . now . . . you want someone to talk with? Just to talk with?"

"I have to start somewhere." The grin wasn't forced, but I was nervous.

"I can live with that. For now." This time, she was the one who took the deep breath. "If you're not playing some elaborate Dzin game."

"No games." I never had played games. There was no point in saying that. I'd been angry, unjustly, at her, and I'd been hurt, but I hadn't been out to play games.

"You wanted directness. Do you still want it?"

"I asked you to be who you are."

"I came here because Andra and Aleyaisha asked me to see you . . . once. On the way back from Omega Eridani, I wished you'd dropped into a black hole. You were—you still might be—an arrogant Dzin prig."

I thought about that. I sipped the Arleen. "You're probably right. I think part of that is cultural and not personal . . ."

"There you go . . ."

". . . but the result is the same," I finished.

"How can you be so calm? I'm attacking you. Ignoring my anger isn't honest, either."

"Do you want me to be honest?" I countered.

The silence fell on her side of the table. Then she laughed. "I suppose I deserve that. Go ahead."

"I know . . . I hurt you. You went out of your way to try to get me to see what Rykasha was all about, and I refused to see it. I suspect it's also partly because you saw me squandering a talent that is incredibly rare and felt I was a spoiled brat. . . . I don't know all the reasons why. You tried to be gentle, but you had to be professional, and being you, you also had to be honest. You had to do what was best for Rykasha, no matter how you felt. It's taken me a while, and I do get a little upset when you attack me. I can't deny that. I still don't think you understand how hard it felt for me. But I can also see that you had to take a lot for a long time . . . and maybe from a lot of others as well."

"Not that long," she said. "But you made me angry . . . and hurt." `

"Why did you come to see me? Rather than link?" My fingers fumbled with the mug, and Arleen slopped over them.

"Andra . . . Aleyaisha, especially. She has a feel for things. I thought she was wrong, but I promised to see you—in person."

"And now?" I found myself holding my breath, not even knowing why.

"You want to be my friend, Tyndel . . . it's going to take some time."

I didn't answer immediately. "I got that idea. I wasn't sure if you'd let me try."

"Are you sure you want this? I'll ask you hard questions. I'll tell you if I think you're deceiving yourself, and I won't honeyglaze it. If you want warm and willing women, all you have to do is finish your training and you'll never have to sleep alone—and never have to say you're sorry. Or explain anything."

"Aleyaisha told me that," I admitted.

"You didn't believe her?"

"I did, and I do. That's not what I want. You can ask her."

"Tyndel . . . you are a case. You know that?" This time, Cerrelle smiled, if briefly, as though I were an impossible puppy dog.

"If you say so, it has to be so."

"Let's see how wonderful you think that is in a month . . . or a year."

"Fine by me." I gobbled down some of the duck before I spoke again. "There are some things that aren't in all the information that's been poured into me, and it's not in the data system." I raised my eyebrows. "You can tell me about being a patrol guard in Elena . . ."

"It's not that exciting."

"I get to be the judge of that."

She took a sip of lemon drink. "It was the best I could do at the time. I can't handle symbolic analogues. I can do everything else, but I'd be blind in overspace, and I was angry, angry that there was something that all my brains and all my determination couldn't get for me . . ."

That explained more, and I nodded. "So you went for the next most challenging job?"

"The next most challenging I could get in Elena. The Dezret border is the most dangerous. Those Saints are always pushing . . . only culture in all Amnord that still doesn't understand what caused the collapses . . ."

I took another sip of Arleen and listened, enjoying the energy of her words, the directness. She wasn't softly direct like Foerga, or gentle like Fersonne, or as sympathetic as Aleyaisha, but as sharp and as honest as a blade. She was right—getting to be friends would take time—and some inadvertent wounds.

Still . . . I hoped we could survive them. I wanted us to survive them.

55

[RUNSWI: 4519]

The universe offers no deception and no encouragement; intelligence creates both.

I looked down at the screen, at the next question: "Why is shock isolation inappropriate technology for a needle ship?"

From theory and skills, Andra shifted my briefings into ship construction and mechanical engineering. More definitions . . . and now schematics . . . swirled through my brain. I blinked and began to sort through the latest mental infusion of information.

Outside the wind moaned, and ice pellets snapped against the permaglass. Already, nearly two centimeters of the sleet coated the ground, except for the walks between buildings, where some form of nanite protection kept the stones clear and mostly dry.

I selected an answer.

Sometime later, the wind still alternated between moans and whispers. The ice pellets had changed to crisp flakes falling faster, and I looked at the last question on the screen and finally chose an answer: "One half the algebraic difference between the maximum and minimum stress across a single cycle (usually a test cycle)."

After rubbing my forehead, I straightened in the chair. The questions were in random order, unrelated to the order in which my brain had accepted the material. That random order was apparently another method to force my brain to do the organizing.

"You're done, Tyndel." Andra stood in the door. "You don't need me to tell you that."

"That's not it. It takes a minute for me . . . to stabilize."

"You're stabilized."

I snorted and stood. "You just want to throw me out into the snow."

"That's Cerrelle."

"You're doing it for her."

Andra gave about a half head shake. "No one with any brains ever does anything that Cerrelle would want to do herself."

I hid a smile and left, heading for the transient quarters and a quick snack before marching back through the snow to the pool.

There, after putting me through the "lighter" conditioning workout, Ileck did have something special for me—differentially weighted boots. So I plunged into the shocking black water more than a few more times before adjusting.

The snow had stopped by the time I walked up the steps to the foyer of the transient quarters, but my hair was frozen from the stiff wind blowing out of the north. If it kept up, the marshes would freeze before long, and that meant the beginning of true winter. Runswi seemed colder than Dorcha, even than Henvor, but not so cold as Lyncol, even though Runswi wasn't that much farther north. The mountains—the wind patterns?

Rather than go out through the snow and chill again, I went downstairs to the limited reformulator in the transients' quarters and had more Dorchan strip beef and Arleen. As I ate, looking out at the glittering white, even without sun, I reflected that snow changed things. I'd been far colder in an outside suit off OE Station, but less than ten centimeters of crystallized water, barely below its freezing point, had dissuaded me from walking four hundred meters to get a better meal—rather, a greater variety in meal selection—when I scarcely would have noticed the chill.

Genetic patterns? Still unchanged by all the nanite rebuilding within me?

After a second mug of Arleen, I walked back to my quarters, where I paced around the sitting room before my eyes turned to the screen. I needed to read more, but I wasn't sure I wanted to start that immediately. I sat down and touched the link studs, doubting that Cerrelle would answer.

The answerer image flashed on.

I waited for the brief words to leave a message, then spoke. "This is Tyndel. You're probably not there, but I wanted you to know I was thinking about you—"

The answerer was replaced by Cerrelle—hair longer than the answerer's image of her, with slightly darker circles under her eyes. "What do you want, Tyndel?"

"You're actually home," I said. "I wanted to talk to you."

"I usually don't answer. I don't like links, but I checked

to make sure it was you. I wouldn't have interrupted the answerer otherwise."

That was some progress. "Thank you."

Cerrelle made a gesture to brush off my words. "What does Andra have you doing now?"

"Ship construction and specifications. It's interesting."

"It should be. It's your neck."

"I know."

"Would you like to come here when you get a break? You will at the end of next week. I've arranged guest quarters for you—where you stayed before. You remember?"

"Yes. I'd like that. I'll be there."

"Good." She smiled. "I'll see you then." The connection broke, proving again that Cerrelle did not like to converse on the link.

I turned toward the window and looked into the grayish white of evening snow, lit in places by lights and reflections of light. Was directness that important to me? In a woman?

The sardonic smile that settled on my face answered that. I might not like that honesty, but the nanites had either changed me or made me understand myself better, and I realized that I could not afford to be close to anyone who would encourage me to deceive myself, even through concern and sympathy.

I still didn't understand why. Maybe it was enough that I understood.

56

Significant images render insights beyond speech.

As I pulled myself out of the pool after the last sprint, still panting, I looked at the deep end of the pool. Now above the clear black water, above the tiles as dark as nielle, Ileck had set two beams spanning the water, one two meters above the surface, the other half a meter to one side, roughly a meter above the water.

Without waiting for my taskmaster to gesture, I pulled on the exercise singlesuit, the weighted pack, and the differentially weighted boots. The weight in the pack and the boots varied every day. I walked slowly toward Ileck.

He motioned toward the pedestal steps that held the uppermost beam, and I crossed the black composite deck to the steps and mounted. When the blackness dropped across the pool, both beams glimmered, the lower one more faintly than the upper.

"Stay on the upper—if you can," Ileck ordered. "You should be running the beam."

I got three balanced quick steps in that first moment of silence before being struck with the music that called forth something like a charge of horses or ancient cavalry. With the music came the projection of glittering, silver-edged dark spears, each radiating chill.

One foot slipped, and I tried to catch myself, then let the momentum take me to the lower bar, where I managed another half dozen steps at a jogging pace before a wave of heat and cold organ music wiped me sideways and off the beam.

"Ooo . . ." I couldn't help the involuntary exclamation

when I hit the water. The electroessence of that jolt froze me for an instant, and I barely managed to get my mouth closed before sinking below the surface. The blackness didn't vanish, and fire jolts made each movement torture. Somewhere above and within the water, a dirge rumbled, mournful and bewailing a death, mine if I didn't manage to drag boots and pack and self to the edge. I could have dropped the pack, but then I'd have to dive down eight meters and recover it.

How long it took to reach the side of the pool, I wasn't certain, but only when my hand touched the tiles did the darkness and the jolts stop.

"You're not trying hard enough to stay on the beams," Ileck announced. "This is not a contest. It is not a game."

I pulled myself out of the dark water, still shuddering from the hot-cold shocks it had delivered before Ileck had lifted the darkness.

He looked at me, disappointed once more.

Dripping water that looked clear as it puddled on the black composite deck, I studied my taskmaster, then asked, "Will you answer a question for me?" I had to work to keep my jaw from shivering as I spoke.

"If I can." Ileck offered a faint quirk of his lips that didn't approach a smile.

"Is there more to having the water jolt me than just conditioning me to avoid pain and stay on the beam?"

"Yes."

I raised my eyebrows, then wiped the water off my forehead. "What, might I ask?"

"To try to condition your body to the severity of failure."

"Are you sure doing that won't just make me more nervous?"

"If it does, then you'll die in overspace anyway."

I stood and dripped water for a time. "You're using various nanite projections to create an illusion of reality here—but wouldn't it be easier just to use something like a nanite briefing spray to give me the entire vision of what you want? Why this way?"

Ileck frowned before he spoke. "In overspace, you will receive sensory inputs. They'll actually be energy signals relayed from the ship's sensors, but you'll feel them as sensory. You'll react based on your training and your senses. Your mind will react one way, and if it's not conditioned properly your body will react another. A Web pilot can't afford that kind of internal conflict. Right now, that's all you should know."

"You're conditioning my body and mind?"

"That's what we're working on."

"You don't sound absolutely sure." I pointed out.

"Nothing is certain until you make your first overspace insertion." He coughed slightly and pointed to the beams. "You need more work."

So I tried to run the beams again.

I failed twice before I made it. So severe were the shocks from the water, the second time, that when I pulled myself out of the pool, I lay in a heap for several minutes and shuddered. I didn't fall the third time.

Nor the fourth, but I staggered a lot, and had to slow down to get across the beam.

When the blackness lifted, Ileck was standing less than two meters from me, looking down on me, as he always did. "Andra is right. You need a break. Take four days." The tall bronzed man turned and walked away.

How many other people in Runswi were doing anything close to the physical exertions he was demanding of me? Or was it because I could do better?

Was he right—that I wasn't trying hard enough?

Probably . . . if you're being honest with yourself.

I pulled off the heavy boots and set them on the drying rack, then the soaked singlesuit, thinking as I did. *Honesty . . . honesty is hard for you, Tyndel.* I nodded. That was why I could talk to Aleyaisha but why I wanted Cerrelle. In a squeeze, Aleyaisha would be sympathetic, would comfort me . . . and let me lie to myself. Cerrelle might be sympathetic again . . . if I ate enough sour eel, but she wouldn't hesitate to let me know if I were headed down the path of self-deception.

But did I want a keeper?

No . . . that wasn't it. It was knowing that she wanted the honesty, enough to be direct and honest, that made me want to be honest. Fersonne had shown me that. . . .

Somehow, the hot shower wasn't as comforting as usual.

57

[RUNSWI/LYNCOL: 4519]

To forget the snows of yesterday is to deny the first flower of spring.

I thought I might sleep late before I left for Lyncol on the first day of the only multiday break I'd had in years. I didn't. I woke early while the sky was dark and cleaned up as it turned lead-gray under heavy clouds that promised more snow.

After a light breakfast downstairs, and after packing a small duffel in hand, I was ready to leave Runswi. Where was the glider station? I could only recall that it had been below ground, about four flights down. While I couldn't remember anything else, I did remember the map I'd gotten when I'd returned. I pulled it out from the drawer under the console and was pleased to see that the glider station was marked clearly—not more than a hundred meters from my quarters, underneath one of the research buildings.

As I looked at the map, I realized again that Runswi, unlike Lyncol, was really not a city or a town or a community. From what the map revealed and what I'd experienced, it was a laborium devoted to science and transport—and one that would have been a dream to the iconraisers of Henvor, had Runswi not been created by demons. Laborium or workplace of the demons, mental truffling wasn't getting me to Lyncol.

I lifted the duffel and left, walking through a gray morning raw as much as cold until I reached the stone archway that had to hold the steps down to the subterranean glider station. The steps were polished stone, polished so they glittered, yet not at all slippery to my boots. Beyond the last flight of steps was a squarish console, ten meters from the platform beyond. I frowned, trying to recall what to do. Cerrelle had done it all before. So I stepped up and tried what worked with the links—tapped in my name and code on the small screen.

This transit is 1 unit. Your free credit balance is 513 units. The words appeared on the screen. I managed not to shake my head. I knew that certain services were deducted from whatever balance I might have, but I really had no idea exactly how far that balance might go.

I stood looking at the empty space where the glider would appear for about ten minutes, until I could feel a slight breeze, and then a wave of air, just before the glider popped through the silvered arc at the western end of the platform. The arched silver cover slid back, revealing what looked to be twenty dual seats, in matched sets, two seats facing two.

Ten people left the glider, but I was the only one waiting. So I took a west-facing seat and waited. A man in a maroon suit scurried down the last of the steps, jabbed at the console, and hurried to seat himself in the four-set in front of me. Less than five minutes later, the covered glider slid into the silvery gray tunnel, and according to my internal timekeepers, something like fifteen standard minutes later I was standing on the stone-walled platform in Lyncol. A man in blue nodded as he stepped into the glider, and so did a woman in the dark green of a Web pilot. She added with a smile, "Good luck."

"Thank you."

I stood for a moment, just surveying the glider station, something I hadn't done when I'd left Lyncol with Cerrelle. Then, I hadn't been listening or looking at much of anything. Unlike the glider station in Runswi, with its single platform, the one in Lyncol had a half dozen platforms, each linked by arched polished granite steps and walkways over the open induction tubes where the gliders were boarded and exited. Every stone glistened, so smooth-polished I could not help wonder if the Rykashan character harbored lithoidolatry. Then, the perfect woods that melded with the stones suggested silvalolatry.

My eyes flicked across the names of the nearest platforms—Elena, Runswi, Berta, Montral, Calgra. Except for confirming names from my basic Rykashan geographic indoctrination, none of them except Elena meant anything. Like all of the glider stations I'd been in, the one in Lyncol was four flights of stairs down, but I wasn't even breathing hard when I stepped outside into a late morning grayed over with heavy clouds from which drifted fat flakes of snow.

Lyncol had snow on the ground, piled nearly a meter deep, except for the cleared stone path that led, as I recalled, down a gentle hill to the transit quarters. I hoped I was headed where I was meant to be.

My breath puffed white in the cold air—drier and more invigorating than the damp chill of Runswi—and I was smiling as I hurried toward the wood-and-stone structure set within the huge and ancient pines. Once inside the foyer, I glanced around until I spotted an open door.

The broad-faced young man in grays looked up from his console. "Greens—you must be Tyndel, the Web pilot candidate. Cerrelle said you'd be here today." He stood, towering almost half a meter above me. "Since you're a pilot candidate, you get the quarters for a half. That's seven units for the three days."

"Do you need me to input anything?" Seven units meant the quarters went for five units a day, since the

Rykashans never charged less than a unit for anything and rounded fractional transactions down, unlike the traders or usurers of Mettersfel.

"If you would . . ." He bent forward and tapped something on the keyboard.

I entered my name and personal code, then straightened.

"That should take care of it. You've been here before, Cerrelle said. So you probably know where everything is. If you don't, let me know. I'm Aximander." His smile was both shy and deferential, surprising to me given his size and obvious strength.

"I will. Thank you."

"Your rooms are on the top left. I'll show you." He led the way out of his office and went up the steps gracefully, if two at a time. With his size, two at a time was easier.

"Are these all right?" asked Aximander after opening the door. "I reserved the ones with the view of the pines and the mountains."

The quarters were somewhat smaller than those in Runswi, and felt older, even if they were spotless. I walked to the window of the sitting/console room. The tops of the rocky peaks to the west were lost in the low clouds, but they'd been there before, and I was certain they hadn't disappeared. "This is fine." I smiled, enjoying the fact that I actually had a choice, limited as it was.

Once the towering concierge of transients' quarters departed, I used the link in the room, but Cerrelle didn't answer. I left a short message with the similacra: "I'm here."

With all the activities Andra and Ileck had crammed into my days, I didn't mind the lack of structure at all. I lay back on the bed and looked at the ceiling, wondering how the son of a mite trader trained to be a Dzin schoolmaster had ended up going to the stars and returning to learn how to pilot more ships there. The ancients had been wrong about that . . . where else had the ancient records been wrong—or altered?

My lips quirked. What about the Rykashan version of history? Where was it wrong or misleading? I yawned and closed my eyes, unwilling to follow that flight of thought, not when I had time off, not when I didn't need to do so.

Thump! I struggled awake, realizing it was nearly noon. Outside the window, the snow continued to sputter down. Swinging my feet over the side of the bed, I stood slowly, as though I were backtreading Ileck's beams when I had first begun, tentative step after tentative step, blindfolded through the darkness. Was that life, removing the blindfold and still treading through the darkness? I shook my head and swung to my feet.

Another *thump* echoed from the door.

"Are you even here, Tyndel?"

"Coming!" I straggled toward the door and opened it.

Cerrelle stood there wearing her thin silver jacket open over the olive-green singlesuit. On her collar was a silver pin—a black T across a spoked wheel. I didn't recall the pin. "Don't tell me. You fell asleep."

I found myself grinning. "I lay down, and I was thinking . . . and then someone was pounding on the door."

"Most men don't think that well on their backs." The humorously sardonic grin faded. "Are you that tired?"

"Physically . . . no. More mentally worn out, I think."

Cerrelle studied me. "No self-pity. Honest attempt. Much better." She motioned toward the foyer. "Are you coming?"

I grabbed my jacket, light green, and closed the door as I followed her down the steps. At the bottom, I caught up with her.

"I thought you weren't going to be a mindtech."

"I'm not." She gestured impatiently, then stepped out into the snow flurries, walking quickly downhill.

"Can I talk to you about Ileck's training?" I asked, hurrying to catch up.

"So long as you don't want sympathy."

"There's a fine line between understanding and sympathy," I suggested.

"I can draw that line, thank you." The words carried a slight lilt, and I glanced at her. Was there a twinkle there, or did I want to see it?

"You want to see it," she suggested.

"You're still able to read what I think?"

"Only once in a while. Most of the nanite capability is gone, but I can read your face. You could do it too, if you worked at it."

"Part of your Patrol training?"

"Yes. It helps."

"You know . . ." I said slowly, "I don't even know what you do now, unless you're trying to shepherd some other refugee into Rykashan society."

"I'm a technical assistant to the Transport Subauthority. Remember . . . green is for transport." She gestured vaguely at herself as if she'd forgotten she wore a shimmering silver jacket.

Not for the first time, I had to wonder how much I had missed or ignored from my first days in Lyncol. "Where are we going?"

"To the Overlook. I'm hungry, and I don't feel like cooking, and it's got the best formulator menu in Lyncol. It's been a long morning, and I don't want to waste the time off."

"Time off? You have to work that much? I owe for being rescued. Do you owe for training, or are you trying to build up a unit balance?"

"That's considered a rather . . . personal question." Her words were as cold as the air around us, or colder.

I threw up my hands. "First, you . . . never mind."

"Tyndel . . . don't get angry with me." She halted and looked at me, and flakes of snow touched her hair, then melted.

I stopped right on the path and turned and looked straight into those piercing green eyes. "Cerrelle . . . I am trying very hard to adjust to a society I was not born into. I am trying to use every bit of information you people have poured into me. I am trying not to ask any more stupid questions or questions I already have the answers to but don't realize that I do. I am grateful for your honesty and your directness. *But* . . . when you know every bit of my past, when you know all of my losses and my stupidities, and then you tell me that an innocent question about your status in this society is rather personal . . . then I think that's hypocritical and self-serving."

She stood stock-still for a moment, flushing red, then white. Then she swallowed. After a moment, she swallowed again.

"I'm sorry," I said softly. "I didn't mean to upset you, but you were born into this society. I wasn't. I've spent five months out of four years with people, and that's not long enough to learn an entire set of new social graces."

She laughed, ruefully, and then shook her head, then laughed some more. After a while, she shook her head again. "Oh, Tyndel . . . you compliment me and insult me, and then, after you tell me the most truthful and direct statement since I met you, you apologize."

I didn't know what to say.

"First . . . you're wrong. I wasn't born here any more than you were. I was born in north Dezret, and I ran for the border before my father could marry me off as a herder's third wife. I didn't learn to read more than the basics until I was seventeen years old. I was diagnosed with a series of genetically predetermined problems that would have killed me before I reached forty. As I told you before, I don't have all the talents necessary to be a Web pilot, and I owe nearly a hundred years' standard service for the medical and educational services I've already received. My current post pays three for one."

I could feel the color drain from my face. No wonder she was angry and impatient with me. I was fortunate she was still even speaking.

"Tyndel . . . I don't want pity. I never wanted to bring any of that up. I don't want you, or anyone, feeling sorry for me. Not anyone. Not ever."

I moistened my lips. "I've a lot of sour eel to consume."

Her forehead screwed up in puzzlement. "What?"

I tried to find a Rykashan equivalent, then shrugged helplessly. "Ah . . . it's an expression that means you were horribly wrong and have to eat all the words you shouldn't have said . . . and it tastes terrible—like sour eels . . . you know . . . bitter and slimy?"

"Eating sour eels . . . I like that. The expression, I mean." After a moment, Cerrelle looked at me, and there was no trace of anger in her voice. "You were wrong about me, you know?"

"I don't think so." My words were tentative. I hated to disagree with her, even if the disagreement were to compliment her.

"You kept talking about my honesty." She shook her head. "I can be honest about you. Or society . . ."

"Not talking about yourself isn't dishonest," I pointed out.

"It is when you use it to mislead people." She gestured toward the path. "I meant it about being hungry. I didn't have much this morning, and I'm getting queasy."

"If you still want to eat with me . . ."

"Don't be self-pitying. I was stupid, and you told me so. I deserved it, but that doesn't give you the right to ask for a pat on the back."

"I was right. You are honest. Which way?"

"This way." Cerrelle led me past snow piled nearly shoulder-high and turned down a narrower lane toward a low hill. "It overlooks a pond. It's frozen now, but . . ."

"It's still an overlook."

"Right."

The Overlook was crowded, with only two small tables for two free out of nearly two dozen. We claimed one by the window as a tall man unbent and left, carrying a mug away.

"You sit while I get something," Cerrelle suggested.

"Fine," I agreed. "You need the food more than I do." She did; she was pale. Low blood sugar? Were the nanite maintenance requirements higher for her because of whatever medical treatments she'd had?

Without a look over her shoulder Cerrelle headed for the low counters that held the food reformulators.

The circular sweep of permaglass overlooked a frozen oval expanse fringed by mounds of snow that were doubtless grasses or bushes in the spring and summer. On the far side of the pond, the snow-covered ground sloped upward for several hundred meters to where the forest began. There was a path entering the forest, but not a cleared one, and it had tracks of some sort, made as if by old-fashioned sleds or skis.

Cerrelle returned and set down a tray with two platters, one heaped with slices of some meat slathered in a greenish glaze with potatoes covered with cheese beside it, and the second with greenery. "Lamb with apple mint glaze, cheese potatoes, and a mixed green salad."

"You are hungry." I stood and made my way to the counters, where I selected a Toze chicken dish out of curiosity, something with peanuts and peppers, along with various steamed vegetables.

After I returned and sat down, I looked at her, taking in the green eyes and the red hair, when she looked up from several hurried bites. "So many things make sense now, and I never saw."

"I didn't want you to see them. You weren't supposed to look for a fellow lost soul. I'm not lost, anyway. Dezret was never home." She started in on the greenery.

I had several bites of the bite-sized chicken, spicier than I normally preferred but good, before I asked, "You never miss anything?"

She took a long swallow of water, followed by a sip of the red wine. "What would I miss? Sharing a husband with two other women? Having three or four children and trying to scrape a living out of land that was worn out twenty centuries ago? Dying young without ever having seen or learned anything?"

"Dorcha sounds like paradise compared to Dezret," I

said slowly, after a sip of Arleen and then a bite of chicken. Most of my platter was empty, more than I would have expected, since I hadn't felt that hungry.

"Women still have to obey men there, don't they?" she asked.

"I don't know that my mother ever obeyed my father if she disagreed." I laughed softly. "Some women feel that way, though."

"Women and girls don't have that choice in Dezret. We—they're handmaidens. Did you know that a woman can't enter the upper levels of paradise unless her husband does?"

"I didn't even know that the Saints had a paradise," I had to admit.

"I doubt they do, but that's what people believe."

Even the Rykashans had believers, I'd discovered, but I merely nodded, not wanting to get into a theological discussion. I'd made enough mistakes for a year in less than an hour.

As we finished eating, Cerrelle looked at me, her head cocked slightly sideways. "Have you ever been on snowshoes?"

"No." I'd seen pictures of them, but no one I knew ever used them, since it snowed so seldom in most of Dorcha—amazing, given that Hybra was less than a hundred kilometers from Lyncol. Then, the warmth of the Summer Sea stopped short of the mountains, well short.

"We'll take the short trail."

After the mess I'd made before lunch, I wasn't about to protest, not one word.

I should have. Being on snowshoes was worse than crossing Ileck's beams. The short trail was an expanse of snow less than ten meters wide that might have been packed once but was covered with a half meter of fine new snow. On each side of the trail were ancient pines that rose a good thirty meters or more into the gray sky from which snow continued to drift.

Every so often, as I strapped the basketlike snowshoes

to my boots, snow sifted off the overhanging pines and fell like a blanket. One of those blankets covered me as I finally stood up after fastening the snowshoes, but I brushed it away with gloved hands and started after Cerrelle, already twenty meters down the trail from me.

The snow shifted under the baskets that held my boots, and I lumbered from side to side as much as forward. I hadn't gone a dozen meters before the front edge of one of the contraptions caught, and I ended up lying sideways and covered with snow.

Cerrelle turned and just stood there, holding on to a pine trunk and laughing.

I struggled to my feet and plodded onward, almost going to my knees once more.

She laughed again, shaking her head.

So I threw a snowball and caught her in the face.

"You!" She threw back, and I lurched sideways, catching an edge once more and sprawling into the too-soft snow.

I sat halfway up and packed a snowball, firing it at her, but tangled as I was in the snowshoes and snow, far more of her missiles struck than mine.

Besides, I ended up laughing.

Eventually, so did she. "A would-be Web pilot, and you can't get fifty meters on snowshoes!" She kept laughing, and that made it even harder for me.

I finally took off the snowshoes and staggered upright. "I'll walk anywhere you want, but not on these."

Cerrelle just grinned, but she took hers off, and we trudged through the semipacked snow for fifty meters or so until we were back on the cleared path toward the center of Lyncol . . . and someplace to dry off and warm up.

And talk.

58

Those who praise honesty have not felt its knives.

Cerrelle and I talked most of the time I was in Lyncol—walking down cold but cleared paths under a quarter moon. Sitting in a hot pool while snow poured out of the night sky and turned to a silver brume when it struck the water's surface. Struggling through hip-deep snow to climb for a view of yet another hill. Watching black-capped chickadees flit through the pines in search of seeds carefully cached seasons earlier, marveling at how they remembered thousands of hoards. Sharing dishes at different eating establishments throughout Lyncol.

I learned more about Dezret—from the wind-deaths whipping off the Salt Desert to herd rotations to ancient temples predating the Devastation to seasonal grasses to the politics of families with junior and senior wives—than about Rykasha. Cerrelle learned some about Dorcha, but I didn't know what Cerrelle learned about me that she hadn't already known. Talk was all we shared, and more than enough for the time we had. I slept alone in the transient quarters, my sleep blessedly phantasm- and dream-free.

She never let me know where she lived, and I didn't push that. Knowing what I had learned, I suspected I could have discovered her dwelling, but what would have been the point—except to make a point?

On the third morning, she met me for breakfast and we walked back toward the Overlook. I had my small duffel in hand as we went down the pine-lined lane in the post-dawn sunlight. The snow of the night before sparkled so brightly I wasn't sure we even cast shadows.

The Overlook was far less crowded in the morning, and we sat in the middle of the sweep of glass, looking down on the shimmering snow covering the ice of the pond.

"You look more rested," Cerrelle observed as she sipped the black cafe she preferred in the morning.

I could sense her nervousness, the edge to her body posture, the slightest acridness of apprehension that had been stronger when I'd first arrived—and that I hadn't recognized then. Now it was fainter but still present. "I feel better." I held the cup of Arleen just under my chin and let the steamy aroma wreathe my face for a moment before taking a sip. "It's been a long time since I haven't had to do something immediately. A day's been the greatest break I've had in years." I laughed. "Unless you count the time lost in travel dilation."

"That doesn't count." Cerrelle took a bite of something that looked like a muffin stuffed with meat and eggs, and far too heavy even for a system of mine that now required nearly twice the food it had when I'd been but a Dzin schoolmaster.

My truffled omelet was adequate, but I could have fixed one better than what the formulator had created. The Arleen was good, and I took another sip.

"Why do you value honesty so much, Tyndel, as if nothing else mattered?" Her piercing green eyes focused on me. "You keep coming back to that. Yet people here don't lie. The system discourages it pretty effectively."

"I haven't seen a Rykashan yet who lied—that I know of," I pointed out. "Yet you seem so much more honest and direct." *And I need that directness.*

"The native demons grow up with it, and they learn to shield it in subtle ways. Subtlety comes harder if you aren't raised with it. When you're not attacking, Tyndel, you're much like them. Dorcha is like Rykasha."

"Maybe the first Rykashans came from the same cultures."

"Not according to the histories. It's more a question of

power, I think. Dorcha is one of the more powerful mite nations, and has been for centuries. Rykasha is the only real nanite culture, and it's definitely powerful."

"With interstellar ships and nanite weapons ... there's nothing else that comes close." I thought about the segments of history I'd read on OE Station. "Do we—I guess it's we—have all those weapons mentioned in the histories?"

"I don't know." Cerrelle shrugged. "The Patrol uses some—tractors and immobilizers. There must be others. The mites have laser cannon and all sorts of explosives, but they stay well away from Rykashan borders." An almost impish smile crossed her lips. "You avoided answering the honesty question. Why do you pursue it?"

I took another sip of Arleen, then found myself holding an empty mug, with nothing to retreat behind. "I ... don't want to guess. When ... you say something, that's what you believe. I can agree or disagree, but I'm not guessing as to what you feel."

"You didn't have to come to Lyncol, you know?"

I thought about that for a moment. "You didn't have to travel all the way to OE Station."

"The Authority paid for it—and for my time."

"But you chose to, didn't you?"

She nodded.

"Then ... I had to come to Lyncol—but I wanted to, as well."

"I'm glad of that."

I paused as I reconsidered her earlier words. "The Authority—they paid? Pilots are that scarce?"

"They're not that scarce ... now, but most are nearly a century old, and there aren't that many new ones—one or two a year, at best."

"Does anyone know why?"

Cerrelle shrugged. "There are rumors—something connected to the Anomaly ..."

"Engee—the so-called god?"

"Whatever it is ... it may not be a god, but we've lost

a few ships along routes that end near the Anomaly. The scientists keep working on it, but whatever they've found isn't common knowledge."

I had to frown at that. "Overspace isn't that congruent with real space-time."

"The ships are missing. Three so far, and there's a deep-space colony of Believers set out there—they went the hard way . . . by photon drive. They run what amounts to a shuttle every few years."

"There was one on the shuttle when I went to OE Station. She said something about the fact that true Believers can't be adjusted."

"They can be adjusted." Cerrelle pushed her plate back just a touch. "Anyone can be adjusted. But adjustment of Believers leads to various forms of insanity that aren't easily cured."

"Oh . . . so a Believer's faith is so deep that it resists Rykashan structures?"

"That's the simple answer, and mostly true."

"But Dzin isn't that deep."

"No."

"Because Dzin is a way of life, rather than a faith per se?"

"Probably. I don't know, but I know it works that way."

Cerrelle told the truth, but her words bothered me all the same. What was it about a Believer that might be different? All people believed *something*. Again, there was information missing or withheld, and I hadn't the faintest idea of what it might be, except in a general sense.

"Believers or not"—Cerrelle stretched and looked down at her empty plate—"I have to work, and you have to go get back to learning to be a Web pilot."

When we left the Overlook, we walked out the lane and up past the transient quarters where I'd stayed after fleeing Dorcha, back uphill toward the glider station.

Cerrelle stopped at the top of the steps. "You can find your own way home. You're a big boy now." She grinned.

"Thanks to you." I grinned back.

She shook her head. "You'd have figured it out. It might not even have taken as long."

"I don't think so."

"You would."

I knew differently, but I wouldn't argue that point. "You made it easier."

"I doubt that. I'll always make your life harder, Tyndel. Don't you ever doubt that."

Harder ... but better ... "I've learned not to doubt your word."

"Good." The smile was better than a hug or a kiss, and I watched as she turned and hurried back downhill.

59

[RUNSWI: 4520]

That which cannot be constructed cannot be annihilated.

Within a few weeks of my return to Runswi, the year turned. Why did the ancients turn the year in the dead of winter, and why had all cultures continued the pattern? None of the databases and libraries accessible through my console had any answers to those questions. Somehow, that confirmed for me that no culture is ever comfortable looking at some of the basic assumptions by which it operates.

I still linked with Cerrelle, but for us, links were short and less than satisfactory, perhaps because neither of us had grown up with the system or because we felt all too strongly the difference between visual representations and full-body reality.

My sessions with Andra had stretched out to every third day, and even Ileck seemed half satisfied with my efforts.

I'd never imagined that I'd be sprinting across narrow beams, dodging fast-moving obstructions and objects with fifty kilograms on my back in pitch-darkness and not losing my balance . . . but most of the time I avoided getting dumped into the shocking black water.

On that day after the year turn, Andra motioned for me to follow her to her work space or office, not the nanite briefing room or the console room. She sat behind a console, and I sat in a green cushioned chair, more comfortable than the briefing chair.

Her words were blunt. "Ileck and I agree, Tyndel. You're ready for the next phase. It's also a big decision point for you."

"Which is?"

"Some nanite-directed and -accomplished modifications to your nervous and sensory systems. Comparatively minor."

Was anything that modified the nervous system minor? "Minor?"

"*Minor* isn't quite the right word," Andra clarified. "The physical changes are modest, and not visible at all, but the impact isn't necessarily minor. Being a Web pilot takes incredible talents and training. You have to know that by now."

"I've gotten some idea. Ileck keeps telling me that. He's always insisting that all the progress I've made is minimal compared to what I'll have to do."

A smile broke Andra's stern visage. "He's exaggerating in one way. Nothing else in the training will be as hard physically. It will be a great deal worse perceptually." She cleared her throat as if preparing to deliver sobering news. "The pilot *is* the ship. That means you need to be able to assimilate and react to outside stimuli instantly, including all the inputs from the ship's sensors and from other sources. Your nervous system's capacity has to be enlarged . . ."

"My brain?"

"No." Andra laughed. "The human brain is over-engineered, most of it, and that part that wasn't, well, we took care of that when you came to Rykasha. The nervous system isn't."

I'd wondered about that more than once, and why it had seemed as though it had taken days for me to regain my strength, but, never having been turned into a demon or Rykashan before, how could I have known? "Just what does this entail?"

Her eyebrows went up and she began to speak. "Without modification, you'd be in a state of perpetual perceptual overload because your sensory inputs and nerve channels aren't designed to handle that much information . . ."

In the end, it was clear enough. Even when not piloting, I'd be able to hear a far greater range of sound and be able to see much farther into both the red and violet, as well as sense to some degree through my skin energy levels. . . . My reactions would be faster, and to protect me from those reactions, my skin would be modified somewhat, effectively creating a low-level nanite armor. I'd be able to link into most Rykashan comm systems without physical contact, were I in fairly close proximity.

"Some of these modifications would be desirable to any human being," I said slowly when she finished.

"It was tried." Andra's voice was flat. "The suicide levels were unacceptable. Only people with the capability of being Web jockeys seem to be able to handle the sensory levels and sensitivity. Think about it . . . more sensitivity means more information. More information means more decision making, decision making where others might not see the need for one . . ."

I nodded, thinking more about Tomas Gomez and Alicia deSchmidt. "So . . . just specialists . . . special operatives and Web jockeys?"

"Some Web jockeys become specialists that way . . . it's their choice. Most don't. There are a few specialists left from the old, old days."

"How can you trust someone with such capabilities?"

"You won't be indestructible, Tyndel—just harder to destroy. Besides, what would be the point? Web jockeys have position and privilege. The way Rykashan society is set up, it's impossible to get more. We don't accept people who are corruptible that way."

That I found almost impossible to believe.

"You were stubborn and stupid, but you were never corruptible. You don't even think that way. No Web jockey does. Some are petty. Some are tyrants aboard their ships, and about half of you are too arrogant for my taste, but you're all very human, and there's never been a case of one being corrupted."

Or of one being caught?

"Tyndel . . . we all live in glass houses with nanite-enhanced scanners trained on us. If the Authority wanted to know what you discussed with Cerrelle, they'd know in hours, if not sooner. They'd even know your lovemaking styles, if they thought it necessary."

"We never—"

"See?" She laughed. "You're even honest about that."

"When do we do this?"

"Now . . . if you're ready."

Would I ever be more ready? I offered a nervous smile. "All right. Now."

"Follow me." She turned and walked down the corridor and then took a set of steps downward. At the bottom, we went through an unmarked blond wood doorway and along another corridor, underneath what looked to be open ground outside. Just how much of Runswi was hidden?

Somehow I imagined a white-tiled room and shimmering instruments and doctors in white singlesuits. My imagination was wrong. The room I entered was five meters square, lit with bright but indirect light, and empty except for a single pallet upon a square pedestal that rose about a meter off the seamless green floor. There were two medical types in red—a man and a woman.

"This is Tyndel." Andra gestured toward the pair. "Doctor Fionya and doctor Colbarr."

Fionya had short mahogany hair that clashed with her red singlesuit. The black-haired Colbarr looked younger, in a way I couldn't describe but felt strongly.

"If you would take off your singlesuit and lie down on the table there," said Fionya.

"Everything?" I asked.

"Everything." Fionya paused, then continued as I pulled off my boots and started to unfasten my suit, "You'll fall asleep here, and we'll ensure that you're comfortable and don't regain consciousness until the optimum recovery point. You may be slightly sore, but there won't be any lasting adverse gross physical aftereffects."

So I undressed, trying to be as impersonal as everyone else. Then I stretched out on the unyielding pallet in a room five meters square, lit with bright but indirect light. I felt like shivering.

Wondering just what I had agreed to, I went to sleep, doubtless nanite-assisted. I didn't dream or have visions or see scalpels . . . nothing of the sort.

It seemed as though I had barely napped when I woke up. Then . . . *then* I saw golden-red arcs of fire against nielle, and the sputtering starry pinwheel. All that appeared and vanished when I blinked.

Both doctors, and Andra, were standing there.

"What do you see?" asked Fionya.

I blinked once more. What did I see? Three people, the same room . . . except that my eyes recorded much more color and *depth*. . . . I blinked a third time. Nothing had changed, and yet everything was subtly different.

"Sit up . . . slowly," ordered the woman in red.

I did, but nothing happened. The room didn't spin, nor did I feel dizzy or disoriented.

"There was something . . . earlier."

"Very good." She studied something she held in her hand, nodding. "All right. If you would stand . . . hold on to the table."

I stood, one hand on the pallet table.

"How do you feel?"

I thought. "There's some soreness, all over, just a little."

"That's to be expected. You were out for three days." Fionya checked the hand-held screen once more.

Three days?

"For the next week, you'll be on a modified schedule," Andra said. "Every morning, you report to medical for a scan. Then you'll get a small briefing, and then a light training session with Alicia. If you're fine at the end of the week, and it looks like you should be, you'll resume a full schedule."

"Alicia? What about Ileck?"

"He has done everything he could. He doesn't possess Alicia's capabilities."

I wanted to laugh. Ileck stood near-on two meters, and looked and moved like an ancient god—big, bronzed, strong, and graceful—and slender, near-erotic Alicia had greater capabilities?

"You have greater abilities, in potential, than Ileck does," Andra continued.

If that were so, it explained a great deal of Ileck's attitude, the impassive and almost withdrawn care. It had to be hard to train people who would do what you never could. *Might do . . .* I still hadn't proved I could do much of anything yet.

"You need to go eat, and then just walk around, read, try to get adjusted to the way you feel. I'll see you in the morning."

I walked out into a cold and bright day, but despite the greater depth in my vision, and the glare of the sun off the snow, while I knew I was seeing more, my eyes seemed more able to handle the glare without blinking or watering.

Cerrelle wasn't there . . . or in my quarters. I knew she wouldn't be, but sometimes hope overrides common sense and judgment. I didn't link. What was the point? I'd survived a modification whose effects I hadn't really even felt yet.

60

Life is born from darkness, not from light.

When I stepped outside my room into the corridor on my way to breakfast the next morning, I stopped, assailed by murmurings and whispers from everywhere.

. . . *click* . . . *hummmm* . . . *click* . . .

". . . trying to reach administrator Challed . . . returning his link . . ."

. . . *scrittchhhh* . . .

". . . doesn't matter who's coming . . . don't put anyone next to a candidate . . ."

I stumbled down to the dining area, trying to ignore the distractions. The formulator clicked and rattled more than I recalled when it came up with a cheese omelet and sweet biscuits. I didn't even want to think about truffled cheese and eggs. The salt on the eggs had a metallic edge, and the Arleen had a smoky taste I hadn't recalled.

There was but a single other person in the dining area of the transient quarters, a man in blue and green—a transport administrator or controller?

CLUNK! I twitched at the sound, managing to hold myself steady. He had only hit the edge of his spoon and knocked it against his platter, but the sound had felt amplified to me. I finished the eggs and the biscuits, not quite all the Arleen, and hurried out of the transient quarters and along the path to the medical building under high thin clouds.

EEEEeeeeeeeeee . . . The sound of a departing mag-shuttle—once so muted—screeched like a drill in my ears.

Doctor Colbarr saw me coming and wordlessly ushered me into a nanite screening room, one of the ones with a collector screen. "WE'LL DO A DIAGNOSTIC FIRST."

I tried not to wince as he touched a stud and a mist appeared that flowed toward me. I squinted momentarily, not recalling seeing such a ghostly brume when screened before.

"YOU CAN SEE THEM NOW—ANOTHER TALENT. DID YOU NOTICE HEARING MORE?"

"Everything," I mumbled, trying to keep my own voice low. "Why didn't I hear all that yesterday?"

"ONSET EFFECT," he announced, as if that clarified everything.

I tried to call up the term. *Delayed impact of increased sensitivity to perceptual stimuli . . . created by axonic physiochemical adjustment . . .*

"PHYSICALLY, EVERYTHING LOOKS FINE." He smiled. "ONE OF THE BETTER DAY-AFTER PROFILES. YOU SHOULD ADJUST WELL."

If I could adjust to such things as the raspiness of everyone's voices . . . and the humming of electroessence everywhere . . . and . . .

"YOU'LL HAVE TO WORK ON MAKING THE PERCEPTUAL SENSITIVITIES VOLUNTARY. YOU CAN, YOU KNOW. JUST A MATTER OF CONCENTRATION."

A matter of concentration? I raised my eyebrows.

"THINK ABOUT IT AS A VOLUME CONTROL. VISUALIZE IT THAT WAY."

His voice still rang in my ears, rumbling like thunder, although I could sense he was trying to speak softly.

"I'll try." My own voice rang and echoed in my ears, even though I'd barely whispered.

Colbarr added, "ALICIA IS WAITING AT THE FRONT OPERATIONS CONSOLE."

Concentrating on the idea of lowering my sensitivity, I nodded.

Ears still ringing, I tried mental commands to myself

and my nervous system or internal demons or nanites. What exactly worked, I wasn't sure, but slowly the hypersensitivity receded somewhat by the time I entered the operations building.

There I met Alicia deSchmidt for the second time, precisely at the same place in the operations building where I'd checked in when I'd returned from OE Station. That was when Andra and Cerrelle had let me walk through gravity I'd been unaccustomed to so they could make a point—one I hadn't forgotten.

"You're Tyndel?" She wasn't even as tall as I was, and her smile was captivating even as I recognized its sheer professionalism.

"Yes, ser." I wasn't about to alienate a special operative, especially one who looked like an adolescent's dream who could drive a knife blade through solid oak barehanded.

She raised her eyebrows. "Do I know you?"

"I watched you drive a steel blade through a table barehanded several years ago."

"Oh . . . the Dzin master." She nodded. "Follow me." She walked briskly down one corridor and around a corner, then through a door and down a circular ramp. At the bottom she followed the next corridor past several closed doors to a door at the end. She opened it and motioned for me to enter the enormous circular room, easily thirty meters across. The walls were black, as were the floor and ceiling, and the arched ceiling looked to be at least thirty meters above me. The only object in the entire space was a pedestal stool or chair attached to a metal pole that meshed seamlessly with the black floor.

"Sit there." Alicia gestured to the chair. It had armrests and a small console of some sort on a curved support rising from the left armrest. "Fasten the harness."

I sat and slipped on the harness that reminded me of those used on the magshuttle that had carried me up and back from the earth orbit station.

She pointed to the console. "You should be able to

operate the console mentally now. Think about powering it up."

I visualized power flowing to the console. Nothing happened.

"A simple command is easier." The dark-haired specialist's words were dry. "Like 'Power.' "

The console energized, and I flushed.

"Always try the simplest solution first, unless you know it's wrong. There." She pointed to the front of the stool. "There is an imaginary line running forward from the direct center of the stool as your reference point. Consider it as either zero or three hundred and sixty degrees. Various stimuli or objects will appear in the room. You are to note their position in degrees and key the location into the console." Her eyes blinked, and a red box appeared by her feet. "What is its location?"

Three hundred forty-eight degrees. "Three hundred forty-eight degrees."

"The input was on the console one point five seconds before you finished speaking. Trust your mind and perceptions. You can't afford that kind of lag. Don't bother to speak."

I shut my mouth.

"Again."

This time it was a black oval.

Forty-seven . . . forty-eight degrees.

"One reference. Just one," she cautioned. "You have to be right the first time. Don't think the word *degrees,* either. The numbers are enough."

A sunflower appeared to my right, barely in my field of vision, and I turned my head as I thought, *Ninety-five degrees.*

"The numbers alone. And don't turn. Learn to trust your senses about what's to the side and behind you. You have to do it without moving. You can't turn an entire needle ship to look at a singularity." She snorted. "And you wouldn't want to. You wouldn't survive it."

Singularities again.

"Now you have the idea. You'll work in darkness from here on." She stepped back and closed the door.

The room darkened, and the pedestal rose, carrying me upward. A slight rush of air confirmed that the floor had fallen away, so that I was suspended in the middle of a sphere.

An arrow flashed straight up.

Two ninety-two.

It vanished.

I licked my lips.

A luminous yellow cube tumbled from overhead.

Seventy-one.

The cube was followed by a bush—lushly green— sprouting out of the side of the sphere as I watched.

"Faster, Tyndel!" Alicia's voice was both spoken and somehow within my skull.

Chartreuse glowed from somewhere behind me. I guessed.

One-seventy-eight . . .

Crack! . . . *Sssss!* Something between an electric jolt and a kick jarred my entire body.

"Don't guess!" snapped Alicia. *"Use your perceptions."*

The objects appeared everywhere—up, down, behind, below—until I lost track of how many and reported their locations automatically.

Then, far later, it seemed, the chair lowered me to the floor—again flat like a normal floor. The lights returned. I wiped my forehead. I was soaked, and I hadn't even been aware of it.

Alicia opened the door and stepped forward, stopping three meters short of me. *Two point nine three.*

"That's enough for today. Tomorrow, we'll start with the first of multiple locations and other stimuli."

Other stimuli? I had the feeling I was going to like Alicia's training even less than I had Ileck's.

"Remember, after this week, you're still required to go back to your physical workouts. Ileck won't be there to push you, but I'll know if you haven't been doing them, and it will show up here."

Of that, I had no doubts. I unstrapped the harness, also damp, and stood up.

"I'd suggest a slow walk up the ramp until you dry out and then a long gentle walk away from people. It helps."

I was sweating and stunk of apprehension, strain, and probably fear, even if I didn't quite know why—except that somehow I did know that all this had to do with my own future survival, symbolic analogue training that it was. The analogues represented danger. That, there was no doubt about at all. Not to me.

Alicia's parting words were, "Drink plenty of liquids, too."

Walking slowly up the circular ramp, I couldn't help reflecting on Cerrelle's hidden help again. I doubted that I would have taken Alicia so seriously had Cerrelle not staged the demonstration by Tomas and Alicia years earlier. I would have liked to have thought otherwise, but I knew better.

Again . . . I owed Cerrelle.

61

[RUNSWI: 4520]

Movement is illusion; so is stasis.

For each of the next four days, after my medical scan, Alicia had demanded greater and greater accuracy in pinpointing the locations of projected objects in the pitch-black spherical operations exercise room. Then she had added the requirement for vertical coordinates, after I had finished my last checkup, when doctor Fionya had pronounced me fit for whatever awaited me.

I knew something else was coming when I walked into the operations training room.

The almost-petite Alicia smiled. "Go ahead and sit down, Tyndel." With her words, the room dimmed into the gloom that befitted an ancient windowless casern rather than a technologically sophisticated culture. I could sense the energy flows from her to the controls, the same sort of linkage that I was gaining with the console and even with the console in my room.

After fastening the harness, I waited in the chair that simulated a pilot's seat, although I knew that it didn't, not from my own pair of needle ship trips.

Alicia was a luminous icon in the dusky blackness. "Today, we'll add moving coordinates. You have to judge where and how fast whatever is projected will intersect your zero reference line. You have to give the location and judge how long before the intersection with you or the zero line."

"Either?"

"There are some things in overspace that you wouldn't wish to put a ship through, but what you can do to avoid them depends on how much time you have."

She winked out, and the chair rose. I swallowed, trying to relax, to accept all the sensory inputs my rebuilt and neurally-upgraded body could gather.

A black spearlike object arched slowly toward me.

Eighty-one, plus thirty-nine, one point three.

A wall appeared dead ahead, not moving at all but apparently growing in size.

Zero . . .

Then it accelerated.

Point two, I added quickly.

"Dead-on objects are deceptive." Alicia's comment didn't stop her or the system from creating a pyramid right in front of me.

"Oooo . . ." The jolt that went through me was worse than what Ileck had used in the black waters of the pool.

"You just lost your ship and your life, Tyndel."

Ignoring the irritation in her voice and my jangled synapses, I tried to use every sense I could muster to pinpoint the veridian cube speeding up behind me.

One seventy-nine, zero, point five.

"Better."

Another disk swelled—red, turning, white-hot enough to feel as though it blistered my face.

Three forty-four, minus twenty, one point three.

A cluster of orange-shaped globules angled up, accelerating as they neared me, accompanied by the frigid cold of space, and the cacophonous rush of a pipe organ march, one too fast for any organ to have ever played.

Forty-three, minus twenty, point two.

The objects kept coming, but, in time, the lights returned, and so did Alicia. "That's all for today."

Again, I found myself soaking wet as I unstrapped the harness. Alicia hadn't created the tension. I had, unable to ignore the importance of what I was attempting to master, knowing that Alicia's training was far more than a series of rote exercises.

"How long for these?"

"Once you've established accuracy in predicting the future locations of moving objects, we'll start your reaction training. Actual velocity varies so much in overspace that even trying to measure it is useless. All you care about is the relative motions and the maneuvering time you have to avoid collisions. You'll understand better when you get into a Web bug." She stepped back, then turned again to face me. "I forgot to tell you. Tomas will be waiting for you in the gymnasium at fifteen hundred, after your workout. You'll need his training as well."

An odd phrasing, but I let it pass. By the time I stood, she was gone, as always, as silently as though she had never been there.

When I left the operations building, a cold drizzle was falling from the thick gray clouds that had moved in from the Northern Ocean. Air and rain were enough above freezing to start melting the ten centimeters of snow that had fallen earlier in the week, and rivulets flowed at the edges of the raised and nanite-heated path. A faint smell of leaves moldering tinged the odor of the cold rain.

Two men in the maroon of land maintenance passed, and I extended my hearing as they retreated behind me.

". . . see that candidate's still here . . ."

". . . seen him swim? Or in the weight room?"

"What do they do . . . need so much training?"

"Don't know, but don't think I want to."

"Not for me . . ."

". . . you'd want the women, Jorj."

"Not at that price."

A half smile appeared on my lips, then vanished. Some people weren't that jealous, unlike those I'd experienced in the lounges with Aleyaisha. The damp cold felt almost welcome by the time I reached the changing rooms of the gymnasium.

The swimming was welcome after running and weight work, especially after working in the pseudo–pilot's chair. All the exercise, strenuous as it was, gave me a sense of well-being and worked out the tensions from all the motion recognition and perceptual training—or perceptual symbolic analogue training.

Once done with the swimming, I made my way back to the gymnasium. There Tomas of the mahogany-red hair was amusing himself with tumbling passes on the pads in the gymnasium—except he seemed to be juggling a pair of razor-sharp blades as he flipped and twisted and finally ended up on his feet—where he threw both fulgent missiles in succession into a small target on the wall. Both were near dead-center.

"Very impressive," I said.

"It's meant to be." He smiled, white teeth contrasting with his olive complexion. His eyes were a light brown, washed out in a way that said he had seen far more than his youthful appearance suggested. "It's also amusing and a challenge to add more elements."

"Alicia sent me. She said you have more training for me. She wasn't very specific."

"You don't need what I'm going to teach you to pilot a needle boat. You'll need it to remain one. You need total conditioning. You can't maintain it on a weightless orbit station. That means you go planetside whenever you reach a destination and have a layover. Some locals are less than accepting of effete earthers, even Rykashans—after all, they're nanite modified as well, and there can't ever be a successful challenge of a Web pilot. Ever." Tomas smiled placidly. "With the modifications to your system, you should be able to avoid most difficulties. My training is designed to ensure other situations shouldn't be a problem."

He handed me a white blindfold.

"More darkness?"

"No. That's to protect your eyes from the glare. Anyone who's nanite-enhanced can step up hearing and sight in normal darkness. It's harder under intense heat and light." He offered a lazy smile I distrusted. "You'll see."

From somewhere he produced a wooden wand, then a second, which he extended to me. "You'll never need to use a weapon, but this is easier on you to begin with. Put on the blindfold."

After having seen him in action twice, I had no doubts about that. Once the blindfold was on and I held the wand loosely in my right hand, I could feel heat—and a blinding light that stabbed my eyes, even through the blindfold.

"I'm going to tap you gently and at odd intervals. I want you to concentrate on trying to use your senses besides your eyes to feel out where I am. Just try to sense where I am."

"Yes, ser."

He laughed. "Tomas is fine." He tapped my left shoulder, and I tried to gather a sensory picture of where he was.

Another tap went to my right thigh. I couldn't hear anything but the faint susurration of his breathing. Where did it come from? Another tap to my left shin.

"Can you sense me?"

With the voice, I located him immediately. *One point four meters, forty-three relative.*

Another tap, this time to the back of my upper right arm.

I concentrated. *Point nine meters, one forty-three.*

An impact harder than a mere tap—to my left shoulder blade.

One point one meters, two zero-one.

"Now . . . try to face me as I move. If you don't follow me, I'm going to tap you harder."

The first tap was to the wand I held, and with the vibrations I could turn to face Tomas, but his "image" faded, lost in the glare and the heat that poured down on me. I caught a whiff of sweat, acrid, not mine, but could not locate it.

Tap! The back of my left wrist stung.

Too many taps landed, despite my intermittent success in trying to keep Tomas before me, for all too many times I did not anticipate or sense his reversals of direction.

"That's enough," Tomas said. The glare faded. "You can take off the blindfold."

I pulled off the damp and white band, my eyes on Tomas. His face was damp, somewhat sweaty. My singlesuit was soaked—again, and I stunk of frustration and apprehension.

"You're getting the feel for it. Learning to read your body's signals is hard. Most demons never go beyond sharper eyesight and listening in darkness. I'll see you tomorrow."

He picked up the fulgent blades from somewhere and began to juggle them, his eyes closed.

I hoped Tomas was right. I had small welts everywhere on my body when I left the gymnasium, welts that once would have been solid bruises—and would be again if I didn't learn faster.

62

Visions are born and die in those who behold them.

On sevenday, Cerrelle was actually waiting when I stepped out onto the glider platform in the depths beneath Lyncol. Instead of a singlesuit, she wore blue trousers and a shimmering white shirt under a sky-gray coat that looked to be wool.

"It's good to see you." I couldn't help smiling as I saw her, as the handful of other passengers eased around us and toward the steps.

She answered my words with a smile.

"This is the first time I've seen you in something that wasn't an official singlesuit." I switched the duffel to my left hand, and we walked up the polished stone steps together.

"There has to be a first time for everything." She paused. "Are you hungry?"

"I've never not been hungry since I came to Rykasha. Where do you want to go?"

"Me, either. The Overlook is close, and it wasn't full when I walked by."

"That would be good."

At the top of the steps, I opened the door, and we stepped into a cold and clear day, a sky bright blue without a trace of clouds. The rain that had fallen in Runswi had been snow in Lyncol, and the piles that flanked the path were more than head high as we walked downhill and toward the Overlook. In the light breeze, snow sifted across the top of the piled snow and onto the path, where it promptly melted—or was melted by some nanite magic.

The tops of the pines swayed ever so slightly, and powdery snow sifted through the needles and sprayed in minute clouds across the lane to the Overlook.

Cerrelle held the door for me. "More people than when I came by earlier."

The tables in the center of the wide glass windows were taken, and we sat at the last one at the south end of the glass. Cerrelle's face was pale.

"You need something to eat," I said. "Go get it. I'll hold the table."

"Just leave your jacket. No one will take it."

Given the honesty, enforced or otherwise, of the Rykashans, she was right. I had to frown as I followed her. I could have done the same in Dorcha. Was there a certain skepticism programmed into us genetically that came out when we didn't think? What else showed up when we reacted? I wasn't sure I wanted to know.

Cerrelle was loading her tray while I was still looking over the limited menu, finally settling on Chicken Mettersfel, flattened and breaded chicken sautéed in wine and smothered with truffles. It came with grass rice and mixed greens.

Cerrelle was waiting as I returned to the table.

"Eat," I told her, "before you collapse."

That brought a smile, and she did lift her fork. I sipped some of the Arleen and glanced out the window. The mounds of snow that flanked the frozen and snow-drifted pool looked lower, until I realized that windblown snow had filled in the hollows. Little swirls chased each other in the intermittent brisk wind beyond the glass. The heat of the hearth warmed my right shoulder.

After several mouthfuls of her roast lamb, Cerrelle looked up. "How are you doing?"

"As they expect, I think. If I weren't, I'd have gotten some indication." I cut some of the herbed chicken and chewed it and some hard cracker bread with sesame seeds fried into it.

"You're learning. I told you you'd be good at it."

"You don't mind my coming for just a few hours?" Outside, the wind picked up and whipped fine snow powder against the window.

"It's better than not coming at all." Her face remained sober, but there was a smile in her eyes, one I wouldn't have seen a year earlier.

"I'm glad you feel that way."

"*You* were the one who didn't feel that way on OE Station," she reminded me.

I winced.

"Tyndel . . . I may forgive, but I don't forget." She softened the words with a half grin, half smile.

"Best I not forget that."

"You have some bruises. There's one on your neck."

"Your friend Tomas. He's taken over my physical training."

Cerrelle winced. "I'm sorry."

She *was* sorry. Her voice and the tension behind it indicated that as well. I thought for a moment. "It would take me years, dozens of years, to match his skills. Where do they send pilots that's so dangerous, and why did they pick me? Because I was so difficult and I owe more?"

She shook her head. "It's not that—not the owed balance. The Rykasha are honest. You worked off three years' worth out of fifteen. A bit less than fifteen for OE Station. That leaves you with six or seven years to make up at a Web jockey's rate. Your training doesn't work off time, but it doesn't count for more time, either. Some training does." The redhead across the table from me sipped the last of the amber liquid in the tall beaker.

"Why not pilot training?" I wondered.

"It's not transferable. A doctor or medical technician could emigrate to one of the outplanets or one of the Rykashan free states and use her training for greater personal gain." Cerrelle gave an ironic smile. "No one but the Authority can afford to operate needle ships."

"So, to obtain the privileged lifestyle of a pilot, I have

to keep working for the Authority." I shook my head. "That's assuming I get that far."

"You will . . . now."

I stood. "I'm getting some more Arleen. Would you like something? What were you drinking?"

"Kienralle."

I'd never heard of it, but I nodded, hoping it was on the formulator menu. It was, and I returned with more Arleen, and another frosted beaker that I tendered to her.

"Thank you."

The Arleen tasted the same as the last mugful, and that bothered me. Why? Because brewed tea varied slightly from cup to cup? Why hadn't I thought about it before? Because I had had more to think about than the strength and consistency of tea?

"That's a thoughtful look," she offered.

"I was thinking about how everything from a formulator tastes the same. It may be excellent, but it tastes the same."

"True cooking never goes out of style."

"Do you cook?"

"Do you?" she countered.

"Some. Not for years, now."

"Men don't cook in Dorcha?"

"Some do. Most don't."

"The same as Dezret. You know, that old pattern was changing, beginning to change when the Devastation happened, but in all the mite cultures the stabilization reasserted the same old gender roles."

"What about here?"

"More men cook, but not many, not with formulators around." Cerrelle laughed. "What would you like to do next?"

Looking at her in the white and gray and blue, for the first time, really, I knew I wanted to hold her.

Cerrelle flushed, the red climbing from the open collar of her shirt and suffusing her lightly freckled face. "Besides that."

I found myself blushing, in a way I hadn't since I'd been a student of Manwarr in Henvor. "Show me something I haven't seen in Lyncol. Something scenic," I added quickly, then found myself blushing more furiously. "Outside, buildings or trees . . ." *Or anything!*

"I can do *that*." She was blushing as much as I was.

We both began to laugh.

Finally, she said, "You can take the man out of Dorcha . . ."

"Or the woman out of Dezret?" I asked.

"I know what you might like to see." She rose, keeping her eyes from me. "Something very old."

"Old? In Rykasha?" I grabbed my jacket and hurried to follow her.

Once on the narrow path from the Overlook, brushed once by a cloud of snow released by one of the pines overhanging the way, Cerrelle walked quickly. "We don't have much time, not for this."

"For what?"

"What I'm going to show you."

I could hear the smile in her voice. We passed the transient quarters where I had stayed, and then another of the buildings with no name, and then another. She walked up the polished reddish stone steps of the fourth structure, one half sunk into a hillside that might have been grass-covered in the summer. Now, the hillside was swirled and drifted snow.

"What building is this?" I asked as I followed her down the wide corridor, lit indirectly from high skylights above.

Cerrelle stopped before a door with a miniature console. "The transport center." She opened the door and stepped into a narrow room, one that held long suits approximating the space coveralls I'd worn to do outside repairs at OE Station, except these were green rather than silver. She handed me one. "These are in case of emergencies."

Then she ushered me out of the room and along the corridor. Before long we were in a maintenance bay where a half dozen silver-green gliderlike shapes rested inertly on a gray composite floor. I studied the craft as we walked toward the nearest. On the base of each were tracks, tracks that circled sprocketed wheels, a design that looked positively antique.

"They're glider-cats. We use them in the mountains. Some of us have our own."

"We're going to the mountains?" I wondered why she had her own glider-cat, but decided against asking.

"We're already in the mountains. We're just going higher." She touched a plate on the side of the glider. "Take the far seat. Put your suit in the second seat."

Rather than go through a door or archway directly outside, Cerrelle guided the glider toward a tunnel on the north side of the building and slipped the glider inside. "We could have gone the long way if you'd had more time, but the last part is what you should see."

"What am I seeing? Besides a transport tunnel?"

"A transport tunnel, and then something I'd like you to see. Let me surprise you."

Since I wasn't going to get a direct answer, I studied the tunnel walls beyond the canopy of the glider-cat, but they blurred by in the greenish gray haze created by the low lights thrown forward from the glider-cat itself. Cerrelle concentrated on the controls, not looking once in my direction. So I finally settled back in the high-backed and cushioned chair and looked at the blank green console before me, then toward Cerrelle's console. That was simple, from what I could tell—the console's flat panel with a small keyboard, the tiller, a pedal for acceleration, and four gauges, one for power, two measuring various temperatures, and one labeled "Trac."

A series of red strobe lights appeared ahead, flashing out of the darkness, blocking the end of the tunnel. Cerrelle keyed something into the console keyboard, and the lights faded. As they did, the end of the tunnel irised open onto a stretch of clear snow. From the depression before us, I could see that the latest snowfall covered a packed expanse of snow—a snow road.

"We're to the east and north of Lyncol now," Cerrelle announced, touching several studs below the "Trac" indicator. A high and barely audible whining began as the glider-cat followed the cut into the trees, first between the bare-branched oaks and maples and occasional pines and firs, a space not that much wider than the two-meter breadth of the glider-cat.

Outside of those tracks we left, there were no other traces in the snow. We traveled less than a kilo before the deciduous trees gave way totally to evergreens clothed in white. Smooth as the glider-cat was, we left behind us a swath of snow clouds. The near silence and the snow created a sense of unreality, almost as though I were seeing the snow and the trees and the snowy peak beyond the trees through a screen rather than through the permaglass of the glider's canopy.

"Beautiful . . ." I murmured.

"It is. You can enjoy it, but there's more." The sound of a smile came behind those words as well, but her face remained concentrated on the controls and the road.

I doubt I'd ever been in a winter vehicle moving so swiftly and not on guideways or tracks, yet Cerrelle kept the glider-cat steady.

"You learn this in the Patrol?"

"One of the things I learned there. They're even more necessary in the west. There's more territory to cover. Much more."

After a half hour, when the way became even steeper and the trees began to thin, I asked again, "Where are we going?"

"Onto another trail."

Trail? As I thought about that, she eased the glider-cat around a corner and onto a ridgeline that was barely ten— more like five—meters wide. *Eight point seven.* The glider-cat moved silently along the twisting but eerily smooth trail.

A burst of snow flew from somewhere, and the entire glider-cat shivered.

"There was once an ancient road, not along this ridge, though. They drove their petrolwagons up here during the summer. It was colder then." Cerrelle did something to the controls, and the glider-cat slowed, dropping almost into the snow.

Colder? I glanced into the afternoon, onto the rocks and the powdered snow that was drifted everywhere. Colder? The wind moaned. The glider-cat shivered, and more snow sprayed across the canopy.

Ahead, along the ridgeline, was something that shimmered. Snow flew around it, enshrouding it, but even when the gusts died down, the shimmering persisted.

"We're almost there," Cerrelle announced.

"Where?"

"The highest point east of Dezret. Sometimes, the winds here reach over two hundred kilometers per hour."

"And we're up here in a glider-cat?"

"They're only running about forty." Cerrelle slowed us more as we neared the top of the peak. "The stabilizers can handle gusts of a hundred, easily."

Were we on the top of the feared Demons' Peak, where the winds ripped men apart? Where people froze in instants?

"There." My red-haired driver eased the glider-cat to a halt beside a shining golden haze, turning the vehicle slightly sideways on a flat expanse of snow thirty meters square—precisely thirty meters square.

Above us and behind the shimmering shield was a structure—an ancient structure. Huge chains, each link a half meter long—or more—rose out of the stone beneath the drifted snow. Each link was reddish, tinged with the rust of centuries, perhaps millennia, yet somehow still massive. There were four chains, one for each corner of the building, and all four passed through the shield—a nanite force-shield of some sort—and crossed the top of the building. The stone-and-timber building, its shape blurred by the shield, was chained to Demons' Peak. Those iron chains—adiaphorus, carious, colossal—were they like the ancients themselves, trying to defy the universe itself through brute force?

I kept looking, though there was little enough to see but an indistinct structure, a nanite shield, chains, rock, and snow.

"There's something about it, isn't there? Not something you can really describe."

"Yes." But, like Cerrelle, I couldn't exactly say what. My eyes went to the west, where clouds scudded toward us with cold celerity, where the tips of lower peaks barely pierced the gray of the oncoming storms.

"We'd better go."

I nodded, and Cerrelle turned the glider-cat, leaving me alone with my thoughts for a time.

More gouts of snow plastered the canopy, and the craft shook more than a few times before we dropped back below the tree line. Once back among the trees and the gloom that would have been shadows had the clouds not blocked the late-afternoon sun, Cerrelle took a deep breath.

"A little close?"

"A little," she admitted. "But I didn't know when you might have another chance."

"I appreciated the scenic drive, all of it."

"I thought you would. Sevenday is about the only time we could have gotten up there without a flock of people around." She smiled without taking her eyes from the console. "Another good part of this is that, since I never finished your indoctrination fams, I can charge the fuel for the glider to that account."

That brought me up short. "You would have paid for that?"

"If I'd had to. But I don't." That brought a grin. "The Authority thinks you're worth it." She flicked something on the arm of her seat, and lights flared out, illuminating the tracks we followed back down toward the tunnel to

Lyncol, tracks that had already drifted over in places.

On the way down the road, even in the dimmer light, I could see how old the trees were, squat pines twisted and gnarled, and tall firs with trunks more than two meters across. Beyond the glider-cat, the wind began to howl, and white flakes skittered across the permaglass of the canopy.

At the end of the road trail, the red strobe lights flashed, but the tunnel doors opened, and Cerrelle eased the glider-cat inside. Her entire body relaxed once we were in the tunnel.

"Thank you," I said again.

"I'm glad you liked it."

"I'm not sure I liked it," I had to confess, "but I'm glad you showed it to me. What was it?"

"A meteorological outpost, from what we can tell."

"But people drove petrolwagons up there?"

"There's a lot the ancients did we still don't understand. It could have been religious. Or some of them might have been ancestors of the rock-climbing self-suiciders."

I chose not to mention Sanselle, but Sanselle was anything but suicidal. The ancients? Who could tell about them?

When we came out of the transport building, the snow had begun to fall in Lyncol as well, lazy fat flakes dropping out of dark gray clouds. In the time it took us to cross the four hundred meters between the transport door and the transient quarters, the wind picked up. Snow turned into a gusting sideways curtain of white, coating my hair, turning Cerrelle's red hair white.

We ducked inside the double doors leading down to the glider platforms and wiped off snow.

"Definitely cutting it close," I said.

"You always have, Tyndel."

"Me? You were driving."

She raised her eyebrows again, and I had to grin. We walked slowly down the steps to the glider platforms. Then we stopped.

"I had a good day." I found myself smiling at her. The departure bells rang twice.

Cerrelle squeezed my hands. "I won't see you much before long."

I frowned.

"You're going to be busy when you get to ship-handling. Very busy."

"So Andra told me."

She squeezed my hands again, and I had to scurry into the second seat in the glider. The doors slid shut, and I was swept eastward into the tunnel toward Runswi.

In the glow of the glider, with the darkness of the tunnel beyond, I sat back in the glider seat, closing my eyes and trying to make sense out of the day. Why had I blushed so much, felt so much like a schoolboy again? Because I didn't have to be so on guard, because I knew Cerrelle had seen me at my worst and would still see me and talk to me?

Abruptly, behind or before my closed eyes, arcs of fire exploded, so bright that it felt as though they seared my ears, yet those golden-red arcs of fire were brighter, closer, and the depth of space far deeper, yet nielle with a fulgence that beckoned, than I had ever sensed before.

I sat up in the dimness of the enclosed glider, eyes wide open, breathing hard. What was it about that niellen fulgurence? *And why now?*

63

The body senses reality; the mind interprets it;
trust your body.

After all the days in the dark simulator with Alicia, suddenly, it seemed, I was standing, waiting for a shuttle to Orbit Two.

Alicia had been as brief as always the day before, telling me, "Report for the zero seven hundred shuttle tomorrow. Be at the operations desk by zero six-thirty. All you'll need is two complete sets of candidate greens, toiletries, and underwear. Your instructor will have everything else waiting for you. The first fam runs three days, usually, but that depends on the instructor and you. Yours might be less, because you have null grav experience, but I wouldn't count on it."

I wasn't. As I stood at the operations building waiting, all I could count on was that I'd learn something new and more difficult than I'd envisioned, or that some other piece of knowledge would rearrange once more my perceptions of the universe and my place in it.

The seven hundred shuttle was a busy one. A good dozen people stood in the area of the operations desk by zero six forty-five. A thin wispy fog hovered across the marsh beyond the permacrete strip, and through the open door that led to the gray shuttle came the sharp cry of a bird. It might have been a heron, but I'd never heard one make a sound, though I'd watched several from the lounge that overlooked the marsh lake.

A black-haired woman in the dark green singlesuit with

the golden web collar pin stepped toward me. "You're Tyndel? The latest pilot candidate?"

"Yes, ser."

Her eyes took me in, and she nodded. "It's harder than anyone can tell you it will be, and easier than what you fear. No one else can do what we do. It sounds arrogant, but it's not, and you have to remember that, outside the Web, you're only a demon." A brisk nod followed. "I'll see you somewhere."

"Captain Siobahna?" called the man behind the desk.

"Here." The pilot gave a last nod and turned, walking out toward the shuttle by herself.

After Siobahna neared the ramp, the desk man called again, "All controllers may board."

A woman in medical red, a man in blue, and a woman in black were followed by a thin blonde in blue.

"Candidate Tyndel?"

I followed the controllers out. Behind me came seven or eight technicians in silver and gray and one in maroon. The passenger section of the magshuttle was as windowless as the two I had taken before and could have been the same, for all the difference I could determine. I did get one of the wider seats in the third row behind the needle pilot and the senior controllers.

Also, as before, the "dull" scent of composite was overridden by the faintest hint of oil, heated metal, and ozone. A last whiff of marsh or salt air slipped into the shuttle before the door silently slid shut. I checked my harness again, trying to catch the low words passing between the controller in black and the one in blue sitting in front of me.

". . . out to Thesalle, this time?"

". . . no . . . headed to Omega Eridani. More problems with the Conan project . . ."

". . . said that one wasn't true Vee-type."

"Nothing's true Vee-type, even Venus, and we've got another five hundred years to go there."

"So why do we do it?"

"Better than bemoaning a universe in which Tee-type worlds are almost nonexistent . . . might as well do something to have our flowers in more than one garden."

Flowers in more than one garden . . . I nodded at that.

"Please make sure your harnesses are fastened. We will be lifting shortly."

After the single warning, the magcraft shivered slightly and then slid forward, gradually lifting into its hover before accelerating down the permacrete toward the east and then taking a high-angle climb to minimize sightings by Dorchan and Dhurr ships traveling the Summer Sea and the ocean beyond. I doubted many lookouts strained their eyes peering into the heavens, or would have dared report what they saw. Except they would have seen little, I realized, because composite was nonreflective to just about any form of energy.

The almost imperceptible whining became far more perceptible as the magshuttle continued to accelerate, rising in volume and frequency until both my teeth and ears felt nearly shattered. I'd tried closing my eyes before, but I tried again—before reopening them quickly. That hot darkness was filled with fragmented images of various objects being hurled at me and recollections of trying to find Tomas in hot blindness while being continually struck.

I left my eyes open and waited until the whining died away, until I found myself being pushed forward in my harness by the force of a brief deceleration, then weightless, drifting upward against the restraints. Finally, I could hear the *clunk* of docking at Orbit Two.

"Smooth trip . . ." came from the seat in front of me.

Null gravity didn't bother me at all now, and I glided out of the seat and toward the opening hatch—behind the black-haired Web pilot, the senior operations controller in blue, the Authority controller in black—at least I thought the Authority controllers wore black—and the medical type in red.

In the tube from the lock outside the shuttle, the black-haired Siobahna had pulled herself to the side to talk to another pilot, and I hung back, tuning up my hearing to catch what I could and letting the technicians slip past me.

"What are you here for, Erelya?"

"Lucky me . . . drew training . . . candidate on board . . ."

". . . he's in back, I think . . . doesn't seem too bad . . ."

"Where to for you?"

"Mithras . . . the new planoforming station there."

"Hard haul, they say . . . and it's a low road . . . long subjective . . ."

"Someone has to . . . better let you get to your charge . . . he's holding back, either because he's polite or eavesdropping."

"Both, I'd guess."

I tried not to flush as the two pilots said good-bye, then I eased forward with my small duffel, using the overhead lines.

"You must be Tyndel." The training pilot had short brown hair scarcely longer than mine, pale gray eyes that looked right through me, and a pleasant smile.

"Yes, ser."

"You don't seem terribly upset by weightlessness. You been in null gravity before, right?"

"Yes, ser. Three years personal objective on OE Station."

"That lets us skip the null grav fam, then, and start with the station orientation." She gave a crisp nod and turned effortlessly and without the gross motor reactions that tended to send people sideways in null gravity.

Dragging my duffel, I followed through the tube and into a long corridor much like the lower level corridor on OE Station.

"Lower level is all cargo and maintenance," Erelya continued without looking back at me. "Second level is passenger entry locks. Third level is operations. Top level are residences. Ops and residence levels run at about point three grav, and that's pushing it. We stay there when we have to be on station. You hope that's not often."

Why? *Because the pseudograv is too low and because centrifugal force substitutes for gravity? It doesn't precisely replicate the physiological impacts.*

"You've used a broomstick?"

"Yes, ser."

"Good. We'll start with the bug. After we suit up." Erelya led the way around the lower and outer edge of the station—all in null gravity.

We passed a transition lock, then two cargo locks, and another transition lock. A technician in silver approached, a new technician, indicated by the not-quite-fluid movements.

"Good day, sers."

"Good day," Erelya answered cheerfully.

I echoed her greeting.

Erelya drew herself to a halt opposite a green hatch—a dark green hatch. "This is the lower level ready room." She eased open the hatch and slipped inside, where, after waiting for me, she pointed to a locker—with the silver name "Tyndel" on it. "That's your gear. Check it out. Put on the suit and the boots. You can leave your duffel there for now."

Except for being green, and fitted rather precisely to me, the outside suit was the same as those I'd worn on OE Station.

"You won't wear a helmet in a needle ship or a bug, but it will be racked where you can reach it easily."

From the ready room, soft helmet in hand, I followed her—she had suited more quickly than had I—back along the cargo corridor to the closest cargo lock. In the lock was an ugly contraption—a composite-hulled, ten-meter-long oblong capsule with large canisters seemingly placed everywhere and dual exhaust jet openings front and back and on the top and bottom.

"This is your starbug," said Erelya. "It's a modified bug with gasjets, but the feel is similar to the ion-electrojets that needle ships use to maneuver. You'll begin to learn how to handle a ship with it."

I'd never been in a bug before, although I'd seen them in the locks on OE Station. Up close, this one was uglier, and more battered than I would have thought.

"Get in." The bug had a hatch rather than a true lock, and Erelya had opened it while I was still studying the craft's exterior.

"That's where you sit." Erelya pointed to the single seat in the middle compartment of the bug, a seat surrounded by blank screens. "This isn't quite a standard bug. The controls are set like a needle ship's cockpit, the part a pilot uses. It isn't big enough for the entire control section."

The bug's control seat looked more like one of the needle ship passenger couches than a vacuum bug-control station, except that there was no overhead matching clamshell. A bug wasn't built for the degree of acceleration/deceleration that required a nanite-cushioned restraint seat.

"You get the part that looks real. I sit up front—" She gestured through the open forward interior hatch toward a much smaller and more cramped console and seat behind a real permaglass canopy. "Someday, if you're good enough, you'll be the one up there." She slipped toward the seat that looked so oversized. "First, the harness and headset there. The harness plugs into the inserts on your suit. I'll show you. Oh, and put your helmet in the open locker to the right."

I eased my way into the seat, stowing the soft helmet, and strapped myself in place. The restraints were designed differently from those I'd had as a passenger, more confining.

Erelya hooked a foot under the rear of the seat and demonstrated how the harness mated with the restraints and how the data leads mated with the receptors on the tops of the forearms of the outside suit. "Your arms won't

leave the seat channels once you begin an insertion, not
until you're back out at your destination."

I slipped on the headset—more like a formfitting partial
helmet—and staggered mentally at the mass of sensory
data. Chill from receptors in the bow and stern ... minimal warmth from the cabin ... twenty percent heat dif-
ferential between the top and stub gas tanks ... diffuse
heat sources in the cabin ...

We were the diffuse heat sources, and I wanted to shake
my head.

The data kept pouring through me.

I'd almost forgotten Erelya until she touched a stud and
the bug hatch closed. "I need to get strapped in and run
through the checklist. All you do is watch. Watch *everything*."

How could I? Not only were my eyes registering what
I saw inside the bug, but I was getting all sorts of images
from the sensors—all four sides of the cargo lock, plus
smaller images of the gas-thrust nozzles. That was in ad-
dition to all the other data—gas pressures and temperatures, interior atmospheric pressure and temperature,
power flows from the fuel cells ...

But the deep, deep *vision* ... that was the strangest and
the most familiar—the bulkheads of the cargo lock, dull
gray composite, yet a blue that was not a blue, chilled but
not so cold as the nielle beyond the lock door, and the
crackling yellow lines that sparkled beneath the inert composite, and webs of white and yellow and orange that
wove the starbug together. I swallowed once, and then
again.

I licked my lips, difficult because my mouth was dry.

"You ready, Tyndel?"

"Yes, ser."

"You're not. No candidate ever is. No point in waiting."

The starbug shivered as the cargo lock cracked and ice
crystals puffed around the hull, doubled images picked up
in the screens before me and in the direct inputs that fed

into the augmented new sensory system the Authority had
given me. As I struggled to reconcile the images, the crystals swirled away. Chill bit at me, and I could feel the
exterior hull temperature of the starbug drop.

"I'll take us clear of the station."

Well clear, I suspected.

"Watch the power, and try to feel what I'm doing." Her
voice shifted—or the frequency channel shifted. "Earth
Orbit Two, Starbug One, leaving lock three."

"Starbug One, cleared. No inbounds this time. Request
duration, Captain."

"Estimate one point five. Local vicinity. Maneuvering
practice."

"Thank you, Starbug One."

The starbug's ten-meter length of composite and gas
canisters slipped through the open lock and into the darkness, dwarfed by the side of Earth Orbit Station Two, a
battered composite gray structure blurred against the black
of space above the ecliptic. Space itself, experienced
through the sensors, was insubstantial yet endless, its
depth emphasized by closer and misty colored webs of
power that girdled and infused the station and the distant
deep white point-disc that was the sun itself. Colors and
power washed over and around me.

Solar radiation, photons, energy—whatever the term—
pattered like rain striking the left side of the bug, each
bundle of quanta somehow registering as heat, or something like it. My eyes twitched, and so did my fingers.

I forced myself back into the mechanical Now where
Erelya was just the latest Rykashan to demonstrate how
the demons didn't have much use for lengthy introduc-
tions to anything, even maneuvering ships in space.

Or for sensing all the unsensed that I'd never experienced before.

I watched, knowing it was the first of many long sessions, wondering—far from the first time—what I had
committed my life to.

And why.

64

Each action creates multiple reactions; act seldom and well.

With deft and quick puff-blasts from the gasjets, Erelya brought the starbug to a halt relative to Orbit Two, nearly five kilos behind us, and less than a kilo and a half from the object before us.

The cold nielle of space burned through the sensors, with the distant disk warmth of the sun off my shoulder and the woven cascade of powerlights enshrouding me. Through both sensors and screens, I studied the dull facade of composite film and the black outlines of the lower cargo locks and the upper passenger locks. The simulacrum was stretched on invisible nanite-projected supports—a facsimile of an orbit station apparently dwarfing the starbug. The entire facade massed less than twenty kilograms, and most of that was the central nanite control box from which the facade microthin film was generated.

"You have it, Tyndel." Erelya's voice was calm, matter-of-fact.

"I have it," I repeated as I felt the lock on my controls lift, the same way in which Erelya had lifted the control lock for the past five sessions.

"You'll see more than most," the training pilot said, her voice coming to me on direct feed through the system, "that it doesn't look like a real station, but this way you can practice without scaring me or damaging yourself and the bug."

All of those were worthy objectives. I also knew that the facade would let me make more grievous errors and thus subject me to greater wrath from my instructor.

"Remember, effectively, the simulacrum has no mass—you touch it with the jets and you'll just push it away, or rip a hole in it and turn it into gray ribbons. Center your approach on the upper passenger lock."

"Yes, ser." My fingers rested in the arm channels, ready to use the manual controls if Erelya decided to call some sort of emergency and require me to navigate solely by the screens before me. The direct links were faster, but I knew I'd be drilled in both types.

How was I supposed to complete the approach? Any direct approach meant side jets, and within twenty meters, any real use of braking jets would shred the simulacrum station.

"To begin with, you'll just sidle up to twenty meters. If your jets affect the simulacrum, then you're using too much braking."

Easy enough for Erelya to say.

"Eventually you should be able to bring in the starbug against the film so gently that the lock will kiss the outline without rebounding. Then we'll try approaches to a closed station lock . . . and eventually we'll start borrowing needle ships after they've finished their runs so that you can get the feel of a real ship. I've talked enough. Bring her in to thirty meters from the lock shell."

I gauged the distance. *Point eight-seven-five kilometers.* Too far to begin with a side approach—I'd end up having to shift gas to the side tanks in order to get enough braking at the end—or come in like a snail, which wasn't the best approach, either.

The "main" stern gasjets got a tweak. On a standard bug all jets had equal power, but the starbug's jets had been adjusted so that the power proportions were equal to those of a needle ship. And needle ships did not have side jets anywhere near as strong as the fore and aft ionjets. That was a matter of safety for stations and those around them.

The distance between the bug and the "station" dwindled. *Point seven-one . . . point six-eight . . . point five-four . . . point four-nine . . .*

I kept running the brake-power calculations.

At point three, I offered a quick blast on the forward jets. The rate of closure dropped. *Point three . . . point two-eight . . .*

But I was drifting down, below a direct line to the target passenger "lock" outlined in black, rather than a real lock with the massive dampers that protruded and formed a cradle of sorts. I offered a slight burst to the bottom jets, and the starbug rose back toward dead even with the lock before I gave the exact same burst of power to the top jets.

Closure was slower, but continuing. *Point one-nine . . . point one-five . . .* Suddenly the simulacrum seemed to loom over the bug, and I could sense again that the starbug was below the lock. I had to turn the bug sideways to match locks, and that took a right forward jet and a left rear one. Then before the bug dropped too low, I sent another minute pulse to the bottom jets and then an even smaller one to stabilize my relative vertical position.

My closure accelerated—*point zero nine . . . point zero six . . .* —and the bug was still swinging.

I reversed the turn thrusts, and the inputs indicated that the bug was parallel to the "station."

But I was still closing far too quickly. *Point zero four.*

The power burst needed to stop closure was too much—*point zero three*—and too close by the time it stopped. Two angular rents slashed across the dull gray sheet of the simulacrum, effectively bracketing the "lock."

Still I had stopped short of the "station"—if close enough almost to have touched it from the hatch, were it open.

"Tyndel . . . your passengers and your third officer would be happy. A quick approach, relatively gentle, and you would have barely bumped the dampers. The station's maintenance officer would be screaming to the station commander about how you roasted the dampers and shortened their life by half."

"Yes, ser. I understand."

"Do you?"

"I had to replace dampers, ser. It took days for one lock."

"They're complex enough that they're lifted from earth. If the dampers on the lock were already worn, you just rendered that lock useless for a year unless the station had a spare on hand. That doesn't make station commanders happy. It doesn't make the Authority happy. It might have you running cargoes through the Trough. That won't make you happy—or anyone you might know, because the dilation's worse there."

Even with all my background information, I didn't understand all the references, such as the Trough, but the message was clear enough. "Yes, ser."

"Tyndel . . . you're making too many corrections. Each jet correction adds another vector to the bug—or to your needle ship. You do it too often, and even *your* nervous system won't be able to judge the correction you need because it'll have more components than you can execute."

Unless I broke off the approach and started all over. I had the feeling that was wasteful of power and definitely frowned upon.

"Take us up a good kilo and out two. Try to stabilize us there before you start the approach."

"Yes, ser." I blotted my too-damp forehead with the side of the suit's forearm, keeping my sweat from the shiny control lines, even if they were supposed to be impervious to anything as mundane as sweat.

Up one and out two—an angled approach, and I hadn't even managed a direct approach right. After moistening my lips and swallowing, I pulsed the jets.

Erelya's presence overhung the pseudonet, almost as enigmatic as the dreams of golden-red fire and pinwheel spirals of stars that loomed over my sleep and dreams.

I added another pulse to the jets, then forced myself to wait, to follow her advice about not piling on vector after vector, to work through another long session in the starbug . . . and no end in sight.

6 5

[ORBIT TWO:4521]

Never mistake a pilot for a guide. The former travels to a goal, taking passengers whether they truly wish to accompany him or not; the latter helps others see both the journey and the destination.

Nearly six months of struggling—half the time in orbit with Erelya, or occasionally other pilots, and the other half of the time struggling back in Runswi with Tomas—followed my introduction to the starbug. Cerrelle and I linked, and even less frequently met and talked, gingerly, like two people balancing on a narrow beam in darkness, uncertain of which direction might lead into deeper night and which toward dawn. That was mostly me, combatting the internal demons of exhaustion and doubt, and fearing success or failure, and still seeking greater apperception.

The starbug struggles came to an end when I found myself in the Orbit Two ready room with Erelya and another pilot, short, almost squat, and stocky, with muddy brown hair and gray-blue eyes with the piercing and washed-out irises that seemed common to all pilots I'd met.

"Captain Aragor is one of the captains of the *Tailor*," Erelya announced. "He'll work with you. I'm just here to observe and to set up the simulacrum."

"Pleased to meet you, ser." I inclined my head to him and bowed slightly.

"It's always good to see another candidate, Tyndel. We never have enough pilots." Aragor smiled warmly. His body posture and eyes confirmed the smile. "Shall we go? You'll need almost two hours for the first fam."

Two hours? Was I going to inspect every cranny of the needle ship?

"Just about," he answered the unspoken question, or perhaps the question I'd felt so strongly that he'd picked it up through his own enhanced nervous system. Or every candidate felt the same way. "Put on your outside suit."

Intellectually and mentally, I knew the *Tailor*. The reality was different, different even from my recollections of what I had felt on my first trip out to Omega Eridani. Somehow, the needle ship was both larger and smaller as I followed Aragor on my broomstick along the *Tailor*'s hull.

Although the jets incorporated variable geometry nozzles, from outside they appeared just as squat black spouts, the four set both fore and aft nearly three times the size of the side maneuvering jets. Outside of the jets' nozzles, the ship's exterior was without projections, a cylinder a hundred meters long, gently rounded at each end. The hull was dull, black, inert composite two thirds of a meter thick, capable of withstanding any man-made impact—*even impacts where the shock would destroy the interior*—capable of withstanding the enormous pressures and temperature fluctuations of overspace insertion and exit.

"Most needles have their hulls rebonded every five years." Aragor's voice was soft in my ears, undistorted by the soft helmet. He turned his broomstick back toward cargo lock three. "The abrasion from insertions." He did not speak again until we had left the lock, helmets in hand, and were headed up to the passenger level to enter the *Tailor*.

"Most people couldn't tell one needle from another, not

from outside, and some not from inside. You'll always
sense the differences. Pilots do."

I hoped I could.

The *Tailor* followed the standard design of all needle
ships, cockpit and passenger section forward and on the
upper level, power sections fore and aft, and cargo in the
larger lower holds. There were no permaglass canopies or
windows for external viewing, not in the ship's normal
configuration, although there was an emergency navigation porthole in the control center, behind a movable section of hull, a port that had never been used on the *Tailor*,
according to Aragor.

The control center, or cockpit, held three of the massive
acceleration couches, forward bulkhead screens, manual
controls before the center couch—that was all that was
visible, though I could feel the sensors and the power lines
and all the connections of the *Tailor*'s systems.

Erelya gestured to the couch on the left. "You sit in the
second's chair until we're well clear of the station." She
took the third couch.

Aragor said nothing as he took the command seat, nor
could I hear anything as he went through the checklist. I
did sense changes in the status of the ship. I could feel
the fusactors come on line, and the locks closing, the fullness of the Rinstaal cells.

Shortly, the *Tailor* slipped away from Orbit Two so
smoothly that I could not feel the change, only sense the
parting of two sets of energy concentrations. Equally
deftly, Aragor eased the ship to a halt, so deftly that I
wasn't sure he had until, abruptly, the pilot eased out of
his couch, his boots a half meter above the deck in the
null gravity. Using the toe of his left boot, he levered
himself down deftly and extracted a pouch from the small
locker in the base of the couch. He clipped what appeared
to be a coupler and then a length of sensor tape to the
input line to the controls. "This allows me to freeze you
off the system and the boards, if I think it necessary. Even
with this, I can't sense what you're doing. I can monitor

what data you call up from the system and the physical
reactions of the system, but not your inputs. Erelya has
doubtless told you why it is engineered that way. I'll be
following the ship's monitors and the screens. If they
show a problem, I'll take over, and"—he smiled ruefully—"it won't be gentle. You'll have enough of a headache that we'll be done for the day. So try to be careful
and not waste the time you have with the *Tailor*. You can
take the command couch now."

"Yes, ser."

"Taking time to familiarize yourself with the ship is *not*
wasting time. Take twice as much time with that as you
think you need."

For all his outward courtesy, for all the softness in his
voice, I could sense the metal core of the man, one that
brooked no argument. "Yes, ser."

"After you feel comfortable you will make your first
approaches to a simulacrum. That's just like you have
been with the starbug. The simulacrum will be modified
in scale to match a true needle ship, but the proportions
are the same so that you shouldn't have that much trouble
adjusting."

I hoped I didn't, and I tried not to fumble as I linked
into the *Tailor*'s net system—and was blinded and deaf-
ened . . .

. . . *white lights strobing from deep within Orbit
Two* . . .

. . . *the faint warmth of the distant sun oozing through
the composite of the hull, the patter of photons clicking
across my skin—or was it the hull?*

. . . *the cage of powerlights fractionally shrinking and
contracting around me* . . .

. . . *the whispering chill of niellen space sucking,
grasping at the heat within me* . . .

. . . *cold points of light set so infinitely distant that each
was a tiny cold bell frozen on a single note not quite
struck* . . .

After the initial onrush, I swallowed and began sorting

through the sensors. While the inputs were all the same as with the starbug, the strength of the outside sensors was nearly overwhelming, and more than half of the inside system feeds felt *deeper*—the ones that had been simulated and were now real.

I went through the checklist, not because the ship needed it but because that was the surest way to ensure I had the feel of everything. Then I scanned all the exterior sensors. Somewhere, along the way out from Orbit Two, Erelya or Aragor had launched the simulacrum. Through the sensors of the needle ship, the simulacrum felt even more flimsy and false, the thinnest construct approximating reality. Beyond the ghostly presence of the simulacrum station was the solid presence of Orbit Two—somehow warm and stolid in the niellen dark.

In time, I looked at the older pilot, then back the other way, in Erelya's direction. "I'm ready, sers."

"Make a standard approach to thirty meters," Aragor ordered. "Figure about ten percent greater response lag than you've been using with the bug. It varies from individual to individual, and you'll need to work that out before we try anything closer. Don't try to stretch it out at the end."

"Yes, ser."

The controls were physically the same, and the ionjets responded almost as had the modified gasjets of the starbug, but the needle ship felt more massive. Once I'd eased the *Tailor* toward the target station's lock, I monitored everything, watching even more closely over the last few hundred meters of the two-kilo approach.

Point zero-six-zero . . . point zero-five-five . . . point zero-four-eight . . . The ionjets eased off, as did the load on the fusactors, and the *Tailor* rested motionless at forty-five meters from the simulacrum. I could have eased it closer, but Aragor had ordered me not to try that.

"Good." Aragor's head turned—that I could sense from the system without looking. "And good starbug instruction as well. Take her out to two kilos, where you began this approach, and try it with a five percent lag, instead of ten."

"Yes, ser."

I eased the *Tailor* away from the simulacrum, gently at first, since a full blast of the ionjets might have shredded the film surface, and back to where I had begun the first approach. Then I recalculated, and then, with a slow deep breath, tried again.

The separation between ship and simulacrum dwindled. *Point zero-four-eight ... point zero-three-nine ... point zero-three-four ... point zero-three-one ...*

After the last puffs from the ionjets, I had the *Tailor* twenty-five meters from the simulacrum lock, without a mark on the film-thin composite.

"One more," said Aragor. "Let's try for twenty meters."

I managed twenty meters—twenty-one, rather. My forehead was slightly damp but not pouring sweat.

"Fold and recover the simulacrum." Aragor gave the impression of a shrug, and he turned in the second's couch. "You seem to have a good touch, Tyndel. We'll see how that works later on. Now, you'll try a stand-off approach to Orbit Two, lock four, the one on the end. Bring the *Tailor* in to a position fifty meters from the station, still side-on to the lock."

"Yes, ser."

"And tell Orbit Two what you're doing."

I nodded. "Orbit Two, this is *Tailor*. Commencing near approach to lock four this time."

"Orbit Two here. Understand series of close approaches to lock four. No inbounds this time. Request you inform Orbit Control when you intend to engage dampers."

"Will report intent to dock, Orbit Two."

"Stet, *Tailor*."

I checked the controls and everything once more before starting the real approach.

Fifty meters turned out to be fifty-two, but I had caught the sense of apprehension and felt I'd best err on the side of distance.

The next approach was to thirty meters, and the third to twenty meters.

After the twenty-meter approach, Aragor said, "All right. Back the ship off to five hundred meters. Once she's stable, disengage the harness. Gently, please."

When I had the *Tailor* away from the station and stable at five hundred and twenty meters, I disengaged the harness, and we changed places.

Aragor brought the *Tailor* into lock three as smoothly as he had taken her out, and without a hint of dampness on his forehead. Once the needle ship was docked and cradled and shut down, he sat up, disengaged himself from the system, and looked at me. "I don't know as I'll see you again, but best of luck, Tyndel."

"Thank you, ser."

Back in the ready room, Erelya added more. "You're doing fine. From here on in, your training schedule is going to depend partly on what needle ships are available for you to use. We'll try more complex approaches to the simulacrum with a real ship—all the types you've done with the starbug. Once you seem to have mastered those in clear space, you'll do them to a stand-off to the station. Then, when it's clear you can put a needle ship exactly where you want it . . . then we'll begin actually docking to the dampers. This can't be rushed, you know?"

I nodded. That was something I had already determined.

"Good." Erelya left me with a faint smile.

66

*A river is water undertaking a journey, yet life is not a river,
nor man a pilot upon it.*

My sessions in Runswi with Tomas slacked off, but
Erelya plied me with more research projects on needle ship systems and overspace and real-space navigation,
and those filled every free minute—or so it seemed. Except I knew, for whatever reason, that I was filling every
one of those minutes because, once I had agreed to be a
candidate pilot, I could no longer pretend whether I succeeded or not didn't matter. I had failed once. I had never
really been a Dzin master, no matter what I had said, no
matter that Manwarr had granted me the title. I knew better, and I refused to fail again.

When I returned to Orbit Two once more, as on so
many other occasions over the past four months, Erelya
awaited me in the ready room with another Web pilot.
"Tyndel, this is captain Sesehna."

At first glance, the woman with Erelya looked the most
un-captainlike of any of those I had seen or worked with.
Small, almost petite, with an elfin face but a slightly
squared jaw, the bare hint of curves beneath the dark
green singlesuit, and a hidden wiriness without overt muscles. Then . . . she looked at me, and I almost froze. The
eyes held the kind of determination and power I would
have equated with . . . I couldn't have even put a name or
a title to someone who radiated that much sheer force of
will. I felt dwarfed, and seldom had I so felt. Yet her smile
was polite and not at all condescending.

"Sesehna is a senior captain," Erelya continued. "She'll

work with you for the next few days, as necessary."

"I am pleased to meet you, ser." I bowed to cover the shock I had taken.

"We're fortunate to have the *Hook* for the next several days," Erelya added. "And Sesehna."

Sesehna inclined her head toward me. "The *Hook* is cradled at the number two locks, passenger and cargo."

I deferred and let my seniors lead the way up to the number two passenger lock, where we entered the needle ship, past the two maintenance crew members standing by to monitor the locks when we departed.

". . . don't see three jockeys together much . . ."

"Last one's a candidate . . . pretty far along if he's being allowed to handle a needle . . ."

Pretty far along? Far enough along to get myself into real trouble? I smothered a silent laugh. Whenever you learned enough about something, you could get yourself in real trouble. Experts always caused more damage when they failed.

Sesehna came to a halt by the command couch and turned to me. "You may make all departure arrangements." She clipped her own harness into the double bracket. "Once you're ready for actual departure, check with me." With the fluidity of a diving bird—or something more graceful—she slipped into the second's couch, leaving me floating akimbo above the command couch.

Erelya silently, once more, took the third's couch.

The *Hook*'s acceleration couches were fractionally closer to the forward bulkhead screens, as were the manual controls before the command couch—really the first deviation I'd noticed from the standard pattern I'd seen in all the needle ships. I used my boot toe to ease myself back into position, and strapped in as quickly as I safely could. Once I was hooked into the system, I flicked through the ship's database, confirming that the *Hook* was one of the most recently completed needle ships—less than ten universe objective years old. I did not hurry as I checked out all the systems of the *Hook*, even skipping from sensor to sensor to gain those full-spectrum images that were so much deeper than mere vision, images that sometimes occurred even when I was not connected to a needle ship.

As I went through the checklist, I monitored the changes in the status of the ship, noting the fusactors as they powered up, the locks closing, and the glittering fullness of the Rinstaal cells. Finally, I turned to Sesehna. "Ser, ready for departure."

"Take us out three kilometers at plus five, zero degrees relative to lock three."

"Yes, ser." I informed Orbit Control and tried to emulate the smoothness of departure I'd first felt with Aragor and later with some of the other pilots, and the *Hook* slipped away from Orbit Two smoothly, if not as silkily as I might have wished.

I used single power jets to bring the needle ship to a halt, leaving her at three point zero five kilometers, rather than fuss with the ionjets for fifty meters.

After scanning the screens and the manual readouts, Sesehna spoke, not looking in my direction. "Make a standard approach to the station, lock number two. A complete halt five meters from the dampers."

Just like that. A standard approach so close it might as well have been a full approach to dampers and cradling—and the unspoken promise that if I even looked as if I'd botch the approach, I'd have a splitting headache and an angry senior pilot.

I calculated, twice, and then again. I ran a signal check to the ionjets, trying to get a sense of any divergence from norm in power/mechanical lags. Then I modified the calculations, notified Orbit Control, and sent power to the ionjets.

The *Hook* slid through the photon-splashed niellen dark toward Orbit Two, first briefly accelerating, then coasting, before I cut in the forward jets for braking.

Point zero-six-zero . . . point zero-five-five . . . point zero-four-eight . . . The ionjets eased off, as did the load on the fusactors, and the *Hook* rested motionless at six meters from the station. Sweat had pooled at the back of my neck and seeped out from there.

"Not bad." Sesehna's head did not move. "Adequate for a start. Take her back out to one point six kilometers at thirty-one plus."

That I could manage and did.

Once the ship was stable, the senior captain made another clipped statement. "A low-power approach. Seven percent power from the Rinstaal cells. Another five-meter clearance."

Seven percent power with a heavy needle . . . that was asking a lot, but I ran through the calculations and then began the setup.

As the *Hook* began to accelerate, the ionjets cut off. They'd been cut manually by Sesehna.

"You've just lost half your Rinstaal cells and the fusactor is dead," she announced. "Finish the approach to five meters with two and a half percent power."

I scrambled through the reordering of everything, and attempted to respond with a dual decel burst. I wasn't going to risk it all on one burst.

After the second burst began, my attention was on the closure and distances. *Point zero-two-eight . . . point zero-one-nine . . . point zero-one-four . . . point zero-zero-nine . . .*

I held my breath following the last ions from the jets, but the *Hook* held at five point five meters from the passenger lock. *Six point one meters from the lower cargo lock.* For a full standard minute that seemed far longer, I waited in silence.

"Take her back to one point eight kilometers at minus fifty."

So I did, stabilizing the ship where Sesehna had directed.

"This time you have eleven percent, and you will bring her in for a full docking." Sesehna paused. "All the way through to full cradling and locks open."

"Yes, ser." I pulsed Orbit Two. "*Hook* commencing low-power approach to docking and cradle."

"Understand docking and cradle, candidate."

"Affirmative, docking and cradle."

Erelya seemed slightly more tense, and I wondered what emergency Sesehna would pull, but nothing happened while I eased the *Hook* inbound, or even after the ionjets cut in to start the deceleration.

Abruptly, the entire net went dead.

Sesehna glanced at me. "Bring her in manually, Tyndel. Full locking. You have no communications, no system."

My fingers found the manual controls under my fingertips, and each finger felt twice its size, and slippery on the rough studs.

. . . *point eight-seven-four . . . point seven-eight-five . . .*

I still had my own abilities to calculate, but now I needed to factor in greater lags and sluggish responses. The first deceleration burst was late and too short, and I scrambled mentally to readjust.

. . . *point four-one . . . point three-seven-two . . .*

I eased in the ionjets once more, conscious of being hot and cold and sweating all at once, my eyes skipping from one manual indicator to another, far slower than assimilating the figures directly.

In the end, the *thump* of docking and cradling was only slightly heavier than normal, and with that impact, I had the net back. I was drenched, beaded with sweat that had welled up all over me and run nowhere, just merged into ever-larger puddles to soak through my underclothes and into my suit.

"Uncradle and take her back out—two kilometers at plus ten."

I followed the orders and waited to see what other difficult approach the senior pilot would request.

"Execute a normal approach."

"Yes, ser."

I watched like an ancient hawk, waiting for another

trick, another emergency, but nothing happened, and I eased the *Hook* into the dampers and cradled the needle without even a bump.

Then I sat in the pilot's seat and tried not to take too deep a breath.

Sesehna glided back, hooked herself down beside me, and unfastened the cutout harness. "Open the locks. We're done." After a minute pause, she added, "You'll do."

I somehow felt those two words were almost a compliment from the senior captain, and as much recognition as I'd be likely to receive.

As she slipped toward the locks that I'd begun to open, Sesehna turned to Erelya. "Another good job."

The senior pilot was at the lock as soon as it cracked, and gone before I even finished the shutdown checklist.

"You'll do all the approaches and departures from now on," Erelya said from beside the command console.

"What comes next?" I slowly released the harness and reclaimed my soft helmet from the locker beneath the command couch.

"The procedures for overspace insertion and exit. That will take a month or so until you know them even if half your brain is gone. Then you get a real assignment."

67

[LYNCOL: 4521]

The difference between truth and honesty is the difference between the riverbed and the river.

When I walked away from the downshuttle at Runswi, the late-afternoon sky was deep blue. Despite the sun, a breeze made the fall day seem cool, almost chilly. My mind was worrying over Erelya's parting remarks—

"Next time you come up, you'll be ready to find out if you're a needle pilot." *Next time?* Why not then? Why offer that possibility but not even schedule it firmly? Just because it depended on the availability of a needle ship? Or was there more?

The wind ruffled my hair, and I brushed it back, finally pushing away my concerns about what else it might take to become a needle jockey and thinking about the red-haired, sharp-featured, and very honest woman who'd helped me find myself. I hoped to get to Lyncol and spend some time with Cerrelle. I glanced up, hoping to see her, knowing I wouldn't because she couldn't even have known when I'd return, not when I seldom knew more than a few hours in advance.

Instead of Cerrelle, the sandy-haired Aleyaisha was waiting outside the operations building. "Tyndel!" She beckoned.

I turned and crossed the dozen meters separating us. "Good news or bad news?"

"No bad news." The full lips pursed into a smile, and the brown eyes were friendly. "You've been busy. I thought you might like some friendly company. So did Cerrelle. She's on her way to Thesalle."

"For long?" I blurted. *Thesalle . . . ?* The green planet, the one that wasn't what it seemed, the one whose strangeness eluded measurement and quantification? *Why Cerrelle?*

"You're not always the controlled Dzin master, I see." Aleyaisha's smile broadened.

"I never was. Not too much." It had been hard to hold on to Dzin when I recalled the two children kissing in the cataclypt of Dyanar, or when I remembered having tea in the Dzin master's house in Hybra, or recalled my cruelty to Cerrelle in lashing out at her when the faults had been mine. Yet . . . for all that, had I ever been a Dzin master? *Not really . . . or not fully.* "Do you know what she's doing on Thesalle?"

"Cerrelle? Only generally. They want someone who

wasn't born a Rykashan to help calibrate the atmospheric baseline effect . . ."

"I'm not sure I like that."

Aleyaisha gave a shake of her head, the sandy hair bobbing away from her head, showing more clearly the elfin jawline. "Every time I see you, you've become more honest with yourself," she said after a moment.

"It must have something to do with being a demon."

"All demons aren't as honest as you are. So I doubt that." She inclined her head. "Are you hungry?"

"Yes. The marsh lounge," I suggested.

That received a nod. Her singlesuit was red this time, with silvered cuffs, and I nodded to myself as we walked along the pathway north and east of the operations building.

"Unless you want to cook," I added, managing not to smile.

"What I cook neither of us wants to eat."

"I'm not sure of that."

"You would be if I cooked, Tyndel. You don't want to be that sure."

I took her word for that.

"How is the training going?" she asked after a silence as we walked up the wide stone steps to the marsh lounge.

"I'm getting close to the end, but Erelya won't—or can't—give me a definite answer as to how much longer I have before I learn whether I'll make it as a needle jockey."

"You will." Her voice held quiet assurance.

"I'm glad you think so. There are times I'm not so certain about that." I held the door for her.

"Few are as hard on you as you are—now."

I understood the "now." I'd coddled myself too much, but who was to say I still wasn't?

When I sat down with my plate of Dhurr pepper chicken and looked through the permaglass into the early afternoon, I found my eyes fixed on a blue heron that stood one-legged on the far shore, across the open water from the lounge. "Do you attract herons?"

Aleyaisha glanced up from her plate of plummed dumplings and through the glass. "Only when I'm talking to you."

I laughed. "You haven't seen one since then?"

"I haven't looked."

"What have you been looking for?"

"You've been a Rykashan for nearly eight years objective . . ." Aleyaisha offered, ignoring my question.

"Two thirds of that personal objective." I took a sip of the steaming Arleen, enjoying it immensely, since tea isn't the same on an orbit station, even an earth orbit station with partial gravity.

"That's still quite a time, Tyndel. Nearly six years and you're questioning whether you belong and whether you should." She sipped the beaker of pale green liquid. "Why didn't you question so much when you thought of yourself as Dorchan?"

Because you didn't want to . . . because you never sought the wider world? Because Dzin taught you to seek meaning in what is, rather than in what isn't? "I wasn't raised to question. That came later." I laughed. "After Cerrelle unscrambled my brains and kicked my ego down to size."

Aleyaisha peered intently into my eyes, exaggerating the gesture and expression. "I don't notice any ego dwarfism."

"You help, too."

She raised her eyebrows, both of them, so comically that I nearly choked on my pepper chicken. "Let's change the subject . . . a little. What is the heart of Rykasha? What defines it? Have you thought about it?"

At times, you've thought about little else . . . "I suppose it depends on what you mean by the heart. Functionally, nanotechnology is the key to Rykasha, since it enables the whole structure."

"You might call that the skeleton or the nervous system . . ." mused the blonde.

The pieces fell together—so obvious. So obvious as to be simpleminded. *Power beyond great power allows honesty and compels those in such a society to demand it.*

"What are you thinking?" A tone of concern edged into her voice as she studied my face.

"About honesty. Why Rykashans have to demand honesty—and greater honesty for those with greater responsibility." I sipped the Arleen, lukewarm rather than hot, but I wasn't ready for another mug of hot tea. "That's your heart, if you want to call it such."

An amused smile replaced the concerned frown.

"Because there's no workable alternative. High technology, and nanotechnology is effectively high technology, requires greater honesty if the society is to survive. Deception, even hypocrisy or excessive manners, is deadly for a society of people of power."

"Oh?" Aleyaisha took another sip from her beaker, then the last dumpling from her plate. "Why would that be?"

"You know, but I presume I'm supposed to explain."

"I don't know if I know. Your answer, that is."

"It's hard to put in words. I'll try. There are but two checks on the abuse of power—greater power and the individual will of those who have power. As power is magnified by ability, the adverse effect of checking power through the use of greater power rises exponentially." I paused. "Maybe not exponentially, but the side effects grow larger more quickly than individual power grows because it takes a greater and greater concentration of power to check power that is abused. That means the only viable means of restraining power is by ensuring power is used responsibly. The only effective means that I can see is to ensure honesty—and Rykasha goes to great lengths to do just that."

"You're assuming honesty reflects integrity," Aleyaisha pointed out.

"I'm defining honesty in the sense of being honest with one's self."

"Can't someone be honest with herself . . . or himself . . . and still deceive others?"

"The Authority does it all the time," I riposted, "by letting people believe partial truths, but the whole truth is there for whoever wants to look. Look at the needle ships: Space is enormous, and overspace has to be dangerous. I can tell that just from the training. Yet nowhere is that stated. There have to be ships that have never arrived, but there's no record, not that I can find. The problem is that most people can't or won't see it because of what they want to believe. But that's not quite the same as setting it up so that self-honesty is required to use power. That's really why you have Alicia and Tomas. Unfailing self-honesty is all that they have left—and honest pride in that honesty."

"You think they're enforcers of some sort?"

"I *know* they are."

Aleyaisha finished the last of the single beaker she had brought to the table. In the twilight, the great blue heron flapped off toward the depths of the marsh. "You're quite a philosopher, Tyndel."

I shook my head. "It took me six years to puzzle it out. That's not great philosophy, not for someone who spent half a life in the halls in Henvor."

"Most who spent that long there would never figure it out, Tyndel." Aleyaisha stood. "You don't mind . . . I've a long day tomorrow."

"I don't mind." As I stood, I looked at Aleyaisha. "Did I pass, honored examiner?"

She began to laugh so hard that her eyes teared. I couldn't help but join her. The couple in the corner stared, but we could have been alone for all that they were there.

Finally, she gasped. "Tyndel . . . you'll do just fine . . ." She shook her head.

"Why? It was obvious, once I thought about it." Then,

that was usually the problem—discovering what the real problem was—the step beyond Dzin.

"It was—but no one else has ever confronted it quite . . . your way." She shook her head. "You are more of a Rykashan than most Rykashans. You denied that to begin with, and you still try to deny it."

"What does that have to do with being a needle pilot?"

"Everything," Aleyaisha answered simply. "Everything. You'll see." She reached up and touched my cheek. Then she began to walk past the empty tables toward the door, and I followed. "Even if I had been the one to meet you and bring you into Rykashan society, Tyndel—it wouldn't have worked. You were too honest for Dorchan society, and you're too honest for me."

Except I hadn't been that honest. I'd been self-deceptive and focused on attaining the title of Dzin master rather than the understanding implied by the title. It had taken Cerrelle to change that, with an honesty that had been almost brutal in its directness. "No one is too honest for you."

She held the door for me on the way out. "You're kind, Tyndel, but it's not so. I almost would have climbed into your couch that first time, because you were still hurting, and I wanted to comfort you. That kind of comfort isn't honest, and you knew it."

"I tried to be honest."

"I know." Aleyaisha touched my cheek briefly, once more, before her hand dropped away as she stepped into the darkness beyond the lights, darkness that my eyes could penetrate as easily as if the full moon had shone. "Good night, Tyndel. Don't forget to stop by medical before the shuttle liftoff."

"I won't. Good night, honored examiner."

"Your turn will come . . ." A soft laugh followed her words.

"Perhaps."

Rather than go back to an empty room, I took a long walk along the marsh path, well past the lounge and along the raised hump of ground that might have once been an ancient river levee. *More Rykashan than most? What is a demon, a Rykashan?*

Someone with nanites swarming through his system and powers beyond the ancients' imagining? Someone whose nanites triggered a Dorchan demon scanner or killed a passlet? Was being a demon as much a state of mind as anything? Being able to accept near-absolute honesty?

The call of something—an owl—echoed across the marsh, a call that haunted but offered no answers.

Even by the time I reached my quarters and my bed, I had no answers for my questions, nor any for the two other questions: Why did such questions matter; why did they bother me?

I laid back on my bed, thinking about Cerrelle, somewhere on Thesalle Orbit Station or Thesalle itself, about Aleyaisha, about honesty . . . about becoming a needle jockey for real.

When my eyes closed, the golden-red arcs of fire were brighter, closer, and the nielle of deep space far deeper, yet with a fulgence that beckoned.

I sat up, eyes wide open, breathing hard.

After a moment, I walked to the window and looked out at the damp brown that was more like gray in the light of the half-moon.

More Rykashan than most Rykashans . . . But what was a Rykashan, or a demon?

I still couldn't answer that, not the way I wanted to.

68

Technically developed self-consciousness isolates the self to an individual
who reduces others to the status of things.

Dekunin ran me through diagnostics at zero six hundred, nodded, and said, "You're fine."

I caught the seven hundred shuttle, as I had for what seemed years, and before that long found myself standing before my locker in the ready room. I opened it. My pale green shipsuits had all been replaced by the darker greens worn by needle jockeys, each folded neatly on the restraining shelves. On the collar of the first new shipsuit was a shimmering golden Web pin.

I turned as someone entered. Erelya floated just inside the hatch.

"Go on. Put it on." Erelya was tense, and I'd never seen her tense.

I pulled off my boots and then slipped off the pale green suit and folded it.

"Just put it in the cleaning bin."

I eased into the darker green suit, the fabric nearly silk-like. It was silk, nanite-generated and modified silk, but silk. After I'd replaced my boots, my eyes went to the senior pilot. "This isn't as simple as you're making it out to be, is it?"

She shook her head. "It is, and it isn't. Only a mind can direct a needle ship—one mind and one mind alone. You know there's no such thing as a copilot. We train you as well as we can. We scan the routes as best we can, and start pilots out on the easier runs . . . but the energy involved . . ." She shrugged. "When we think you're ready, you get a ship and a run."

And everyone hopes you've been trained well enough that we all get where we're going and back.

"Exactly," she responded.

Sometimes, it was clear, pilots could read thoughts— or close enough. Sometimes I could, even, with Cerrelle and Aleyaisha, but more so with Cerrelle.

"Let's go up to operations," Erelya continued. "You need to meet Astlyn. Then you'll meet your officers."

Your officers? That sounded strange, strange enough that I felt almost numb inside, but I took my soft helmet and gear and followed her along the corridor and up the transverse shaft.

"Your ship will be the *Mambrino*," she continued over her shoulder.

The *Mambrino*? I repressed a laugh. *Certainly appropriate for you, master of Dzin and seeker after illusions.* "It's one of the older needles. Less of a loss if things don't work out?"

"More of a loss. The older needles are more stable in overspace, but that's not the point, pardon the pun. It's suited to you. We try to match ships to pilots. You'll see."

Her matter-of-fact tone chastened me. "I'm sorry."

"You wouldn't know."

But you should have guessed. "I'm on my own, and you have no idea whether I'll make it or not, or whether I'll destroy a ship . . ."

"That's right. The Authority bets a ship and a cargo— ten million life-credits on each new needle jockey." From the shaft hatch, Erelya glided left along the upper-level corridor.

The Authority really bet that amount on each insertion—the odds were merely much worse on a needle jockey's first run. And now I was the one swallowing and wondering.

"The cargo is valuable . . . not irreplaceable, but still close to it . . . planoforming nanotemplates, that sort of thing. You know already, Tyndel, that *any* interstellar cargo is nearly irreplaceable. So are needle jockeys." She touched the edge of a blue-and-black-rimmed hatch and motioned for me to enter.

A single figure waited in the operations room, standing in the light gravity beside the central console. He was black-skinned, with brown eyes that were guileless and simultaneously looked right through me.

"This is Astlyn. He's the senior operations controller here. Astlyn, this is Tyndel."

I could see a collar pin—the Web pin, except with two four-pointed stars on each side. My internal information store let me note that he was both a needle pilot and a junior member of the Authority.

"Tyndel, I'm pleased to meet you. I hope we'll be seeing a great deal more of you. Erelya has confidence in you."

"I hope to be worthy of that confidence." *What else can you say?*

"So do I. Erelya is seldom wrong." Astlyn's thin eyebrows lifted slightly. "I would not like to see her wrong."

That was almost a command—bring back the needle ship.

"Nor I, ser."

"Good." With a nod, he turned to Erelya. "I leave you to introduce the officers."

Why did he need to see you? Just to let you know there is a senior controller? So that he could tell the Authority?

"He's the one who authorizes first flights," Erelya said dryly. "So . . . if you fail, it's both our heads." After a pause, she continued. "On your next flight, you'll meet your crew in the ready room and introduce yourself on your own."

As if on some sort of cue, two officers entered the small operations room.

Erelya gestured toward the round-faced blonde in the singlesuit that was darker than my candidate greens had

been but lighter than the silklike Web jockey singlesuit.
"Berya will be your second."

"Pleased to meet you," I offered, studying Berya, taking
in her air of competence. Supposedly either the second or
third officer could maneuver a needle in real space with
the manual controls, in case something happened to the
pilot in overspace, and doubtless the officers on the *Mambrino* would be more experienced than most, given my
inexperience.

She nodded, returning my smile with one somewhat
forced. "Erelya says that you're good."

We'll see, won't we? "I hope to live up to her confidence."

The squat black-haired man glided forward, inclining
his head.

Erelya explained. "Souphan will be your third. He's
actually going to Santerene for a more permanent assignment, and you'll pick up another third for the return."

"The cargo's already loaded," Souphan noted. "Full,
but not pushing mass limits."

"Good." Both Erelya and I spoke simultaneously.

She smiled. "I'll leave you three to the business of getting the *Mambrino* ready for departure."

"Thank you," I said, and nodded to the other two officers.

Berya returned the gesture and led the way from the
operations center. The three of us made our way back
down the shaft and to the passenger level.

As we reached lock three, where the *Mambrino* was
cradled, I finally said, "I appreciate your expertise and
your confidence."

"That's what we're here for, captain." Berya's smile
was professional, if guarded.

Souphan tapped out the entry code on the touchpad,
and the ship's lock opened. "I'll be below, ser, doing a
last check on the cargo and the stays."

That definitely made sense from Souphan's point of
view—with a new Web pilot at the controls.

Belatedly realizing that I should have unlocked the ship with a direct control, I began my inspection with the passenger compartment, and continued through every space, just as I had with Erelya. And as with her, I didn't find anything unusual.

Back in the control center, after strapping myself into the command couch, I checked the harness, then the headset, before running through the systems checks.

"Passengers are boarding," Berya announced. "Five of them—all working on the Santerene Three planoforming project."

"Thank you. Anything else I should know?"

"They don't know this is your first insertion."

"Let's make sure it stays that way."

My words did bring a smile to the lips of the round-faced second, if but for an instant.

I was ready to uncradle the *Mambrino* before Souphan returned, but I rechecked all the systems and tried to get a better feel for sensors and responses in that interim.

"We're ready for departure." The dark-haired third strapped himself in.

"I'll notify ops," I told them.

Berya was already making the announcement to the passengers. "Make sure your harness is securely fastened. We will be departing shortly." Berya's voice came through both center speakers and through the system.

I beamed operations. "Orbit Two, *Mambrino*, ready for departure."

"*Mambrino*, area clear, no inbounds this time, understand destination Santerene."

"Orbit Two, destination Santerene, uncradling this time." When the cradles released, I gave the lower ionjets the slightest puff, enough to undock us, followed by a side puff, phasing in more ionjet power as we separated.

"Orbit Two, *Mambrino* clear of lock three. Departing this time."

"Stet, *Mambrino*. Controller Astlyn sends his best."

"Orbit Two, thank him for us."

I moistened my lips and stepped up the power flow from the fusactors. Even at full power, the acceleration from the ionjets was limited, unlike the photonic system, but we had to be well clear of anything—a minimum of two hundred kilos—before I could bring up the main drive system even on minimal power.

When I did extend the photon nets, brought the configurators on-line, and then switched from ionjets to photonic drive, more than ever the mass of the cargo loomed under and behind the control center, and me, with a feel that made the term "jockey" seem more appropriate than I had realized, far more appropriate.

I eased the needle's nose upward, trying to establish the orientation necessary for Santerene, as the acceleration built for insertion speed. Then came the excitation power-up, lattice after lattice raising the needle toward overspace.

"Minus ten for insertion," I announced quietly as the growing acceleration pressed us back into our couches and the clamshells above clicked out of their restraints.

"You *must* be in your harness at this time," Berya announced.

"Minus five." Scanning the passenger cabin, I could see and sense that all passengers were secured, and recalculated again, trying to ensure an orientation as perfect as possible.

"Minus three."

The clamshells and nanite foam filling were in place, sealing us against the pressures, cushioning us against the growing acceleration—more than ten gees and building. I could feel the barriers between now and overspace thinning . . . thinning.

I twisted the untwistable—as Aragor had put it—and slipped the *Mambrino* beyond the Now into a momentary silence.

Overspace itself wasn't the sightless black I'd been prepared for by Alicia's and Tomas's training, but the backdrop was dark purple with a tinge of green—like a storm twilight without the definition of clouds. Where I stood/ flew/floated seemed at the top of a hill, one that sloped down from me toward a distant beacon. Behind me, I could sense the pulsations from the enormous moon beacon and identify the pattern.

Slowly . . . it seemed so slowly, I locked on the distant beacon pattern before me, catching the pattern pulses and verifying the ID of Santerene. I could sense other beacons—perhaps a dozen, scattered at various distances, distances I knew to be deceptive.

From where I/we/*Mambrino* soared, I could sense that the overspace gradient to Santerene was all downhill— almost like a grassy slope to a flat . . . I stepped/guided forward.

A lazy black sun slowly climbed from below me—*two-eighty-eight, minus seventy-seven*—out of the purple mist below.

I eased myself—the *Mambrino*, one and the same— ever so slightly sideways and forward, through the cloud of lilacs, past the sounds of a German polka and through the veil of a vanishing march.

A run . . . a gallop, and the slope slid by beneath me.

Somewhere beyond the distance, I could sense a pinwheel of stars and a golden-red arc of flame, but they were there . . . not beckoning, not threatening—just somewhere out beyond overspace.

Another sun—yellow-black—turned and flared toward me, but all it took was a slight lifting jump to slip past that bumblebeelike humming and drop onto the gradient downslope once more.

The beacon that I somehow *knew* was Santerene grew warmer, and, then . . . simply, I retwisted the untwistable, and we exited overspace.

The control center flashed black, then blinding white, then settled into the standard gray of composite and plastics and electronics.

That's it? I blinked, discovered that I was soaked and that my body was slightly sore. The gee meters ranged from plus fourteen to plus twenty-three, gees I hadn't been aware of experiencing.

"Smooth," said Berya. "Easiest quad I ever made." She half turned on her couch toward Souphan. "This is the way they all ought to feel."

Erelya hadn't told me, but I wasn't surprised that the officers accompanying a needle jockey on his first insertion received more than normal compensation. Berya's comment indicated that she'd accompanied more than a few beginning jockeys.

I grinned and almost asked what she was piling up credits for before I decided against the flippancy. Instead, I cranked up the fusactors and eased out the photon nets as the *Mambrino* began to accelerate downward toward orbit control off Santerene.

Once we were on a steady inbound course, I flicked off my inbound report. "Santerene Orbit, this is *Mambrino* inbound, captain Tyndel, second Berya, and third Souphan. Five passengers. Condition green. Estimate arrival in . . ." I had to pause and calculate the dilation impact, minimal as I suspected it would be, and the transmission lag time. Even the standing wave tightbeam was subject to lightspeed constraints. Then I gave myself some margin. ". . . twenty standard minutes."

The *Mambrino* was still accelerating inbound when Santerene's return transmission arrived.

"Captain Tyndel, we have the *Mambrino* at the locks in approximately fifteen your time. Commander Krigisa will be waiting to welcome you."

"Stet. Fifteen minutes."

Station commanders didn't normally welcome every needle. That I knew from OE Station. So Krigisa had to know I was new. I wondered how, since nothing traveled between systems faster than a needle ship. Of course, standard procedures demanded I announce the crew and the number of passengers, and any high officials of the Rykashan Authority. And the commander probably knew all the needle pilots by name, and her run was the easiest around. So an easy run and a new name . . . meant a new pilot. I hoped that was all.

I folded the photon nets at ten thousand kilos, but with enough mass so that I could complete all but the smallest fraction of decel by five hundred. It worked, and I cut in the ionjets for the last maneuvering as the clamshells retracted from the couches.

"Santerene Orbit, *Mambrino* ten out. Commencing final approach."

"You're cleared to lock two, *Mambrino*. Local beacons are burning."

"Understand cleared to lock two."

From there the approach was routine, and the needle ship kissed into the cradles with hardly a *thump*. I managed to avoid releasing the sigh I felt as I unstrapped and then sat up.

"Smooth, captain," offered Berya.

"Thank you. I'd hoped it would be, but you never know."

"No, ser, you don't," added Souphan with a grin, one of relief.

"You get to greet the station commander or the maintenance officer, captain," Berya reminded me gently as I eased myself erect in the null grav. "We just take care of cargo and passengers and shipkeeping." After a pause, she asked, "Any maintenance problems?"

I had to think, but I'd detected nothing. Was that because I still wasn't sensitive enough to the nuances or because there were none? "None that I know of."

"Wouldn't have thought so. Usually show up after exit, and you brought us out clean."

How much had been me and how much the *Mambrino*—that I wasn't certain, but for the moment, it hadn't mattered.

The passengers had all already debarked by the time I'd finished the shutdown and reclaimed my gear. I still had to wait to do the postflight after Souphan ensured the cargo was off-loaded. A golden-skinned muscular woman, easily a head taller than I, waited by the upper passenger locks. She wore the golden Web collar pin, unlike the commander of OE Station. "Captain Tyndel, I'm Krigisa."

I inclined my head. "Commander, I'm pleased to meet you." *And most happy to be here to see you.*

"This one of your first runs?"

"My very first, actually."

"How was it?"

"Smooth. My second let me know, politely, that not all future runs will be that smooth."

"Some of that is the jockey . . . but some is not." She gestured. "After you finish your postflight, I'd appreciate it if you would join me for a meal—whatever you like, since I've no idea where your internal clock is set."

"I'd be happy . . . and dinner would taste good."

The invitation was a pleasantry to cover a debriefing, a command pleasantry, but far more courteous than a standard debrief.

Unloading took the maintenance crew nearly two hours, and I reflected that Fersonne and I could have cut a third or more off that time without straining. Finally, it was complete, and I finished the postflight, finding nothing the matter despite a concerted effort to ferret out anything.

Souphan and Berya were waiting by the lock.

"We'll be returning in twenty hours, station objective," announced the second.

"Cargo?" I had to wonder what there was of value to return to earth.

"Eight passengers, and a bunch of biological samples, plus some nanotemplate equipment too complicated to repair or rebuild out here."

All that made a sort of sense, and I nodded. "See you in . . . what . . . seventeen hours."

Berya nodded. I let them precede me, and we parted ways on the second deck.

The table in the commander's dining quarters was already set, its elegance muted by the null gravity adaptations, including squeeze bottles.

Krigisa—obviously linked to the station's sensors—opened the hatch herself and beckoned me to enter. "I took the liberty of having Arleen tea for you . . . and Dorchan lemon chicken . . ."

My smile was rueful. "Does all of Rykasha know my tastes?"

"No. I'm the only station commander who does." She gestured to the table.

I used the sticktites to ensure I didn't drift away, but waited until she lifted her own squeeze bottle before drinking.

"You know needle pilots are rare . . ." began Krigisa.

Just how rare struck me then. The Authority was more willing to risk a crew and a ship and a cargo than to place a second senior needle pilot on the *Mambrino*. Yet Krigisa was or had been a needle jockey. "You were one of the first?"

"Not the very first . . ." She smiled ironically.

"And you're here to bring back ships that somehow make exits with injured or incapacitated pilots." I frowned. "Berya is probably better than most seconds in handling a needle in real space."

"You're right in both cases."

"How often?"

"Not too often." Commander Krigisa smiled.

"What do you need to know?" I took another sip of the Arleen.

"I'd like you to describe overspace to me—the way you saw it."

I started with the green-based purple backdrop, the downhill gradient, the distant beacons, and went on from there, including the lazy black sun and lilac veils. ". . . and then I retwisted the untwistable, and we popped out." I shrugged. "I think I could have waited a shade longer, but . . ."

"It's better not to wait too long," she observed. "What were your gee meter readings?"

"Fourteen to twenty-three."

"That is low." She nodded. "Who was your principal ship instructor?"

"Captain Erelya."

"She's one of the best. How did you find the *Mambrino*?"

"We're a good fit." That was the way I felt.

The gentle questions continued.

"Did you have any trouble distinguishing the beacon IDs . . ."

". . . evasive tactics you used . . ."

". . . how far when you folded the nets . . ."

Abruptly, she looked straight at me. "I think I've asked enough. You'll be a Web jockey for a long time. We should eat, because you'll need some rest before you turn around. That's the downside of Santerene. Nowhere planetside to go. I must spend half my time in the high-gee capsule. Part of it even has a console for me." Krigisa laughed.

I hadn't thought about that, and had to wonder how many other things I'd discover over the years and insertions ahead. But I did begin to enjoy the chicken.

69

[RUNSWI: 4522]

Science cannot be "true" in the absolute sense, and that is why a society based on science alone cannot survive, for the people require absolute truths. Symbolic uncertainty is the downfall of civilization.

Cerrelle was waiting when I got off the downshuttle at Runswi. She was sitting on a bench inside the operations building, out of the late-winter sleet that rattled against the windows. For me four days had gone by, personal objective, and slightly more than a season had passed on earth.

"Tyndel." The way she said my name and the smile warmed me. She'd cut her hair short, not that it had been long before, and, even in the forgiving late-day gloom, she was pale.

"Are you all right?"

"Now. Thesalle isn't for everyone." Her voice was uneven.

I winced inside. If strong-minded Cerrelle had been shaken by Thesalle, the planet clearly wasn't for everyone.

"Are you still interested in seeing me?"

"What?" *Cerrelle . . . as direct as ever . . . as you're barely off the magshuttle.*

"You're a needle jockey—one of the elite. I'm a midranking troubleshooter and baby-sitter for the Authority. I'll never be more."

"You're also the most honest person I've ever met, and I need you and that." I held out my hands.

She didn't move, but my words raised a ragged grin. "At least you put me before the honesty."

"You need an electrocart. Can you eat?" I paused and studied her, wondering what had happened to her. "You need to eat."

"I do, but my appetite isn't what it should be. I wasn't sure I'd have time to eat, but the shuttle was late."

Instead of being charming or persuasive, I reached down and out and lifted her off the bench and into my arms. For a moment, she stiffened, but I didn't press beyond a gentle hug, and she finally hugged me for a moment before stepping back and looking straight into my eyes. "You could have anyone, but I won't share you."

I nodded. I'd understood that long before she'd said a word. "Let's find a cart."

There were two waiting, but the driver in the first nodded to us, his eyes on my pilot's greens.

"The marsh lounge . . ." I offered.

"It will have to be the main lounge," Cerrelle corrected me. "They're repairing the marsh lounge—or expanding it . . . or something."

The cart driver looked back at me.

"Main lounge."

"Yes, ser."

After I helped seat Cerrelle and eased in beside her, she leaned next to me and whispered, except it was more of a subvocalization that only I—or another pilot—could have caught. "Yes, ser . . . yes, ser . . . that's the way it will be from now on, Tyndel. Don't let it go to your head."

"You won't let it."

"Oh . . . I will. I won't say a word. I'll just leave."

"You just got here—or I did."

"*You* know exactly what I mean."

"That's what I mean about being honest." I grinned at her, still worried about the pallor that dominated her face.

"Later," she said, looking at the driver in the front seat.

"Promise?"

"I promise."

Cerrelle didn't lean on me as we walked into the lounge, but she did take my arm, and I could sense that she was unsteady. What had it been about Thesalle that had created such a problem? And where else had I heard about the place? *On OE Station* . . . Thesalle was the place that had an effect that no one could quantify. More than half the tables were taken, but there was one in the near corner, and we eased toward it.

". . . must be one of the newer Web jockeys . . ."

". . . has to be older . . . she's attractive . . . but not a raving beauty . . ."

". . . new jockeys have 'em hanging on them . . ."

I tried not to flush.

"You see, Tyndel. By choosing me, you've aged yourself." Cerrelle smiled, but the expression was forced.

"I was already aged, and I've always looked beyond the obvious to what counts. You count." I held my arm so she could use it to sit. "What would you like?"

"I can get it. I'm not helpless."

"Humor me," I suggested.

Her smile was halfway between irony and relief. "Any kind of pasta that's not Dhurr-spiced ... with meat of some sort. Cerise ... no ... a pale ale of some sort."

I bowed my head. "Your wish ..."

"... is not a command, Tyndel. Get the pasta."

I got her pasta and ale, and then returned for my own orange beef with saffron rice, and Arleen tea.

"How long before you go out again?" she asked after several mouthfuls.

"Three weeks ... I'm supposed to spend half of every day of the last two before I leave training with Tomas." I paused. "What about you?"

"Four weeks' convalescent leave—that's what's left."

I studied her with every sense I had. "You've been in medical. When did you get out?"

"This morning."

"You're not supposed to be out."

"Aleyaisha bent the rules for me ..."

"If you took it easy?"

The nod came hard to my redhead.

Are you sure she wants to be yours? "What's wrong?"

"Something about the nanite balance ... Thesalle upsets it for some. They don't know why. If you want more details, I'll tell you later. Tell me about your trip." She took another mouthful of the pasta.

"Are you sure?"

"Humor me, this time."

We both smiled.

By the time I finished recounting my trip and eating my own orange beef, she had pushed her plate away, leaving about half of the pasta and trying to stifle a yawn. She looked more pale even than earlier.

"You need some rest."

"I do need to go home," she confessed.

"Not by yourself."

"I can manage."

"Aleyaisha told you that if I wouldn't help you, you had to go back to medical." I smiled.

"You're getting too perceptive," she grumbled. "I'm only asking for help getting home. That's all."

"For now," I agreed.

"For a while," she countered.

I didn't want to argue, and she was in no shape for much besides rest. I had to wonder just what had happened to her, but I'd asked twice, and she was clearly not going to tell me until she was ready—as usual. Still . . . most demons were resistant to just about anything, and she didn't seem to have any overt physical trauma.

"Home" was a great deal farther away than I realized. First came the tunnel glider to Lyncol, and then the free glider-cat I had to steer along a winding path for kilos out of Lyncol until we reached a lake, its ice-and-snow-covered surface shimmering under the full winter moon. The snow was depressed by the pressure of a single set of glider prints, partly drifted in.

"There." Cerrelle pointed to a chaletlike structure jutting out of a rock outcropping and overlooking the iced-in lake. Below the chalet was a long slope down to the lake itself, a stretch clear of pines that might have been a lawn—at least in summer.

I eased the glider-cat along the edge of the lake through the unbroken snow that covered what had possibly been an old road, and then up to the chalet. A glider door in the side of the chalet slid open as we neared.

"You never told me. . . . It's impressive."

"This is my one luxury. I didn't want to . . . not until after you made your first insertion. I've seen it happen. Pilots change. Not all of them, but some do."

"And me?"

"You seem about as hardheaded and obstinate as ever."

We laughed as I eased the glider into the low-ceilinged hangar. The lights came on, and the door closed behind us even before I could open the canopy.

Cerrelle staggered.

"You shouldn't . . ." I caught her and half carried her up two flights of stairs to the bedroom, still trying to determine how much help she needed and where help turned into imposition and intrusion. On the way, I took in the smooth polished woods and the openness of the main floor, and the sparseness—a deliberate austerity, I knew.

The lights followed us, and I could sense the link to Cerrelle.

As I stepped into the bedroom, Cerrelle stiffened. "I can get into bed. Go get me something to drink. There's a formulator down in the kitchen . . . a drink menu . . . the green tea . . . tastes bitter, but it should help."

After easing her into a sitting position, I slipped back down the steps to puzzle out the kitchen. By the time I returned with the tea, she was stretched out under a deep blue comforter, propped up with two pillows, looking through the glass wall at the silent white expanse of the lake.

She took the tea, and the lights flicked off, leaving us in the darkness. A single light twinkled in the darkness beyond the wide window overlooking the snow-covered slope that led down to the lake. "Feels better lying down."

I pulled a chair next to the bed and took a sip of the green tea—not so good as Arleen, but soothing. "What's Thesalle like?" Perhaps she would tell me without my prying too overtly.

"It's beautiful, shifting shades of green, even at night, and the air is perfumed." She paused for some tea.

"It doesn't sound dangerous." I paused. "When I was on OE Station, there were some scientists—or controllers—talking about it . . . how they couldn't quantify something, an unknown hallucinogen . . ."

"I don't know about that. I felt off balance the whole time, and it just got worse when I got back."

"Do they know why?"

"My nanite balance got disrupted." She shrugged, almost resigned. "Aleyaisha says it happens to some Rykashans, but they don't know why."

"Hmmm . . ." I sipped the green tea, which wasn't bitter at all, not to me, waiting.

"They had to replace my entire nanite system, the way they did when you first got here, and I'm still readjusting. I don't have to pay for it, though, not this time." Cerrelle took another sip of the green tea, her eyes still fixed on the silent and moonlit lake.

"Can you tell me why they sent you to Thesalle?"

She shrugged. "I was sent with some newer and more sensitive atmospheric measuring equipment. It was designed to look for the organic equivalent of nanites."

"Molecular-level biotechnology?"

That got a nod. "And they thought they might get a different result from someone not born and raised a Rykashan."

"Did they?"

"I don't know. I wasn't in much shape to care when I got back, and today . . ."

"Was your first day out of medical?"

Another nod affirmed that.

"Thesalle . . ." I mused. "Here Rykasha has enough technology to do what the ancients never managed, but something on the planet is beyond that technology, so much so that demons can't even discover what it might be."

"No one has spent that much time on it. Whatever it is, it affects only a few people. We just don't have that many resources. The Galaxy alone is huge, Tyndel, and we spend an incredible percentage of our resources on interstellar travel."

"I know." That was why the ancients never had gotten that far. One reason, anyway.

She held up the mug. "Would you mind?"

"Not at all." I set my cup on the carved table by the bed and stood, walking through the darkness to the kitchen area and the small food formulator, thoughts circling through my mind.

"That brings up another question," I said as I brought her the second cup of green tea.

"Oh?"

"Rykasha has the technology to subdue or destroy all the mites. Hasn't anyone ever thought about it?"

"Who hasn't? But what would be the purpose? The mite cultures are stable." A faint smile crossed her lips. "Besides, the gene pool is wider and faster evolving. We wouldn't have people like you."

"Or you," I pointed out.

"You're more valuable."

"I don't think so." And I meant it. "I still can deceive myself; you never do."

"I do. We all do. That's not all bad." She paused for a sip of the tea. "Think about it. Self-deception is the strength of all humans and all human cultures. We delude ourselves into believing that the universe has meaning, that we have a role and an importance in it. We dream grand dreams."

"Is that self-delusion or self-preservation?" I asked. "How could most people survive without believing that there's an inherent meaning to their lives?"

"That's true of the mite cultures. We both know that. So many things people take as truths are built upon deception. Is there a god? How would we know? No one has any proof of a god, not in the scientific sense. All the major religions of the ancients were built upon revelations or interpretations of purely human or natural occurrences as the hand of god and not upon verified facts."

"You don't think it's not true in Rykasha?"

"There are certainly some people who believe in the old superstitions, but look at how we handle something like Thesalle. At least some of the mites would call it the will of God because it's beyond our understanding. The same's true of engee. We just try to understand and try to accept that we can't understand everything without immediately running and hiding behind superstition."

"That's another form of honesty," I mused. "But it's hard. We're not that honest by nature. Even demons."

Cerrelle laughed softly. "You don't think the Authority hasn't considered it."

"Considered what?"

"Tyndel . . . you're a Web pilot. What if you have a ship out there and you run into another form of intelligent life? Can you imagine a culture whose members could not deceive themselves? How would they deal with us? Knowing that they could trust no word . . . no action, knowing that we could trust anything they said, what would they do? What could they do?"

I paused. Such an occurrence was unlikely. Surely, it would have happened earlier. Still . . . "I suppose there would be only two workable alternatives—ignore us or destroy us."

"Always the extremist, my dear. Why do you think that?"

Her use of the gentle and possessive appellation brought a smile to my heart, and my lips. "In contact with humans, a truth-telling culture would either be perceptive enough to see through our continual deceptions and face continued frustration and exasperation, or, if less able, fall prey to our deceptions and machinations, or possibly become contaminated with such deception."

"They could . . ." Cerrelle yawned and eased the cup toward the table.

I took it and set it on the far side. I had another thought. Could there be an advanced alien civilization that was not based, as ours was, upon deception? Our whole technological advancement was in a sense based upon creativity and at least a portion of creativity was a form of deception . . . of denying the "truth" of reality and seeking more.

"Tyndel . . . the guest room is across the hall."

I rose, taking the hint, then bent and kissed her cheek. "You sure you'll be all right?"

"I'm sure. I'm tired, but I feel better already."

So did I.

With a smile, I closed the door behind me, far more awake than my sleepy redhead, with questions of Web insertions, honesty, grand dreams, alien intelligences, and the mystery of Thesalle all swirling through my mind.

70

[EARTH ORBIT TWO/BETA CANDACE: 4522]

Each journey is the same journey, yet those who travel together
go separate ways.

After we had spent several quiet weeks mostly at the lake—where I continued to sleep in the guest room— the Authority had notified a recovered Cerrelle that she would be going back to Elena to "baby-sit" another convert, one from Dezret. Because I had another trip scheduled first, though, she had been the one to see me off at the operations strip in Runswi . . . after I'd stopped for my medical screening, this time handled by doctor Fionya.

"How do you feel about going to Elena?" I'd asked Cerrelle as we waited for my shuttle. "After all, I was a baby-sitting job."

"You were a pain." She hugged me. "You still are." She smiled. "But you're better."

Smiling back, but silently wondering about that, I had hugged her in return, and then walked toward the shuttle for Orbit Two, at the head of the line, still conscious of how shiny the golden Web collar pin was.

Erelya met me as I glided out of the shuttle at Orbit Two. "Astlyn's waiting for you in operations."

"I thought you wouldn't be guiding me around anymore?" I grinned.

She smiled back. "This is the last time—unless something special comes up. That doesn't happen often."

The operations room was the same featureless composite gray, as chill and empty as the one time I'd been there before. Astlyn was alone, waiting for us. He inclined his head. "Tyndel."

I bowed my head briefly in return. "Ser."

The black-skinned senior operations controller smiled. "You're headed for Nabata—off Beta Candace."

Nabata? I racked what I'd learned. Tee-type world, recently colonized, two main continents, hot, dry, despite being a water world.

"Your cargo is the latest round of biotechnical efforts to develop grasses that match the native biology, plus the supporting equipment so that the bioteam there can carry things forward without the time lags. You'll also be carrying a full load of passengers."

"They're the ones who will operate the equipment," Erelya added.

All of that made sense. What didn't make sense was Astlyn telling me that.

"That's along the Web gradient for the Anomaly." Astlyn paused. "You've heard of it?"

"Just in general terms," I admitted.

"Most people have." He nodded, the brown eyes serious. "You need to know more. We don't bother with this briefing until someone is a pilot and until he or she is beyond the first run." A hologram sprang into being—almost at his shoulder. "Alpha Felini—that's the official term for the Anomaly. It's about ten light-years away from Sol—in roughly the opposite direction from Santerene, in case you're interested."

I studied the image. In the center of the unfamiliar star field was a glowing haziness—somewhat like the fuzzy golden ball of light that I'd sensed right after I'd been "infected" with the first, old-style nanites. The image expanded and focused in on the golden center. Abruptly, the ball turned into a central core of golden-red fire—a miniature sun—or was it miniature? Around the sun were long arms of red fire. I'd seen that image in my thoughts and elsewhere all too often.

"This is accelerated several hundred fold from real time," Astlyn explained.

The arms of fire sparkled as they swept through seemingly empty space, although I knew no space was totally empty.

"Actually, for practical purposes, the space behind each arm is effectively empty. Each of the arms is a field of some sort, and what you're seeing is low-level antimatter annihilating low-level matter. The result is energy and virtually empty space."

"And a great deal of disruption in space and overspace," added Erelya.

"And the sun?" I asked. "It doesn't look normal."

"New matter. We think it's more 'energetic,' if you will, but that could be a bias from the energies involved."

I digested all of that. "There's something creating and using antimatter to generate energy and sweep space, and creating new matter. Engee?"

Astlyn nodded.

"Exactly," Erelya confirmed.

I took a deep breath. "Just *what* is engee? There's nothing in any data system about the Anomaly or engee." I almost added "not any system I've found," but decided against that.

Erelya and Astlyn exchanged glances.

Astlyn cleared his throat. "We *believe* that engee is an assemblage of self-assembling and replicating nanites of a variety developed by the ancients. While there has been no way to verify this, there are enough indirect indicators to make that conclusion. There is not enough information to put what we suspect on the full Rykashan datanet . . ."

As he talked I pondered his words. Why not on the full net? Because people would be concerned or upset? I could understand that intellectually, but the universe was so vast it seemed unlikely that it was empty, and if something was there . . . it was there. *That's Dzin, and most people—even Rykashans—don't see it that way.*

". . . while not conclusive, one would have to act as though there is some form of intelligence there . . ."

"Which the Followers believe is God, their god at least," I suggested.

Astlyn nodded.

"And it has enough power to create a solar system?"

"Yes."

"Why?" I pursued, wondering if I were pushing too hard. *Probably.*

"We don't know why; nor do we know the mechanics of how, although the theory is relatively old." Astlyn waited.

"Why are you telling me this?"

"Because you're a needle pilot, and because you're headed along that general gradient, and there seems to be an even greater fascination on the overspace level. And because none of this is a surprise to you, or any pilot," added Erelya. "You've seen visions of this, haven't you?"

"At scattered intervals ever since I came to Lyncol," I confirmed, then asked, knowing that they wouldn't have briefed me if there weren't a danger, "How many pilots have you lost?"

"Just three, but that represents three ships and a substantial resource commitment." Astlyn cleared his throat. "You must know that."

"There's another problem," added Erelya.

Astlyn frowned.

"New City."

I didn't hide my surprise. I'd never heard of whatever New City might be.

The hologram vanished before Astlyn spoke again. "A number of people have built ships, photonjet-powered. Somehow, without Web pilots and excitation systems, the ships arrive there. There, and nowhere else. They're building a deep-space city near this Anomaly. They say it will be a new solar system in time, created by the only True God."

"Demons . . . people . . . believe that?"

"It could be." Astlyn laughed harshly. "They'll have to wait a long time. At the present rate of accretion it still is likely to be millions of years before engee has enough matter there for a new system. Even if you assume an exponential rate, it's around ten thousand years—and the disruptions to the Web, overspace, and normspace will render the area rather uninhabitable, even for individuals with full nanite protection."

Astlyn's explanation left much unexplained.

"Is there a possible way to use the Web without an excitation and insertion system—or a pilot?"

"It's possible an untrained pilot could bring a ship from Sol to the Anomaly about half the time," Erelya theorized. "We don't know of any way that it could be done in the time frames that we've observed without a Web insertion system."

"But it happens?" I pursued. "What about the missing pilots?"

"There's been no sign of them or their ships," Astlyn replied. "No exit disruptions, either."

That all brought up the last question. "Why me? This is my second trip as a needle pilot."

"Medical thinks you have a higher resistance than most of the others." Astlyn did not sound totally convinced.

"You've opposed anything you didn't like all along," Erelya added dryly.

I managed to resist smiling.

"This is the second attempt with this cargo," Astlyn said. "You'll be carrying almost a full load of passengers also."

Those two items gave me a reason to swallow.

"Is there any trace . . . ?"

"The ship could be almost anywhere in normspace," Astlyn pointed out.

Or it could be drifting in overspace until it collides with enough mass to create a real normspace mess.

"It would be years if we saw anything optically."

"More like centuries," suggested Erelya.

I nodded slowly.

"Do you have any other questions?"

Dozens, if I'd thought of them, but none would have changed anything.

As I made my way down to the ready room, I had to ask what Astlyn and Erelya knew that neither was saying, and what I didn't know enough to ask.

One familiar figure was waiting—a round-faced blonde. "Glad to see you, Tyndel." Berya smiled and gestured. "This is Durmak." The wiry man with the golden skin and mahogany hair had to have come from Dhurr extraction.

Durmak nodded. "Ser."

"Glad to meet you, Durmak. Have you done the Nabata run before?"

"No, ser. I've done the Trough, though."

Trough? *The Epsilon Cygni—Ballentir run . . . climb over an overspace gradient . . . considered the most difficult insertion and exit.*

"This should be easier." Not quite sure about that, I glanced at Berya, wondering if she happened to be getting another bonus. "Might as well get moving."

I gathered the rest of my gear, and we slipped out of the ready room and down the shaft and to the passenger level. This time, the *Mambrino* was cradled at the other end, lock one, and I used the directlink to send the entry code to open the locks.

"With your permission, ser?" asked Durmak.

I nodded, and the third headed to the lower decks to recheck the cargo, while Berya rechecked the passenger area for our full load. I went through the passenger compartment, and continued through every space, just as I always had, and, as usual, I found nothing out of the ordinary. That brought me back to the control center, where

I strapped myself in and began to run through the systems checks.

"Passengers are all aboard, locks closed," declared Berya as she returned to the control center.

Durmak followed her. "Cargo is set and the lower locks sealed."

After a last recheck of the systems, I was ready to un-cradle the *Mambrino*. "Ready for departure."

"Make sure your harness is securely fastened. We will be departing shortly." Berya's calm voice was clear through both center speakers and through the system.

"Orbit Two, *Mambrino*, ready for departure."

"*Mambrino*, no inbounds this time, area clear. Understand destination Nabata."

"Orbit Two, destination Nabata." With the release of the cradles, I slipped the ship away from the station with the ionjets, adding power gradually as the separation increased.

"Orbit Two, *Mambrino* clear of lock three. Departing this time."

"Stet, *Mambrino*. Clear trip."

"Orbit Two, thanks." I stepped up the power flow from the fusactors, bringing the ionjets to full power until we were clear enough to spread the nets for the photondrive. Then, once the configurators came on-line, I switched from ionjets to photonic drive and began to establish the orientation necessary for Nabata as the acceleration built for insertion.

"Minus ten for insertion." The clamshells above us— and above the passengers—clicked out of their restraints, waiting for the signal from Berya to drop into place.

"You *must* be in your harness at this time," announced the second officer.

"Minus five." With all passengers secured, the clam-shells dropped into place.

"Minus three."

After setting the orientation, I pushed the acceleration closer to fifteen gees, more on a feel than a requirement.

Even before the lattices were all locked, the barriers between the Now and overspace had thinned. Slipping the *Mambrino* beyond the Now, into a momentary silence, was smooth, so smooth that it was an instant before the dark purpled green of overspace swam up around me, with the great white pulses of the moon beacon receding behind me.

As I'd been briefed by the system, the gradient toward Beta Candace—and Nabata—was supposed to be a slight incline for the first portion, and then a steep drop, and that was what I sensed, except the incline was long, longer than that coming back from Santerene.

First, while I/we climbed, came the lock on to the distant beacon pattern, verifying the ID of Nabata. I could sense other beacons—perhaps a dozen, scattered at various distances, distances I knew to be deceptive.

In that timeless depth, we reached the "crest" beyond which lay a void of uncertain depth, a depth that I/we/ *Mambrino* must cross. Sparkling lines of fire, like fireflies or an incandescent brume that shimmered in the winter sunlight over a silent lake, cascaded around me, around the *Mambrino*, and a whispering rumble, holding words that I could not quite decipher, folded around us.

Ignoring the urge to twist the ship around the fire veil, I could sense that it was without the substance of singularities, and without the depth of cold mass of stars, nebulae, or heavy planets that intruded upon overspace, and pushed off the cliff top and into a glide over the purpled drumming depths that separated us from the white-yellow beacon that was Beta Candace and Nabata.

Time condensed, folded, then stretched, simultaneously.

Silent voices beneath and beyond the vanishing brume made a last plea and then vanished.

And, nearly on top of the beacon, I untwisted the unNow, and *Mambrino* dropped into normspace, with a slight sense of falling.

I swallowed.

So did Berya, loud enough that I could hear it over her inline.

"We're here," I pulsed the second and third.

"Good."

Not even a hint of raggedness came through the nets as I reoriented the ship into a "climb" upward toward the system ecliptic and Nabata Orbit Control.

"Nabata Orbit Control, this is *Mambrino*, inbound this time. Captain Tyndel, second Berya, and third Durmak. Sixteen passengers. One-six, I say again. Condition green. Estimate arrival in . . ." I still had to pause to calculate. ". . . twenty-five standard minutes."

The *Mambrino* had just begun deceleration when the return transmission arrived.

"Captain Tyndel, we have the *Mambrino* at the locks in approximately twelve-plus your time. Subcommander and maintenance chief Jukor will supervise unloading."

"Stet. Understand subcommander Jukor."

"A subcommander. Must want the cargo," Durmak said.

I nodded, realizing that Nabata Orbit Control wouldn't know that the previous needle hadn't made it—not for certain—but the number of passengers was a good indication of some difficulties.

We were there—almost there. I frowned to myself. What about coming back? Or did it really matter to the Authority? The whole cargo and passenger list had been set up as if there wouldn't be too many trips to Nabata.

I shrugged. There was little enough that I could do except make sure we returned to Orbit Two intact.

71

*To tell another what one has sensed is to paint a scene
without color or perspective.*

The return trip to earth and Orbit Two was without in-
cident, and the *Mambrino* fairly soared through the
purpled green of overspace with almost no cargo and but
two passengers. Orbit Two Control did request my presence in operations after postflight and shutdown. Again,
Astlyn and Erelya were waiting in the gray-walled and
almost dank operations room.

"It's good to see you," Astlyn said. "How was the trip?"

His words conveyed true happiness that I had returned
in one piece, and I had the feeling that his warmth wasn't
just for the fact that I'd gotten a necessary cargo to Nabata
and brought back an expensive needle ship. All the same,
I understood the concern beside and behind the warmth.
Needle ships were what held the Rykashan stars and colonies together, and the Authority could not afford too
many missing ships—either in resource or psychological
terms.

"It's good to be back." I shrugged. "A bit strange on
the way out, routine on the return."

The black eyebrows lifted over the deep brown eyes.

"I can't say there was anything exactly new." That was
certainly true. "There might have been a voice whispering
beneath overspace—but I couldn't make out anything. I
wasn't about to try."

"Any color to the voice?" asked Erelya.

"No. It seemed to throw up a gauzy veil of sparkling
things. I went straight through it."

"Was there any impact on the hull or the ship? Afterwards, that is?" Astlyn pursued.

"No. Not a sign."

The black-skinned controller nodded.

"Engee?" suggested Erelya.

"What do you think, Tyndel?" Astlyn's voice was neutral.

"There was *something* there—something not like anything else I've sensed in overspace." I had to shrug. "I don't have enough experience to know more."

"Was . . . is there any record in the ship's systems?" Erelya pressed.

"I couldn't find any indications. The second didn't sense anything at all."

The two nodded at each other.

"Is there anything else we should ask you? Or you'd like to ask us?"

"Have other pilots sensed this sort of thing?"

"Five that we know of."

I nodded. Another thought occurred to me. "Do most pilots sense overspace as a deep black?"

Erelya nodded. "Most do. You're one of a handful that see more than blackness and highlighted objects."

"I can't think of anything else," I said.

"Let me know if you do." Astlyn nodded and withdrew, leaving me with Erelya.

"Now what?" I asked.

"You check the schedule on the pilot's screen—you can reach it from any console in Rykasha—and keep checking once you're back in Lyncol or wherever. You'll have at least two weeks' notice, unless it's an emergency. You seem to fit with the *Mambrino*, and Berya likes you. So she'll probably stay as your second." Erelya glanced at me. "Unless you'd rather try someone else?"

"No. Berya and I seem to work well together. That's fine."

"Your third this trip—Durmak . . . I have to debrief him to see how that will go."

"He seemed edgy. I couldn't say why."

"He just might be the edgy type. Or he might not be suited to continuing on as a needle officer."

"Or I might make him edgy," I pointed out.

"That's possible, too." Erelya smiled. "Now . . . there's one other thing I want to make perfectly clear. If you sense *anything* unusual in overspace, you need to report it to me or Astlyn as soon as you return to Orbit Two."

"Yes, ser."

She smiled. "Go catch the next shuttle planetside and get some rest—and keep in shape with Tomas or someone else."

"Yes, ser." I grinned at the senior pilot, wondering if Cerrelle were back from Dezret.

72

[ACTEAN: 4525]

Life offers no theology. There is but music and dance.

Three insertions later, I found myself on Actean—the place where Fersonne had wanted to use her life-credits to settle. That thought struck me as I was leaving the orbit station with Berya.

We had a new third officer—Alek. He was more settled than Durmak had been, but he stayed on the station, for a time, to supervise unloading and loading, and would come down on one of the cargo runs to join us on the three-day layover.

Actean had enough of a planetary magnetic field that the orbit station used magshuttles, and I pulled myself into the shuttle behind Berya, but we both managed to straighten up and halt in time to avoid gliding into the dark-haired man who waited for us.

"Captain Tyndel," offered the bearded shuttle pilot. "Miletos Arachos. Miles for short. You been on Actean before?"

"No. I've spent most of my deep-space time out toward Omega Eridani." That was true, if misleading; so I had to go on. "I was a station tech before I was a pilot."

"Good to see you here. You and Berya are the only passengers this run. Make yourselves comfortable. Be just a bit." With a nod, he turned and closed the hatch.

"I didn't know about OE," Berya murmured as we settled into the couches.

I had to grin. "That was in the lowly position of maintenance tech."

"Dzin masters are stubborn, I've heard."

"Former Dzin masters."

"Once a Dzin master, Astlyn said, always a Dzin master. I think I believe him. When you take the *Mambrino*, Tyndel, you *are* the ship. That only happens with Dzin or Toze masters." A quick smile flashed across her face. "They're the only ones I'm comfortable with."

"Who did you officer for before me?"

"Used to be Mru-Chin, but he retired after four centuries."

"You've been at this a while? Miles already knew you."

"Say . . . half a century personal objective. I've been here a few times. He's one of their three shuttle pilots. Nice man. Has an interesting family."

I'd sensed she favored me, but I was definitely flattered. "You don't have to do this now, then—being a needle officer."

"What else would I do? Besides, I enjoy it—under a solid captain, and new as you are, you're solid."

"Please make sure your harnesses are secure." After the announcement, and with a slight hum and a click, the shuttle eased away from the orbit station and down toward Actean. Through the ship's scanners, all I had been able to sense had been a Tee-type water world, nothing more, and I wondered what the planet itself might offer.

The upper atmosphere was rough, and several times we were thrown up against the harnesses before we reached the lower and smoother section of the descent. Usually, it was the other way around. Before long, the shuttle glided to a stop. The gravity felt good.

"We're here, folks. Actean tropical." Miles stood in the hatchway between cockpit and cabin, a crooked smile across his dark-tanned face.

"Thank you, Miles." I nodded.

"A little rougher than usual," Berya noted.

"Surprised me, but there have been some flares." The shuttle pilot shrugged. "It does happen, but it's still smoother than with those fireboosters they use some places."

Outside, forty meters from the magshuttle, in the bright and yet somehow hazy sunlight, stood a single building, a long and one-storied rectangular structure constructed of oversized reddish brown bricks and topped with a slatelike roof—except the slates were rusty-red. There was a slight heaviness, just a trace, that reminded me that the gravity on Actean was a shade higher than on earth, perhaps five percent, nothing that my system and beefed-up nanites couldn't handle, I hoped.

To the west of the strip was a long and low line of hills covered with trees that seemed to shade toward blue rather than green. I glanced northward, toward a taller range of mountains, glistening with white. The landing strip was practically equatorial. Actean, on average, was colder than earth, and although the tropical belt was quite temperate, the northern continents were anything but.

The sun held a shade of orange, and I called up what I knew. *Actean . . . fourth planet around Dyana . . . G-3 with a mass of approximately 1.2 Sol . . . first planet terraformed through Brynk-Hezoff transformations . . . borderline for habitable zone . . . required greenhouse screening . . . four major continents . . . one equatorial, one temperate, two polar . . .*

"Captain . . . new on this run?" The speaker who interrupted my reverie was a stocky and black-haired woman wearing a kind of uniform consisting of tan shorts and shirt, and hiking boots.

"Yes." I grinned. "I go where they send me."

"I'm Malya. The needle officers' places are to the west, maybe four kilos, on the hill. I'll be the one to take you two there." Malya glanced at Berya. "You know the layout."

My second officer nodded.

The cart was a fuel-cell-powered four-seater with a canopy-type roof and no sidewalls. Berya and I sat in the second seat, duffels in the open cargo bin behind us.

"Captain," Malya said, not looking from the narrow, composite-paved path along which she guided the cart, "you're welcome to walk wherever you want. The only things really dangerous are the local replizards, but they'll shy away from most people. They don't like the way we smell or taste. If you startle one, just back away slowly, but they're hard to miss. Bright red, and there's not much undergrowth. Both the local sheep and the lizards like to eat it. I'd wear long sleeves in the forest, though. Some folks have a reaction to some of the saps. They're Tee-derived, mostly, but they can give you a fierce itch and an infection that's hard even for nanites to deal with." She shrugged. "Other than that, Actean's a pleasant place."

"Don't you get a lot of immigrants?"

"Not many. Life-credit cost to get here means you're either born here or you've been deep-space officers or crew. Good folks. The locals that aren't we send to the north continent."

"It's not too pleasant there?"

"It keeps them out of trouble," Malya answered.

The cart whined as it began to climb the inclined section of the path that angled upward along the tree-covered slope of a ridge. The trees closest to the path were no more than three or four meters tall and had low-spreading branches from which fanned wide spade-shaped leaves that were nearly as blue as green. The grass beneath was wiry, and I could see no undergrowth or bushes, even after we reached the ridge top.

"We have three bungalows here," Malya explained as she slowed the cart and gestured toward the small buildings that almost grew out of the rock and grass and low trees of the ridge. "Captains usually take the one on the knoll. It's a shade quieter, not that anything's noisy here. The path over there goes to the overlook. You can see Ribbon Falls from there. It's only about two hundred meters along the path."

We stood and stretched, then took our small duffels from the cart bin.

"The quarters are stocked with anything you'd need, but if you need something, use the console and link."

"Thank you." Berya and I spoke almost simultaneously.

"I'll be the one picking you up day after tomorrow," Malya called as she turned the cart and headed back down the ridge path.

"Guess we get settled," I offered.

"Right. I'm tired." Berya nodded and carried her duffel to the dark-stained wood structure at the far end.

I stifled a yawn and made my way to the bungalow on the knoll. Light flooded the quarters, illuminating an open area that held a hearth, a kitchen/formulator area, and a sitting area. A sliding permaglass door separated the sitting area from a deck overlooking the trees on the slope below. To my right, a half dozen steps climbed to a sleeping area and a fresher.

In a way, I wondered about the almost luxurious nature of the quarters. Then I shook my head. Needle pilots held the human Galaxy together. Each ship was close to prohibitively expensive. Understated luxury was cheap by comparison and an easy way to ensure well-rested and fewer unnecessarily stressed pilots.

Not wanting, somehow, to settle into the quarters at that moment, after setting the duffel inside the door, I followed the packed clay path past a cultivated circular area filled with flowers, all of them blue and short-stemmed, and through the low trees to the overlook. The overlook itself was but a rectangle of local red stones. To the west, the trees had been removed to allow a clear view of the falls.

A ribbon of white spray cascaded out of the vine-covered cliff and arched down toward the churning water of a pool a good three hundred meters below. More spray wreathed the pool, enough so that I couldn't make out where the river wound through the valley forest below, except that it must have gone westward, since the valley sloped in that direction.

Sounds percolated through the foliage, but whether they were from insects, birds, or local fauna like the replizards there was no way to know.

The light breeze out of the north held a trace of chill. I turned and watched the clouds forming around the distant snowcapped peaks. How long I watched, I wasn't sure, but eventually I blinked and looked back at the cascade.

Fersonne would have liked Actean.

My eyes burned, and I blinked again, several times, before turning and walking back toward the empty bungalow.

73

[LYNCOL: 4526]

Beware of those who truly garden . . . for they see people as plants.

Cerrelle had wanted a garden, though I suspected she had asked as much to please me as for herself, but gardens were something I did know from my years in Dorcha, and it was the least I could contribute since she wouldn't allow me to transfer more than a small fraction of my rapidly growing free account balance to her credit, even though I'd effectively moved in with her.

So I was determined to make the garden special. The hardest part of a garden is to visualize what kind of garden will suit a location, and how it will fit so that it appears it would have grown there naturally, even though no garden is natural.

The early-spring sun was hot, almost like summer, as I moved stones to create the back wall. Without realizing the leverage, I twisted my elbow moving one of the larger stones. After a moment, the pain subsided, and I shook my head. I had felt the agony, knew that I'd overstrained both my own capabilities and even those of my reformulated miniature rebuilders. I still had trouble dealing with the idea of an entire mechanical universe inside me, and one of those problems was that my musculature was comparatively stronger than my skeletal system, although the rebuilding I'd undergone to become a pilot made the discrepancy less than that enjoyed by most Rykashans.

I hoped the garden would become one of my pastimes when I wasn't Web-bound, but even training, transport, and gardening couldn't keep my mind from occasionally going back to Henvor or Mettersfel.... or Hybra ... or— less and less—Foerga. At times, I didn't think of Foerga for weeks, or months, and those memories had faded into pleasant reminiscences, mostly, reminiscences of a kind of childhood that I hadn't realized was childhood. After a deep breath, I concentrated on the small yew, and where it would bring together the harmony of the stones. Dzin helped.

"Tyndel? Are you all right?" Cerrelle's voice was quiet, pitched barely above the whisper of the late-afternoon breeze through the pines behind the chalet.

"Fine." I squatted, studying the stones I'd already moved and set in place.

"I saw you wince. You're trying to do too much. I didn't want a garden overnight, you know?" She glanced at the line of stones, each massing at least a good seventy kilos, then at me. "You're pressing it."

I didn't look her in the eye, instead glanced downhill toward the lake, glinting in the early-spring sun. "A garden takes years, but I wanted to get it set up."

"You could take a few days . . ." She favored me with a smile.

"I haven't acted when I should have before . . ."

"That was different. You're different now."

"I'm glad you think so." *Are you? How do you tell, when you consider everything from the subjectivity of personal observation?* I shrugged. At times, I still wondered why she'd insisted on saving me despite myself, why she'd enlisted Andra, Aleyaisha, and Alicia in the effort. *Because no one born in Rykasha understands the need for and agony of honesty?* "Do you want to take a swim? It's still cold."

"Cold water I don't mind. As long as you *walk* to the beach."

I stood and stretched, then walked toward the chalet to change.

Afterward, after the chill of water and air that had helped the elbow and muscles, the breeze across the small terrace was just cool enough, with the scent of pines, for us to sit and sip the tea I'd brewed from a kettle and not heated with a reformulator.

"You people all do make good tea."

"I'm glad I can do something well." I grinned, and she laughed, and I poured more tea. Friend, monitor, lover, and whatever else, she was honest, and for that I was glad, a gladness I was finally coming to embrace.

Before long, I'd have to get ready for the *Mambrino* and the next trip across the Web, the next separation that took days for me and months for Cerrelle. Maybe that was why I needed to create a garden, a manifestation of one aspect of me, to leave behind, something more permanent against the impermanence of dreams.

74

Human beings presume questions have answers; the universe does not address such presumption.

A young woman in a tight-fitting silver singlesuit kept trying to catch my eye, both at the operations building in Runswi and after we boarded the shuttle for Orbit Two. I politely kept my eyes elsewhere, which wasn't hard, worried as I was about the abrupt schedule shift that had the *Mambrino* set for a "DTBA." Any "destination to be announced" wasn't reassuring.

Cerrelle hadn't liked it either, but she'd only sighed and given me a kiss, and then a hug . . . for starters. Love-making hadn't been desperate . . . but there had been an undercurrent of concern.

Then Bekunin had added a few more diagnostics to the medical check. So when I saw Erelya in the corridor outside the magshuttle lock, I knew there was trouble. "Operations?" I asked.

"I'll explain then." She nodded and surveyed me. "What did you do besides keep in shape?"

"I'm still working on a garden. It started out for Cerrelle, but it's as much for me as her."

"Sometimes things work out that way. Usually for the better." She didn't say more, and I didn't ask.

Commander Krigisa was waiting for us in the operations center—alone, as Astlyn always had. "Good day, Tyndel. You've been busy since I last saw you."

"I try." *Five earth objective years and something like four and a half round-trips to various systems . . . and lit-*

tle more than a year personal objective time. "Where's Astlyn?"

"We don't know." Krigisa shrugged sadly.

"He took a needle ship? Past the Anomaly? You're the new operations coordinator or whatever?"

Krigisa nodded. "He didn't want to send anyone else past Alpha Felini."

"How many more needles are missing?"

"Two," Erelya admitted. "One besides his."

I could understand the grave expression on her face. Interstellar travel was still not quite routine, but losing two needles in a year when previously the losses were more like two in a decade indicated problems that could threaten the whole Rykashan stellar transport system.

"This is the last direct run to Nabata, and after this you'll go from somewhere else?" My question was almost a statement.

"Epsilon Cygni," confirmed the commander. "We can't afford losses like that, not at ten-million-plus life-credits a ship."

"But you really need a last cargo to hold for them—planoforming technology and templates to cover the delays caused by double dilation?"

"The effect is almost quadruple dilation by going over the Trough and then triangulating upslope in overspace," said Krigisa. "The cost of an indirect flight now, since they're unprepared on Nabata, would be equivalent to about three ships. So we need one last direct transit."

"Why me?" I suspected, but wanted her to say it.

"Only those pilots who've actually *heard* something on previous runs—except for Astlyn—have disappeared. Since you haven't . . . we're fairly sure you can make at least one run to Nabata."

"How sure?"

"As sure as anything is," replied commander Krigisa.

I wasn't certain if there were any surety.

"You won't be taking any passengers," Erelya added. "We've reconfigured the *Mambrino* to carry more cargo.

The techs at Nabata Station will have to reconstruct the passenger area for your return."

"You're not to make a direct return, either," added Krigisa. "You'll be carrying this datacube to the station commander that explains the situation in terms of overspace hazards. I'd prefer that you not expand upon that." She handed me an oblong case not much bigger than my palm.

As I took the case, I understood the logic of both. If I didn't "hear" anything on the way outbound, then I could make another direct run from earth in an emergency situation, and there wasn't much sense in speculating on the nature of the "hazard"—since nobody really knew what happened except that needle ships were inserting and not emerging. At least not anywhere near Nabata or anywhere else we had discovered.

"You'll come back via Epsilon Cygni and Ballentir," Erelya added. "Do you have any more questions?"

I had a lot, but they weren't the kind that they could answer. "No. I may think of them later, but not now." My smile was crooked as I left.

I levered/glided my way through the transition locks and down the shaft into the null grav of the lowest level of the station.

Both Berya and Alek were waiting in the ready room.

"It was too good to last." Alek grinned.

"Uneventful runs, you mean?"

"Those are the best kind," he affirmed.

"Not always," said Berya.

"We're going to be stuffed with cargo," I pointed out.

"We are already. They're using the passenger cabin," Alek replied.

"Heavy," murmured Berya.

Without any more empty words, we gathered our gear and headed from the ready room to the *Mambrino*, cradled at lock three.

Alek and Berya both split off once we were in the ship to recheck the cargo stowage, while I went into the control center to begin power-up before making my own preflight.

Once the ship was operating under its own fusactor power, I began my inspection in the passenger area. The couches had been removed and stored in more compact form in the back of the cabin, while the front held boxes and crates locked in place with cargo ties and restraints.

In continuing through the ship, I found everything as it should be, with the exception of the passenger area. When I got back to the control center, I strapped in and began to run through the systems checks.

"Upper locks are closed," Berya said as she began to strap in.

Alek was close behind. "Cargo set. Lower locks sealed."

"You two ready for this?" I asked.

"That's not the question, captain," said Berya cheerfully. "If you're ready, then everything's fine."

"I'm ready." *You hope you are.* I made a last check of the systems, then pulsed Orbit Control. "Orbit Two, *Mambrino*, ready for departure."

"*Mambrino*, no inbounds this time, area clear. Understand destination Nabata."

"Orbit Two, destination Nabata. Cargo only, no passengers." When the cradles released, I eased power to the ionjets.

"No passengers."

"Orbit Two, *Mambrino* is clear. Departing this time."

"Stet, *Mambrino*. Good trip."

"Orbit Two, thank you." I pushed the power flow from the fusactors, bringing the ionjets to full power until we were out far enough to spread the photon nets and bring the configurators on-line. With the switch to photonic drive, I began establishing the insertion orientation as acceleration built. Without passengers, I decided on the maximum insertion velocity possible, but even with full power, the acceleration was slow, and the ship felt heavy, near the maximum load even for a needle.

"Minus ten for insertion." The clamshells slid from their restraints, then dropped over us.

"Minus five." I adjusted the orientation minutely.

"Minus three." The acceleration continued at nearly twenty gees, and the lattices locked, early, but I didn't slack off. We'd need that converted momentum, every bit of it. The barriers between the Now and overspace were nearly nonexistent, but I left the *Mambrino* in the Now until it was no longer possible to hold the needle there, until the lattices crackled and the fabric of real space seemed to groan.

The needle bucked for a nanoinstant as we slid into the momentary silence of overspace, an overspace more green and less maroon than usual, as if lit more brightly by the pulses of the moon beacon behind and below us.

Perhaps it was the insertion velocity, but the initial overspace gradient toward Beta Candace was nearly flat, and I could sense that the drop-off at the end of the incline was far steeper than on my last trip. I pushed that aside and centered on the distant beacon pattern, matching and confirming that it was indeed that of Nabata.

The seemingly near-flat incline began to steepen as I/we/*Mambrino* neared the break point beyond which was the bottomless void separating us from Beta Candace and Nabata.

Points of glitter flashed around me, instant pinpoints of blinding light, but I held my course, held and soared the void toward the still-distant pulse of the destination beacon. The pinlights intensified, until the green-purple of overspace was submerged in an endless expanse of light that revealed nothing.

A wordless question rumbled around me, a question without the music of overspace or the menace of singularities or star masses intruding into the Web.

Then, as suddenly, the glare dropped into sparkling lines of fire, like fireflies, or a dawn brume lit by winter sunrise over a frozen lake, and the voiceless, soundless question faded into the background, and the familiar purpled green of overspace rose up around me, around the *Mambrino*.

The drumming purple-churned depths that had separated us from the white-yellow beacon of Beta Candace and Nabata were past, and, once more, at insertion's end, time shrank in upon itself, then stretched, simultaneously.

Just short of the strobe of energy that was the beacon, I untwisted the unNow, and *Mambrino* dropped into normspace.

I slowly released my breath. "Beta Candace," I pulsed the second and third.

"Good," murmured Alek.

I reoriented the ship into a "descent" to reach the system ecliptic, and Nabata Orbit Control, then rebuilt the photon nets and began to accelerate in normspace. I didn't bother to transmit our arrival for a time.

"Nabata Orbit Control, this is *Mambrino*, inbound this time. Captain Tyndel, second Berya, and third Alek. No passengers. Full cargo. Full cargo, I say again. Condition green. Estimate arrival in one-five standard minutes."

We were half through with deceleration when I received the reply.

"Captain Tyndel, we have the *Mambrino* at the locks in approximately eight-plus your time. Subcommander and maintenance chief Jukor will supervise unloading."

"Stet. Understand subcommander Jukor."

"The subcommander again," Berya said.

I nodded, already concentrating on the switch to ionjets and the approach, slower than usual. With all the mass stuffed into the *Mambrino*, I needed to watch the deceleration profile. Ionjets didn't give the response, and we didn't need to crash into the station.

I did sigh once we were safely cradled. Then, after the short shutdown checklist, I went to the lock to meet the subcommander.

The short stocky subcommander with the blond, fuzz-cut hair half bowed. "Glad you could make it, captain. We were wondering. It's been nearly two years, and we haven't had any word."

"I'm glad to be here." *That's true enough.* "I have a

datacube for the commander—from the Authority."

Jukor's square face blanked. "I'll have Messer take you up."

"Thank you." I wanted to tell him not to worry, but what I could have told him would still have concerned him, and it was the station commander's decision how to handle it.

"Messer?" Jukor motioned to a young-looking man in gray coveralls, the kind I'd worn when I'd been a maintenance tech on OE Station. "Would you show the captain to the commander's office?"

"Yes, ser."

I followed the tech without a word, up shafts whose patterns were all too familiar, up to the station's upper level.

Commander Gerala was a wiry and dark-skinned woman who looked down on me, or would have in normal gravity, by a good head or so. Jukor had used the station link to warn her, clearly, since she didn't betray any surprise when I extended the datacube. She took it with a rueful smile. "When needle jockeys are personal messengers, the news isn't good. Do you know what's in the cube?"

"In general terms. There's a hazard problem on the direct line from Sol to Beta Candace. Needles don't have the power to make radical course shifts in overspace. The Authority will be supplying you from E. Cygni."

"You made the direct run," the commander observed.

I waited.

Gerala frowned. "Weren't you the next-to-last one to get through—four years ago?"

"I made a trip four universe objective years ago. I don't know who came after that." I gave a wry smile. "With the dilation, I have a hard time keeping track of my own trips."

"I can imagine." She shook her head.

"If there's nothing else, commander . . ."

"I'll let you know if I have any questions."

I made my own way back down to the ship and had barely finished rechecking the *Mambrino* when Berya stuck her head into the control center.

"Messenger for you, captain."

The messenger was a man in blue, a controller, who floated just inside the lock. "Ser, the commander would very much appreciate your presence in her office."

Berya's smile was an exercise in both control and carefully concealed worry. Controllers weren't used for messengers, even on orbit stations.

So I made my way back through the same shafts I'd so recently traveled and hauled my body back into the commander's presence. She wasted no time.

"If what commander Krigisa states in this happens to be true, then I cannot fault the logistics . . . and I do appreciate the cargo you brought. Subcommander Jukor was rather . . . astounded at the mass. A hot young pilot on a risky run . . ." A wintry smile creased her lips. "But . . . two to three years more before the next supply run? That's a five-year lag or more in the project . . . and we don't possess the equipment or expertise if something goes wrong in the final stages of the project."

"I thought Nabata was habitable . . ."

"It's hot and borderline. We're still having to supplement the water cycle with ice comets from the outer belt. Atmospheric pressure is too high, and . . . that's not something you have to deal with." She shrugged. "Can you tell me how bad this 'hazard' is and how long it's likely to last?"

"It's somehow cost two needle ships out of the last four or five scheduled here." That was true and would eventually come out.

That brought a long pause. "That bad?"

"Yes, commander." *That bad.*

"Does anyone know how long this will last?"

"No." That was also true. "They don't know the cause at this point, either."

"Has anything like this happened on any other runs?"

"Not that I've heard. There aren't any other needles missing recently. Or there weren't when I left Orbit Two."

The questions continued for a time, but I kept to the facts.

Finally, she looked straight at me. "You've been very patient, captain Tyndel. It's clear that you've told me all you know, and it's also clear that you risked your life and your ship to bring that cargo and this information." Gerala took a long breath. "I don't like it, but we do what we must. I may send back several people who wouldn't be scheduled to leave until next year—if they wish. Would that be a problem?"

"Not so long as your techs can help put the passenger cabin back into working order. The couches were removed and stowed to provide space for more cargo."

"We can do that." The wintry smile returned.

In time, I made my second trip back down to the ship, where the maintenance techs were already working under Alek's supervision to reconvert the passenger cabin. By then, I was really ready for some rest—a nap, anything.

75

[BETA CANDACE/E. CYGNI: 4527]

Words are not a conversation; conversation is not dialogue; dialogue does not always lead to honesty.

Almost no cargo and ten passengers—that was what the *Mambrino* held when I eased the ship away from Nabata Station. Commander Gerala did not see us off, leaving the task to subcommander Jukor.

I'd never made what might be called a "sideways" transit, but the data was in the system, correctly, I hoped, and I set up the acceleration and orientation for E. Cygni and

Ballentir Station, and the clamshells descended and locked, and we slipped through the needle hole of the Web and into the purpled green I perceived as overspace, finding almost a ridgeline toward a beacon. I verified the beacon twice, and then again, since I'd never approached E. Cygni from anywhere.

Even before the beacon check was done, massed organ marches blasted at me from below the darkness of the ridge across which we sped.

The spears of twin singularities shivered below the *Mambrino*, cold and menacing.

Then came another unvoiced, soundless question, one I answered mentally, "What do you want?" But my thoughts and reactions were on the singularities.

A dialogue, as you might put it. The words pounded through my skull. The dark spears marched anglewise toward *Mambrino*.

"About what?" I eased the *Mambrino* into an upward arc, as if that might help.

Honesty, which you value highly, and the involvement of higher powers, or cultures . . .

The massed steel-strung twang of singularities rattled through me, and beneath the harmony/disharmony came words, words unbidden, words unsummoned.

My lack of involvement is assumed to represent a lack of ability for such involvement.

"Lack of ability?" My words were half uttered, barely considered as I and *Mambrino* danced along the lines of light and darkness.

The nanite-demon people have the ability to affect non-demon cultures. What makes you think that ability has not been exercised?

I was sure it had been but did not answer, instead evading, sidestepping, a block of black crystal that tumbled end-over-end in the white darkness.

For what purpose . . . mere vanity? Do you trust the honesty of your Authority? If so, if that power is to be trusted, why not greater power?

"Not all power is the same." I would have swallowed if I could have.

Not all power? Or not all users? Or does power shape its user? Those drifting words carried amusement I could not address or consider.

Is an Authority more than a demon? More than a grouping of demons? Is it to be respected because you have conquered the Web? If but in the darkness where there is no dust? . . . Gods use the Web . . . old gods and new gods . . . whether there is dust or not. Think of the power any god must employ to dip into the dust-strewn regions of life.

From there the words rolled on, and through me, as though I had heard them before. Or perhaps they were my own arguments. About that, I wasn't certain, only upon Engee's parting words, if they were from Engee and not from somewhere deep within my own snarled mind.

Think on what I have said, needle jockey.

With those words, the connection was broken and I was back among the sonic blocks and the music of lilacs and windroses and apple blossoms . . . and the singularities that marched upward swiftly and toward the *Mambrino*.

I untwisted the twist of the Web, and we dropped out to the beacon of Ballentir, too high above E. Cygni, but safe.

"Captain . . . what was that energy spike?" asked Berya. "I could sense it even in overspace."

"Later," I temporized. "Later." *Energy spikes . . . Engee . . . and not even on the Beta Candace run.* I'd need to report, a solid report—after I brought the ship into E. Cygni, after I explained the "hazard" of the earth–Nabata run to the station commander, after I got back to Orbit Two.

Then, if I could, I needed to think . . . and talk to Cerrelle.

76

[E. CYGNI/ORBIT TWO: 4529]

The void is coeval with all things and is not subject to being obstructed by things, nor does it hinder the coming and going of all things.

From Ballentir Station, we picked up two more passengers, happy to leave six months earlier than the next scheduled run, and my first trip over the Trough was backward, down an incline, an overspace gradient steep enough that I certainly wasn't looking forward to going the other way.

There were no other attempts at "conversation" by Engee, if what I had "heard" had indeed been such. Breakout in normspace was above the ecliptic and normal.

"Orbit Two, this is *Mambrino*. Estimate arrival in twenty your time. Captain Tyndel, second Berya, third Alek, twelve passengers. I say again, one-two passengers. Cargo less than one tonne." After a moment, I added, "Inbound from Ballentir."

We continued inbound for more than ten minutes, well into the end of deceleration, before there was a reply.

"*Mambrino*, this is Orbit Two. Say again, previous departure point."

"Previous departure point was Ballentir. Before Ballentir, Nabata. Estimate arrival at Orbit Two in eight standard."

"Stet. Eight standard. Area is clear. No inbounds, cleared to lock one."

"Stet. Docking at lock one."

"They didn't want to believe our previous destination," suggested Alek.

"All they had to do was check the dilation intervals," snapped Berya. "Junior controllers shouldn't be questioning needle captains."

That might have been, but I knew that someone would be.

The usually ubiquitous Erelya was not waiting for me. Rather, commander Krigisa was, except she didn't wait but glided into the *Mambrino*'s control center even before I'd fully finished the postflight.

"You're looking well, Tyndel, especially for a three-insertion run." She nodded. "I'd like to see you in operations after your postflight." As quickly as she had arrived, she was gone.

"What did we do?" Berya looked at the empty hatchway.

"Nothing. The commander's worried about dangers to needle ships and what I might have sensed in overspace."

"That energy spike?"

It was my turn to nod. "There have been some odd . . . sightings . . . along the Beta Candace run. I need to report. I was asked to watch things closely." *Not precisely true . . . .* "Actually, I was asked that when I first became a pilot. Maybe all pilots are."

Berya didn't press me, for which I was grateful, as I gathered my gear.

Both Erelya and Krigisa were waiting when I hurried into operations. Both faces were drawn, and their eyes almost hollow. For not the first time, the gray of the room reminded me of the caserns of the ancients, of the deep cellars beneath Henvor and under the Hall of Unremitting Alertness.

"How did it go?" Krigisa's face was concerned, faintly.

"I had no difficulties. There was the same sparkling veil. It's a trace disconcerting but not enough to distract me."

"What about the voices?"

"This time . . . I did hear them—but not on the Beta Candace run."

The commander's face turned impassive, her expression like those of the demons on the cataclypt of Dyanar, and I wondered why I had thought of such after all the years that had passed since I had left Henvor.

"Go ahead. Don't leave out *anything*, Tyndel." Krigisa's words went beyond a command.

"All I got on the Nabata leg was the impression of a question. Not even a verbal request. Just this question. I ignored it. I didn't know if I should, but I did."

"Did this . . . voice . . . or whatever threaten or did it move singularities against the ship . . . ?"

"Did the transit get harder?" Erelya's question tripped over the last words of the commander.

"No, sers. Nothing happened then. We came out of overspace without any problems." I paused, then dropped the words I knew would make a difference. "But . . . on the sideways leg to Ballentir, there were words. On the homebound leg, there was nothing."

"What words? Do you think it was Engee?" asked Krigisa bluntly.

"I don't know. It was certainly some entity with great power, and one that understood both mite and Rykashan cultures."

"Engee *spoke* to you?" asked Erelya. "What did it . . . he say?"

"He said that he wanted a dialogue about honesty . . . after that, I listened, but I didn't. I concentrated on bringing the ship through."

"Can you remember *anything* specific?"

I concentrated. "He said several things . . . that we assumed his lack of involvement represented a lack of ability . . . that Rykasha has been meddling in non-Rykashan cultures. He asked me to . . . assess the honesty of the Authority, and if I found it trustworthy to ask whether I also shouldn't trust a greater power . . ."

"A greater power? He's asserting he's a greater power, then?"

"There was that implication," I admitted, "but it was never stated."

"What else?" Krigisa's voice was clipped.

"He suggested that not all power and not all users of power were the same, and then he went on to suggest that if I could respect the Authority, which had only been able to conquer overspace in the relatively dust-free sections of the Galaxy, surely one should respect a power that could reach anywhere through overspace."

"It's mad . . . or deceptive," suggested Krigisa.

"What do you think, Tyndel?" asked Erelya.

I swallowed, then opted for honesty, as if I had any other choice that would leave me whole. "I think whatever it is is powerful. I couldn't prove it, but I don't think it's deceptive. And it wants something beyond dialogue. I don't know what that something is."

"Could you be imagining this?"

"I could be, but I don't think so."

"Did you have any trouble with breakout at Epsilon Cygni?" asked Erelya.

"No, ser. That was smooth. So was the inbound to Sol."

"A dialogue about honesty?" mused Krigisa.

"And about power. He was very direct in suggesting that Rykasha had meddled with the mite cultures, and yet worried about his meddling with Rykasha. That part was clear. After that, I was more concerned with the ship, and I didn't follow the exact words, or thoughts. There was something about honesty in the dust-strewn regions of the Web."

"Distraction? An intellectual Siren . . . an intellectual discussion . . . could it be that simple?" asked the operations controller, looking at Erelya.

I didn't think so, but I waited for the question to be directed to me. After a moment, they both looked in my direction and waited.

"I could have been distracted," I said, "and there were singularities on the route. But I'd think that an experienced pilot wouldn't have been distracted."

"Anyone can be distracted. Then, you seem to 'see' better in overspace," reflected Erelya. "Were you tempted to move the ship—or asked to?"

"No."

"Were there any manifestations of this . . . dialogue?"

"There was some sort of power spike that the second picked up, or sensed, but the instruments and the system records don't show it."

"Berya's pretty level." Erelya glanced at the commander.

The questions went on for a long, long time, but all those that followed were merely attempts to verify what I'd said before.

After a time, Krigisa glanced at Erelya. "Can he take another ship out?"

"Can you, Tyndel?" asked Erelya.

"Why not? Haven't others heard voices? Besides, the run back from Epsilon Cygni was clear."

"I don't know," mused Krigisa. "We don't know enough."

"We can't shut down everything," pointed out Erelya. "If we ground every pilot who senses anything, then we won't have enough to supply the technology and expertise to either the colonies or the projects. Do you want to explain that to the Authority? Do they want to explain that to everyone?"

Both women winced, as though explaining difficulties in interstellar travel were a far greater problem than I thought. After all, the needles were doing the near impossible. Sooner or later, there had to be problems. That had to have been obvious for a long time, hadn't it?

"Besides," Erelya continued, "Tyndel's the only one who's actually reported a contact and made insertions afterwards."

"This one, I'll have to think about." Krigisa turned to me, a dark figure all too symbolic of the Authority. "First, you're going down to medical at Runswi to get a full examination, and you'll repeat everything in a way that can be verified. Senior Captain Erelya will observe all of this. Then the medical types will examine every possible physical cause that could create a false set of overspace images. We'll also examine all the sensors and ship systems. If you get a clean report, while we evaluate everything, at the very least, you'll have a double layover. You should anyway, after a trip like that. Then," her voice softened, "we'll let you know what we decide about your future as a pilot."

Erelya nodded to me, and I left, marveling at how the operations room again seemed like a casern from the past and wondering if I would ever pilot another needle ship. I couldn't believe I would, and yet, I didn't doubt that I would.

And I kept recalling how the operations room had seemed like an ancient casern, and I wondered what awaited me at the medical facilities in Runswi. I worried about that a lot, far more than about Engee . . . but then we often consider our own place first.

Still . . . I couldn't believe that any power that great and that curious was malevolent . . . or even that interested in doing harm.

77

[LYNCOL: 4529]

Grasp emptiness, and emptiness is form. Grasp form, and it is emptiness.

My medical "debrief" took more than three days, and more than half of it I didn't remember.

The only thing that mattered was that, at the end, Erelya and Aleyaisha both looked at me with clear eyes, and Erelya said, "You're sane. You're better adjusted than most pilots, and that means we have a problem bigger than anything since the Devastation."

They did. I didn't. I'd already had to face a culture and individuals beyond my comprehension. Somehow, another experience like that didn't bother me, not too much, but that was Dzin. If it is real, then its existence must be accepted. Engee was real. A good many of the Rykashans were going to have trouble with that, especially if Engee were as powerful as I suspected.

Once they released me, I sent a link message to Cerrelle, then went to find the tunnel glider. The one I took from Runswi was crowded—half-full was crowded for Rykashan transport.

Cerrelle met me at the tunnel station platform—that odd architectural combination of polished gray stone and warm golden woods—the gray of the ancients and the living gold of . . . what? Demons? Even more antique druids?

Her heavier winter coat was unfastened, and those piercing green eyes did not quite meet mine. I smiled, for I was truly glad to see her, but, once again, she hesitated. I didn't. I hugged her warmly.

"You're back. I wasn't certain . . . and then your link came . . . I was afraid to take the message."

"You shouldn't be." I kept holding her.

From across the platform I caught a murmur. ". . . wish a needle jockey would look at me like that . . ."

". . . all the young types after them . . . don't notice the experienced ones around much . . . keep to themselves, their family . . . bet those two have children somewhere . . ."

"No . . . but I'd like to," I murmured in Cerrelle's ear.

"Like what? To get to the lake?"

"That will do for now." She hadn't heard the words my more acute hearing had picked up, and I didn't feel right about explaining it all. I hugged her again. She felt real and solid in an uncertain universe.

"Not here."

I flushed. I hadn't meant that, not directly, but amplifying on that would have just gotten us both embarrassed.

"You're blushing . . ." She grinned. "I like it when you do that. You're not the composed Dzin master, needle jockey."

"I never was. I keep telling you that."

"Maybe I need to hear it more often," she answered as we walked up the polished stone steps.

While the path leading from the tunnel exit was clear, fine snow drizzled around my face out of the heavy gray clouds. The snow on either side of the way was higher than my head and showed little sign of melting.

"It's been a cold and snowy winter," Cerrelle said. "They're talking about another little ice age."

Three years plus, three and a half, and I was back in winter. I'd barely felt summer before I'd left. Sometimes, life felt like that.

"The glider-cat's in the transport hangar."

Cerrelle took us into the low stone-and-wood transport building, past open doors, and murmuring voices, and the scent of electronics and people, and then down another set of steps into the lower hangars, where the glider lay in a bay between two others—both larger. After Cerrelle opened the canopy, I stowed the small duffel in the rear of the free-range glider. She closed the canopy, and I settled into the seat beside her.

After she had the glider-cat on the tree-cleared but snow-covered way to the lake, she glanced momentarily at me. "Now . . . tell me what happened."

"They asked me to take the Beta Candace run. That's the one past Alpha Felini—the Anomaly. Engee, if you will . . ." I went on to explain the lost needles and everything that had happened, including the medical debrief. By the time I had finished, Cerrelle was guiding the glider on the last stretch toward the lake. Her face was drawn. "You . . . they . . . Erelya was right about this being the greatest challenge since the Devastation."

"I can see why people would get upset . . . I suppose."

"You suppose?" Her eyebrows rose, although she kept her eyes on the snowy track. "Is that Dzin . . . or don't you understand?"

I sighed. "I understand, but I don't. Anything that powerful could have done a lot before this. What real changes will it make? The worst it could do would be to disrupt interstellar travel. That won't affect anyone much on earth. It will hurt a few thousand people on the orbit stations and the borderline outplanets. Most of the colonies are self-sustaining. They have to be . . ."

Cerrelle laughed as she eased the glider-cat up the snow-covered slope to the chalet. "I doubt that most people will be anywhere near that calm."

"I know. I know. But it's all true."

"Truth often doesn't impact people's emotions. Do I have to remind you of that, Dzin master?"

I flushed. She was, again, definitely right about that.

"Think of all those excited people the way you felt when you discovered Rykasha," she suggested.

That thought wasn't exactly reassuring.

A thin line of white circled from the hearth's chimney, barely visible against the clouds whose gray had begun to lighten, even though the fine flakes of snow continued to fall.

"The fire will feel good." *In more ways than one.*

"I thought so. I put on four of the heavy oak logs before I left."

Once we were inside, I left the duffel by the steps and hugged Cerrelle again. This time, she didn't protest. After a time, she murmured, "This has upset you. You're affectionate, but not usually this affectionate, and it's not . . ."

"Lust?" I suggested, letting a wry grin cross my face.

"I don't mind lust, at the right time. Or place." She smiled back. "You want to talk about it?"

"After I get some real Arleen."

"It's laid out, by the kettle."

Even though the kettle was heated through nanite action, somehow boiling water and steeped tea tasted better than formulated tea, and all the scientific rationales for why there should be no difference didn't explain the greater satisfaction of brewed Arleen. I carried two mugs to the couch before the hearth and the fire, to which Cerrelle had added another set of logs.

Beside the woman whose directness and honesty had inspired mine, I enjoyed a sip of the brewed Arleen.

"This . . . nanogod spoke to you?" she finally asked. "The debrief showed that, too?"

"Yes. The first few times, I thought or wondered if . . . well . . . like you lost your nanite balance on Thesalle. I wondered if all those little nanites were scrambling my nerves and I was making up thoughts to cover the static."

"What changed your mind?"

"Static isn't that rational . . . and then there were the power spikes on the system, and I wasn't the only one who noted them."

"Static could have affected the others."

"Not with other pilots hearing things. They finally found a record in the lower level systems, something about derivative power flow memories, Erelya said."

"A real god?" Cerrelle laughed, half humorously, half bitterly. "After all the generations of rationality that has almost eliminated unreasoning faith in the supernatural?"

"He's not a god. A powerful intelligence isn't a god," I pointed out.

"Too many people won't see it that way . . . and if it gets to the mite cultures . . ."

"It won't change anything," I pointed out. "Most believe in a supernatural being anyway. The danger is greater in Rykasha. Erelya said it . . . was the greatest problem since the Devastation." I shook my head. "You said it, too."

"You don't think so?"

"Engee exists, whatever Engee is or has become. This being . . . this intelligence has power. We have powers that people before the ancients would have called godlike or angellike or demonlike. Somewhat greater power doesn't make a deity."

"Spoken like a true Rykashan. From a man who wasn't sure he was one." Cerrelle raised her fine eyebrows into an arch. "How many true Rykashans are there?"

"Not as many as the Authority thinks."

"They will. They'll calculate it down to the last head."

I had to smile, momentarily, but the smile faded. "That still doesn't bother me. After the initial flurry, most people will get over it. Something else does. He . . . it . . . wants something. Why does a creature with that kind of power want something from me? Or any needle pilot?"

"Do you have any idea what?"

I shook my head. "Besides, how will I ever know? He's only contacted me in overspace—so his powers are limited that way. You don't think they'll let me near a ship anytime soon, do you?"

"What do you think?" Cerrelle asked, gently, after another long silence.

"I don't know. They've lost every pilot who's heard the voices, except me." I stood, needing more Arleen, and walked to the kitchen, where I poured a second mug, before returning and settling beside Cerrelle, ruffling her short red hair for a moment. "I suppose that's up to the Authority."

"They'd be wise to let you go." She frowned. "I'm not sure you'd be wise to oblige them."

"I haven't come close to paying my obligation," I pointed out.

Cerrelle nodded. She knew about obligations—hers made mine look minuscule.

"I have a double layover," I said. "At the very least. That's because they want to think it over. Also, that's because I did the sideways transit, and that rates double."

"Good." She edged close to me, close enough that I could brush her cheek with my lips.

I did.

"I missed you."

"I missed *you*."

The discussion about Engee was postponed . . . but only postponed.

78

[LYNCOL: 4530]

Studying the physics of light is not illumination.

Standing on the main level of the chalet, amid blazing sunlight reflected from the expanse of white outside the long glass windows, I looked at the console, letting my mind do the searching for the needle pilot's assignments. I could have linked directly, but I liked the old-fashioned image, though I would have once called it an iconraiser's screen, many years back, back when anything beyond the basics of the ancients' technology raised the old fears of the Devastation, back when intercity gliders were the fastest transport I'd known and the stone-sided demon traps of Henvor had provided a sense of security against the unknown.

Erelya had notified me a week earlier that no other contacts with Engee had been reported and that I could pilot again—along with dropping a strong caution about mentioning Engee and also letting me know that I had to pass another physical screening in Runswi before taking the shuttle to Orbit Two.

The image flashed into place, and the information was stark enough: Tyndel—Alexandri Gamma/Thesalle (4/12/30).

Cerrelle looked over my shoulder and winced. "Don't stay planetside longer than you have to."

"Bad memories?"

"No memories, really, except hazy ones, and that's worse."

No memories? What were we but memories governed by a form of intelligence, seeking to make our lives in some way memorable? Trying to attain dreams that would secure such remembrance?

Pushing that aside for the moment, I scanned the lists of assignments. Nothing was out of the ordinary—except that there were no direct runs to Beta Candace. Somehow, that wouldn't make much difference. Not to Engee.

I flicked off the link, mind-directly, rather than with my fingers.

"That still fascinates me," Cerrelle said. "Even if I know the theory, it's something else to see someone you know and love do it."

My thoughts lingered on the word *love* for a long moment before I replied. "Mind over matter, but it's a mind aided by a great deal of nanite-sized matter." I laughed.

Then I frowned. *What is Engee but a creation aided by a huge amount of nanite-sized matter? What is the difference between Engee and a needle jockey?*

There wasn't an answer to that, not at hand, but I wondered, then set aside that as well, and enfolded Cerrelle in a hug born out of my own uncertainties, as if she were a rock in the storming sea, shade in blinding light.

79

[THESALLE/ORBIT TWO: 4531]

*Myths dissected by logic and science die, and so does the culture
that lived by them.*

The transit to Thesalle had been uneventful, as uneventful as any insertion and exit, but once I had gone planetside . . . then . . . then I had understood the disorienting effect of the planet. I'd stood in middle of the square of Machedd and looked up and seen green everywhere. The air was green—a mistlike green, unlike the heavy veils of green that cascaded down the terraced slopes—and the five-sided mountain was green—five green flush sides that rose eight thousand meters over the valley, so regular one would have thought it had been sculpted rather than weathered into shape. Except when I counted again there were four sides, and a recount gave me seven. Post-Web sensory scrambling? Or that unnamed and undiscovered hallucinogen mentioned by an Authority scientist years before, that hallucinogen presumably still undetermined.

I'd never figured that out, and Dzin hadn't helped that awareness, nor had the red golden-fires that had flared through my system as I had stood in the four-pointed green square and looked up at the mountain overlooking the town. In the end, I accepted that I wouldn't know how many sides the mountain had, and had gone and gotten some sleep.

Berya was hollow-eyed when she met me outside the *Mambrino's* lock the following day.

"How did you rest?" I asked.

"Didn't . . . not well. Should have stayed on the station."

The control spaces were quiet as we prepared for departure and the return to Earth Orbit Two.

Departure and insertion were smooth, easy, and overspace was an even lighter green-purple than usual, a green-purple of unusual clarity as the *Mambrino* and I eased our way down the incline toward Sol, past the Baroque-like deep melodies of a barely formed singularity and across the first of the triplet gulfs. As we hung over the first gulf, there was a rumbling . . . that sense of an unvoiced question, a sense that I ignored until we were clear of a yellow velvet ice trumpet that had narrowed into a spear and tried to impale the ship.

Even the mighty are limited . . .

"That's a tautological paradox," my mind replied. I concentrated on avoiding the deadly rectangles that followed the spear. "True mightiness would have no limits."

Any being within a universe is limited by that universe. Any ordered action in any universe results in a total increase in disorder. Even gathering and creating information is an ordered action, and as such, there is no way even a god can create more information than is destroyed through the creation process. Golden-red starfire punctuated the words.

"Then how can any being increase knowledge?" I eased the ship into a climb over the dissonant wake of a singularity.

By linking two universes, by using the energy from a collapsing high-entropy antimatter universe to power the creation of order within this universe.

"That would take more than a god." I dismissed the thought and concentrated on the white/black warmth of the lunar beacon, and on untwisting the unNow and breaking out into normspace.

"Energy spikes, again." Berya's words were bleak as I eased the *Mambrino* toward earth and the orbit station on its photonjets. "You felt them, didn't you, captain?"

"Very much. I'm sure operations will want to know." I tried to keep my own thoughts focused as I considered Engee's message.

Ordering information within any universe destroys more information than it creates . . .

That was probably true, but how much of the destroyed information was usable? Usable by whom? And when? Add to that the power implied by Engee's last words . . . *By linking two universes, by using the energy from a collapsing high-entropy antimatter universe to power the creation of order within this universe.*

I shook my head. That kind of power was impressive, and I had no doubt Engee had already been using it. That explained Astlyn's comments about the "more energetic" matter of the Anomaly. Then, too, there was the fact that Engee had used those no-time moments of red and gold fires of the deep to sear through me at the pinnacle of overspace, from the distance of Alpha Felini to a point in overspace that all the science of Rykasha could not have precisely located. Yet Engee had.

I took a deep breath as I shut down the photon nets and brought the ionjets on line, then triggered a transmission to Earth Orbit Two. "Orbit Two, this is *Mambrino*. Estimate arrival in fifteen your time. Captain Tyndel, second Berya, third Alek, six passengers. I say again, six passengers. Cargo less than three tonnes. Request conference with operations upon arrival."

We continued inbound and had less than twenty percent of deceleration to go when Orbit Two replied. "*Mambrino*, this is Orbit Two. Understand you wish conference with operations. Is that affirmative?"

"That is affirmative."

"Request status, *Mambrino*."

"Status is green. Green, I say again."

"Stet. Cleared to lock four upon arrival. No inbounds this time."

"You meeting about the energy spikes, captain?"

"Unfortunately . . . yes."

Berya nodded. "Some ships don't make it past them, do they?"

"That's what operations suspects, but we don't know for certain. That's why they want to know about anything like that." I didn't want to say more; I'd not wanted to say that, and I certainly wasn't looking forward to dealing with commander Krigisa or even senior captain Erelya. I might feel that Engee was more curious than dangerous, but that kind of power wasn't going to set well on Orbit Two.

Shutdown and postflight were mostly silent, because I was silent except as necessary, thinking about the meeting ahead. And I'd asked for it, not that I'd had much choice, not if I wanted to remain honest.

In the gray-walled casern of operations, there were three people waiting—Erelya, commander Krigisa, and Aleyaisha. There was also a complete diagnostic console, also gray, a shinier newer gray. The air was cool, dry, like that in a casern or a desert crypt. That Aleyaisha was there meant more trouble, not for me but for needle ships in general, because they couldn't have gotten her up from Runswi in the time since I'd requested a conference.

I didn't even bother to ask the procedure, just nodded at the red-clad Aleyaisha and eased myself over beside the console. "Any time you're ready."

She lifted the diagnostic spray, and the silver mist wafted over me and into and through me, then began to reform on the receiving screen. I watched as the sandy-haired medical type studied the screen.

"He's in perfect physical health," Aleyaisha finally noted. "He has been before every run. Even his muscle tone is at the top."

"Nothing out of the ordinary?" asked Krigisa, worrying the forefinger and thumb of her right hand together.

"Not that the diagnostics show."

The three of them looked at me as though I might be human once more. Then Krigisa nodded at Aleyaisha, who eased back to the other side of the console, effectively leaving me with the two senior officers.

"I presume you had some sort of contact," Krigisa began.

"I did." I glanced in the direction of Aleyaisha. "I presume I'm not the first, lately, either."

"Three others, but we've only lost one more ship."

One . . . on top of the others? I nodded politely, but the reason for Aleyaisha's presence was clear.

"Any more . . . dialogues?" inquired the commander.

"Nothing on the outbound, but a fairly elaborate set of . . . observations coming back."

"What?"

I smiled, if nervously. "A general observation on entropy . . . so to speak . . . and then a solution that might explain the puzzle Astlyn outlined to me years ago."

"Go on."

"If it's Engee, he . . . it . . . is tapping a reverse universe somewhere, one that runs backwards from ours, using its high-energy entropy as a power source to build his system. That's if I understood what he was trying to convey. He calls it the only way to create more information than is being destroyed by the information creation process, a way to avoid losing the memory of the universe . . . or something."

"Avoid losing the memory of the universe? Odd," murmured Erelya. "That's his concern with all that power?" She frowned.

"He says he's pumping energy from another universe into that Anomalous system? The theory says that wouldn't work," said Krigisa.

"Something's pumping energy there," pointed out Erelya. "And if he has that kind of power . . ."

"I don't know. I'm certainly not an expert on universal physics. It might not work. He might just be throwing words, or I might be imagining them, but that was what I heard. I listened, but I kept my mind on the ship."

"If Tyndel heard them, he heard them," Aleyaisha confirmed from the other side of the console.

"It doesn't mean this . . . creature is telling the truth."

"Why would it lie?" asked Erelya. "Something is creating matter *and* energy in the Anomaly, seemingly from nowhere. This provides an explanation."

"Why would it tell the truth? Why would it tell us—or Tyndel—why?"

"Because it wants something and because greater power demands greater honesty for survival, and it has greater power, and it's survived," I suggested.

For a moment, the casern that operations had become, at least in comparison to overspace, was silent.

"Did it say what it wanted?"

"No. That's just an impression," I had to admit.

"Are you sure this wasn't because of Thesalle . . . its

impact?" asked Krigisa, still worrying forefinger and thumb together.

"Outside of visual disorientation . . . no." I offered a grin. "I never did figure out how many sides the mountain over Machedd had."

"No dizziness? Nausea? Physical weakness?"

I shook my head.

"He's telling the truth on that, too," Aleyaisha confirmed.

"You say we've lost another needle—just one?" I asked, watching Krigisa.

"Just one."

"You're doing this with all pilots?"

"Have you a better idea?"

Find out what Engee wants and give it to him, except you don't know what he wants. "Not right now."

Aleyaisha nodded once more.

"How can you take this so calmly, Tyndel?" asked Krigisa, her voice carrying both interest and a tinge of exasperation and anger, as if she felt I didn't understand the gravity of the situation.

"You forget, commander, that I've already had to learn this once before."

She frowned for a moment.

"Rykashans have abilities far superior to those of Dorchans. Finding another being of superior abilities isn't so frightening to me. You all forced me to learn." I smiled rather than continue. *And it's amusing to see how you all face it.*

"And you think that makes you different?" asked Krigisa.

"He has made three separate returns after hearing discrete messages. No one else has managed one," added Erelya.

"It could be that I'm not tied to either God or no god. I'm a former Dzin master, one who's never been quite at home in any belief system."

"That's not a physical explanation," pointed out the commander.

"State of mind determines the physical ability to master overspace," countered Erelya.

I wanted to smile at her almost feisty response. Aleyaisha did, but erased the expression quickly.

"The universe exists independent of the anthropic principle . . . so does overspace," continued Krigisa.

There was a significant difference between existence and understanding, between reaction and proaction—or were intelligence and planning merely illusions? Were we genetically programmed to respond, merely rationalizing our actions after the facts? I didn't think so, but even my assessment could have been an illusion of sorts.

"That's not the question," Erelya responded. "It's why Tyndel can keep making runs after contact by Engee. It's possibly also why no other former Dzin masters have had a problem."

"We don't know that Dzin is the reason."

"It will do for now."

Krigisa turned to me. "What about the color of overspace? Has it changed?"

"It's slight brighter now, more of a lighter deep purple-green . . ."

"Have you noticed any changes in the perceptual gradients . . ."

The technical questions went on for what seemed more than a standard hour, until the room drifted into another silence. "Can I answer any more questions?" I asked politely.

"Not unless you have some other factual or data-based input," answered Krigisa.

"I've told you what I know."

"You'd better go, Tyndel. You're suspended from active flight status pending the results of a complete medical evaluation in Runswi as soon as you arrive." Krigisa's voice was tight when she finally dismissed me. "And I'd appreciate it if you would restrict your speculations."

"Yes, ser."

The debate was still going on when I left, for yet another in-depth medical evaluation in Runswi, but I had no doubts. In time, I'd fly at least one more insertion, and probably many more.

Once out of operations, I used my mental links to access the shuttle schedule board directly. Then I began to hurry, not wanting to spend another eight hours on Orbit Two.

As I slipped toward the handful of people lined by the lock, the shuttle's second—they had but two officers—caught sight of my greens.

"Captain . . . if you'd board now?"

"Thank you. I'm sorry. I was held up."

"It's not a problem, ser."

Behind me, I could hear voices.

". . . who's that?"

". . . name is Tyndel . . . say something special about him . . . no one says what . . . young, but there's a waiting list to officer under him . . ."

I frowned—a waiting list for me? Because I'd managed to survive at a time when a few needles had disappeared? That could have been mere chance. Was it because people were looking for some reason to think I was special? As I eased into the front couch in the magshuttle's passenger section, my thoughts skittered over the debriefing and the words I'd just heard. *Something special? Honesty out of fear? Fear that you won't be honest? Fear that your honesty is a fraud?*

I could sense the fear of others as well, especially of Commander Krigisa—the fear that the absolute power represented by Engee was a threat to Rykasha. Fear that the whole overspace system was about to crumble—or that faith in it was. That was almost the same thing, given that faith and the ability of the needle jockeys were what made the technology work.

If the Authority lost faith in the needle jockeys . . . if the other jockeys lost faith in themselves . . .

I'd asked, once, what a Rykashan was and found no answer. I had part of the answer—a Rykashan was someone who dreamed beyond the confines of earth, dreamed and worked to realize the dream, not just contemplate it.

Every society, I understood, had to have faith in something beyond itself, beyond the day-to-day. For the ancients, it had been religion, irrational and constricting as it had been. For Dorcha, it was the way of Dzin. For Klama, the way of Toze. For Dezret, the way of Ryks.

And Rykasha? *The stellar dream . . . the dream that nothing is beyond the souls and aspirations of demons? Such fragile arrogance . . .*

80

[LYNCOL: 4531]

Belief in destiny becomes an excuse for inaction or a rationale for self-centered action.

Late fall was in the air, the mold of leaves fallen and about to freeze, the ice curtain of winter about to drop across the calm shimmering surface of the lake. Cerrelle and I sat inside, protected by the glass, warmed by the sun, a mug in my hand, a tall beaker in hers. In a way, it was totally incongruous.

There was the possibility of an enormously powerful intelligence that might well change all of Rykasha merely by its presence. The interstellar travel system of Rykasha was certainly threatened, and we sat and drank. Yet . . . what could either of us do? I was a needle ship pilot who, because I'd been honest about what I'd sensed, was effectively grounded until the Authority made up its mind what to do with me. Cerrelle was a mid-level transport troubleshooter considered far below the problem facing Rykasha.

"Things are getting worse," I mused.

"How bad?"

"They had Aleyaisha up on Orbit Two to monitor every part of every needle jockey after each inbound." I took a sip of Arleen and thought, my eyes looking out at the surface of the lake, where, on the far side, the winds had begun to whip the silver surface into low whitecaps. Soon, the wind would reach our shore. "You never told me how fragile the system is." I turned sideways and studied the clean and strong profile, my lips curling into a smile as she brushed back a vagrant wisp of short red hair.

"I wouldn't have used that word."

"Fragile? I suppose not. In some ways, Rykasha is almost indestructible . . . except it's not. Societies run on myths, and one of the great myths is that we hold the stars the ancients couldn't. What happens if, one by one, we lose ships and pilots? The myth dies."

"That's what happened in Dezret," Cerrelle said, taking a delicate swallow of the icy veridian liqueur. "The Saints believed that they were the sons of God and that the world would be theirs, and that all would come to accept their vision of salvation, and that the land could be used and abused without consequences. It didn't happen that way, and the lake turned to salt and the rivers dwindled, and the winds blew harder, and the outsiders laughed . . . and slowly the men turned bitter, and the women were beaten into acceptance, those who didn't flee, and the winter gales brought down the temples, and no one has the time or the tools or the strength to repair them. Yet the records here show that the climate has not changed that much in millennia."

"Their perception did?"

"The lake was shrinking when they settled the area, in geologic terms, but they wouldn't see it. So much of their belief . . . their myth . . . wasn't in accord with reality, and they couldn't or wouldn't change it, and then it was too late." Cerrelle nodded. "Isn't that what you mean?"

"It's what I worry about. Overspace is dangerous. They don't really say that in training, but the training makes it clear. A few needle ships were vanishing over each twenty-year period or so, and those losses were downplayed, accepted. But two a year is far more than one a decade. There were only ninety-five pilots and sixty-one needle ships, and we've lost five ships, and pilots, I think, in the last three years. Or maybe six or seven." I frowned, trying to add up what I'd heard over the past years, because the numbers weren't in the data system. "That's what I've been able to discover. That's more than a tenth in less than five years. One's been built in that time. We can't keep taking those losses and still support the planoforming projects or supply the few high-tech items that will keep the smaller colonies from slipping back into low-tech states . . . or barbarism."

"That's why Krigisa and Erelya are worried," Cerrelle pointed out. "That's why you're worried."

"In some ways, I worry more about the mythic side." I took another sip of Arleen. "If the star dream goes, what's there to replace it? Engee? Then how are we any different from those of Dorcha . . . or Dhurra . . . or Klama?" I set down the mug. "Yet there's nothing I can do. Part of me worries that my own honesty keeps me from piloting. What if I'd just said I'd sensed some vague energy?"

"Then you'd have been grounded for lying, and in bigger trouble," Cerrelle pointed out. "Aleyaisha may be sympathetic, but she would have to have reported that, and the equipment is sensitive enough to reveal deception on that scale. Remember, they have your entire medical and psychological profile at hand."

"It still bothers me." I picked up the mug and looked across the lake, so placid, as if nothing in the universe had changed since it had been formed by glaciers fifteen thousand years earlier.

"The man who didn't want anything to do with needle

ships is now worried about their demise." A faint smile crossed her lips, and the piercing green eyes sparkled.

"That man has seen what dreams mean and do. His problem was that he didn't understand them because he'd been schooled that dreams of aspiration were dreams of vanity."

"All dreams are dreams of vanity," she pointed out. "All dreams are a search for meaning beyond impermanence. Even a long-lived demon is a mayfly on a universal scale."

"I don't know that I like being a mayfly."

"That's why you're building a garden you want to be so beautiful that no one will wish to remove it."

"That's part of the reason. I don't want to be impermanent in your mind and life, either."

She reached out and touched my hand, then curled her fingers around mine. "You won't be impermanent."

Even as I worried about a universe far bigger than the demons conceived, possibly far more hostile to dreams, especially stellar dreams, I squeezed her hand in return, taking comfort in the small island of warmth in which we basked, impermanent as it might be, waiting to see what my fate might be . . . what all our fates might be.

81

[LYNCOL/ORBIT TWO: 4532]

Each person believes in self-uniqueness: snowflakes are equally unique.

The year turned, and the snow fell, and the lake froze, and my name did not appear on the schedule board. I managed links to Erelya twice, and the senior captain was most polite and mostly not very informative.

"We've verified the information, Tyndel, and your status is under review."

That was the gist of what she'd said—twice. So I kept working out, in the gym, in the pool, and running through the deep snow that continued to fall.

Cerrelle's name showed up on another board, one that sent her off to Vanirel, looking in on another demon convert, this time from Thule. Vanirel—home of Fersonne, who'd only wanted her own place on Actean. Vanirel . . . another cold land, colder even than Rykasha—or really the region of Rykasha where I was, since the cold lands of Amnord and Thule were components of Rykasha.

I missed Cerrelle, but I kept telling myself that she had more than me to worry about . . . especially since it had been established that I was a Web pilot who knew what he was doing. With my schedule and the winter and the snow, I hadn't done much on the garden besides finish the back stone wall and place a couple of yews. So we conversed on the link when we could—not exactly satisfactorily.

Vanirel—I no sooner decided that I'd take a trip to see her when the screen chimed and I found myself facing Erelya through the screen at Cerrelle's chalet.

"Yes, ser?"

"Are you ready to take another run, Tyndel?"

"Yes, ser. What changed everyone's minds?"

A wintry smile cracked her face. "The fact that nothing's happened. The fact that needle ships continue to depart and return."

"Any more messages from . . . our entity?" I asked.

"A few hints, but only hints."

"So . . . now that Rykashan interstellar travel isn't instantly threatened—" I broke off, realizing that she'd been on my side. It had largely been commander Krigisa who'd put me on the shelf. "I'm sorry."

"Quite understandable, Tyndel. You were honest, and shelved, and the word apparently got out." The smile got colder, although I didn't feel it was directed at me. "So I thought it might be time for you to take another run. We need your talents anyway."

"What run?"

"Epsilon Cygni, over the Trough with some very heavy cargo. In four days. You up to that?"

"Yes, ser." For many reasons, I couldn't say no, especially with what Erelya had conveyed indirectly, but I wanted a little confirmation. "You say there's been some discrepancy between the medical reviews and the flight reports?"

"I didn't say that, Tyndel. That's strictly your conclusion." An ironic smile followed. "It is difficult to hide something from a Dzin master. That's why I want you piloting the *Mambrino* on this run." The emphasis on the pronoun "I" was there, but so slight as to be almost unnoticed.

I nodded. "I'll do my best."

"And, Tyndel . . ."

"Yes, ser?"

"You have to pass a long medical this time. You'll need to be in Runswi by noon of the day before. I doubt it will be a problem, but the commander insisted."

I understood that . . . and more. So . . . rather than take a suborbital magshuttle to Vanirel, I ended up two days later in Runswi, where doctors Fionya and Bekunin applied every examination technique they could find. Apparently, they couldn't find anything wrong, because the next morning I was on an orbital to Earth Orbit Two.

Once on the station, my first stop was the ready room, too gray for my taste, but in recent years, gray had become less and less intriguing.

Berya was tight-faced and turned when I appeared, pursing her lips before speaking. "Tyndel."

Now, former ignorant Dorchan or not, former would-be Dzin master, I could tell she was less than happy. "Good morning, Berya. Anything interesting?"

"A special Epsilon Cygni run . . . and Alek muttering about mass. He never mutters."

"Captain Erelya said it was heavy cargo. She didn't say what. You want to tell me what sort of heavy cargo?" I forced a grin. "Or is the captain the last to know?" E. Cygni was a tough run because it was a stiff climb, almost the opposite of the Santerene insertion, well above the insertion gradients. I'd seen it well enough from the other side, and hadn't been in any hurry to go the hard way.

"Fusactor spines." Berya offered a wry smile that faded quickly. "I'm glad it's you, Tyndel."

I gave a short nod. "I need to talk to Alek . . . if he's muttering."

"He's not on the ship . . . he's in station ops."

I turned and headed back up the transverse shafts, back to the gray casern of operations. Alek was standing in the hatchway to operations, talking to a thin figure with an oily smile.

"Captain . . . this is Ensor, assistant ops officer. He's standing in for commander Krigisa."

I nodded. That figured. Krigisa didn't want to see me, because if something went wrong, then the blame would go to Erelya and Ensor.

"I've heard about you, captain Tyndel." Ensor's voice was as oily as his lank brown hair and his unvarying smile.

"Fusactor spines?" I managed to keep my voice level, angered as I was at the oily assistant ops officer, and surprised as I was to find the anger there. Why was I upset? Because of the politics? Because it went against my feeling that honesty was important to Rykasha?

"They need an entire power net on Ballentir." Ensor shrugged. "Just discovered an incipient flare pattern, and they want to salvage what they can. And . . . as you know . . . needle transport has become slightly less certain . . . recently."

"Why us?" I knew the answer, but I wanted to see how Ensor reacted.

"Captain Tyndel, they're worried about time. Besides, the *Mambrino*'s the only ship this side of the Trough that's free. The *Costigan*'s never been the same since that problem it had going to Omega Eridani. And we never did get enough fusactor equipment to Nabata. You may recall that."

"Thank you." I managed a polite nod. From body posture and voice tone, it was clear that Ensor had been kept in the dark. I'd been there when the *Costigan* had barely survived a singularity, but wondered if Ensor knew I knew.

The station's junior operations officer smiled tightly. "If you're not up to handling Epsilon Cygni, I could call in someone else, a senior pilot like captain Sesehna. Or talk to commander Krigisa."

"I'll handle it." The last thing in the universe I wanted was to ask for help from Sesehna or Erelya.

The tightness around Alek's green eyes and narrow mouth eased. Ensor kept grinning.

Fusactor spines? Was I wrong to take the insertion? Berya and Alek deserved my best, but was it good enough to take spines across the Trough? Good enough to act as bait for Erelya before Engee lured or otherwise distracted another needle jockey?

"You're sure? You're new at this," Ensor pointed out.

"I've been at it long enough." I looked at Alek. "You ready to go?"

"Yes, ser."

"Good to meet you, Ensor," I lied, knowing he knew I lied.

"And you, too, captain." He cared even less for me than I did for him.

"What were you talking to . . . Ensor about?" I asked Alek as we headed back down the shaft. "How much mass they're loading onto us?"

Alek's mouth quirked. "I told him you wouldn't be happy if he loaded spine cases in the passenger compartment."

"You were right."

"He backed off. I think it was his idea, not the commander's."

We were nearly back to the *Mambrino*, locked on the lower ring, beside the *Costigan*, before the third spoke again. "The spines weren't my idea, Tyndel. I didn't volunteer us."

"I know. I was asked almost a week ago if we'd take heavy cargo. I didn't ask how heavy." I offered a laugh. "I should have. Ensor was right about one thing. I am new to the politics of being a needle jockey."

Alek smiled faintly. "Politics doesn't deliver the ship."

"No." I paused. "Make sure everything's locked in place. This is going to be one rough run."

My third officer nodded.

At the lock, Berya looked from Alek's face to mine, then pursed her lips. "We're going?"

"We're going."

She nodded. "Thought so."

After my preflight, I went into the control center while Alek finished checking the holds again and Berya covered the passenger area.

First came the harness. I plugged it into the silvery stripes that ran along the outside of the uniform suit sleeves and down the front of the thighs. Last, I eased on the helmet. They call it a helmet, although it's more like a skintight plastic cap and weighs maybe half a kilo, if that. Once on-line with the system, I rechecked the foam release nozzles, then the lines and plugs to the sensiharness and helmet. Plastic, that's the needle, composite and plastics pretty much end to end, with the bare minimum of metal—except for the power plant. Metals increase your specific attractions to the vortices. That's what happened to the *Costigan* and what everyone thought had hit the *Obelisk* decades earlier. At least, that's what they think happened. It makes sense, since any needle jockey can feel the pull from the fusactor.

"Everything all right, captain Tyndel?" Berya's voice came through the system as somehow scratchy.

"Fine, so far. How many passengers?"

"Eight. High-level techs, I think, except for a controller. He doesn't look happy."

"He knows what's in the holds." I glanced toward the other two couches. Berya was secure, and Alek was strapping in.

Even before I had started to uncradle the *Mambrino* from Orbit Two, I could almost sense the lurking mass of the spines, looming up behind me like a dark hulk ready to swallow the *Mambrino* whole. That much metal? It made a stupid kind of sense, especially if some had to go to Nabata. Do it once, and get them out there. Then any kind of in-system ship could carry them down to Ballentir—or anyplace else beyond the Trough. E. Cygni was not only high but more than halfway to anywhere and beyond the worst of the vortices along the Trough. The pull of that much metal also made sense . . . perhaps . . . if I were bait for Engee.

"Orbit Two, *Mambrino* disengaging this time. Outbound for Epsilon Cygni."

"Stet, captain Tyndel. Understand outbound for Epsilon Cygni. No inbound traffic this time."

"Stet."

Once we were well clear of the station, I began to boost the ionjets to full power, calculating and rechecking the orientation and acceleration I'd need for the climb over the Trough.

"On full ionjets," I passed along to Berya and Alek. "We'll start photonjet acceleration early so I can build it up more gradually." I didn't want any jerkiness with that kind of mass behind and below us.

As I spread the nets and transitioned to photondrive, I could feel the Web, waiting beyond, just beyond that flash of power that would shift the *Mambrino* up an energy level to where there's no matter, just energy fields. That was stupid, of course, because the ancients had proved millennia earlier that there was no matter, only energy. But in overspace, in harness, you can feel it all.

It doesn't last. Even with full power from the fusactor and the Rinstaal cells, there's not enough energy to keep a needle that excited for very long, just long enough for the insertion, the jump above the Now, and the quick dance through that web of sound and scent. Just enough to make it worthwhile.

"All passengers must be secured at this time."

The clamshells dropped, sealing us against the acceleration.

"Ready for insertion?"

"Stet."

There was just the faintest hiss before all the force lines centered on me, on the lines of power that made me the nerve center of the ship, of a ship that climbed upward and around eddies of solid energy.

The *Mambrino* screamed through the veil into the sense-scrambled realm of light and darkness, where black was so often white, and where silence was music, and music silence. I danced the unsupported climb over the Trough, over a dark vibrating triplet of singularities, singularities that twanged the symphonies of the ancients on steel strings, rumbling menace from deep in the Trough as the *Mambrino* and I soared, and gasped, and pirouetted through ice and fire and lilacs and heavy rose perfume to the white comfort of the beacon beyond.

And not a word from Engee. I wasn't sure whether to be worried or relieved.

Then as the fired strands of the Web faded, to the chorus of tiny bells that echoed a march I knew not, I slipped us out and into the white-flashed and twisted Now of real time, with Ballentir Station far above us. Low as we were, we were close enough to E. Cygni, and all in one piece, fusactor spines and all.

"Web exit complete," I reported, my voice scarcely hoarse at all. "Photonjets on-line."

"Are you all right, captain?" Alek's voice scratched through the speaker.

"Fine," I lied. Lilacs still sprinted through my nostrils,

burning a pathway to my brain, and dull echoes of matter-based kettledrums resonated in my ears. Already my back muscles had spasmed, and my eyes burned. The straps felt like chains. "Those spines are a hell of a load."

"What happened?"

"Singularities." I hated singularities, hated them and loved them, because they were clear black crystalline spears aimed at your guts, but spears that permeated the Web with the scent of spring lilac even as they stressed the channels and blocks a ship ran, even as their steel guitars threatened to disassemble you.

Now, in the back of my mind, on the real-time level, the inputs told me about the alarms and the safety web alerts and the gee-foam that had flooded the ship. Not that it mattered, really. I'd either cleared the singularities or I hadn't.

"How many?"

"Three." I swallowed. My guts were protesting more than usual. But then it hadn't been a normal trip. I'd had to climb all the way, the hard way, thanks to the damned spines.

"Thanks, captain . . ."

In the background before Alek closed the link, or maybe it was a residual from the Web, I caught the next words. ". . . frigging lucky . . . Tyndel . . . may be new . . . but be blood soup, otherwise . . ."

Maybe. I'd managed another insertion above the Now and under the Web, over the Trough, and the return would be downhill and smooth without all the heavy metal.

Maybe . . . unless Engee discovers you're back in over-space . . .

82

Those who believe in "truth" are invariably disappointed.

We got a week planetside on Ballentir—one of the first colonized worlds and the most earthlike, although there were no tall trees, but the downshuttle port was on a plateau overlooking a gray-green sea. I took a lot of walks and runs, and thought about Cerrelle, and wished I'd gone to Vanirel earlier, before it had gotten too late to go at all. I tried not to think about Engee and the disappearance of needle ships.

Berya went sailing, and I never saw Alek.

Then, suddenly, it seemed, we were back at Ballentir Orbit Station, readying the *Mambrino* for the return. Even before the locks were closed, the cradles released, my thoughts kept drifting back to Engee, wondering when I'd next hear from the being/god/Anomaly, wondering if Erelya's instincts and my feelings were correct, hoping in a way they're weren't.

"Ballentir Control, this is *Mambrino*, uncradled this time. Departing for Sol. Six passengers, minimum cargo."

"*Mambrino*, clear to depart. No local traffic or inbounds this time. Good trip."

"Ballentir Control, thank you."

Once the needle was clear of the cradles and the dull composite bulk of the station, I stepped up the fusactors' draw until the ionjets were at full power, easing the *Mambrino* in a trajectory that would allow spreading the photon nets and bringing the configurators on-line as quickly as possible.

"Please make sure that you are in your couches," Berya cautioned the passengers.

In time, we switched to photonic drive, and the clam-shells began to descend.

"Minus ten for insertion." I stepped up the acceleration and established the insertion orientation. Even with pas-sengers, without cargo the ship felt light, and absolute velocity increased rapidly toward the maximum insertion speed possible.

"Minus five." I made a last adjustment to the orienta-tion.

"Minus three." The lattices locked. The barriers be-tween the Now and overspace continued to thin, until the lattices themselves whispered and crackled, and the fabric of real space seemed to groan.

The needle slid smoothly into the momentary silence of overspace, an overspace almost a glowing but deep green, without maroon at all, except for the gap of the Trough below us and the distant but shivering thrumming sound of the singularities that were always present some-where in overspace.

Have you thought on what we discussed, needle jockey?

The words shivered me, but I concentrated on keeping the ship on its arc over the Trough. What had we dis-cussed? Did it matter? What mattered was that Engee stopped disrupting Web traffic. "When will you stop plucking pilots out of the Web?" Again, my words were spoken, yet not spoken, but more than merely thought.

When I find one who will do what I cannot—one like you.

"I'm not special." As ship-self, I continued that dash along the unseen narrow path toward the warm and com-forting, pulsing lunar beacon.

You see more than the others. You can guide your little needle without grasping for light in the darkness.

"What do you want—of me?"

Your cooperation.

"And if I don't provide it?"

I will continue to seek others . . .

I wanted to sigh. "You don't offer many choices."

The universe offers fewer.

That wasn't arguable, one way or another. "Then let me exit somewhere safe for my officers and the needle." If the Anomaly/Engee wanted to get a needle pilot, it needed to do so without jeopardizing others and the whole Rykaskan interstellar transport system.

As you wish . . . I could sense that swirling cloud of protostar dust and fire that was created by Engee—perhaps it was Engee.

And from outside overspace, from normspace, a smaller arm of fire reached out from the edge of that cloud and wrapped itself around the *Mambrino*.

The needle ship shivered, and the control center strobed black and white, and, had they registered, the gee meters would have pegged, and then I/we tumbled out of overspace and into the Now. We were in normspace, though the excitation lattices were locked—or power was being shunted from them. I depowered the insertion system, wondering what I'd let everyone in for.

"Captain . . ." Berya's voice sounded hoarse. "We were plucked right out of the Web . . ."

I was silent, scanning the skies with all the *Mambrino*'s systems.

"There's no beacon," I whispered, "but there's a star . . ." *The Anomaly . . . Engee's system . . . but where to?* For lack of anything better to do, I spread the nets and eased the needle inward toward the protostar.

The moments ticked by in the silence, and the star drew nearer.

"Rykashan ship, this is Follower Control. Rykashan ship, this is Follower Control."

"The Followers?" muttered Alek. "Where are we? They've got a station?"

"Follower Control, this is *Mambrino*. Go ahead."

"What do they want?" hissed Alek.

"We are at your zero-seven-one, minus forty. We have full cradling and locking facilities."

With that, I could locate the small beacon and the energy signatures, and adjusted course.

"What do I tell the passengers?" asked Berya.

"Tell them that we've made an unanticipated stop at Felini Station."

"Felini Station?"

"That's as good a name as any." *And much better than New City.* "We've been tendered an invitation that I decided not to refuse." I eased the ship downward and began to accelerate, gently, mentally shaking my head. In overspace, agreeing to Engee's invitation had seemed a good idea. Now . . . ? But anything that could lock and depower the excitation systems wasn't going to let us leave until I did whatever it had in mind.

The station was anything but conventional. Rather than a massive cylinder, it was more like a reinforced spiderweb. Where were the docking locks? Did it have any?

"Follower Control, this is *Mambrino*. Interrogative docking locks?"

A flash of green light flared from one side of the spiderweb, almost painful through the optics of the needle's system. "*Mambrino*, green light indicates lock two."

"I have it. Thank you."

"Cradles and locks are Rykashan standard."

"Thank you," I repeated.

My approach was gentle, as I feared any impact might shiver the fragile-appearing station. We barely kissed into the cradles, and the cradling was so uneventful as to be frightening, down to the familiar faint *clunks* and the hissing as the ship and station pressures equalized. Shutdown was routine, and there were no further communications from the station.

"Now what?" asked Berya as she unstrapped.

"I go see what they want."

"You?"

"They want me. I'm not sure why, but that energy spike

was a request that I make myself available."

"A request . . . ?"

"And a threat," I added. "If I don't, then Engee or who-ever's pretending to be Engee will keep picking off nee-dles."

"Are you sure that's not what hasn't happened before?" asked Berya.

"No . . . but before this, none of the missing needles ever turned up in known space." I shrugged. "I have to go on feel here."

Berya nodded slowly. "I hope you're right."

So did I, but it wasn't the time to doubt my sanity, not at all. Still, I did enter a course profile into the system. It might take subjective weeks for the needle to return to Sol, and that would be more than a decade elapsed time, but they wouldn't have to spend the rest of their lives on Follower Station—or New City, as Erelya called it.

Then, I made sure I was at the ship's lock when it opened, although what I could have done was another question.

Besides two crewmen in gray singlesuits trimmed in gold, a heavyset man in a totally gold singlesuit waited on the other side of the lock, a broad smile on his face. Something about his posture bothered me, subcon-sciously, but I could not explain what it was.

"Welcome, captain. We're glad to see you. I'm Bream." I nodded.

"We have a canteen, and an actual waiting area here." He chuckled. "It has been waiting a long time. We don't get many transients."

"I imagine."

Berya's face was grim, her eyes going from me to the Follower and back to me. "Why are we here?"

"You will understand. It is God," Bream said in a matter-of-fact tone.

If such a belief happened to be the impact that Engee had on rational, nano-educated demons who'd had a life-time to adapt to high and low nanotechnology, I wasn't

sure I had any interest in meeting Engee. On the other
hand, I didn't seem to have much choice, not if I wanted
there to be any needle jockeys left. *Aren't you rating
yourself highly?* I shook off the self-critique.

Berya opened her mouth and then shut it, practical second officer that she was.

"Are you ready, captain?" asked the gold-suited Follower—Bream.

"In a moment." I turned to Berya. "I should be back.
But . . . there's a manual course return to earth in the system. It will strain the *Mambrino*'s capabilities, but it will
work."

"We'll be here."

I nodded, again hoping she was right.

Once I eased across the lock threshold and staggered
into full gravity, I understood what had bothered me about
the Followers' postures. Gravity—they had artificial gravity of some sort, not provided by acceleration or spin.
Control of gravity . . . what else did they have? What
other dreams had they attained through Engee?

The waiting area beyond the lock tunnel was spacious,
immaculate, the floors a deep blue, the walls cream and
gold, the indirect lighting from glow strips bright.
Comfortable-looking chairs flanked low tables, and there
was even an antique bookcase on one wall. Yet I had the
feeling I was in an ancient temple or the Hall of Unremitting Alertness in Henvor. In the middle of an impossible stellar system?

"You are to go to the communications center," added
Bream.

If Engee wanted me to do something, I suspected he
could have done it from anywhere. So why was I to go
to the communications center?

*Because they like rituals, and it pleases me to acqui-
esce.*

Who could argue with that? To any effect, that was? I
followed Bream, walking down the angled, gold-trimmed,
blue corridors—hexagonal—in total silence, except for

whispering feet. A vague tickling flashed in my head . . .
as though neurons were clicking. Not silence at all, but
nanotelepathy?

Yes. You are proving yourself worthy.

Worthy? I wasn't sure I wanted that at all. The gravity
bothered me. Theoretically, gravity control wasn't possible, not in any useful way. So why were we here, on a
station circling an impossible solar system? Supposedly,
the Followers were almost riffraff, yet they had clean air,
clean corridors, clothing, and artificial gravity—and they,
or their "God," had been able to snatch me out of overspace.

Not they, but I . . .

I wanted to wince, even as I saw the Followers turning
toward me, their eyes wide. *They* could sense Engee, all
of them. Could they "hear" him/her/it?

*"Him" will do. No, they can but sense that I have
reached out for you, and they are awed.* A sense of a
chuckle followed.

"What do you wish of me, of a flawed demon?" I
thought-spoke the words, rather than state them aloud.

*A task . . . a task that only a pilot and a Dzin master
and you could achieve.*

That did not reassure me.

*There will be no need of further such, should you suc-
ceed.*

Translated loosely, unless I succeeded in whatever Engee wanted, Rykasha was going to lose more needle ships.
I'd known that already, but the confirmation wasn't welcome.

"Here." Bream halted at a hexagonal door, which
opened at his gesture.

Beyond the door was an open space—a hexagon with
each face a good fifty meters on an edge. I blinked—it
was really an octagon of open space—or . . . I wasn't certain.

"Just walk through and to the gold platform in the center," Bream explained.

I wanted to ask how, since the platform seemed suspended in midair, but instead I shrugged and put one foot forward—onto an invisible surface. Not without trepidation, I crossed the emptiness to the platform, toward a sparkling mist so faint as to be barely visible.

"I'm here," I said, and gave the equivalent of a shrug . . .

. . . and found myself in a swirling maelstrom of color.

"What do you want?" I asked for the fourth or fifth time, trying to ignore the swirls of color that flashed around me.

Your cooperation in ensuring that my methodology for establishing order will result in a total increase in informational quanta rather than the normal entropic decrease.

"What can a needle pilot do that you can't?"

Be somewhere else and understand enough for observation and analysis. You might say that I am requesting that your consciousness act as an exploration platform.

That gave rise to far too many questions.

The lack of boundary in the universe—any universe, because each universe is without boundary—results in increasing disorder both as the universe expands and, should it do so later, contracts. Early scientists erroneously believed that there was a symmetry between expansion and contraction and that order would again increase with contraction. In a sense, it does, because at the final contraction to a point all the low-entropy energies of the universe are reunited in one massive and ordered singularity—which explodes and begins the cycle again. But not all universes contract, nor must they. An expanding universe eventually loses all information to entropy, and intelligence is a form of information. You could call the second law of thermodynamics the thermodynamic arrow of time, in that what intelligence perceives as time always proceeds along the direction of entropic decay.

But? I wondered if Engee were nothing more than an insanely rational nanite-intelligence agglutination.

The key is perception. If time and energy flows do not proceed in the same direction, then, under normal conditions, intelligence cannot exist, and there is no perception.

I didn't exactly like the phrase "normal conditions."

So I will modify an avatar of you, which you will effectively become, and you will report all that is necessary.

I didn't finish the swallow as the swirling brilliance descended upon me.

The area around me turned black, then white, the color alternation repeating at an ever-increasing rate into strobing slashes. Between the slashes, I could sense a ripping, as though I were being torn to shreds and rebuilt, or perhaps being scanned and separated into two images, one white, one black.

That duality was what my mind insisted was happening. But which image was *me*? Or was I either, or a disembodied intelligence watching my own destruction?

Not exactly. You are not you, because the arrow of time is reversed so that you can see what you see . . . or will see.

The alternating slashing strobes increased, to the point that the air or vacuum or whatever surrounded me seemed almost to scream as I felt myself lasered—like a beam of light—down a red-rimmed black tunnel toward a white spiraling whirlpool.

Abruptly, I found myself in darkness, a darkness that extended in every direction, and the incredible cold began to seep through me. I tried to move my right arm, but I couldn't tell if it moved or not.

Tossed into deep space to freeze? For what? My eyes seemed to coagulate in the cold of deep space, and I marveled that I hadn't frozen solid nearly immediately. Yet I could sense faint flickers, just at the edge of my vision. Cosmic radiation, exciting the dying retinas of my eyes . . . gamma rays . . . ?

The blackness closed over me, even faster than the chill that had turned me into a quick-frozen soul, or worse, feeling every energy pulse in this dying universe . . . faint as they might have been.

White light, more intense than plunging into the sun, washed over me, and every subatomic particle of my body flared in agony. Electronic acid etched my nervous system, and awls of ice stabbed through the backs of my eyes.

Then I found myself back in the swirls of color, neither hot nor cold.

I shuddered. Which Tyndel was I—black or white?

You are as you were. That other you no longer exists, since only the informational quanta crossed back through the wormhole.

Why?

Because the independence of that other entity, that avatar of you, was necessary to obtain the information I sought . . . and because it pleases me to demonstrate that "I" meet the traditional criteria of "God."

"You're not claiming to be God?" From what I'd seen, the nanogod was acting like an ancient deity.

Acting like the conception of an ancient philosopher who could not comprehend the universe does not a deity make, any more than having your cells repaired constantly by miniature organic technology makes you a demon. The faint sense of a chuckle followed.

The chuckle bothered me.

Nanogods shouldn't have a sense of humor?

Engee could have a sense of humor or not. I just hoped I could get back to the *Mambrino* and return the needle to Earth Orbit Two.

Why not? You acted in good faith, if with fear.

I blinked and found myself standing on the shimmering gold platform in the middle of nowhere in Follower Station. What was I supposed to do now?

Whatever you want. You could return to Dorcha, not as your previous self, of course, or to Rykasha.

Dorcha?

If you study yourself, you will sense the difference.

Since "you" had to be transmitted in quantum form, I took the liberty—call it payment for services rendered—of reconstituting you in a slightly more durable form. The functions provided by the nanites have been integrated on a cellular level. I would caution you. You remain a destructible individual, although that destruction would be far more difficult for outside agencies, but you will register as a totally old human on a Dorchan demon scanner and as a converted human on a Rykashan scanner. That will also increase your cellular life expectancy.

Cellular life expectancy—a polite way of saying that I was far more likely to die in an accident or be killed than for my body to wear out or run down.

Exactly. You could live for several tens of thousands of years more, internal objective clocking, that is. Your ship is reenergized. You may leave as you wish. Unlike the rumors, I do not turn humans into subprocessing units. They're rather inefficient at that.

I shuddered, then walked across the empty space, a nanite-based force-field I could sense, and the hexagonal door opened.

Bream bowed. His face was pale. "As you wish, angel of light."

"I'm ready to leave." I paused. "How long has it been?"

"Three standard hours, ser."

Three hours, to ensure that Engee could change the fate of the universe? Or was that conceit? I laughed softly, and kept walking. I knew my way back.

As I neared the cream-and-white walls of the waiting area, Berya hurried toward me, not quite running. Then she stopped short.

"I'm back."

She studied me silently, for a long time. "You *look* the same, Tyndel. But you're different. I can't say why, though. It's something."

Being tossed into another universe to report quantum data and freeze might change even a demon, I reflected. "I'm still me."

Berya fingered her chin. "Can we go?"

"Any time."

Berya turned to the six passengers who had watched me return. "Captain says we're ready to board." She glanced at me again, speculatively. "Alek's in the control center. Figured that one of us ought to be there at all times."

"That was a good idea."

"I'll button up the locks," she said, glancing back at where the gold-clad Bream stood silently, his faint smile somber.

I'd finished the systems check when she returned to the control center. "Passengers are secure; locks secure, captain."

"Good. We're about ready." I pulsed the release commands to the cradles, hoping they responded. They did, as they did on any Rykashan station.

"Follower Station, this is *Mambrino*. Clear of locks, departing this time for Sol."

"A happy journey, captain and angel of light. God will always be with you."

"What was *that* all about?" asked Alek across the shipnet. "Angel of light?"

"I managed to make their god happy. So I'm an angel." I snorted.

"Is Engee a god?"

"He's a being of immense power. I don't know that I'd want to go beyond that. After all, compared to the humans of ten thousand years ago, we're beings of immense power." I eased up the power on the ionjets, wanting to get clear of Alpha Felini as soon as possible, for reasons scarcely clear to me. "I doubt that our technology could destroy Engee, but the swords and arrows of our ancestors couldn't destroy us."

"They couldn't destroy you, Tyndel," Berya pointed out. "Alek and I are still vulnerable to that sort of thing. Maybe you are an angel." Then she laughed.

I swallowed a sigh of relief at her laugh and torqued the ionjets to full power.

As the *Mambrino* eased clear of the Follower station with the artificial gravity that should not have been, clear of the energy fluxes and the sparkles of matter being re-energized, of local entropy being reversed, I spread the photon nets and began an acceleration to raise us above the incidental dust density.

"All passengers must be securely restrained." The clam-shells began to descend with Berya's announcement.

I scanned the cabin, but the passengers were all locked in place. They had probably strapped in as soon as we pulled away from Follower Station, if not before.

As we slipped into overspace under close to maximum acceleration, needling through the barriers with lattices that flamed, I had a lingering thought. What about the changes Engee had made to me? Did they affect the gene structure?

Of course. Your descendants, should you choose to have any, will retain the improvements. I suggest you have descendants, if only to save some later needle pilots from the difficulties inherent in my finding one such as you.

"That's almost blackmail."

It is honest. It is not truth, but honest.

"You shy away from truth . . ."

The basic concept of "truth" as exhibited in human culture indicates the deceptive nature of your species. If an object exists or an action indeed took place, then why do you need to protest the "truth" of its existence unless you need to distinguish that truth from events which did not take place? And why would you need to make such a distinction unless you are in the habit of frequently representing that which was not as having been?

Even in my pilot's couch, I winced at the accuracy of Engee's assessment. He and Cerrelle had certain characteristics in common.

"Why did you do all this?"

To keep the universe from fulfilling its purpose . . .

I eased the *Mambrino* sideways, avoiding the vortex-blocks spinning away from a yellow-cold spear singularity, waiting for the explanation that might come but not ignoring the ship or overspace—an overspace that seemed almost light green, with everything in even greater relief and better perspective.

The universe's purpose, although that implies a sentient volition which I have not been able to ascertain, appears to be formless entropy. Intelligence opposes formless entropy. More focused and mobilized intelligence can effect more opposition . . .

"You were doing quite well at that without our assistance."

For now . . . but nanites and nanotech deities lack one factor in their makeup that organic intelligences possess.

I waited again.

Some higher "ethics" of the majority of human philosophies seek "beauty." What is beauty? The sense of another chuckle followed.

I didn't know where Engee's inquiries led. Or I was too bemused to follow the logic and dared not remove my attentions from the overspace and the Web around the ship? Not now.

What do beauty and truth share?

I wasn't sure they shared anything except that some humans pursued them and others rejected them.

Come now, former Dzin master. You cannot have failed to notice that both are subjective. Both in the extreme are unattainable ideals. Both move people, not always in the most socially desirable paths.

I was having trouble with the dialogue, if that were what it happened to be. "Unattainable ideals will oppose formless entropy," I finally suggested.

Unattainable ideals propelled by the one factor I lack. Emotion?

Passion is a more accurate term. I wish to survive. I can act upon what is known, but passion acts in search of what cannot be attained.

That was nonsense. Men sought women; women sought men. Men and women sought greatness, empires, art—all things attainable.

No. They attain things which substitute for the vision of the unattainable. That is why the truly great are so often miserable, because they realize at last that their best achievements will always fall below their visions. Yet without those visions . . . After the briefest of pauses, the monologue continued. *You as a human can pursue good, or perfection, but you cannot expect others to follow you. They will encourage you and offer meaningless expressions of praise, but few will emulate your example. To pursue excellence is an admission that one is not perfect and that perfection needs far greater effort. Most self-aware entities wish praise for their present state of being or achievement, not the acknowledgment that they will always fall short of excellence or perfection. Therefore, the pursuit of excellence is always lonely. Those who achieve some small measure of perfection are ignored, or praised and quickly forgotten, or deified so that other entities can rationalize their lack of perfection by their lack of deity.*

I was abruptly chilled and tired. All true—or accurate—but why did Engee even care?

If you evolve, so must I.

With that, the link . . . connection . . . whatever . . . snapped.

As much threat as promise, as much danger as hope . . . and that was life.

I eased the *Mambrino* out of overspace and down toward the lunar beacon, toward earth . . . passion . . . and Cerrelle.

83

Form is emptiness; leave that emptiness without falling into it.

O rbit Two, this is *Mambrino*, inbound from Epsilon Cygni via Alpha Felini. Captain Tyndel, second Berya, third Alek, with six passengers." As we accelerated upward and toward the lunar beacon, I intensified my scanning, attempting to pick out Orbit Two optically—to find that cylinder of composite that had so come to remind me of gray and ancient caserns.

"Are you going to tell us what happened?" asked Berya into the quiet.

"I was persuaded into doing a task for Engee. I did it. He's promised he won't interfere with any more needles." *And you hope he keeps that promise . . . at least for a few centuries.*

"Can you trust it?"

"It was worth the risk. It cost us probably six months lost dilation time, and there doesn't seem to be any damage to the *Mambrino*."

"Do you know how they got gravity on that station?" asked Alek. "There wasn't any spin."

"No. No one told me." *You didn't ask, either.* "I was rather occupied."

"Real gravity . . . in the middle of the Anomaly . . . that's frightening," said Berya quietly.

I could understand that . . . but I trusted my senses enough to know that it had been real, and what was . . . was. And that meant only that Engee had mastered a technology we hadn't.

"What was this task?" Alek injected.

"Observing another universe."

Berya laughed. "You had to ask, Alek."

I was saved by the incoming transmission.

"*Mambrino*, say again intermediate station."

"Intermediate station was Alpha Felini, also known as New City. You may confirm that with senior captain Erelya and commander Krigisa." I grinned as I replied, knowing that the confirmation would certainly get her attention, and I wanted her to get the word before any of the passengers talked. I also wanted the word out beyond the commander, distrustful demon that I was.

"*Mambrino*, we copy Alpha Felini, or New City."

"Stet."

The reference to New City definitely got the commander's attention. Krigisa and two figures in black were waiting at the lock.

"Your officers will go with controllers Bilek and Nyra, captain, and I would appreciate it if you would accompany me." The commander's voice was polite but not terribly warm. "The passengers will be accommodated in another fashion."

"Of course, commander." I doubted that either controller could have restrained me physically, but where would I have gone? And why?

Neither Berya nor Alek looked particularly cheerful, but they didn't have half the problems I would.

"Medical first," insisted Krigisa as we turned toward the shafts.

A black-haired and petite woman in red waited inside the low-spin gravity of the second deck space.

"Doctor Josara, this is captain Tyndel. As I requested . . ." Krigisa nodded toward the doctor.

"You want an immediate and complete diagnostic panel." The doctor turned to me. "If you would step this way?"

I stepped to the square mat by the blank screen and waited as Josara released the spray of diagnostic nanites, and as they returned to the shimmering screen.

"Well?"

"He scans normally," Josara announced. "He's tense, but . . ."

Who wouldn't be?

"Is there anything there that shouldn't be?"

"The scans don't show anything. His cellular balance is better than normal after a triple insertion trip." Josara smiled, a polite smile, but one that seemed pleased to report my good health. "Everything is off the top."

Krigisa nodded. "Let us go."

"Operations?" I asked.

That got another nod.

After we went through another transition lock and along a back corridor I'd not known about, she ushered me into what had to be her private space, barely larger than an oversized closet, with a full wall screen view showing Luna's disc not quite touching the blue and white of a full sunlit earth.

"Why did you broadcast Alpha Felini?" Krigisa's dark face was shiny, her eyes hard. "And then emphasize New City?"

"I couldn't see any way to keep it quiet." *And didn't want to.*

"You could have requested restraints for the passengers."

"I don't operate that way, and, frankly, I didn't think about it." *And if you had, it wouldn't have changed anything.*

"Do you think it's good that people know about Engee—everyone?"

"People already know." I missed Astlyn and his quieter approach. "They won't know any more or any less from this."

The commander eased into the chair, barely held there by the low gravity on the upper station level. "Why don't you start at the beginning."

"There was no sign of Engee on the outward insertion to Epsilon Cygni . . ." I went on to explain everything . . .

including the way Engee lifted the *Mambrino* out of over-space and the apparent task Engee had set me. All I left out were the aspects of changes to me personally.

Then I had to answer dozens of questions, most of them details about Follower Station and its systems. I finally managed to ease in one of my last points. ". . . and he said that he wouldn't bother any more needles."

"You trusted . . . this intelligence?"

"I didn't have that much of a choice. I thought that if I did, and it worked, then . . ." I shrugged, ". . . we had a solved problem. The Authority can't afford to keep losing needle ships."

"There are certain implications," suggested the commander.

"Several," I agreed. "We can't keep Engee or Follower Station a secret, or the fact that it has a gravity field."

There was a long moment of silence. "You said that the Followers had artificial gravity? Are you sure?" asked Krigisa.

"You can ask Berya or any of the passengers. They felt it."

"You let them debark?"

"Only to the waiting area," I said. "I told you that. What was the point of not letting them stretch their legs? If Engee could pull a ship out of overspace—"

"Do you have any idea how these . . . Followers came up with a gravity field for a station?"

"No. I was rather occupied dealing with Engee. I suspect that Engee has come up with at least some technology we could use." I smiled. "I do have a suggestion."

The black-skinned commander raised her eyebrows. "Yes?"

"Consider making regular needle trips to Felini's station—or Follower Station. That's what they call it."

"I doubt the Authority is prepared to consider that."

I offered my best argument. "It would be dishonest not

to, and that dishonesty would eventually undermine our whole system."

"Are you telling the Authority what to do?"

I thought for a moment. "Yes." I grinned. "For twenty years, they've told me. At least, twenty universe objective years of my life. Besides, I don't think the Authority has any choice."

"That assumes Engee will allow visitors."

"If he doesn't . . . then nothing's changed."

"You're not to make this public," Krigisa said. "Not until I meet with the Authority. I suspect they'll want to see you as well. After you have another complete medical and psychological battery at Runswi."

I could understand the Authority's concern. After spending millennia attempting to refute the existence of gods, the Authority was faced with admitting that either a god existed or that a form of intelligence with superior abilities existed. There was concrete proof for one of those conclusions, and neither one was likely to be palatable.

"You're suspended from active flight status until this is resolved."

Again, but I'd hardly expected anything else. "Is that all?"

"Everything we know is being changed, and you act as if nothing had changed. Don't you understand?"

"I understand that there will be a great uproar among some people." I shrugged. "And, in the end, very little will change. If we can get the secret of generating gravity fields, more of the universe may be open and another avenue of technology will improve. But you can't get to the stars that much faster than we do, and there really won't be that much effect on the average Rykashan or mite." I paused. "Or even on the Authority."

"You forget about beliefs," she pointed out.

"The rationalists will accept Engee as a being with some superior abilities, still governed by the rules of the universe. The various kinds of believers will adopt him as a new god, and nothing will change because the only Followers he listens to, and the only ones he probably can listen to, are those in New City, and people on earth or in the colonies will find that, as usual, there's no difference in the answer to their fervent prayers."

"I truly hope you're right." The commander shook her head.

I waited. Nothing else I could say would make a difference.

"You'd better go and get those tests, Tyndel." Krigisa's voice was tight. "And keep your speculations and information to yourself."

"Yes, ser." *For now . . . and excepting Cerrelle.* I nodded.

Perhaps Cerrelle would be at the chalet. She would understand. She might even laugh.

84

[LYNCOL: 4534]

Humankind is myth.

When the doctors and psychologists finished with me, they sent a report to commander Krigisa that I was in wonderful physical and mental condition. When she didn't respond, I suggested—strongly—that it would be better for everyone if I just disappeared to the lake. All in all, I didn't get to the lake until almost a week after my return to Orbit Two.

There, the leaves had begun to turn, and the frost hadn't burned off when I stepped out of the glider. I'd missed two straight summers—four, actually, when I thought about it—and I still hadn't done more than the basics on the garden.

Cerrelle stepped from the driver's side and closed the canopy. I walked around the glider, and she took my hands for an instant. Then she wrapped both arms around me. I let her, and we clung together in the small hangar in the chalet that felt like home even before we went upstairs.

Inside, we stopped before the hearth, where she had the wood burning. I added another log.

"You've made light of it, but it was a hard trip, and dealing with Krigisa had to have been harder."

I took a deep breath. "It started with the fusactor spines—all that metal—and then . . . well . . . I told you everything that happened."

She pointed to one of the pair of armchairs that faced the window and the afternoon view of the lake. "You told me what happened. You haven't told me how you feel. I'll get you some Arleen."

"That would be nice." I sat down in the padded armchair next to hers, let the warmth of the fire flow through me, removing the last hints of the grayness.

"Now . . ." She handed me a big gold mug I'd not seen before. "Here's your tea. It's not so good as yours."

"Who's self-pitying?"

"Tyndel . . . I deserve a small measure of self-pity occasionally, especially when you're doing grand things among the stars and I'm baby-sitting confused refugees."

"You did a good job with me."

"I did the best I could, but you weren't easy."

"It still worked."

We both laughed.

Cerrelle, always honest.

The tea smelled and tasted good, and, for a long time, I just sipped and looked from Cerrelle to the golden and red leaves framed in the glass beyond the hearth and the burning logs. I took another sip of tea as, outside, the gray clouds closed off the autumn blue of the sky and the leaves began to drift away from the oaks.

Finally, I began to talk, about the trip, the medical

exam, the debriefing. As I reached the point where I recounted leaving Krigisa and Earth Orbit Two for the shuttle down to Runswi, Cerrelle asked quietly, "That's the second time you've told me everything that happened. You're avoiding how you feel. How do you *feel* about it, about Engee, and Rykasha? And how will your being a genetic superman affect *us*?"

I frowned. "I don't think I even considered myself a genetic superman. All Engee did, really, was to ensure that I would pass on genetically the nanotech improvements that our children could get anyway." I smiled. "Without the muss and the costs."

That did get a smile in return. "I'm glad you said *our* children."

But who else's would they have been? Who else could I possibly have come to love so much? Who else understood?

"And . . . about Engee and Rykasha?"

"Tired . . . relieved it's over."

The faintest of frowns crossed her face.

"I know, honest woman, it's not over. Nothing's ever over." I shook my head slowly. "I suppose . . . there's always something mightier and grander out in the universe—or the universes. Calling it God is a way of personifying it and making ourselves feel more important. Engee's appealing as a god because he . . . it . . . needs us to have meaning in his existence, despite his greater physical powers in the universe. The Authority doesn't want to deal with it at all . . . but they don't have a choice. Not if they want Rykasha to survive." I smiled. "The Authority will have to come to terms with Engee's existence, and, after the initial shock . . ." My words drifted to a halt, and I took a sip of the Arleen.

"Shock?"

"First, there's the business of his being able to link with other universes and bleed energy through. That was always theoretically possible, but now . . . now people know it can be done, and no one knows how." I took another sip of the tea. "I think it will be a long time before they figure out how that can be done. The artificial gravity fields are different. In a way, they're more of a shock. Except for gravity control, the rest of New City can be explained in terms of technology and insights brought by the Followers or by the knowledge that Engee could have attained through self-examination and passed on." I paused and looked across the lake.

"Go on . . . don't leave me in the middle of a thought," Cerrelle prompted.

"That means"—I smiled more broadly—"that the Authority will have to recognize Engee as something—another culture, an equal . . . and they'll have to recognize the Believers, the Followers of the Angel of the Lord, or whatever they officially call themselves. Oh, the Authority can still require some service obligation, but it would be difficult—and stupid—not to set up some way of letting at least some go to New City. The Authority's not stupid." I smiled. "And for millennia people have been pursuing the dream of conquering gravity. Gravity dreams, if you will. But the Authority can't beg, or steal, or borrow, the gravity technology without contact . . . so . . . sooner or later, probably sooner, some accommodation will be worked out. Over time, that will change things." I set down the empty mug. "And for a while, it will make Rykashans a bit less arrogant."

"That pleases you," mused Cerrelle.

"I'd like to see a muting of the Rykashan arrogance. This might help."

"It might." An amused smile crossed her face. "Do you think they'll send you out on another flight—ever?"

"Not for a while . . . but they will. They will." I took a last sip of the tea and set the mug on the table. "After it becomes clear that Engee kept his word."

Cerrelle looked at me. "You have to finish it."

I knew what she meant. "In Dorcha, yes. Because I never really said good-bye to the past. What about you?"

"I did before I left Dezret. You never did."

As usual, she was right, but I didn't have to finish it at that moment. So we sat in the warmth of the chalet and watched the sun set behind frosted hills on the other side of the lake.

ΣPILOGUΣ

In the shadow of the Cataclypt of the Rykasha, not of Dyanar as I had once erroneously thought, two children kissed, and a demon watched, and smiled.

That cataclypt, where I had once seen two other children kiss, had not changed, but the dark gray stone was different . . . softer . . . edges blurred by rain and time. In thirty years, rain could not have made that difference. My eyes went to the carvings, to the images of the winged men that represented the ancients, and to the tailed figures in the background, background figures more clearly defined than the foreground angels.

Art? Artifice? Or a hand that had left hints, hints I had been too young and too full of Dzin to see when I had first come to Henvor. Once I had recalled a day when I had kissed Esolde behind the grape trellis in her parents' garden. Esolde was now mid-aged, a medical doctor of high reputation in Halz, her hair possibly graying. And I remained brown-haired and sharp-featured.

On that day of my posting, more than three decades past, with the slow swirl of the river below and the dampness of the morning mist in my nostrils, I had let the two kiss unmolested. At the time, I had wondered. Later, I had thought it had been the beginning of my undoing. Now . . . now, I had just watched two children kiss in an innocence I still could recapture on a lake to the north . . . because honesty begets innocence of the deeper kind.

My eyes went back to the cataclypt, and after studying the carvings, again noting the less-defined shapes of the ancient angels and the harder-edged forms of the demons, I turned to retrace my old path along the foot-polished stones of the River Walk. The mist was thicker this year, and no warmth came from the brume-hidden sun.

Old as Henvor is, old as it seemed, cold as the early winter day was, the mist fell gently on my shoulders, like a blessing, as I walked northward beside the Greening River. All the myths of the time before the Great Hunger and Devastation, all the stories that had seemed so impossibly distant, all seemed fresh-printed on the pages of a history text barely written.

My face solemn, I smiled within as I walked the river path before returning to the north, to a Rykasha that had yet to learn what I had discovered twice—that there is always a greater knowledge, a greater challenge, and that deception is everywhere.

Deception . . . all life is deception, for without deception few can face the cold impartiality of the universe or the fact that it will go on and we will die, never benefiting fully from what was or at all from what we have struggled to create, but striving against the darkness of self-deception. Yet . . . the struggle in itself has meaning because the universe only exists. Merely existing, the universe lacks meaning, and only a deceptive being can bring meaning to the impartial fact of meaninglessness.

And, as I can, that is what I will do, knowing that we, or the ancients, have created a being that some call God. Our old dreams have been found wanting, even as we are more than gods, and more than truth, for truth does not exist, and never has. I will fail, and failing, will succeed. I will die, later or sooner, and what I understand will be lost, for when men and women seek truth, what they find is as deceptive as lies, and neither truth nor lies exist outside of a deceptive soul.

I watched when two children once kissed in a cataclypt, and what I did not see has made all the difference.

Jake Lloyd reading ENDER'S GAME.

Get caught reading

A Message from the
Association of American Publishers